D0615292

941.08 F312
Fearon, Peter
Buckingham Babylon   22.50

MID-CONTINENT PUBLIC LIBRARY
North Independence Branch
Highway 24 & Spring
Independence, MO   64050

WITHDRAWN
FROM THE RECORDS OF THE
MID-CONTINENT PUBLIC LIBRARY

NI

Buckingham Babylon

BUCKINGHAM BABYLON

*The Rise and Fall
of the House of Windsor*

Peter Fearon

A Birch Lane Press Book
Published by Carol Publishing Group

MID-CONTINENT PUBLIC LIBRARY

3 0000 11104243 2

Copyright © 1993 by Baron Hall, Inc.
All rights reserved. No part of this book may be reproduced in any form, except by a newspaper or magazine reviewer who wishes to quote brief passages in connection with a review.

A Birch Lane Press Book
Published by Carol Publishing Group
Birch Lane Press is a registered trademark of Carol Communications, Inc.
Editorial Offices: 600 Madison Avenue, New York, N.Y. 10022
Sales and Distribution Offices: 120 Enterprise Avenue, Secaucus, N.J. 07094
In Canada: Canadian Manda Group, P.O. Box 920, Station U, Toronto, Ontario M8Z 5P9
Queries regarding rights and permissions should be addressed to Carol Publishing Group, 600 Madison Avenue, New York, N.Y. 10022

Carol Publishing Group books are available at special discounts for bulk purchases, for sales promotion, fund-raising, or educational purposes. Special editions can be created to specifications. For details, contact: Special Sales Department, Carol Publishing Group, 120 Enterprise Avenue, Secaucus, N.J. 07094

Manufactured in the United States of America
10 9 8 7 6 5 4 3 2 1

Library of Congress Cataloging-in-Publication Data

Fearon, Peter, 1951–
    Buckingham Babylon : the rise and fall of the House of Windsor / by Peter Fearon.
        p.   cm.
    ISBN 1-55972-204-5
    1. Windsor, House of. 2. Elizabeth II, Queen of Great Britain, 1926– —Family. 3. Great Britain—Politics and government—20th century. 4. Monarchy—Great Britain—History—20th century. I. Title.
DA28.35.W54F43 1993
941.08′08′621—dc20   93-11342
                                                                        CIP

MID-CONTINENT PUBLIC LIBRARY

North Independence Branch
Highway 24 & Spring
Independence, MO 64050

To my darling wife, MARCY,
My co-author in life,
With whom I am desperately in love

The author is pleased to acknowledge
the outstanding contribution of Ken Chandler,
editor of the *New York Post,*
to the preparation of this volume.

Contents

Buckingham Babylon

Prologue

A Change in the Beat
of the Clock

A t about six-thirty in the evening, on Tuesday, January 22, 1901, a small, frail, nearly blind eighty-one-year-old woman took her last breath in the powerful embrace of her grandson, Kaiser Wilhelm II, Emperor of Germany. Britain's prime minister was told on a crackling line to 10 Downing Street, and then a crowd of reporters, waiting in the freezing, gaslit night outside Osborne House, were given the bulletin. There was an unseemly stampede down the hill to the town of Cowes as the reporters shouted: "Queen dead! Queen dead!" Her birth had been proclaimed by heralds in the age of candlelight, horse travel, and town criers. Her death was announced by telephone and telegraph in an age of trains, motorcars, and electricity.

There had been nothing England's Queen Victoria liked so much in life as arranging a good funeral, and she had paid meticulous attention to the details of her own, from the assortment of talismans that would share her coffin to the purple cashmere draperies that would be hung along the processional route in London. She decreed ceremonies of "such splendor . . . that those who were her subjects might look upon the moving scene in common grief and might remember it to the end of their days."

It was to be history's first truly global event, marked by services and formal mourning from Tokyo to New York, Paris to Peking; in every Royal court in Europe from St. Petersburg to Lisbon; and in every corner of Britain and her vast empire of 10 million square miles, a

3

quarter of the earth's landmass. The greater part of her 400 million subjects had known no other monarch in their lifetime.

She had died peacefully at the isolated, melancholy retreat she and her husband, Prince Albert, had built on a hilltop on the Isle of Wight, off England's south coast. Two weeks later, her oak coffin, covered with a gold pall embroidered with the Royal standard and mounted on a crimson dais, was taken on board the Royal yacht *Alberta.* The leaden weight of the English winter lifted for a day, and the February wind stilled.

With a bright winter sun beginning to drop behind her, the white yacht, accompanied by a convoy of destroyers, crossed The Solent to Portsmouth through an avenue of Royal Navy warships that stretched for eight miles. At the eastern end, the Queen's ships were joined by warships of the French, German, Portuguese, Russian, and Japanese navies. Each ship fired a series of broadside salutes as the *Alberta* passed by. The spectacle, wrote the Countess of Denbigh, who watched from the deck of the *Scot* in the line of battleships, "left behind a memory of peace and beauty and sadness which it is impossible to forget."

People dropped to their knees in fields along the way as the Royal train, its black blinds drawn, made the slow journey to London's Victoria Station the following day. A funeral procession of unprecedented size and majesty accompanied the coffin across London through bareheaded, silent crowds to begin the last leg of its journey to Windsor Castle. Each minute for an hour and twenty-one minutes, cannon fire echoed from Hyde Park, off Victorian and Georgian façades across London, as "X" Battery of the Royal Horse Artillery fired a salvo for each year of the Queen's life.

Immediately behind the gun carriage bearing the coffin came a small army of Emperors, Kings, Princes, and Grand Dukes, most of them related to the dead Queen Empress through a complex web of marital alliances, primarily designed, in vain, to ensure the peace of Europe.

At their head was a massive, bearded figure in scarlet, his forty-eight-inch barrel chest covered with every kind of decoration and insignia, each meticulously located in relation to the other with obsessive care for rank and place. He was the new King and Emperor, Edward VII, Victoria's dissolute son, described by the American writer Henry James as "the arch vulgarian . . . Edward the Caresser." Newspapers that had once described him as a "whoremonger," a "wastrel," and "unfit for the throne"—this latter opinion shared by his own mother—now remarked on his "nobility and kingly dignity." At his right, on an immaculate white charger, was the dead Queen's bellicose and arrogant grandson, the German Emperor Wilhelm II, dressed, ironically, in a British field marshal's uniform. He looked "pale and sad but . . . a very emperor," wrote the *Times*.

At the King's left was Queen Victoria's favorite son, Prince Arthur, the Duke of Connaught, furious that his nephew, the Emperor, was dressed in a British field marshal's uniform, while he, who had led the Scots Guards in battle in Egypt, wore only the uniform of a general. He had to demand his right to help place his mother in her coffin or the Kaiser would have done so, with his one good arm, by himself.

Posting straight-backed behind them, in a clatter of hooves and scabbards, came the full flower of Europe's Royal dynasties: Kings of Greece and Portugal; the Archduke Franz Ferdinand of Austria; Grand Duke Michael of Austria, the Czar's brother, in a dazzling white uniform; the Crown Princes of Norway, Sweden, Denmark, Rumania, Bulgaria, and Siam; and the scions of scores of German principalities and dukedoms. Among them was the teenaged Charles, Duke of Saxe-Coburg Gotha, the British-born grandson of the Queen. In an undreamed of future, he was to become an ardent, dedicated Nazi, a war criminal, and a key figure in the downfall of a future English King.

"It was a gallant spectacle . . . a rapid vision," declared the *Times* correspondent, "a splendid following—flowing cloaks of blue, silvery grey or black . . . purple sashes, resplendent uniforms, dancing plumes."

The only hitch in the complex pageant occurred at the last stage. A contingent of Royal Horse Artillery had been waiting at the railroad terminal in Windsor to carry the body to the castle for burial at the Royal Mausoleum at Frogmore. The long wait in the withering cold unsettled the horses. One after another they reared up and broke their traces just as the procession moved off to the accompaniment of Chopin's funeral march and a Royal Artillery battery salute. The coffin looked ready to fall from the gun carriage. There was an unseemly struggle as the officers and enlisted men tried to regain control, watched by the increasingly impatient (King) Prince Louis of Battenberg.

The German-born husband of Princess Victoria of Hesse, Victoria's granddaughter, dressed his horse over to the King, leaned from his saddle, and said something in his ear. The King was seen to nod in agreement. "Let him handle it," he ordered. Battenberg, who had left his native Germany at fourteen to join the British navy, dismissed the outraged artillery officers. He ordered Lt. Algernon Boyle of the HMS *Excellent,* head of a naval honor guard, to instruct the bluejackets to drag the gun carriage away. To assist, Battenberg himself strode to the funeral train, slashed a length of communication cord with his sword, and handed it to Boyle.

For the vast majority of those who witnessed it, the funeral represented the passing of an age, which for the middle classes and Britain's still-ascendant nobility was one of unsurpassed brilliance and security, pomp and prosperity. The Queen's birth had been attended by the Duke of Wellington, whose victory at Waterloo had ushered in a century of the Pax Britannica, an era more of victory than peace, one of unparalleled military and economic supremacy and expansion. Her obsequies were attended by the doomed crowns of Europe, already embarked on the road to revolution and war.

Ford Madox Ford described her death as "a change in the Beat of the Clock." The poet Robert Bridges wrote that the keystone "had fallen out of the arch of heaven."

Victoria had inherited the throne in 1837 from a succession of hated Hanoverian monarchs, each madder and more tyrannical than his predecessor. Her own father, Prince Edward, Duke of Kent, was a deviant of the most degenerate character, born into a family that has become a byword for rapaciousness. In an age of brutal punishments, he had been recalled from a succession of military postings for the sadistic fanaticism and undisguised glee with which he disciplined his troops, ordering floggings of up to 999 lashes. The fourth son of King George III, he was living in a bleak, self-imposed exile in Brussels when catastrophe struck the English Royal House.

George III had fifteen children, yet the dynasty was on the brink of extinction. His five daughters had produced no heirs. Only three of the Princes were legally married: Frederick, Duke of York, who was childless; Ernest, Duke of Cumberland, an incestuous tyrant married to a woman who had murdered her two previous spouses; and George, the Prince Regent. The Regent's only offspring, Princess Charlotte, had married the German Prince Leopold of Saxe-Coburg. Their children were expected to be the last hope of the English monarchy. But Charlotte died in childbirth, and her baby, a Prince, was stillborn.

Encouraged by the prospect of hard cash in the form of a grant from Parliament, Prince Edward, heavily in debt, set aside his French prostitute, Julie St. Laurent, with whom he had lived for twenty-seven years, to marry another Saxe-Coburg, Princess Victoria of Leiningen, sister of the unfortunate Leopold. In 1819 they had a daughter, Victoria.

In 1837, still a teenager, Victoria ascended a throne debased by her Hanoverian predecessors. She moved from her home in Kensington Palace, away from her interfering mother, to the vast palace at the end of the Mall. It had been the site of a monastery of the order of St. James the Less, seized by Henry VIII. Land nearby still bears the name St. James Park after the order. It had been a silkworm farm under James I. The place had also served as the site of Goring House, home of the Earl of Norwich; Arlington House, home of the Earl of Arlington; and Buckingham House, home of the Earl of Buckingham. George III bought it for his bride, and it was refurbished as Queen's House. When Queen Victoria was born, it was known as the Palace of Pimlico. But when she moved in as Queen, it was widely referred to as Buckingham Palace.

The British monarchy had never been so secure as at Victoria's death. The four princes who were to succeed her and reign until the second half of the twentieth century were all alive. Her son, Edward VII, the last British monarch to lend his name to an era—Edwardian—rode in her funeral procession. His son, George V, then Duke of York, who was to be the first Windsor and whose right to the throne would be challenged in his Coronation Year, remained at Osborne recovering from the measles. The future Edward VIII, the grandson of the Duke, sat in the congregation for the requiem at St. George's Chapel, Windsor. He was to plot against the very people he ruled and spend much of his life in a wandering and embittered exile.

Next to him was his brother, the future George VI, whose childhood abuse was to leave him with a permanent handicap. The two children would remember the funeral only for the interminable waiting and the tomblike cold. "At six, one's sense of destiny is limited and one's appetite for historical pathos even more so," he wrote later as the Duke of Windsor.

Held up to a window to witness the procession to the Queen's last resting place at the Royal Mausoleum at Frogmore was the one-year-old Prince Louis of Battenberg, son of the quick-witted naval officer who had earlier saved the day. As Lord Mountbatten of Burma he would one day plot unashamedly, but unsuccessfully, to have the Royal dynasty replaced by his own and would be asked to lead a coup against the British government.

Within a few years of the spectacle, the intricately woven tapestry of European monarchy had unraveled. The Romanovs of Russia would be massacred by the Bolsheviks. The Hohenzollerns, the Imperial family of Germany, went into exile in Holland. The Kaiser, who had cradled Victoria in his arms so lovingly, was lucky to escape extradition as a war criminal. Archduke Franz Ferdinand, who had ridden a few feet behind the Kaiser in the funeral procession, would be assassinated in 1914 with the shot that triggered the Great War. The Hapsburg rulers of the Austro-Hungarian Empire, who had reigned in central Europe for six hundred years, were to be deposed, their Empire splintered.

Lesser monarchies came tumbling after. The fate of the three great dynasties was largely the fruit of military defeat. But in England, too, the political power of the aristocracy would soon be dramatically limited and demands made for the dismissal of the Royal House, Saxe-Coburg Gotha. They were essentially a German family which was to survive in Britain only by reinventing themselves as paragons of the staid English middle class rather than bearers of aristocratic values. They would thrive under a new, thoroughly English sounding dynastic name: the Windsors.

As the Windsors, the British Royal Family would become the most successful, the most widely recognized, the most respected—and the richest—royal dynasty in the world. Their personality cult was to obsess not just the British public and their old colonial relations in the remnants of the Empire but countries like France and the United States, otherwise proud of their republican heritage, and even nations like the former Soviet Union, where the cult of Royalty had theoretically died in a hail of gunfire with the Romanovs. The panoply of Royalty, once only a symbol of power, had already become an end in itself by the time Queen Victoria died. The Windsor family celebrations would become the most widely witnessed events in history. A vast propaganda machine was built to keep the cult alive, creating, destroying, approving, and altering Royal history.

Hidden behind the Windsors' façade of moral rectitude and much-trumpeted qualities of leadership is the world's most dysfunctional family. Their story is one of hypocrisy, boundless ambition, sham marriages, routine infidelity, child abuse, acute emotional disturbance, drug addiction and substance abuse, alcoholism, irrepressible greed, revolutionary plots, Nazi sympathies, even murder. And casting its shadow over each generation, a recessive gene of manic and sometimes deviant sexuality.

Part One

EDWARD VII
Bertie (1901–10)

One

"The Arch Vulgarian"

The prudery associated with the Victorian era has little to do with the character of Queen Victoria, who was a sensuous woman with a matter-of-fact attitude toward sex. Among her many gifts to her husband, Prince Albert, was a painting by Winterhalter showing a number of plump, half-naked nymphs, among whom were idealized likenesses of herself in her sexual prime, which he hung in his dressing room. When she was advised by doctors to have no more children after the birth of her last child, Princess Beatrice, she pleaded with them in the frankest of terms not to order her to forgo sex. And when her nine children had produced several grandchildren and they, great grandchildren, she remarked that all of them were breeding "like the rabbits in Windsor Great Park."

She did, however, have an eccentric view of the nuances of public propriety. For the Prince of Wales to attend the first two "great days" of the Epsom races was acceptable, she wrote, but for him to attend the remaining two days would be "evil."

The excessive modesty associated with the Victorian era, the extremes of which led to the covering up of shapely furniture legs, stems from the entrepreneurial class, with its predominantly Calvinist values of industry, prudence, and self-denial, attitudes which trickled down the social structure. Prince Albert, Victoria's consort, was intolerant of any moral lapse, however. His mother had been separated from her children and banished from her husband's home for adultery with a courtier. His brother had contracted a venereal disease. In matters of illicit sex, records one biographer, the Prince Consort was "unbalanced." But his son, Bertie, who was to become Edward VII, shared none of his father's attitudes. He was a compulsive adulterer his entire life—what today would be called a sex addict—sleeping with upwards of seven thousand women, many of them the wives of his friends and courtiers.

When he was thirteen, Bertie visited the court of Napoleon III, where he was impressed by the fragrant beauty of the Empress Eugenie's ladies-in-waiting, particularly when they curtsied to him in their décolleté gowns, showing what was "veiled at Windsor" and a good deal besides. The elegance and luxury of the Second Empire court at Versailles had no match anywhere in Europe, certainly not in his mother's relatively sedate home. Enjoying kindness and adult friendship for the first time with the French Emperor, Bertie told him, "I should like to have been your son." When he wanted to extend the visit, the Empress Eugenie remarked that his parents would miss him. "They don't want us," he told her.

As a child, Bertie had been deprived of a normal mother's love and father's approval for which all children strive. In this way, Victoria and Albert created a pattern of disastrous parenting which persists among Britain's Royal Family and is at the root of many of their recurrent problems.

Prince Albert, Victoria's husband, is widely accepted as the architect of the modern British monarchy, above party and beyond corruption and personal political ambition, bound by the onerous obligations of rank. He did not envisage a modern monarchy devoid of all but ceremonial function but one in which the monarch was a permanent and active chief executive. He believed sincerely that as a future king, his son should have all the best qualities and attributes of a Renaissance man. He was particularly concerned that the future King develop a personality far removed from that of his Hanoverian forebears. He set strict and unrealistic educational goals, and when these were not reached, he turned up rather than released the pressure. His motto was 'Never Relax. Never Relax. Never Relax.' Thus, Bertie's most formative years were turned into a sentence from which there was no appeal, to a prison from which there was no escape.

When his frustrations expressed themselves through outbursts of violence, his father concluded that Bertie was insane and had him examined by a leading phrenologist, who determined that while the heir to the throne was not yet mad, there was a possibility of his developing the feared Hanoverian disability.

Like other British Royals after him, Bertie probably had a learning disability. He certainly developed a distaste for everything that smacked of intellectualism and probably never read a book for pleasure. He did not even develop a complete command of English. German was his first language. He mastered several dialects, and he spoke German at home and to others who could speak it, less so in his later years. He was particularly fond of German endearments. To those of his subjects who could not speak German, he spoke English with a heavy R-rolling accent.

He developed an acute sense of style and fashion. Some of his fashion innovations, such as the dinner jacket and the English affectation of not fastening the bottom waistcoat button, persist to this day. He helped to popularize smoking cigarettes, rather than cigars, after dinner. And, by extension, he introduced the drinking of brandy to close a meal—its taste suiting cigarettes better than port.

By his early twenties, with his round, boyish face, still unvalanced by a beard, and with heavy, drooping eyelids and sensuous lips, he cut an elegant, flamboyant figure. He had an encyclopedic knowledge of all the nuances and arcane subtleties of manners and honor and a taste for all the less imaginative arts: gambling, hunting, sports of every kind, and all forms of self-indulgence. As an adult, Bertie spent his life living the childhood he had been deprived of, satisfying his by then gargantuan appetites—at the dinner table, at the gaming tables, and in the beds of his innumerable lovers.

Throughout his life he was able to consume dozens of oysters in minutes and digest the richest food in enormous quantities with no apparent effect on his iron constitution. Wags joked that the Prince's motto 'Ich Dien' ("I serve" in Welsh), had become 'Ich Dine.' He mixed himself incendiary cocktails of spirits and champagne and smoked more than twenty unfiltered cigarettes and at least twelve enormous cigars a day, starting before breakfast. However, his greatest appetite was for sex.

An incident in Darmstadt, Germany, when he was fifteen, gave a mild foretaste of what was to come. The teenaged Prince was discovered drunk, forcing himself on a local girl in public, an incident serious enough to be reported to Gladstone, the then prime minister, who termed it "a squalid debauch."

When Bertie made an official visit to Canada and a rather less official one to the United States in 1860, his appearance in New York became the season's number-one social event. Leonard Jerome, millionaire speculator and part owner of the *New York Times,* served as one of the organizers of a grand ball in his honor at the Academy of Music. There is some irony attached to this event: Jerome's daughter, Jennie, then seven and one day to be mother of Winston Churchill, would eventually enjoy a lengthy, adulterous affair with the Prince.

The Duke of Newcastle, Bertie's chaperon, remarked at the unseemly enthusiasm and undignified competitiveness with which New York's socially prominent maidens hurled themselves at the Prince. None appears to have been successful, thanks to the Duke's watchful eye. But the New York newspapers reported that Bertie escaped from His Grace long enough to spend a riotous time in the city's brothels.

The Curragh Camp Affair took place the following year, 1861. Queen Victoria was to claim, unfairly and quite cruelly, that it led directly to the death of Prince Albert, the Prince's father.

Bertie had been sent to the Curragh Camp in Ireland for several weeks' military training. The regimen set for him made typically unrealistic demands on his intellect. He was to learn the duties of all grades of officer, rising in two-week stages from lieutenant to battalion commander. He was to live away from the barracks so that his association with officers his own age would be minimal. Even time to be spent reading was written into his schedule. Little wonder he rebelled at the first opportunity.

At the end of his training there was a wild party in the junior officers' mess. A woman whom most of them had enjoyed at one time or another, Nellie Clifden, was smuggled into the camp and, ultimately, into Bertie's bed. The incident might have ended there had Bertie shown some moderation, but he was incapable of doing so. He took her to England and continued to sleep with her, even at Windsor, when his parents were at Osborne. She, in turn, made no secret of the fact that she was having sexual relations with the young heir to the throne. Those in the know joked that she was "Princess of Wales."

The news that Bertie had an ongoing relationship with "an actress" who "frequented the lowest dance halls in London," by which was meant she was a prostitute, was conveyed to the Prince Consort by Baron Stockmar, the Queen's closest adviser. The affair had already become the talk of London's clubs and smoking rooms. Lord Torrington, a well-connected gossip, filled in the color. The news came as a blow to Prince Albert, who, ashen and drawn, told Queen Victoria what he called the "disgusting details."

In any of the other Royal Houses of Europe, or among the other aristocratic families of Britain, the incident would have been regarded as a reprehensible but perhaps inevitable episode in the life of a young man. But the Prince Consort was incapable of viewing it in such a light. He wrote to his son in the severest possible terms, calling his behavior "evil" and telling him he was the cause "of the greatest pain I have yet felt."

Prince Albert launched into a tirade, a projection of his most lurid fantasies, about the damage that would be caused by the relationship. The woman would get pregnant at some point in her life. People would inevitably believe that it was the child of the Prince of Wales. She would go to court. The heir to the throne would be called as a witness, "cross-examined by a railing, indecent attorney." The sordid details of their relationship would be paraded before the outraged public.

"She will be able to give, before a greedy Multitude, the disgusting details of your profligacy," he wrote. The monarchy would be disgraced. The Prince of Wales would be "chased and hooted at by a lawless mob.

"Oh, horrible prospect, which this person has in her power any day to realize! And to break your poor parents' hearts!" Prince Albert's letter to his son is a remarkable document, a Victorian guilt trip in which the Prince Consort wallows, like John Donne in his sermons on corruption. Later, Queen Victoria was to endorse this view. "I agree with all that Papa foresaw," she wrote.

The news came at the worst possible time for Prince Albert, who was already overworked, overwrought, depressed, and sick, and which might explain a reaction that was extreme even for him. He had collapsed on a visit to his native Coburg, predicting that he would never see his native land again. The King and heir to the throne of Portugal, who were relatives and friends, had died of typhoid. Albert had been overwhelmed with additional duties. His personal intervention had barely averted Britain's entering the Civil War on the Confederate side.

Within weeks of the Curragh Camp incident, the Prince Consort was dead. Typhoid was the immediate cause, but it has been speculated that he had been suffering from cancer for some time. Queen Victoria believed a broken heart over Bertie's misdeeds had weakened his constitution. She ever after held him responsible.

"Bertie . . . does not know that I know all," she wrote to her daughter Victoria, the Crown Princess of Prussia, adding, "Oh, that boy—much as I pity I never can nor shall look at him without a shudder. . . ."

Bertie was sent on a four-month trip to Palestine, no doubt in the belief that the waters of the Jordan might wash away his depravity. Upset as he was at his father's death, he was happy to receive news of Nellie in letters from friends.

Even before the Curragh Camp affair, the Prince Consort and Queen Victoria had ordained that Bertie should marry as soon as possible, and a search was undertaken for a future Queen. The field was relatively small. Queen Victoria thought it improper for a member of the Royal Family to marry even the most highborn subject and unthinkable for the heir to the throne to do so. Catholics were barred, which excluded several of the most prominent Royal Houses of Europe. Only someone with admirable physical attributes was likely to satisfy Bertie's inclinations for any length of time. The only candidate given serious consideration was Princess Alexandra of Schleswig-Holstein Sonderburg-Glucksburg.

Princess Alexandra was the beautiful daughter of Prince Christian, later to be King Christian IX of Denmark. Queen Victoria described her as "a lovely being whose bright image seems to float. . . . Unfortunately she is very deaf."

She was shallow, which would have been by no means a deal breaker for Bertie, but her hearing problems, which grew worse with time, made her appear stupid, for it was difficult for her to follow conversations. Bertie, though he loathed learning, was attracted throughout his life to intelligent, articulate, and amusing women, and that Princess Alexandra was not. "That she is very clever I don't think" was Victoria's verdict on her, but whether she felt that failing would prove an advantage or not is unclear.

That Victoria and Albert were willing to marry the heir to the throne into the Schleswig-Holstein house and so early in his adult life indicated the urgency of the need to find a wife for him. Schleswig-Holstein lies on the narrow peninsula south of Denmark and offers both North Sea and Baltic ports. A key to Prussian expansion, it was likely to be claimed by Germany in the near future. Victoria and Albert were even willing to overlook the fact that the family of Alexandra's mother, Hesse-Cassel, was renowned across Europe for the orgiastic gatherings they hosted at their castle near Frankfurt.

Such was the opposition to the match among the German Royal Houses that Prince Albert's brother, the Duke of Saxe-Coburg, spread gossip that Princess Alexandra was not a virgin. But it took only the news that the Czar was also interested in Princess Alexandra as a wife for his son for Victoria to make her move.

Princess Alexandra and the Prince of Wales were married on March 10, 1863, in St. George's Chapel, Windsor. He was twenty-one; she, seventeen. Children came in rapid succession. In December Alexandra gave birth to a son, two months premature and weighing under four pounds. Queen Victoria decreed that he should be called Prince Albert Victor. Another son, George, later King George V, was born a little over a year later, in 1865. Alexandra lied to Queen Victoria about her due date so that the Queen would not be present at the birth. Three daughters followed, and in 1871, Alexandra gave birth to a third son, who died after only a few weeks.

At first, Alexandra joined Bertie's restless search for diversion and entertainment. Not even her first pregnancy slowed her down. But as time went on, she joined her husband's wanderings less and less.

She developed a limp, which was widely mimicked. Her deafness became more profound. Her mind never matured, and she retained the emotions of an adolescent her entire life. The indications are that the Royal couple abandoned sexual relations after the sixth pregnancy. Bertie took a succession of lovers. Alexandra, though faithful, amused herself with platonic relationships with chivalrous admirers. And she found herself more conspicuously alone, forced to accept her husband's innumerable infidelities, some more quietly than others.

Marriage had made Bertie free for the first time in his life. The fetters of his youth vanished. If Queen Victoria and Prince Albert believed that Princess Alexandra could keep Bertie in check, they were wrong. While the isolation and close supervision of his childhood made him rebellious, he now faced a new problem in that Queen Victoria refused to give him anything to do. He had few official functions, and the Queen rejected pleas from successive prime ministers to allow him some access to state papers. As a result, he had nothing to do but enjoy the myriad temptations available. Europe became his playground. His eclectic circle of friends became known as the Marlborough House set, after his magnificent residence in London's Pall Mall.

The substrata of the upper classes was based on the elusive concept of "breeding"; on wealth and how that wealth was obtained; on achievement in arms or in certain acceptable pursuits, such as hunting or racing; but most of all on behavior. And behavior did not mean moral rectitude. It meant adhering to the arcane catechism of ethics that the

Victorians regarded as good manners. A man whose gambling debts were beyond him or who had disgraced his class with cowardice might be expected to shoot himself. A man who had committed a crime associated with the baser classes, such as stealing a paltry amount, might be expected to do likewise. A woman—or a man—who had committed a social sin, such as marrying beneath herself or himself, might be expected to go into exile from public view in that Elba of the socially ostracized, the French Riviera. And a man who had an adulterous wife might be expected to console himself, in turn, with a mistress.

Many of the marriages among the Victorian aristocracy were arranged by parents. Divorce was regarded as scandalous. Adultery, if kept discreet, was less so. What separated acceptable from unacceptable activity was the subtle minuet of behavior that took place around it. This made for a good deal of hypocrisy. As both Prince of Wales and later as King and head of the Anglican church, Bertie refused to speak publicly to couples who were contemplating divorce on the grounds that divorce was breaking an oath. But he never shied away from sleeping with married women.

Often husbands were complaisant either because their marriages were not love matches and they had their own distractions or because the attention paid their wives by the heir to the throne lent them additional social status. For those who were not complaisant, there was, in any case, little recourse. For a man to create a public scandal with a divorce action would have destroyed his own standing in society unless he had been so thoroughly wronged as to put the train of ethical behavior into reverse. For a woman to start a divorce action would have meant both social and financial suicide. Victorian divorce laws were weighted heavily in favor of the man. His wife was as much his property as his brandy. Sometimes, however, he had to share it.

Victorian society was not only stratified; it was organized by a rigid calendar of social and sporting events: racing at Ascot, Auteuil, and Longchamps; sailing during Cowes Week; the opening of grouse-shooting season. Times of the year were set aside for sojourns in Biarritz, in Paris, and at Marienbad; for the round of balls in London; and for weekends—Fridays to Mondays, as they were called—at one or the other of the palatial country houses of the Marlborough House set. In the course of one season, the Prince saw thirty plays and attended twenty-eight race meetings and forty balls, galas, and other social functions. The calendar of major events was unchanging. To be excluded from the group of fifteen hundred or so whose social metabolism was set to this chronology was to be denied a raison d'être.

This carousel of pleasure revolved amid grinding and degrading poverty and deprivation. London particularly was notorious for its vast army of homeless—thousands of families who sought nightly refuge in Trafalgar Square or lived on benches in Green Park. The luckiest members of the lower orders lived in a single room with an entire ménage. Sanitation was primitive; health care, rudimentary. More than half the children born in the poorest districts of London died before they were a year old.

That the equation of perpetual want amid conspicuous plenty did not lead to the revolutions that took place elsewhere is due in part to the stability of Britain's basic institutions, including the Crown. No shattering military defeats would discredit the ruling cliques, as in France. Yet the fear of revolution was never far off. In 1885, when the winter was harsh and unemployment unusually widespread, a mass meeting of the unemployed led to a riot in Pall Mall and a pitched battle with the wealthy members of London's leading clubs, supported by police.

The following year, when Queen Victoria celebrated her Golden Jubilee, Metropolitan Police Commissioner Sir Charles Warren felt obliged to remove the homeless from the city's squares and parks for the benefit of visiting dignitaries and West End traders. The result was another battle, this time in Trafalgar Square. Hundreds of police and troops charged a mob of club-wielding poor. One hundred and fifty civilians were injured, and three hundred were arrested, many of whom were jailed at hard labor.

This showed admirable restraint on the part of the authorities compared to the way unruly citizens in Paris, Vienna, or Madrid were dealt with, but to the Victorian landed classes, they were disturbing indicators that revolution was exportable.

While the Queen was ensconced at the apex of the political and social structure, the Prince of Wales stood at the apex of Society, the federation of the rich and the highborn at play. As such, he was able to create some of his own conventions and live down the many scandals that were to be associated with his name. To an extent he opened the portals of the upper caste to those whose admittance had been barred: bankers, industrialists, sportsmen, even bookmakers. In part, this change in the social rules was due to the fact that he had not been brought up with many aristocrats his own age and was therefore unaffected by their rigid snobbery. Furthermore, since he was heir to the throne, all people were equally beneath him socially, from the noblest duke to the jockey on the Derby winner. He was also adept at switching roles: Playboy Prince one moment, Anointed of God the next. He danced an undignified cancan in the Moulin Rouge with La Goulue. But woe betide his closest friends or his own acknowledged mistresses if they attempted a familiarity when he felt it inappropriate.

So varied and so numerous were Bertie's forays into the bedrooms of the era's most beautiful women that some complex interrelationships came into being. He had a lengthy, sporadic affair with Lady Randolph Churchill, mother of Winston. He also had an open affair with Mary Cornwallis-West, wife of a prominent colonel. That affair may have been open in more ways than one. One account claims that the Prince and Mrs. Cornwallis-West were seen making love al fresco in the woods on the Duke of Westminster's estate in Cheshire. Mrs. Cornwallis-West had a son, George, for whom the Prince of Wales stood godfather. It was widely believed that George was the Prince's illegitimate child. So when Lady Randolph became engaged to George Cornwallis-West, it was not just the significant age difference between the two that prompted the Prince to personally intervene to try to talk them out of it. The marriage went ahead.

Bertie was equally at ease in a brothel in Paris, in the salon of a high-class courtesan, in the drawing room of a Duchess, or moving silently down the corridor of a country home to the room of an official mistress, that is to say, one recognized as his mistress by their friends. Even to these women he was incapable of remaining faithful. He had private rooms, containing concealed beds, constructed in public restaurants where he would "entertain" women for the evening. One Paris brothel, the Chabanais, kept a raised armchair, the *fauteuil d'amour,* for his use with women who were, in his words, "good on their knees."

French detectives followed him everywhere when he was in Paris, Nice, or Biarritz, noting liaisons with the nymphomaniac Princesse de Sagan, the Comtesse de Portales, and the Comtesse de Boutourline, wife of the prefect of Moscow, among many others. After Cesar Ritz opened the Ritz Hotel in the Place Vendome in 1898, the Prince of Wales would stay in the Royal Suite. Cesar Ritz was so eager for the Prince to make the hotel his Paris pied-à-terre that when he complained about the shape of the toilet seats, Ritz had them all redesigned. One of

Bertie's conquests at the Ritz, a woman identified only as Suzette, was immortalized by Escoffier in crêpes suzette.

He was seldom discreet. As early as 1866, when he was twenty-five and married only three years, he visited St. Petersburg and astonished the Czar's court by his philandering. He had to support Lady Susan Vane, who bore him a child. He had an open affair with Sarah Bernhardt but was unable to take her, as others did, in the coffin she kept for the purpose. At something over three hundred pounds, he weighed too much.

He was forced to purchase letters he had written to Giulia Bennini, "La Barucci," a Paris courtesan, who vied with La Belle Otero and Cora Pearl for the title "the Greatest Whore in the World." The Prince, of course, was in a position to know which of them best deserved the title. He had had La Belle Otero, as had many of the crowned heads of Europe, and had summoned her by sending his calling card with a clock face showing 5:00 P.M. drawn on it. Cora Pearl was presented to him curled up on an enormous silver platter, naked but for her string of pearls.

The letters to La Barucci, which he bought from her brother, Piero, after haggling over the $7,500 asking price, were not the only correspondence that came back to haunt him. The Prince had had an affair with Mrs. Harriet Mordaunt, as had several others. When her husband, Sir Charles Mordaunt, M.P., took the desperate step of suing for divorce, the Prince's letters to her were entered into evidence, and although he was not named as a co-respondent, he was called to testify. He told the court he had had no familiarity, nor had he committed any crime, with Harriet Mordaunt, answering counsel's pointed questions with a loud "No! Never!" There was thunderous applause, rapidly suppressed by the judge.

It was certainly perjury. He had visited Lady Mordaunt on numerous occasions in 1867 and 1868, under circumstances that were typical of a Victorian affair. He never came in his private carriage, which had his coat of arms and would have attracted attention. He was always received alone. Sir Charles was always out. He always stayed between one and two hours, and Lady Mordaunt invariably left orders that they were not to be disturbed.

When the letters—which included a Valentine—were read in court, however, they were innocuous, although signed: "Yours ever."

The Prince was threatened with much more incriminating letters in the breakup of the marriage of the Earl of Aylesford. The seventh Duke of Marlborough's son, Blandford, had had an affair with Lady Aylesford while her husband, "Sporting Joe" Aylesford, was in India with the Prince. Upon his return, Lord Aylesford left his wife, whom Blandford had made pregnant. The Prince of Wales insisted that Blandford divorce his own wife and marry Lady Aylesford.

Lord Randolph Churchill, Blandford's brother, took his brother's side. He called on Princess Alexandra at Marlborough House and threatened to publish love letters the Prince had himself written to Lady Aylesford when they were having an equally torrid love affair. Possibly Lord Randolph was already aware of the attention the Prince was paying his own wife, Jennie Churchill. Complicating matters was Blandford's infatuation with his sister-in-law, which had already caused an explosive family row. The Aylesford Affair became so heated that the Prince offered to go to Holland to fight Lord Randolph in a duel. Lord Randolph accepted, with the proviso that the Prince send a second to fight for him, as he had no wish to kill the heir to the throne but would be happy to shoot down the Prince's nominee.

That was enough for Queen Victoria. She stepped into what she called "a dreadful, disgraceful business," and sent Lord Hartington, later to be the Duke of Devonshire, to mediate. One of the most respected aristocrats of his generation, he was among the few men the Queen could trust with the mission. He was also a man of the world in such matters and had long been having an affair with the Duchess of Manchester. He asked Lord Randolph to let him see the letters, and when he had read them, he thrust them into the fire. "You may say what you like and do what you like," Hartington told Churchill. "I have acted in the best interests of both sides."

The feud between the Prince and Lord Randolph Churchill continued for some time. The Prince refused to visit any home in which the Churchills were welcome, and few were willing to take the Churchills' side. It was that boycott that convinced the Duke of Marlborough to accept the post of Viceroy to Ireland so that Lord Randolph, with Jennie, could join him as private secretary. The unfortunate Lady Aylesford gave birth to Blandford's illegitimate son in Paris. Disraeli described the Prince as "a thoroughly spoiled child."

The most celebrated of the Prince of Wales' long-term mistresses was Lillie Langtry. She was born Emilia de Breton, daughter of the philandering dean of Jersey, a British island off the coast of France. An early love affair with a Jersey youth was terminated when her father informed her that the young man was her half-brother, of whom there were several dotted about the island. The dean's sexual conquests in his little domain ultimately forced him to live in Britain, perhaps the only instance of someone being exiled from a tiny island to a large one.

Lillie married an older Jersey businessman and moved to London, but it was two years before she had a chance meeting with the artist Millais and agreed to pose for him. He launched her spectacular career as a "professional beauty." He called one of his paintings, exhibited at the Royal Academy, *The Jersey Lily*, and the *nom d'amour* stayed with her. Lillie had the perfect Pre-Raphaelite looks so prized in the period and was as much a sex symbol in her day as one of the contemporary supermodels is in ours. The Prince had one of his friends, Sir Allen Young, arrange for them to meet at a dinner party. They were soon lovers.

The Prince was not the only member of the Royal Family to find his way to Lillie's bed. She was to bear a child, Jeanne Marie, by Prince Louis of Battenberg, the husband of Queen Victoria's granddaughter, Victoria of Hesse. Thus, she was the half sister of Lord Louis Mountbatten, uncle of Queen Elizabeth II. Battenberg's German relatives made Lillie a financial settlement in return for her silence. Jeanne Marie grew up thinking her aunt was her mother, and it was only when she was in her teens that she accidentally discovered the truth.

In 1879, a scandal sheet, *Town Talk,* published a story that Edward Langtry, Lillie's long-suffering husband, had filed for divorce, citing the Prince of Wales and two minor members of the aristocracy as corespondents. Some weeks later, *Town Talk* claimed that the petition had been withdrawn. Mary Cornwallis-West had been libeled in another story and sued. The editor, Adolph Rosenberg, was arrested, and the Langtrys, encouraged by the Prince, served their suit for libel while he was in jail.

By that time, the Prince's affair with Mrs. Langtry had become public knowledge. It was said that the home secretary, responsible for public order, with additional powers of censorship, had forbidden jokes to be made about the relationship in music halls. One newspaper published the single sentence "There is nothing between the Prince of Wales and Mrs. Langtry" in one issue and the phrase "Not even a sheet" in another. Another publication sarcastically bewailed the fact that store windows displayed pictures of professional beauties, such as

Mrs. Langtry, "side by side—or even beneath" that of the Prince of Wales. Rosenberg admitted publishing the libels but denied knowing they were false. He was sentenced to eighteen months in prison.

Lillie Langtry was to be replaced by Frances "Daisy" Maynard, later to become Countess of Warwick. Frances Maynard was originally recruited into the Royal circle as a possible bride for Queen Victoria's youngest son, Prince Leopold. The Queen had relaxed her objection to members of her family marrying her subjects, allowing her daughter Louise to wed the heir to a Scottish dukedom. Negotiations had reached an advanced stage when Leopold persuaded Daisy to turn him down in favor of a friend, Lord Brooke, who had also been wooing Daisy. Leopold himself had romantic interests elsewhere. He even stood as Lord Brooke's best man.

Perhaps no scandal involving Bertie best illustrates the subtleties of acceptable and unacceptable behavior in Victorian aristocratic society than the affair that brought Frances Maynard into the Prince of Wales's bed.

After marrying Lord Brooke, she took a string of lovers, among them Lord Charles Beresford, a close friend of the Prince's. Beresford had taken an active role in the feud with Lord Randolph Churchill. He brought the Prince's offer of a duel to Lord Randolph and was likely to have been the Prince's nominee had Queen Victoria not intervened.

The son of the Earl of Waterford, Beresford was a flamboyant naval officer with an ego that matched his courage. He had become a national hero during the short, decisive war against Egyptian rebels with a piece of main chance bravado that could have cost him his career. In 1882, Beresford was commanding the gunboat *Condor* during the bombardment of Alexandria, an effort to quell an uprising by Egyptian rebels. The *Condor* was kept away from the action while bigger battleships pounded the fortifications. But when the Egyptians brought larger guns to bear from a fortress out of range of the main British formation, Beresford seized his opportunity.

He sailed unordered under the Egyptian artillery, correctly guessing that he would soon come too close to be hit. The *Condor* destroyed a key fortification just as Beresford was about to be recalled.

In the same campaign, he led a party of marines into the city to find Alexandria in chaos, with rebels burning and looting everywhere. He restored order with only sixty men, using a subtle Imperial cocktail of violence and diplomacy, ordering public executions, floggings, and some judicious paroles. He performed other heroic feats in the war in the Sudan.

Parallel with his military career, Beresford was a Member of Parliament for Waterford, a constituency his family controlled, and he made himself a national figure in that forum, too.

Beresford and the Prince had been close for years. He introduced the Prince to horse racing, which became Bertie's primary occupation after womanizing, and bought him his first racehorse, Stonehenge. His brother, Marcus Beresford, was later to run the Prince's stables. Beresford had accompanied the thirty-three-year-old Prince to India in 1874, and their hunting adventures there became legendary. In turn, the Prince had saved Beresford's career when he was about to be court-martialed for writing to British newspapers that British policy in the Mediterranean was too soft.

Like the Prince, Beresford was a notorious philanderer. He was worshiped by his men and showed them a kindness and concern unusual in a traditionally harsh service. But when it came to women, Beresford could be cruel. Something of his attitude can be gathered from the fact that he claimed he liked to make women cry because it made him laugh when their stays creaked.

When the friendship between the Prince and Beresford was destroyed, the resulting feud almost cost Beresford his career and the Prince his claim to the throne. It began with Frances "Daisy" Maynard and her obsession with Lord Charles Beresford.

What made this affair stand out from the rest was that Beresford and Lady Brooke contemplated divorcing their respective spouses and marrying each other. When Lady Beresford got wind of the seriousness of the affair, she put a stop to it by pointing out to her husband the consequences a divorce would have for him. His military, and probably his political, career would be ruined. He would likely have to leave England. Her own social standing as well as that of Lord Brooke would be injured. And a divorce action might involve the Prince of Wales as a witness. It was not too late to turn back. To go on would be insane. Undeterred by Egyptian artillery, he was outmaneuvered by his wife's reasoning.

The affair cooled, at least on Lord Charles Beresford's side. The Beresfords were reconciled, and Lady Beresford became pregnant. When Frances heard this new development, she was outraged. She wrote him a letter expressing anger more appropriate to an abandoned wife. She claimed one of her children was his and demanded that Lady Beresford's husband leave his wife and join her in France. Had Beresford himself received the letter, he would probably have tossed it into the fire. But he was away, and the letter was opened by Lady Beresford. She immediately put it into the hands of a prominent society attorney, George Lewis. Lewis fired off a warning letter to Frances.

It was Frances who dragged in the Prince of Wales. The Prince took his role as head of society seriously—much more so than his duties as Prince of Wales and heir to the throne. He agreed to retrieve the letter for her. There was a reason more compelling for him than avoiding a scandal in his set. Frances could not help noticing that the Prince was casting his lustful eye on her. There was nothing he liked more than helping a beautiful woman when the reward might be so rich.

The Prince awakened George Lewis in the early hours of the morning and demanded to see the letter. Lewis was unethical enough to show him the letter, but not unethical enough to destroy it, even at the Royal command. The Prince's next stop was Lady Beresford. She told him she would destroy the letter if Lady Brooke would give up Lord Charles and exile herself from London's social scene for a year.

The Prince was furious. Not only was it a harsh punishment in itself; it would have prevented the Prince from pursuing the lust he now felt for Daisy Brooke. It was she, he told Lady Beresford, who would be exiled from society if she failed to hand over the letter. He proceeded to have his friends ostracize Lady Beresford.

Lord Beresford, whose hot temper was renowned, now came to his wife's defense. He stormed over to Marlborough House, had a furious argument with the Prince, called him a coward to his face and a string of vulgar names, and pushed him backward on a sofa. The two would have come to blows had Beresford not been physically restrained. Beresford soon left in command of a new ship, the *Undaunted*, in the Mediterranean. But the feud had only just begun. At that moment a new scandal erupted, one that was to subject the Prince to the kind of public outrage Prince Albert had once predicted.

Two

The Ultimate Sin

F rances Maynard, Lady Brooke, became the Prince of Wales's lover while the dispute between the Prince and Beresford was still developing. But Frances Maynard—everyone called her Daisy—was more than just another lover. The Prince went through a private little ceremony with her that made them, in their own eyes, husband and wife. He would write to her several times a month when they were apart, even referring to her as "darling wife" and "Daisy wife." It was a double betrayal—of his legal wife, obviously, but also of his mother and dead father. For he gave her in lieu of a wedding ring an inscribed man's gold ring, one of his father's last gifts. "To Bertie," it said. "A. & V. R." By September 1890, when the forty-nine-year-old Prince made a fateful visit to a country estate called Tranby Croft, the thirty-nine-year-old Daisy was an established *maîtresse en titre*.

This meant that she would always be placed close or next to the Prince at dinner unless the Princess herself was present. It was not uncommon for husband and wife to be given separate rooms in country houses to which they were invited, and this was invariably the case when Lord and Lady Brooke came to stay. The Prince would be placed conveniently, and discreetly, in a room next door, if possible, to his lover. It was also common for a bell to sound early in the morning to allow those who strayed from their own bedrooms during the night to return to them before the servants arrived.

The Prince never missed the classic flat races of the season, which included the Derby and the St. Leger. The St. Leger of September 1890 took Bertie and his Marlborough House retinue to the bleak north England town of Doncaster. Having the Prince as a guest for a few days was not an inexpensive undertaking. Each of the Prince's circle of friends, who would expect to be invited, too, would arrive with his own servants, as many as four apiece; the Prince would be joined by six. Most hostesses would want to put on a great show, and it was not uncommon for whole suites to be redecorated to the Prince's taste prior to his arrival. His usual host, the obsequious Christopher Sykes, had almost bankrupted himself entertaining the Prince and his circle and could no longer afford to do so.

Instead, the group stayed at Tranby Croft, the country home, copied from the blueprints of an Italian villa, of a wealthy shipbuilder, Arthur Stanley Wilson. Daisy was not present. Her stepfather, Lord Rosslyn, had died, and she was preparing to travel to Scotland for the funeral. The Wilsons were determined to make the Prince's stay memorable, and their hospitality was particularly lavish.

Some eighteen months earlier, the Wilsons' daughter, Susannah Menzies, had given birth to a son, Stewart Graham Menzies. Many years later, when he was Sir Stewart Menzies, head of MI6, the British intelligence agency, he was widely regarded in the intelligence community and at the highest levels of the civil service as Edward VII's son. He bore almost no resemblance to his siblings and had what was later to be known as "Windsor blue" eyes.

One of the other guests that week was Sir William Gordon-Cumming, a lieutenant colonel in the Scots Guards. At forty-three, he had been in the army for more than twenty-three years and had a heroic record. He had fought in the Zulu wars and figured prominently in the climactic engagement of the campaign, the Battle of Ulandi, in which the Zulu Empire was crushed, the Zulu army mercilessly massacred, the monarch, Cetshwayo, put to flight, and his capital razed.

He had fought with panache in Egypt under the command of the Prince of Wales's uncle, Prince Arthur, Duke of Connaught, in the Battle of Tel-el-Kebir. He possessed a stately London home, Scottish estates of some forty thousand acres, and a healthy private income. He had been a friend of the Prince of Wales for several years and stayed at Sandringham, the Prince's country home. Like many of the Prince's friends, he was an insatiable womanizer. When he tried to seduce Leonie Jerome, Winston Churchill's aunt, she refused him. He was dismissive of her chastity. "All the young wives try me," he told her.

Others staying at the house included Lord Arthur Somerset, Lord Edward Somerset, Lord and Lady Coventry, Gen. Owen Williams, Christopher Sykes, Lady Brougham, the wealthy trader Reuben Sassoon, Lt. Berkeley Levett, who was in the same regiment as Gordon-Cumming and served directly under him, and relatives of the Wilsons.

After dinner, there was music and entertainment, and a considerable amount of champagne, port, and brandy had been consumed. Bertie, Sir William Gordon-Cumming, and several others settled down to play the Prince of Wales's favorite card game, baccarat, or "backie," as he called it.

They used the Prince of Wales's beautifully crafted casino chips, embossed with his three-feathered coronet emblem, which had been a gift from Sassoon and which the Prince carried with him on weekend trips.

Baccarat is a simple game of chance played with a shoe of four packs of cards. What skill is involved rests in gambling, not playing. The object is to reach eight or nine with two cards. There is a croupier, a banker, a dealer, and players, two of whom actually take cards, the others betting with or against the bank. Each hand of cards is known as a "coup." When the events of the weekend were ultimately to place the players in a crowded Court of Queen's Bench some months later, Sir Edward Clarke, Q.C., was to describe it as "a most uninteresting mode of losing your own money or winning anyone else's." Socially, it was not the most acceptable form of gambling. The senior Wilson had once lost a considerable amount of money at baccarat and banned its play in his home. Good manners prevented him from enforcing the ban on his Royal guest.

Play began at about 11:00 P.M. on the first night. The Wilsons had no baccarat table, and so three whist tables of unequal height were pushed together. The players crowded around to gamble and remained there, hugger-mugger, for about an hour and a half. The bank was fixed at $500. Not a high-stakes game, but $500 would pay the annual salaries of two valets.

Arthur Stanley Wilson, the son of the host, was seated next to Sir William Gordon-Cumming. He saw something in the lieutenant colonel's play and turned to Lieutenant Levett, who was sitting next to him. He said in a whisper: "This is too hot!"

Levett asked him what he was talking about.

"The man next to me is cheating."

Levett told him that was impossible.

"Well, then, look for yourself!"

Levett watched the next coup while Wilson looked away. The lieutenant came to the same conclusion. "My God!" he whispered. "It is too hot!"

When the game had broken up and Sir William had retired, one hundred pounds ahead, the two discussed the incident for about an hour. What they had witnessed, or thought they had witnessed, was Sir William surreptitiously increasing and decreasing his stake after the cards had been declared. It was a form of cheating known as *la pousette.*

It would be a breach of any code of honor; indeed, it was a criminal offense. But in Victorian society, for a senior military officer from an elite Guards regiment, like Sir William, to stoop so low as to cheat at cards, and in the presence of the Prince of Wales, was more serious than that. People had been forced to shoot themselves for less. If it were to be shown to be true, Sir William faced dismissal from the army, blackballing from his clubs, and social isolation. None of that could be done discreetly. If revealed, a scandal would ensue, and it would inevitably involve the Prince.

The following morning, the younger Wilson told his mother what he saw. She warned him not to cause a scandal in her house. He ordered the butler to mark out a baccarat table with margins so that stakes at that night's game would be in plain view. He then told his brother-in-law, Edward Lycett Green, a pompous, hot-tempered master of hounds with the local hunt, what he had seen.

That night, the Prince teased Sir William about having won the night before. "How did you come to win so much?" he said as he shuffled the cards.

"I could not help winning with a tableau such as this," Sir William answered, showing the record he had been keeping of the previous night's hands.

Meanwhile, Lycett Green watched Sir William's play and believed he saw the same cheating Wilson and Lieutenant Levett had witnessed. He rose from the table and left the room, sending a note to his mother-in-law that he had observed Sir William cheating. She focused on the game, and she, too, saw evidence of cheating. The Prince had seen nothing but at some point remarked irritably, "I wish people would put their stakes where they can be seen," apparently referring to the way Sir William held his hands over his stake.

At the next day's race meeting, Green told the two Somersets, and it was decided they should bring in Lord Coventry, as the elder and most respected of the house party. Coventry, in his turn, brought in General

Williams, as both were old friends of Sir William's. They confronted him before dinner that night, and Lord Coventry told him: "A very unpleasant thing has occurred. Certain persons have accused you of causing a foul play at baccarat." Even the word cheating was beneath him. Sir William denied it and demanded to see the Prince.

The dinner bell intervened, and everyone dined as if nothing had happened, although the atmosphere was decidedly cooler than on the previous two evenings. The guests who had not been told about the unfolding drama doubtless knew something was afoot. After dinner, the news was given to the Prince in private, and events took an inexplicable and, for Sir William, disastrous turn.

Sir William was called in. "I have heard that certain persons have brought a foul and abominable charge against me, and I emphatically deny that I have done anything of the kind," he told the Prince.

"What can you do?" the Prince said to him coldly. "There are five accusers against you."

Sir William replied that he would insult his accusers on the race course the next day—an open challenge to them to bring a more public charge or back down. Eager to avoid a public row, Bertie told him not to be a fool. "What would be the point of that?" he asked. "There are five to one."

Sir William was told to wait in his room while his fate was decided. Although Sir William was at no point directly confronted by his accusers, and indeed, he did not ask to be, his accusers apparently took part in the discussion of what would happen to him. Lycett Green demanded that Sir William be publicly charged, but he was overruled. Instead, the Prince, Coventry, and Williams agreed on a compromise, which, as it turned out, was as foolish as it was shabby. If Sir William were to sign a document promising never to play cards again, nothing further would be said, and the accusation need not be revealed. Lycett Green insisted that the document clearly contain an admission of guilt, and the others agreed.

The document was hastily drawn up. The Prince withdrew, leaving Coventry and General Williams to secure Sir William's signature. He was called in and shown what was proposed:

> In consideration of the promise made by the gentlemen whose names are subscribed to preserve silence with reference to an accusation which has been made with regard to my conduct at

baccarat on the nights of Monday and Tuesday, the 8th and 9th of September 1890 at Tranby Croft, I will on my part, solemnly undertake never to play cards again as long as I live.

Sir William complained that the document was tantamount to an admission of guilt, but his friends told him that signing was the only way to avoid "a horrible scandal." They may have been thinking more about the scandal that would fall upon the Prince's head rather than Sir William's.

He signed, but in doing so, he made it clear he was standing by his claim of innocence. The document was taken back to the Prince, who also signed it, followed by Coventry, Williams, the Somersets, Wilson, Lycett Green, and Levett. Sir William was then told he had better leave the house the following morning. Within days, the Prince, incapable of keeping anything secret, had told the story to Lady Brooke. She, in turn, spread the tale, earning her the nickname "Babbling Brooke."

Sir William soon regretted signing the document. First, he was told to keep out of the Prince's sight and to cancel his visit to the Duke of Fife's Scottish estate, Mar Lodge, where he would have run into the Prince and other members of the Royal Family. His doing so triggered more speculation. Then he received an anonymous letter from Paris signed "From One Who Pities You," saying, "They had talked too much in England." There was an error in it, but the letter said just enough to convince Sir William that the writer knew everything. "If you come to Paris or Monte Carlo be very reserved and do not touch a card."

He began to feel a chill in the mess when he entered. Conversations seemed to stop when he approached his fellow officers. Tables to which he might have been invited filled up. Old friends seemed lost in the *Times* at the Guards Club, the Turf, and the Marlborough.

Sir William was outraged that he had signed a humiliating document in return for keeping his good name and now found himself defamed and ostracized. He wrote indignantly to the Prince, Coventry, and General Williams, his old friends who had guaranteed their discretion: "I have only two choices—vanish or cut my throat."

Shortly before the New Year, 1891, Sir William filed suit for slander against his original accusers: Arthur Stanley Wilson and his mother, Berkeley Levett, Lycett Green, and his wife.

The Prince, entering his fiftieth year, heard of Sir William's suit while he was celebrating the New Year at Sandringham. Lord Randolph

Churchill—now back in the Royal fold—Jennie Churchill, and Lord and Lady Brooke were among the guests. The Prince was superstitious about the rituals of the New Year, and bad news made him depressed. He knew he was certain to be called as a witness, and he became increasingly distressed as the trial date drew nearer.

He was intelligent enough to understand that the immediate issues of Sir William's guilt or innocence were likely to be swamped in the speculation about and criticism of his own actions. He was no longer a relatively young man about town, as he had been during his last court appearance in the Mordaunt case. Now in his fiftieth year, he could expect to become King at any time. That he was something of a rake was well known, although the details were not public. The resurgence of Queen Victoria's popularity following her Diamond Jubilee and respect for her character merely served to emphasize the differences between them. A public scandal would inevitably spark a debate over his fitness to succeed her. He even tried to get Lord Salisbury, the prime minister, to influence the trial, but Salisbury refused.

The trial opened on a gloriously sunny June day in 1891, by which time various versions of the story had already been published, including the full text of the document Sir William, the Prince, and the others had signed. The court was packed with titled spectators, many of them wielding opera glasses. Sir Edward Clarke, the solicitor general, represented Sir William in his private capacity as a barrister. Among the defense barristers were Sir Charles Russell, a deadly interrogator, and Herbert Asquith, the future prime minister. The case was heard before one of that generation's finest legal minds, the lord chief justice, Lord Coleridge.

"This court is not a theater," Coleridge barked during a burst of applause during the tense proceedings. But as the *Illustrated London News* pointed out in its reporting of the case, theater was exactly what it was. The Prince of Wales was present for most of the trial. At one point, Sir William made a point of turning his back on his friend and future King just as, he no doubt felt, his friend had turned his back on him.

The case was opened by Sir Edward Clarke with an eloquent summary of Sir William's military record, his service to the nation, his rank in society, his honor as an officer and gentleman, and the lack of any credible motive for having cheated for a relatively small sum. The Prince, Lord Coventry, and General Williams could not have believed Sir William was guilty, or they could not, as honorable men, have agreed to cover it up, he argued. What Sir William had been doing, he said, was playing a common system in baccarat—*coup de trois*—in which a stake is increased with each winning coup. But in their efforts to distance the Prince from controversy, Lord Coventry and General Williams pressured an innocent man to settle for less than justice.

Sir William took the stand. Many military officers are incapable of wearing civilian clothes with panache, but he was not one of them. He stood boldly in the dock, coolly challenging the fates, one hand encased in a tight gray leather glove, the other ungloved, elbows resting on the bar of the witness box. He gave his account of the two evenings' events—his immediate outrage at the charges leveled against him, his fruitless interview with the Prince of Wales, and the pressure to sign the document. He swore he had never cheated.

But he was badly mauled by the tenacious Sir Charles Russell in cross-examination. Sir William's letters, including his thoughts of suicide, were read in court. They sounded loaded with self-pity. In a rapid-fire exchange, Sir Charles drew Sir William into a trap, establishing the many years of friendship and intimacy with the Prince, Coventry, and Gen. Owen Williams. These men believed him guilty, and he signed an admission of guilt at their request. Why, if he were not guilty? His own counsel had set up an escape route for Sir William—that his friends acted as they did to protect the Prince. For whatever reason, he failed to use it, repeatedly stating that the only scandal discussed was his own. Then why had he not demanded to be confronted with his accusers? Sir William shilly-shallied. Again, why had he signed the document knowing everybody would believe him guilty?

"Not everybody," he said.

Sir Charles ripped into him. He had already stated that the document was an admission of guilt.

"I lost my head on that occasion," he explained.

Looking at Sir William, who had fought hordes of assegai-wielding Zulus, it must have been difficult to understand that explanation. To lose his head over the accusations of three young men—one of them a subaltern—and two women!

The fifty-year-old Prince of Wales watched the performance with evident satisfaction. But he was to fare little better himself. He appeared uncomfortable and diffident—more in the dock than in the witness box. He seemed to be waiting for a question that he did not want to answer and gave his testimony in tones that could barely be heard.

His German accent shocked those who had not heard it before. One contemporary writer reported: "It was curious to observe in his deep voice the early studies in his father's language."

Under Victorian trial rules, juries could direct questions to witnesses through the judge, and it was a jury member who asked the most pertinent question. As the Prince was about to leave the witness box, he was called back. Did His Royal Highness believe it when told his friend had cheated?

"They seemed so strongly supported—unanimously so—that I felt I had no other recourse open to me," he said.

He came away fortunate that deeper inquiries had not been made but with his reputation tarnished. He had failed to take proper charge. He had used poor judgment in taking part in a cover-up that could not succeed. He had allowed himself to be convinced by flimsy evidence. He had let down an old friend to save himself. And hovering over the whole proceedings was the image of an heir to the throne who became the banker at a gambling table in a smoke-filled room, playing with chips adorned with his own noble insignia.

And if there was any doubt that the reason Lord Coventry and General Williams pressured Sir William to sign the document in exchange for silence, it was dispelled by an entry Lord Coventry made in his private diary: "We desired, if possible . . . to keep the Prince out of it."

English law forbids comment on a court case while the case is proceeding, but the *Illustrated London News* cleverly bypassed the rule. Next to a report on the continuing trial, it carried an essay which purported to be about the title that should be accorded the daughter of the Duchess of Fife, the latest Royal grandchild. It segued gracefully into a thinly disguised critique of the heir to the throne. It raised the specter of republicanism once the Queen was dead, and went on:

A period of social disturbance is not far distant. It may not be a period of violent disturbance. It is far less likely to take that character if the throne is firmly maintained as a center of stability; and therefore it becomes a matter of profound importance that the royal family should guard against every accident, near or remote, that might be provocative of popular discontent or lowering to the dignity of the Crown. . . . We have seen that possibilities of weakness lie at a distance which cannot be called extraordinary.

The Tranby Croft jury listened to six days of testimony before Sir Edward Clarke made his final appeal to the jury on behalf of Sir William. His family motto was *Sans Peur* (Without Fear), and that is how he came before the court, he said. His most scathing attack was on Lord Coventry and on General Williams—false friends, he called them. "There is a strange and subtle influence in Royalty," he said, "which has adorned our history with chivalrous deeds done by men of character and honor at the peril of their lives, to protect a Prince . . . here it led to a cruel injustice."

He rounded on the Prince himself. "Some people might think there is no scandal in playing baccarat, but . . . when houses where baccarat was played were liable to be visited by the police, it was to be lamented that it be played in such circumstances." It was "against the conscience . . . of the mass of the people." At the end of his address to the jury, the whole court rose in applause, quickly suppressed by Lord Coleridge.

It was an appeal of extraordinary power, so that the next day, Lord Coleridge told the jury he was glad a night had passed before he himself had to sum up. His final remarks, supposedly impartial, clearly directed the jury toward the defendants' case. Lord Coleridge quoted Samuel Butler:

> By Jove! I am not covetous for Gold
> But if it be a sin to covet honor
> I'm the most offending soul alive!

He proceeded to demolish Sir William Gordon-Cumming's behavior as that of a man who did not covet his honor enough to refuse to sign an admission of guilt. The implication was clear. No innocent man would have done so. The jury took only ten minutes to find for the defendants.

"The bronze face and statuesque form did not flinch," the *Illustrated London News* said of Sir William's reaction to the verdict. "He slowly left the court and passed to his doom, a Spartan to the end."

The crowd in the packed courtroom heard the verdict with less sangfroid. The jury were hissed and booed and, as they tried to leave, jostled, forcing the police to intervene to save them from attack. Attacks on the Prince's behavior came within hours.

The Tranby Croft case marked the nadir of the Prince's popularity. The press attacks were severe partly because the Prince's behavior had been dishonorable and partly because the press leaped at the opportunity to criticize him for those aspects of his personal life they could not otherwise mention. The Tranby Croft case was an issue they could legally address; the stories of his many infidelities were issues they could not.

The *Times,* in a thundering editorial, remarked that it would have been better for the nation if the Prince, rather than Sir William, had been forced to sign the document swearing never to play cards again.

"If he is known to pursue questionable pleasures . . . the serious public who after all are the backbone of England, regret and resent it," the editorial said.

The president of the powerful Wesleyan Conference, Dr. James Moulton, called a public meeting on the night of the verdict to "consider the gambling tendencies of the age." He denounced the Prince's behavior, saying it was "a matter of deep regret that the heir to the throne should be given to one of the worst forms of gambling that existed."

The Reverend Charles Williams, former president of the Baptist church in England, told his faithful that "all deplored that the Prince of Wales should be the leader of a gambling concern." Messages and resolutions condemning the Prince poured in from all over the country.

Arthur Wilson fared little better. He had been suspected of being one of the gossips who had allowed the scandal to leak in the first place. Of his entire family, only Susannah continued to rise in society and retain amiable contact with the Prince of Wales, further fueling suspicions that she had been his mistress and had borne him a son.

Sir William drew little comfort from the Prince's difficulty. He hurried over to the home of his twenty-year-old bride-to-be, a New York cotton heiress, Florence Garner, and offered to release her from their engagement. She refused. The following day, they were married, very quietly, at Holy Trinity Sloane Street, while contractors working inside the church were on a break. Three days later, a three-line announcement appeared in the *Times,* saying that Sir William had been dismissed from the army. Sir William and his bride left London for Gordon-Cumming's Scottish estate, where they lived in isolation, barred from society forever.

His American wife, unable to adjust to the life of a disgraced spouse exiled to a Scottish hillside, vegetated. Ultimately, Gordon-Cumming had two mistresses move in with them.

The Prince, meanwhile, had to sweat it out in public. He was booed and hissed at the theater and at Ascot races. The prime minister, Lord

Salisbury, refused to support him, knowing that public opinion against the Prince would then focus on the government. Queen Victoria suggested that the Prince write an open letter to the archbishop of Canterbury condemning gambling. Lord Salisbury told her that no one would believe it. He finally wrote a private letter to the archbishop, which was judiciously leaked, expressing a newfound "horror" of gambling and saying he no longer allowed baccarat to be played in his presence. Horse racing, he told the archbishop, was a different matter. Henceforth, the Prince did swear off baccarat and switched to bridge.

One man keeping a particularly eager eye on the Tranby Croft case was Lord Charles Beresford, Daisy's former lover. The dispute over the recovery of Daisy's letter to Beresford had not diminished, and Beresford's wife, who had tried to have Daisy banished from society, now found herself ostracized. In his cabin on the *Undaunted,* he pored over newspaper reports of Tranby Croft, and his fury at the Prince was fueled by regular letters from Lady Beresford detailing each new social slight.

On July 12, 1891, Beresford wrote to his wife, enclosing a letter to be sent on to the Prince of Wales via Lord Salisbury. It accused him of being "a blackguard and a coward."

The letter for the Prince went on:

> I have no intention of allowing my wife to suffer for any faults I may have committed in days gone by. Much less have I any intention of allowing any woman to wreak vengeance on my wife because I would not accede to her entreaties to return a friendship I had repudiated. . . . The days of duelling are past but there is a more just way of getting right done and that is publicity.

Beresford threatened to denounce the Prince of Wales and his affair with Daisy and other women on his return to England.

The substance of the threat, as it must have been interpreted by Lord Salisbury, was that Lord Beresford intended to defame the Prince and challenge him to sue. The Tranby Croft case had already shown Beresford what kind of mauling the Prince would take if even more sordid details of his private life were revealed. The story of the Prince of Wales's defense of an immoral woman whom he had made his own mistress against an honest woman who struggled to save her marriage was explosive. Beresford demanded a public apology—meaning in front of the Prince's friends—and the dismissal of Daisy from court.

Lord Salisbury wrote Beresford, trying to calm the waters. He told Beresford he would destroy himself if he tried to ruin the Prince. He hinted, too, that his career might be more glittering if he forgot the feud.

But the new scandal already had a life of its own. Egged on by Beresford, Lady Beresford's sister circulated a typewritten pamphlet detailing the Prince's entire affair with Daisy, including a verbatim copy of Lady Brooke's letter to Lord Charles. It was so sensational that hostesses held secret gatherings at which it was read aloud. There was, of course, no suit for libel.

Princess Alexandra heard about the new scandal on a visit to her relatives in Denmark. She had stood by the Prince through his other difficulties and supported him unquestioningly during the Tranby Croft affair, but now his open favoritism of Lady Brooke and the undeniable reasons for it were a public embarrassment. She changed her plans to return home and went instead to visit her sister, Dagmar, the Czarina Marie Fedorovna, at the Livadia Palace in the Crimea. She declined to tell Lord Salisbury when she might return.

This was a catastrophe. A public breakdown of the heir's marriage would have thrown the succession itself into question. A quick resolution was now urgent, and Salisbury convinced the Prince to take whatever way out that could be found. He met with Beresford and guaranteed that his naval career would be unaffected, perhaps even enhanced, if he gave in to diplomacy. Salisbury drafted letters for both Beresford and the Prince to sign.

Salisbury's letter to the Prince from Beresford provided an anodyne version of the affair which gave Salisbury plenty of room to ghost a reply from the Prince that it had all been a misunderstanding and that he "had never had any such intention to wound her [Lady Charles's] feelings." The original letter from Lady Brooke was burned.

Fate intervened to bring Princess Alexandra back to England. Her younger son, Prince George, Duke of York, developed typhoid, and she rushed back from the Crimea to nurse him. But she was furious with her husband for allowing the sordid affair with Daisy to get out of hand. It remains unclear whether she was aware of how emotionally involved her husband had become with his other "wife." But a series of blistering arguments ensued, culminating in the Prince of Wales daring Princess Alexandra to sue him for divorce. He had been in the divorce court before as a witness, he told her, and she could take him there again as a defendant.

It was a bluff, because Queen Victoria would have moved heaven and earth to stop it. It would almost certainly have forced the Prince of Wales to step out of the line of succession, but it would also have separated the Princess from court and her children.

They agreed to formalize an agreement that had remained unspoken. She told him he could have as many women as he wanted. From that point on, their marriage became little more than sentiment and ceremony. Princess Alexandra retained a deep affection for her husband, and he, respect for her. If anything, their public attitude toward each other improved, while privately they grew further apart. But the looming constitutional crisis was averted.

The Prince never fully forgave his old friend. Some four years later, the Prince's horse, Persimmon, won the Derby as an outsider at 20–1. Lord Marcus Beresford, Lord Charles's brother, was in charge of the Prince's stables, and in the midst of the celebration in the winner's enclosure, he knew no request would be denied by the Prince. He asked—his eyes welling with tears—if the Prince would accept the congratulations of his brother. He did so, a little diffidently, and Lord Charles was friendly, polite, and even a little humble.

Immediately afterward, the Prince decided he had been disloyal to his "own lovely little Daisy wife" and wrote her a letter explaining why he had received Beresford before she heard about it from anyone else. This was one letter that did not trigger a scandal for the Prince.

Instead, it was to cause one, some years later, for his son, George V.

There is a postscript to the Beresford feud which shows that private affairs can sometimes have spectacular consequences for public policy. Lord Charles was ultimately to rise to the rank of admiral and commander of the Channel fleet, making him the second most important officer in the navy. His flagship, ironically, was the *King Edward VII*. He was to embroil himself in another bitter feud with the admiral of the fleet, John Fisher, whose foresight prepared the Royal Navy for its greatest challenge in a hundred years—the German navy.

In this feud, Bertie, by now King Edward VII, sponsored Fisher against Beresford and saved Fisher's career. "They would have eaten me alive," Fisher acknowledged, "if it had not been for Your Majesty."

Had Fisher fallen and Beresford triumphed, the Royal Navy would have entered World War I less prepared. The result of the great naval clash at Jutland, when the Royal Navy narrowly triumphed over the German fleet, might have ended in a catastrophic loss to England.

Three

Farewell the Strumpets

Bertie began his reign in 1901, upon the death of Queen Victoria, with acts of betrayal and vandalism. He was approaching sixty. He ignored his mother's wishes to take his given name, Albert, as his title and announced he would style himself Edward VII. No one believed his explanation, which was that he so admired his father that he wished his name to stand alone in history as "Albert the Good." He proceeded to sweep through his new home, Buckingham Palace, eliminating Albert's influence wherever he could. Some of this work was much-needed renovation—installation of garages for motorcars, wiring for electricity, telephones, and new plumbing, all in keeping with the technology of the new century.

He destroyed all the traces—busts, pictures, and mementos—of John Brown, his mother's controversial servant and companion, whom he despised. One vast portrait of Brown in full Scottish dress hung at Balmoral, the Queen's Scottish estate. Edward VII poked his cane through Brown's heart before destroying it. Victoria had believed that Brown had been sent as a companion for her from the beyond by Prince Albert, but whether theirs was a sexual relationship remains in question. Certainly Edward VII loathed Brown's influence on his mother.

The new King also deported his mother's Indian servants, including one known as the Munshi, who he believed, as did many others, exerted an improper influence on her in her later years. He abandoned Osborne House, Victoria's hideaway on the Isle of Wight, which for him held so many unhappy memories. He did so despite Victoria's specific wish that her descendants retain it as a Royal residence in perpetuity. Eventually, Osborne House became a naval training school and a convalescent home for superannuated sailors.

He then set about rewriting, or rather destroying, history. It had been Queen Victoria's wish that Princess Beatrice, her youngest daughter, edit her diaries. She doctored and copied out sections of the journal the Queen had kept from childhood until the last days of her life, destroying the original manuscript as she went. What would have been a gold mine for historians was consigned to the fire. King Edward went further, ordering many of her letters both to members of the family and major political figures, such as Disraeli, tracked down, returned to him, and burned. He also had letters he himself had written to Disraeli as Prince of Wales returned and destroyed. He did so on the grounds that the writer owned the material. When he destroyed communications to himself, however, he contended the recipient owned them.

Lord Knollys and Lord Esher, his two closest aides, were assigned to comb through all state papers and private correspondence for any references that might prove compromising during his life or after his death. When Catherine "Skittles" Walters, a society courtesan, was close to death, Lord Knollys was sent to her home to recover hundreds of letters Edward VII had sent her over a period of some thirty years. He had given her what amounted to a state pension, and detailed records of these payments were destroyed.

This systematic destruction of priceless and irreplaceable historical records as well as compromising billets-doux has few equals in modern history. It was a mountainous task and went on well into the reign of Edward's successor, George V. When Queen Alexandra died intestate in 1925, all of her personal papers were also consigned to the bonfire of Royal vanities. Despite all that is known about Victorian political and social life from other sources, Edward VII's passion for destruction ensured that there would always be gaps in the record and many secrets unknown.

The attempt to alter and manipulate the modern historical records of the British Royal Family continued throughout succeeding generations. Time and again, potentially embarrassing documents have been ordered destroyed. Even those retained in the Royal Archives are subject to stringent censorship. No biographer is given access to the Archives without an agreement to submit a manuscript for palace approval. As a result, no professional historian, as opposed to a biographer, has attempted a thorough, objective study of a British monarch after George IV, whose ten-year reign ended in 1830.

Edward VII came close to having one of the shortest reigns in British history. Eight days before his scheduled June 26 Coronation, he came down with appendicitis. An appendectomy was a major operation in 1902, and a man of sixty-one as obese as Edward VII was considered unlikely to survive. Surgery became inevitable when his appendix ruptured on the twenty-third and peritonitis was diagnosed. Without surgery he would have days to live.

Queen Victoria had been superstitious and a notorious occultist, and Edward VII and all his successors harbored similar faith in Gypsies, mystics, and mediums—a bizarre character trait for the head of the established Church of England. He had good-luck charms hung in festoons from his bed in each of the Royal residences and carried a stock of them when he traveled. His servants, entourage, and hosts knew many of his superstitious foibles, such as his horror of a crossed knife and fork and his fear of the number 13. So before consenting to an operation, he consulted a clairvoyant who told him that Victoria was going to die shortly and that he would follow her within days. She did in fact die the same week. Queen Alexandra, who had similar occult interests and believed herself both clairvoyant and clairaudient, summoned a more celebrated psychic to counter the predictions of the first. This psychic, Cheiro, who had officiated at numerous Royal séances, had earlier predicted that the King would live until he was sixty-nine. He told the King he would survive.

The King, though he must have been in considerable pain, still had his doubts. He refused to die uncrowned after waiting so many years for the throne. He was adamant that the Coronation go on as planned, even at the risk of his life. His doctors told him bluntly he would die before he reached Westminster Abbey and that the guests already filling London hotels for the event would inevitably attend his funeral if he continued to behave in a stubborn fashion. Queen Alexandra ultimately helped hold him down while he was chloroformed. The operation proved successful. Meanwhile, palace officials, in what was to become a pattern of public deception, had issued a bulletin that he was suffering from lumbago.

His illness and recuperation of several weeks meant that the Coronation could not take place until August 9. Many European heads of state could not stay in London for such a long period, nor could they return so quickly once they had left. So the Coronation was robbed of much of its splendor. Only the Imperial and colonial contingents took part in the traditional procession to Westminster Abbey. One courtier noted tactfully that the ceremony, devoid of so many European Kings and Princes, "had something of the character of a family festival."

Edward VII began his reign one of the poorest of British monarchs. Queen Victoria had not kept him penniless, and the estates of the Duchy of Cornwall, which belonged to the Prince of Wales, provided what should have been a more than adequate income. But his constant private travel, his unequaled generosity to friends and sometimes strangers, his enormous household, his lavish entertaining, his gambling, at which he often lost large sums of money, and his expensive taste in women meant that he easily went through his income and made regular inroads into his capital. Despite keeping his stable in profit, he had constant recourse to French moneylenders and on occasion secretly sold jewelry and *objets d'art* to raise ready cash.

As a result, he had virtually no capital when he took the throne and was horrified when Queen Victoria's largest bequests went to his children, his siblings, and their offspring. Parliament rescued him with a capital payment of $2.5 million.

Edward VII set about being King with gusto, but he showed some reluctance to give up the title of Prince of Wales, which he had held for so long. The traditional title of the heir to the throne, it should have passed to his son, the Duke of York, but the new King delayed bestowing it on him as long as possible.

His enthusiasm for his new role was short-lived. Long denied access to state papers, he demanded to see as many as possible, and while he took no interest in domestic and trade policy, he insisted on his constitutional right to be consulted on important state issues. But the constitutional monarchy envisaged by Parliament was a far cry from the constitutional monarchy proposed by the Prince Consort, Edward's father. In a series of battles which were, in effect, to create the modern ceremonial monarchy, successive governments sought to exclude him from the decision-making process as much as possible, ignore his input, and on occasion openly defy him.

Several times, individual ministers, and at least twice the entire government, threatened to resign and create a constitutional crisis over relatively trivial matters. As the King's irrational temper tantrums grew wilder and less predictable with age, ministers sought to exclude him further, creating more uncontrollable rages, when he would throw objects.

When the British government insisted that the King bestow the

Order of the Garter on the Shah of Persia to cement a shaky alliance, Edward VII insisted it was a Christian Order and could not be bestowed on an "infidel." Ministers designed a special version of the Order, devoid of Christian symbols, which the King found even more offensive. At one point, Edward hurled the diamond-encrusted badge of the Order through the porthole of his yacht, *Victoria and Albert.*

Matching his fits of towering rage were equally unpredictable troughs of depression, both symptoms of alcoholism. Several times he gloomily talked of abdication. He believed his government refused to take him as seriously as it had taken his mother, and it struck him that, now in his sixties and having waited twenty years longer than he expected to ascend the throne, the job now seemed empty and frustrating.

Many of his old friends and political allies were dead, and there was no one in the political arena willing to defend him from repeated attacks in the House of Commons. A reactionary even by the standards of his times, he was an implacable opponent of liberalizing movements, both in the administration of the Empire and at home, where he violently opposed voting rights for women. This is a paradox, given his lifelong attraction to intelligent, opinionated, and independent ladies.

By far the most traveled of English monarchs, he considered himself an expert on foreign policy, especially since he was related to the key heads of state in Europe. He was well informed on the complex web of foreign policy issues and vital interests, and he was responsible for the personal diplomacy that led to an alliance with Russia against Germany. He was humiliated again and again, however, by the fact that most of his relatives were much more powerful in their states than he was in his. The surviving legacy of his reign was the renewal of the alliance with France, the Entente Cordiale. He was not, as was widely held, its architect, but as a successful roving ambassador and sincere Francophile, he helped lay its foundations.

By the time he ascended the throne, Edward VII's relationship with his "darling Daisy wife"—by now titled Countess of Warwick—had waned, although he maintained a platonic friendship with her. Her newfound interest in working-class politics would culminate in a career as the "Socialist Countess," allying herself with the infant Labour party. Her place in Bertie's affections and his bed had been taken by Alice Keppel, the wife of George Keppel, the untitled son of the Earl of Albemarle. She was twenty-nine when she first met the then Prince of Wales in 1898. He was twenty-seven years her senior. Beautiful, vivacious, and intelligent, she remained his recognized mistress until his death in 1910.

Alice Keppel was the daughter of a British admiral and had an exotic heritage. Her maternal grandmother had been Greek, married to the governor of British possessions in the Aegean. Alice inherited something of her Mediterranean looks, passionate nature, and fiery personality. She had striking chestnut-red hair, a pristine complexion, haunting blue-green eyes, and a voluptuous figure. Edward became emotionally dependent on her, and as might be expected in a May-September romance, he was intensely jealous when she paid attention to anyone other than him.

As well as regular weekends and amorous afternoons, the King and Mrs. Keppel would spend several weeks a year together in Biarritz and Paris, ostensibly at separate villas but nevertheless as man and wife. Queen Alexandra knew of the affair, as she had known of the others, and tolerated it—a good deal more amiably, in fact, than she tolerated Mrs. Keppel's predecessors. His more casual affairs continued, and the ever-present threat of public exposure hovered over his reign.

Mrs. Keppel probably exerted more influence on the aging and unpredictable King than any other woman, including the Queen. She interceded in his repeated battles with the Foreign Office on behalf of the government and gave private advice to Prime Minister Herbert Asquith on how best to handle the monarch. She even acted as something of a diplomat and spy. She was placed next to the Kaiser at a state dinner to sound him out on a variety of his opinions and reported back to the King. She passed on the gossip she learned at embassy gatherings to the Foreign Office. She also helped keep Edward VII sane during the worst political crisis of his reign, perhaps the century, one which may have hastened his death: the bitter constitutional struggle between the democratically elected government in the House of Commons and the unelected peers in the House of Lords.

The first years of the new century brought sweeping social changes. The industrial classes, whose right to organize had been severely limited in the nineteenth century, had begun to flex their political muscle. The Labour party was in its infancy. Political reforms had challenged the power of the aristocracy. The upper house of Parliament, the Lords, composed of hereditary peers answerable to no one but their class, inevitably clashed with a House of Commons responding to a growing electorate. English aristocrats saw nothing antidemocratic in an upper house of unelected oligarchs with the power to veto the will of an elected government. They would argue that their rights stemmed from property ownership and outweighed rights born from mere citizenship.

The concept that the vote of a footman or coal miner could be equated with the judgment of a Duke was considered radical and socialist, at best ridiculous and at worst evil. Working men were expected to touch their caps as they passed their betters in the street. To care for their welfare was one thing, but to be swayed by their opinions was equivalent to a farmer being guided by the reasoning of his pigs, a sensibility that has not altogether disappeared from British life. It was a view reinforced by the belief that the social order had been ordained by God and that man would change it at his peril.

According to the hymn "All Things Bright and Beautiful," sung in most Anglican churches every Sunday:

> The Rich Man in his Castle
> The Poor Man at the Gate
> He made them high or lowly
> And ordered their Estate

In political practice, while all peers of the realm were able to vote in the Lords and the peerage had produced many prime ministers, only a handful ever attended the House. The Lords and Commons had worked more or less harmoniously so long as the monolithic institutions of British life and the ascendancy of the landowning class remained unassailed.

But in 1906, a Liberal government, headed by Sir Henry Campbell-Bannerman, won election by a landslide. His tenure as prime minister was brief, and in 1908 he was succeeded by his Liberal colleague Herbert Asquith, who had represented the defendants in the Tranby Croft case. The Liberals were committed to sweeping social reforms. But the House of Lords, which has a permanent Conservative majority, created itself a bastion against all Liberal legislation.

For three years, Liberal programs mandated by the electorate were vetoed or emasculated by the Lords. It became a constitutional class war—peers versus the people—with all the militant rhetoric of Imperial warfare.

It was not a struggle the King could long avoid, and he took a great deal of the criticism directed at the intransigent aristocracy as a personal attack on him. In 1909, partly out of revenge and partly to finance welfare reform and no doubt to lay a trap for his noble opponents, the chancellor of the exchequer, David Lloyd George, proposed a "People's Budget." In it, he proposed new income, land, and estate taxes, which severely punished the landed class. A tradition which carried the stature of law held that the Lords would or could not challenge a budget. After acrimonious debate that dragged on throughout the summer and fall, the Lords rejected the budget proposals, provoking a general election and a constitutional crisis with the King firmly at the center.

King Edward, impelled by his breeding, background, and training, sympathized with the Lords. But he believed that the Lords were certain to lose a direct confrontation and feared that the results would be disastrous for the aristocracy, and for the monarchy, because it could mean a resurgence of republicanism, always simmering on the back burner. He had tried desperately to get the Lords to pass the budget, even offering to dismiss the government and dissolve Parliament after a few months, which he had no right to do. Now a general election would be fought on a divisive class issue. A Conservative victory threatened to be hollow, tainting the democratic process and setting the scene for future vengeance from the Liberal and Labour parties. A Liberal victory would pose a more imminent threat.

If the Liberals were returned, they were pledged to pass a bill reducing the power of the House of Lords. In order to get the House to pass it, they would have to force the King to create hundreds of new titles, which would devalue the entire aristocratic class.

The new year came as the crisis grew more desperate. King Edward VII was particularly superstitious about the New Year rituals and insisted on clearing the house before midnight and reentering first after the clock had chimed the hour. As 1909 became 1910, the sixty-nine-year-old King strode toward the main door of Sandringham, his country estate. His fifteen-year-old grandson, David, later Edward VIII, had slipped in first by a back door as a practical joke and swung the main door open to welcome him. The King was deeply disturbed and took it as an omen that he would not survive the year.

In secret negotiations with the Liberal prime minister, King Edward VII continued to take the side of the House of Lords, even threatening, yet again, to abdicate in protest rather than place his seal on legislation reforming the Lords. If the Liberals were reelected and the House of Lords remained intransigent, he would refuse to create a slew of Liberal lords unless there was a second general election on the constitutional issue. In the event of the Liberals again winning a majority, he would, reluctantly, create the new peers. This put the Liberal party in the position of having to win three consecutive mandates from the electorate in order to enact their program, whereas the Conservatives needed only one and the Lords none at all. Somewhat gallantly, Asquith said nothing of the King's position during the election campaign and did everything he could to keep the sovereign above the fray.

The Liberals won with a severely reduced majority, and the crisis remained unresolved. Worse, the Irish members now had the balance of power and were demanding autonomy for Ireland as the price of their support of the Liberals. Now the King feared a breakup of the Union as well as the emasculation of the aristocracy.

In March 1910, the King's health began to deteriorate rapidly. He was approaching his sixty-ninth birthday, and his lifetime of excess had finally begun to catch up with him. He tired easily and breathed laboriously and was susceptible to chest infections. Nevertheless, he insisted on traveling to Biarritz for his annual sojourn with his mistress, Alice Keppel. His plans triggered a bitter argument with his sixty-four-year-old Queen, who wanted him to go to Corfu with her to visit her brother, the King of Greece. She left without him. He stayed in Biarritz for several weeks, the longest unbroken period with Mrs. Keppel he was to enjoy.

He returned to England at the end of April and quickly came down with bronchitis. He dined out for the last time with Alice Keppel on May 2 and returned to Buckingham Palace, never to reemerge. Queen Alexandra, traveling slowly back from Corfu, returned to the palace on May 5, shocked by how ill her husband now seemed.

For weeks, he had rarely been out of Alice Keppel's company, and now that his wife was back, he was reluctant for his mistress to leave him. At the time of his previous serious illness, in 1902, he had written to Mrs. Keppel saying that if he was dying he was sure she would not be kept away. Mrs. Keppel now used the letter to return to join Queen Alexandra at his bedside on May 6. That morning, he suffered a heart attack.

The Queen received her husband's mistress, and the King persuaded them to kiss each other. Then Alice Keppel sat at his bedside holding his hand, while the Queen turned her back to gaze out of the window. As the King grew weaker, Mrs. Keppel became hysterical, and Queen

Alexandra ordered her to be forcibly removed to another room, where she collapsed. He was cheered momentarily by the news that one of his horses, Witch of the Air, had won the 4:15 at Kempton Park races. Appropriately, his response, "I am very glad," were his last words. He lapsed into a coma. Just as the clock struck the quarter hour at fifteen minutes to midnight, King Edward VII died. In the minutes after his death, Queen Alexandra consoled herself over both his death and his infidelities: "He always loved me best," she said to an aide, adding, "At least now I know where he is."

The following morning, the King's grandchildren, David, fifteen, and Albert, fourteen, aware that the King was seriously ill, rose early and looked out the window of Marlborough House. Less than half a mile away, they could see the Royal Standard flying half mast above Buckingham Palace and realized that King Edward had died during the night. They were summoned to their father's study, where they found that the new King, George V, had been crying. Recovering himself, he began to break the news to his sons. David interrupted him and said they had seen the flag flying at half mast and knew what had happened.

"What's that you say?" said the new King, distracted from his morbid narrative.

"The Royal Standard is flying half mast above the palace," David said.

"But that's all wrong!" Frowning and muttering, "The King is dead! Long live the King," he ordered an equerry in a powerful naval officer's voice to have the flag run back up the mast immediately.

It was a peculiar echo of Edward VII's own early hours as King. Crossing The Solent on the *Victoria and Albert* behind the yacht carrying Queen Victoria's coffin, the new King had asked his captain why he was flying the standard at half mast. "Because the Queen is dead, sir," he replied. "Nonsense! The King lives! Run it up the mast, man!"

Edward had been King for nine years, but he had been a colossus on the social stage for half a century, a colorful, commanding, and largely popular figure despite the spectacular downturns in public favor. In a self-deception that is quintessentially British, those who knew his frailties now chose to dress him in borrowed robes. There was a welter of sanctimonious tributes and eulogies, a portrait that none of his thousands of mistresses, brothel companions, hordes of gambling partners, and racing cronies could possibly have recognized as "Tum-Tum."

His grandson, Edward VIII, said he was the last man in England to spend his life having a thoroughly enjoyable time. One contemporary attributed his ability to retain his popularity in spite of many trials and scandals to the fact that he was so obviously wayward and human.

The King's death, in the midst of a constitutional crisis, immediately turned into a political issue and threatened to turn the tide against the Liberal government. The Kaiser, in London for the funeral with a posse of other European heads of state, claimed in dispatches home that the Liberals were now reviled for having "killed the King." It was a genuine impression, for his informants were the leading aristocrats who had turned the House of Lords into a political *Festung*. But the Liberals' hold on the electorate remained for the time being undiminished.

The new King, George V, with a maturity and firmness of character that his father had never possessed, inherited, at forty-five, a throne facing its worst political crisis in seventy years. But if anyone believed that his qualities would keep the Crown free of the kind of scandals that had punctuated his father's life, they were spectacularly mistaken.

Part Two

GEORGE V
(1910–36)

Four

Knaves of Hearts

T he new King, George V, had spent the first twenty-seven years of
his life not thinking for a moment that he would one day be King.
Edward VII's second son, he had become heir on the untimely death of
his elder brother, Prince Albert Victor, Duke of Clarence, known in the
family as Eddy. So many of the contemporary records of Prince Albert
Victor's life were destroyed or edited after Queen Victoria's death, and
so intense was the pressure to describe his flaws in euphemisms that
Albert Victor has become a shadowy figure. The gaps in the record have
given rise to sensational speculation, much of it misplaced, both about
his life and the manner of his death.

Listless, languid, lethargic, unstable, and dissipated are all words
used to describe the Prince in his lifetime. The truth about Prince
Albert Victor is that he was an alcoholic and drug addict from his teens.
His emotional instability, his mood swings, his unpredictable fits of
violence and rage, and his more usual lethargic demeanor are all attributable to laudanum and morphine abuse, which was common among the
English aristocratic classes in the nineteenth century. He may also have
become addicted to cocaine, which he chewed and smoked in South
America, and marijuana, to which he was introduced in India.

Albert Victor had been born prematurely and severely underweight in
1864, and he never fully recovered from this difficult start in life. Both
his parents and his tutors despaired of teaching him anything beyond
the most rudimentary academic skills. He relied heavily on his younger
brother Prince George, later King George V, to help him out of every
difficulty. Like his mother, Prince Albert Victor could only hear at a
particular pitch. Deafness made him appear stupid, lazy, unresponsive,
and inattentive, which tried the patience of his father and tutors.

Prince George spoke at a pitch both his mother and brother could hear, so he became essential to them both. Incredibly, Albert Victor's hearing problems appear to have gone unrecognized until he was an adult.

Queen Victoria's views on both her grandsons from her wayward son Bertie fluctuated. They were "ill trained and ill bred," according to one journal entry and "dear intelligent. . . . unpretentious children" according to a letter to her daughter, the Crown Princess of Prussia.

Prince George, as the Prince of Wales's second son, and therefore unlikely to have any constitutional role, was enrolled in the navy at twelve years old. It was essentially Prince Albert Victor's inability to get through life without his younger brother's help that embarked him on a naval career, too. The Prince of Wales had never forgiven his own father for forcing him to separate from his beloved brother Alfred, and he may have refused to commit the same error with his sons.

It was also crucial to get both Princes away from their mother's influence. Not only was Princess Alexandra herself immature; her three daughters were also locked into adolescence their entire life, due almost entirely to their mother's attempts to keep them children well into adulthood. As it was, Prince George still wrote his mother childlike letters after reaching manhood, asking her to visit his empty bedroom at Sandringham and signing himself "your little Georgie boy."

The brothers were sent to a naval training ship, *Britannia,* and while still in their mid-teens, they embarked on an extraordinary series of voyages on the *Bacchante,* a 4,000-ton corvette, its captain and crew hand-picked as appropriate shipmates for the heir presumptive and his brother. The *Bacchante* was to keep the Princes away from England for all but a few weeks of the three years from September 1879 to August 1882, taking them to southern European and North African ports in the Mediterranean, the West Indies, South America, South Africa, Ceylon, Australia, New Zealand, Japan, and the South Pacific in three voyages.

It could have been an excellent education. A tutor, John Neale Dalton, went with them, but he was no better a teacher than his charges were pupils. They left children and returned men, but they had the academic achievements of an average eleven- or twelve-year-old. Dalton, in an outrageous attempt to cover his own deficiencies, published an account of the voyages which purported to be written by the Princes but which had been clearly written by himself. Content that the public believed the Princes were better educated than they were—

Prince George was actually barely literate—the family accepted the forgery.

It was probably in 1880, on his third voyage, which took him to the Far East, that sixteen-year-old Prince Albert Victor fell prey to drug addiction. While it is true that Dalton tried to keep a close check on their behavior on shore, Prince George in later life admitted to several visits to port brothels, and both Princes returned to England with extensive and elaborate tattoos, so his watchfulness was clearly ineffective. On his return, Prince Albert Victor had difficulty concentrating on anything for more than a few minutes at a time, and his emotional swings—probably attributable to intermittent withdrawal symptoms—were notorious among his family and friends.

While Prince George continued his naval career, Prince Albert Victor completed his education at Trinity College, Cambridge. However, Prince Albert Victor appears to have hardly opened a book while he was there and instead used the prestigious university as a finishing school. He was awarded an honorary degree in law. It has also been suggested that he developed homosexual relationships while at Cambridge, in particular with his tutor, J. K. Stephen, although it is possible his bisexual tastes were developed on board the *Bacchante.*

Following Cambridge, he took up a belated army career but was incapable of managing even a company on maneuvers, and he shocked his superiors with his ignorance. Continuing in the army, the Prince of Wales, who would become Edward VII, wrote to Queen Victoria of his son's future, would be "a waste of time." By the age of twenty-four Prince Albert Victor suffered from gout, a likely side effect of his substance abuse. His father at one point tried to have his son sent away on another series of lengthy voyages.

When Queen Victoria suggested her grandson be sent on a tour of Europe, his father countered that the colonies would be a better choice because his son would be away longer. But a trip to India, during which Prince Albert Victor indulged all his self-destructive appetites, left him pale, underweight, and exhausted.

The Victorian cure for a life of "dissipation"—often used as a euphemism for drug abuse or sexual excess—was usually marriage, and the search was begun for a future Queen. The most obvious choice was Princess Alix of Hesse, known as Alicky in the family, who was his cousin. Knowing something of his reputation and personal problems, she tactfully turned him down in favor of the Russian heir apparent, Nicholas. She thus became the ill-fated Empress Alexandra, who was to die with the Russian Imperial family in 1918.

In 1886, Republican France had exiled most of the remaining members of the French Royal House, the Bourbons, among them the pretender to the French throne, the Comte de Paris. In 1890, encouraged by his doting mother, Princess Alexandra, and his three sisters, the twenty-six-year-old Prince Albert Victor began an affair with Princess Helene, the pretender's twenty-year-old daughter, triggering a constitutional crisis.

Helene was friendly with the Prince's sisters, and she had confided to them that she had become sexually obsessed with their brother. After several amorous interludes at Sheen Lodge, the home of the Duke of Fife outside London, and at Mar Lodge, Fife's Scottish estate, he proposed to Helene and was accepted. At the suggestion of Princess Alexandra, the couple tried to bypass their respective fathers by appealing directly to Queen Victoria for her approval. Princess Alexandra guessed correctly that the aging Queen would see something of her own love affair with Prince Albert in her grandson's affair with Princess Helene. Romance triumphed, at least for a time, over propriety. However, Helene was a Catholic, and a legal bar, then as now, prevented the Prince from marrying anyone professing the Roman faith. Helene obligingly offered to convert, which delighted Queen Victoria, but her father refused to allow her to do so.

Prince Albert Victor persisted. At Queen Victoria's insistence, the government even discussed various legal ways in which the marriage might be accomplished. Princess Helene appealed to the Vatican for a dispensation which would allow her to keep her faith while marrying the Prince and raising their children as Protestants. The Prince even offered to step out of the line of succession in order to marry her but was dissuaded by his brother, Prince George. Prince Albert Victor and Helene were forced to give each other up.

However, during the entire period Prince Albert Victor made love to Princess Helene, he also indulged in an illicit affair with Lady Sybil St. Clair Erskine, daughter of the Earl of Rosslyn. He wrote numerous letters in which he instructed her to cut his crest off the letterhead so no one would guess the identity of her lover. He also enjoyed two mystery women lovers, one in Southsea and one in the St. John's Wood district of London, whom he shared with his brother Prince George.

Prince George described the latter, with unintentional irony, as "a ripper."

Another suggested wife for Prince Albert Victor was another cousin, Princess Margaret of Prussia, known as "Mossy." But the Prince found her unattractive. It was Queen Victoria who hit upon the solution: Princess Victoria Mary of Teck, known in the family as "May." She was the daughter of Queen Victoria's cousin, Princess Mary Adelaide, who had married the Austrian Francis Duke of Teck. The Teck line, direct descendants of King George III, lived in relatively reduced circumstances in London.

Princess May, then twenty-four years old, had already become somewhat long in the tooth by Victorian aristocratic standards. She was invited, without her parents, to Balmoral, the Queen's remote Scottish estate. After ten days, the Queen pronounced herself content and the Princess compliant. In November 1892, the Prince of Wales ordered his twenty-eight-year-old son to propose to her "for the sake of the country."

It had taken only two weeks from the time the Princess was first considered as a bride to the proposal by Prince Albert Victor. Although the two had known each other since childhood, they had never been friends, and the match was clearly arranged. It was felt necessary, however, to promote the union as a love match, possibly because Prince Albert Victor's affair with Princess Helene was still fresh and widely known.

An indication of the family's desperation to see Albert Victor married can be deduced from the fact that the wedding was scheduled just ten weeks from the day of the betrothal and in the depths of winter, February 1893. As Princess May spent more time with the Prince and got to know more about his character, she began to have second thoughts. She wrote to her mother, "Do you really think I can take this on?" Eager to see her daughter crowned Queen of England someday, she insisted that she could.

The winter of 1892 was particularly harsh. An influenza epidemic swept across northern Europe, taking thousands of lives. Several members of the Royal Family suffered mild forms of the illness. When Prince Albert Victor returned from a morning's shooting at Sandringham with a temperature, on January 7, 1893, Prince George advised him to go to bed. The next day, his twenty-eighth birthday, he got out of bed for a few minutes to open gifts but was still unwell. Two days later, his lungs had become inflamed, and his breathing was labored. Despite a momentary improvement, within the week he was dead. In his final delirium, watched over by Queen Alexandra, he shouted over and over again for his former lover, Helene.

His death, in the midst of frantic preparations for the Royal wedding, came as a devastating blow to the Royal Family and the nation, although he would have made an unlikely King. "An overwhelming misfortune" was how Queen Victoria described her grandson's death.

> When you think of his poor young bride, who had come to spend his birthday with him, came to see his death, it is one of the most fearful tragedies one can imagine . . . it would sound unnatural and overblown if it were put into a novel.

Although he was not well known to the public, he was beatified in death in a way he could never have been in life. The funeral took place in Windsor, Princess May's bridal wreath of orange blossoms covering the coffin. A wreath of beads spelling the name "Helene," sent by his former love, was placed over the tomb. The Prince and Princess of Wales, heartbroken, ordered that his rooms at Sandringham and at Marlborough House remain as he left them. A heroic sculpture of the Prince, in the uniform of the Tenth Hussars, lying like a fallen soldier on an Imperial battlefield, was placed over the tomb.

Songs and poems of accolade to the dead Prince were circulated in rural areas of southern England. In one spectacular demonstration of mourning, his former tutor at Cambridge, J. K. Stephen, refused to eat after hearing of the Prince's death and died of starvation three weeks later.

The death of Albert Victor turned Princess May from an obscure peripheral member of the Royal Family into a tragic and romantic figure in the public mind. If Queen Victoria felt that the heir presumptive's untimely death was the stuff of novels, how would she have described the plans already being hatched for his bereaved bride-to-be? Even as the funeral was taking place, the idea of her marrying the new heir presumptive, Prince George, was being whispered.

In the years following his death, numerous legends about Prince Albert Victor have circulated, the most sensational being that he was Jack the Ripper. Beginning in the summer of 1888, a series of gruesome murders of prostitutes in the Whitechapel district mesmerized London.

Each of the victims was slashed and mutilated, some with an expertise which suggested some medical knowledge. The murders, never solved, have preoccupied theorists ever since.

In 1970, Dr. Thomas Stowell published an article in the British forensic science publication the *Criminologist* claiming that the Ripper had been Prince Albert Victor. He claimed he had based his researches on the papers of Dr. William Gull, one of Queen Victoria's physicians. He did not name the Prince in the article except as "S," but it was clear that his references were to him. Shortly after publication, Stowell died, and his family destroyed all his notes. According to the theory, Prince Albert Victor had contracted syphilis in the West Indies during the voyage of the *Bacchante* and by 1889 was in the terminal phase of the disease. Gull's notes, recorded by Stowell, say: "told [blank] his son had syphilis."

According to Stowell, the Ripper murders were committed by the Prince while in the grip of madness induced by the disease. The Prince does have a strong resemblance to one of the descriptions given by contemporary witnesses and a striking resemblance to one of the contemporary Ripper suspects, Montague Druitt. The murders also coincide with the Prince's periods in England. But there is no hard evidence of any kind to link him with the crimes. He has a cast-iron alibi for at least three of the murders, when his whereabouts were known and he was far from London.

When his brother died, Prince George, twenty-seven, was still weak from his own battle with typhoid that had almost taken his life a few weeks earlier. Deeply shocked, he had not expected to be in the direct line of succession and did not want to be. In the summer of 1893, following the death of Prince Albert Victor, the course of his life irrevocably changed. He was created Duke of York, one of the traditional titles held within the Royal Family. His brother's title, Duke of Clarence, remained vacant and was never again conferred on a Royal Prince.

Somewhat surprisingly, one of the first steps taken to train him in his new role as heir presumptive was to send him to Heidelberg to learn German. While there, he represented his grandmother, Queen Victoria, at the golden wedding celebrations of the Duke of Saxe Weimar. As honorary commander of a crack Prussian regiment, he wore his Prussian uniform, German military orders, and *Pickelhaube,* the traditional spiked helmet of Prussian soldiery.

Death had taken one Royal Prince and threatened to take the life of another in the space of a few days. Queen Victoria was seventy-five; her heir apparent, the Prince of Wales, whose lifestyle would have taxed the most ferrous of constitutions, was fifty-two. It was judged crucial for Prince George to marry and produce an heir to keep the dynasty on a secure footing. Queen Victoria pressed a match with Princess May, Prince Albert Victor's intended bride.

It was arranged for Princess May to vacation on the French Riviera to recover from the death of her betrothed and for the Duke of York to make an incognito visit. The future King George V courted her somewhat diffidently, his semiliterate letters displaying little initial interest. Even so, he proposed that spring, and they were married in July 1893.

From a dynastic point of view, it was a happy match. As Queen Mary, the strongest-willed, most intelligent, and best-educated woman the Royals were to admit into their ranks, she became the matriarch and architect of the Windsor dynasty and the guiding force behind its survival through its most difficult years. That they ultimately loved each other is beyond doubt. Prince George, with a limited intellect, came to rely almost entirely on his wife. As with many arranged marriages, it was an intelligent and successful match.

Queen Mary bore Prince George, later George V, six children: David, who was to become Edward VIII; Albert, later George VI; Princess Mary; and Princes Harry, George, and John. As parents they were remarkably deficient. The Royal children were brought from the nursery twice a day to see their parents. But their father seems to have been more concerned that he was not disturbed by their crying than how they were faring as infants.

It was their neglect that was responsible for the fact that both infants—Prince David and George—were disgracefully abused for three years by their insane nurse, with neither of their parents even remotely suspecting that something was wrong. The nurse, or nanny, Mrs. Green, had been unable to have children of her own and had been abandoned by her husband. She had served adequately on the staff of the Duke and Duchess of Newcastle and earned a positive reference. As is often the case with young and inexperienced parents, the Duke and Duchess of York, as they were now known, were hostage to the children's nanny. She set the rules and schedule, leaving the parents as spectators to the raising of their children.

When the eldest child, David, was taken to see his mother and father in the evenings, he would invariably cry hysterically, and the impatient Duke would order him returned to the nursery. The Duchess would become even more dependent on the nanny, who was the only person able to control the child. In truth, Mrs. Green was obsessed with her charge and had come to regard him as her own. She would pinch the child's flesh whenever he was due to see his mother, causing him to cry. In this way she triggered negative feelings in the baby about his mother, and he would cry as soon as he saw her. Her behavior also ensured that the natural mother gave up what little control she was willing to exercise. It has been suggested there was sexual abuse in addition to their physical discomfort.

The torture in the nursery became worse after Albert was born. Mrs. Green regarded the new child as an interloper and a distraction. She would neglect him, feeding him irregularly and insufficiently and leaving him unattended for long periods. David was three years old and Albert two when another member of the staff discovered what was going on and reported it. Mrs. Green was dismissed and soon suffered a complete emotional breakdown.

That such abuse could have occurred in an institution or even a large palace household for so long a period would be astonishing. But the Duke and Duchess were living in York Cottage on his father's Sandringham estate, a house no bigger than a country vicarage and where, he supposed, "the servants slept in the trees," for there seemed to be no room in the house. By the time it was discovered, permanent damage had been done. Both children were prone to unpredictable bursts of violent temper, which continued well into adulthood when David was crowned Edward VIII and then abdicated to marry Wallis Simpson. David's later problems in his relationships with women may be attributable to abuse by his nurse, and his brother had recurring digestive problems, a stammer, and painful shyness, all stemming from his infant experiences.

As the two children grew, their father, the future George V, ran his household along the lines of a warship at sea, checking the barometer each night and each morning and barking orders as from the bridge. He continued to bully his children.

Rebuked by a friend, Lord Derby, he is said to have replied that his father was afraid of his father, he was afraid of his own father, and he was going to make sure his children were afraid of him. Whether or not this story is apochryphal, as George V's official biographer asserts, it is true that he had a poor relationship with his sons. One of them persistently rebelled, and the other became shockingly withdrawn and ineffectual—another example of poor parenting in the Royal Family that was to be repeated in later generations. Perhaps just as shocking was their treatment of the last child, John. He was epileptic and emotionally unstable, and his unpredictable fits became more alarming as he grew older.

The Royals had a deep-rooted fear of hereditary diseases. Queen Victoria and her offspring had spread hemophilia throughout the European Royal Houses, with particularly tragic results in Russia, where the heir to the Russian throne had contracted the affliction. And it was widely believed that the madness of the Hanoverian monarchs was capable of revealing itself in subsequent generations. So it must have seemed to his parents that Prince John was the product of some errant Hanoverian gene.

Perhaps the violent, raging outbursts of which both his brothers were capable only emphasized Prince John's apparent madness. Prince John was sent into seclusion, with a nursing staff to care for his basic needs. When he died, at fourteen, after one of his epileptic episodes, his mother described it as "a great release . . . I cannot say how grateful we are to God for having taken him in such a peaceful way."

When the Duke of York became King George V on May 6, 1910, he was ill equipped for the political crisis that had paralyzed the nation's legislative process. Lloyd George sensed that the new King had been kept in the dark by his father, Edward VII. He convinced the King that his father had agreed to create the necessary new peers to steer reform legislation through the Lords. It was a bold lie. The late King had in fact demanded a new general election before he would agree to such a move. But it worked. King George V agreed to create the new peers if the Lords continued to barricade Liberal legislation. Faced with the adulteration of their class, the Lords backed down. The battle was over.

The class tensions caused by the crisis had helped fuel a resurgence in republicanism, rarely more than a fringe element in British politics. Throughout the summer and fall of 1910, the *Liberator,* a scurrilous republican quarterly, had promulgated a rumor that had been around for almost twenty years: that the 1893 marriage of the present King and Queen was bigamous. Shortly before Christmas, 1910, Edward Mylius, publisher of the *Liberator* and author of articles on the allegedly bigamous marriage, was hailing a cab on Oxford Street when he was arrested by two Scotland Yard detectives.

The details varied with each retelling, but the substance of the rumor was this: at some time in the late 1880s, when Prince George was in his mid-twenties, he had fallen in love with a commoner, either on Gibraltar or Malta. She had become pregnant, and, presumably to legitimize the child, they had contracted a secret morganatic marriage. A morganatic marriage is one between a titled male and a commoner in which the man's rank and right of succession are not conferred on his spouse or children. In one version, the woman was a British admiral's daughter; in another, an American heiress. The point of the story was that when the alleged marriage had taken place, Prince George's older brother, Prince Albert Victor, was alive, and Prince George did not expect to one day become King. But when Prince Albert Victor died in 1892, Prince George was thrust into the direct line of succession. He then set aside his morganatic marriage and married Princess Mary of Teck.

The story had first surfaced in 1893, shortly after his betrothal to Princess Mary of Teck. It had been published in a London newspaper, the *Star,* at least twice that year. Prince George had made a joke of it. The rumor was published again a number of times and in various forms, notably in Australia's *Brisbane Telegraph,* with no official reaction.

The British Labour leader Keir Hardie had even made a veiled reference to the affair in Parliament. When Prince Edward was born in 1894, the Commons was called on to record their congratulations. Hardie, a republican, dissented. As an uproar erupted around him in the House, Hardie poured scorn on the life of privilege the future King Edward VIII might expect to lead. Warming to his theme, he went on:

> In due course, following the precedent that had already been set, he will be sent on tour round the world and probably, rumors of a morganatic marriage will follow [cries of "shame" and "sit down"] . . . and in the end, the country will be called upon to pay the bill.

Edward Mylius, a staunch republican agitator and journalist, was more interested in promoting a scandal than uncovering whatever truth lay behind the rumors. His accounts in the *Liberator* of the alleged marriage were more detailed than any published before. He identified the woman as Mary Seymour, daughter of British admiral Michael

Culme Seymour, and claimed the marriage had taken place in 1888 on Malta. He sent scores of copies of his *Liberator* articles to members of Parliament, churchmen, and other leaders. Buckingham Palace at last responded. Mylius was charged with criminal libel. That the palace chose to reply at all after so many years seems remarkable. But the weight with which the hand of justice fell on Edward Mylius is even more astonishing.

He was arraigned under a system—already obsolete in 1910—that required no affidavits to be presented by his accusers. Bail was fixed at the enormous sum of $100,000. When Mylius briefed defense attorneys, he was told they would not represent him unless he pleaded guilty. No barrister in London would take his case. He was kept incommunicado, which severely limited his ability to defend himself. And he insisted, for ideological reasons, that he should be allowed to call the King to testify.

An attorney who represents himself has a fool for a client, runs the old legal axiom. But a layman who represents himself has a fool for a client and for an advocate. The full weight of British justice came down on Mylius a little over a month after his arrest. In a trial before the Lord Chief Justice, Lord Alverstone, Mylius insisted on calling the King to the stand and was refused. The court then heard testimony from the family of Adm. Culme Seymour to the effect that the King could not have been married to his daughter. Mylius refused to cross-examine any of them. It took the jury just moments to arrive at a guilty verdict, and Mylius was jailed for a year.

At the close of the trial, a statement from the King was read to the court by the attorney general, Sir Rufus Isaacs, saying he had never been married to anyone but the Queen and would have given evidence had it not be unconstitutional for him to have done so.

Mylius was not a great deal more accomplished as a journalist than as a lawyer. He had made little effort to check his story. But there was a defense available to him that any attorney could have mounted. As a response to reports that had already been published elsewhere and not denied, Mylius could have claimed, his *Liberator* articles were fair comment, offensive to monarchists, perhaps, but within his rights.

The extent to which the courts railroaded Mylius was recorded by no lesser person than the solicitor general himself, who had originally advised against the prosecution but ultimately took part in it. Sir John wrote:

We were lucky . . . if Mylius, instead of justifying . . . had explained he was only repeating what thousands of reputable people had been repeating for years without prosecuting, we could never have established the falsity of the lie.

The reason Buckingham Palace insisted on the risky prosecution just a few weeks before King George V's Coronation remains obscure. Winston Churchill, then home secretary and no friend of the King's, had recommended the prosecution. He was present at the trial and personally communicated the result to the palace. Everyone involved in the prosecution was congratulated and over several years rewarded by the King. Isaacs and Simon received the Royal Victorian Order for personal service to the Royal Family. Isaacs later become lord chief justice despite being embroiled in a financial scandal—what today would be known as insider trading. Sir John Simon was appointed privy counselor. Sir Arthur Bigge, who persuaded the Home Office to make Mylius serve his full term, was created Lord Stamfordham.

When he was released from Brixton Prison, Mylius continued to promote the story and published an account of his trial, which repeated the libels, in a pamphlet called *The Morganatic Marriage of George V.* This time the palace did nothing. Had Mylius hit on some kernel of truth that the Palace felt had to be crushed in the months before the Coronation? The effect of the prosecution was to silence speculation. Its success ended it. There was no further investigation into George V's private life prior to his marriage to Queen Mary.

Five

Royal Blackmail

O n July 7, 1914, King George V met with three of his closest
advisers in his study at Buckingham Palace. He called it the
writing room. The King sat at his meticulously arranged desk, his chair
turned slightly to the left, with Lord Stamfordham, his private secretary, the Earl of Albemarle, his equerry, and Sir Charles Russell, the
King's solicitor, seated in a crescent around the monarch.

The Archduke Franz Ferdinand of Austria had been assassinated in
Sarajevo some ten days before, and the repercussions from the event
seemed to intensify each day. The situation in Ireland was deteriorating. Protestants in the northeastern region had armed themselves to
fight against proposals for Irish autonomy, and nationalists in the south
had armed themselves to demand autonomy. The army's officers in
Ireland were close to mutiny over the prospect of having to fight the
ultraloyalist Northern Irish.

But the secret meeting between the King and his advisers that sultry
Tuesday morning had nothing to do with the international situation or
the prospect of a civil war in Ireland. As discreetly as he could, Lord
Stamfordham told George V that the king was being blackmailed and
might be forced to comply with his blackmailer's demands. The extortion was being perpetrated, Stamfordham told him, by Edward VII's
former lover, Daisy, Countess of Warwick, and a disreputable journalist, Frank Harris. A Conservative Member of Parliament and leading
British industrialist, Arthur DuCros, and a prominent London lawyer
were also involved, but to what extent was not yet clear. Possibly others
were involved in the plot as well.

Stamfordham showed the King a maroon folder containing five photographs, each showing a page of a letter in close-up. The letter was

written on the stationery of the Marlborough Club in Pall Mall, which had been founded by Edward VII after another leading gentleman's club, White's, had refused to lift a ban on smoking in the morning room, not even for the then Prince of Wales. The script was indisputably Edward VII's. All in the room were familiar with his distinctive and barely legible italics. It began: "My own lovely little Daisy . . ."

As the King read his father's love letter to his former mistress, he stroked his beard with the palm of his hand. As he did so, the Earl of Albemarle shifted uneasily in his seat. He knew the late King's record as a womanizer only too well. He was the brother-in-law of another of the late King's mistresses, Alice Keppel. There was silence as the King read on. Finally, he reached the last line on the fifth page. "Goodnight and God keep you," it said. "My own adored little Daisy Wife."

It was by no means a sexually explicit letter. It was the note Edward VIII, while still Prince of Wales, had written to Daisy, explaining why he had spoken to Lord Beresford after Persimmon's Derby win. But the first and last lines alone were enough to cause a scandal. And it was the worst possible time. There is no record of George V's reaction to the letters. He admired his father and adored his mother. But he could not have had any illusions about his father's scandalous personal life.

Weighing his words carefully, Stamfordham gave the King the details of how the letter had come into his hands and how the blackmail demand had been made.

Since her affair with the late King had ended, Daisy had fallen on hard times. As noted earlier, she had become the "Socialist Countess," helped to fund the Labour Party, opened the doors of her two stately homes, Easton Lodge and Warwick Castle, to socialist groups, and contributed to dozens of socialist and charitable causes. But she also kept up the lavish lifestyle she had had when she was Edward VII's mistress. One of her more outlandish expenses was a zoo and aviary on her estate at Warwick. She also maintained a private railroad station and branch line built to her estate at Easton Lodge to allow guests to avoid the inconvenience of using the public station.

Regularly entertaining the Prince of Wales was an enormous expense in itself, and part of Daisy's justification for her subsequent actions was that her financial difficulties had begun when she started to spend lavishly to keep up a lifestyle fitting for the mistress of the Prince. For twenty years, Daisy had spent extravagantly, invested unwisely, and borrowed heavily. By the spring of 1914 she was being refused credit by common tradesmen in stores in Leamington, near Warwick Castle, where once she was welcomed by an obsequious staff. She owed nearly $425,000, some $13 million buying power in today's money. Bankruptcy, foreclosure, and disgrace were weeks away.

During her affair with the Prince of Wales, she had met Frank Harris, the journalist who was later to become famous for *My Life and Loves,* his explicit autobiography. She had contacted him during the spring of 1914 and told him of her dilemma. Never discreet, she revealed she had kept all of Edward VII's love letters. He told her that her memoirs, if they included the letters, could fetch up to $500,000 in the United States.

Publishing her memoirs would be social suicide, but it would clear her mounting debts. And Daisy quickly grasped that there might be a way to get the money and avoid publishing the letters—by arranging for the palace to buy them back. One of her creditors was Arthur DuCros, a founder of the Dunlop Tyre Co. Harris also knew DuCros, but it is not known whether it was Daisy or Harris who first thought of approaching DuCros.

On June 25, 1914, Daisy met with DuCros at a house in Eaton Square in London, ostensibly to "reassure" DuCros that she would soon be able to pay him the sixteen thousand pounds she owed him. She showed him copies of a number of Edward VII's letters and told him of her plans to publish her memoirs and, with them, hundreds of other letters from her former lover. Some of the other letters, she indicated, were filled with court gossip that would make sensational reading. DuCros later said he tried to talk her out of the plan, but she remained adamant. She told DuCros she had already struck a deal with Harris. She left a copy of the Beresford letter with DuCros.

But if Daisy really did wish to publish the memoirs, she had no reason to tell DuCros about it except in the hope that word would get back to the palace. As both a leading industrialist and Conservative Member of Parliament, DuCros had access to a spectrum of powerful political figures, and Daisy knew what he was likely to do next. He wrote immediately to Lord Albemarle, who was a fellow member of the Carlton Club, a gathering place for Conservative gentlemen, and asked for an urgent meeting. He then went to Paris for the weekend, but there is no record of his having contacted Harris while he was there.

That weekend, the Archduke Franz Ferdinand and his Czech-born wife, Sophie, survived an assassination attempt as their motorcade drove through Sarajevo to the city hall. A grenade had grazed Sophie's head, rolled behind their car, and exploded. The would-be assassin, Nedjelko Gabrinovic, one of twenty-two scattered along the parade route, had been caught just as he tried to swallow a cyanide pellet. A few yards away, another conspirator, Gavrilo Princip, thought of shooting Gabrinovic to silence him but could not get close enough. It seemed the assassination plot had failed. It was only a matter of time before Gabrinovic, under torture, revealed the names of his conspirators.

Some two hours later, the Archduke sped away from city hall en route to a hospital where those injured in the explosion were being treated. The chauffeur, rattled by the day's events and unsure of the new route, passed a turn onto the Latin Bridge and was ordered to stop and back up. He did so just as Princip was leaving a cafe. Princip saw his chance and fired. It was the first act in a drama that would bring the death of millions more. At the time, however, it seemed that it would have few consequences other than for the succession in the Hapsburg House. "Terrible for the poor old emperor," George V recorded in his diary that night.

Albemarle believed the meeting with DuCros was going to be about the deteriorating situation in Ireland—DuCros was from Belfast and a fierce opponent of home rule—but he soon realized it was far more serious. DuCros told him of Daisy Warwick's plans to publish her memoirs and gave him his copy of the letter, pointing out there were hundreds more. Albemarle said he would be in touch. Albemarle left the meeting suspecting that DuCros was somehow in league with Daisy, not for the money, perhaps, but more likely to have leverage over the situation in Ireland.

Some days passed, and the only contact was a letter from Albemarle telling him the King was in Balmoral, Scotland, and nothing could be done until he came back. Then DuCros received a phone call from Lord Stamfordham asking him to come to St. James Palace. Stamfordham made him go through his story again, grilling him on his own involvement. He asked how much Daisy owed him and whether he had been pressing her for money. He was particularly suspicious because DuCros had connections with both Harris and Daisy. DuCros had been put into an invidious position. He tried to reassure Stamfordham that he had not pressed Daisy for money and said it was beneath him to accept money earned either by extortion or by publication of the memoirs.

Lord Stamfordham ushered DuCros out, some of his suspicions

eased, and summoned Albemarle and the King's solicitor, Russell, to the meeting with George V. When Stamfordham had finished outlining the affair to the King, the three turned to Russell. Russell told them their legal position. No crime, so far, had been committed. There had been no overt demand for money. But clearly, the letters were for sale to the highest bidder. The Countess of Warwick could not be legally kept from publishing her memoirs. Some social pressure might be brought to bear on her, but at this stage, with her debts uppermost in her mind, that was likely to fail. She could, however, be prevented from publishing the letters themselves under the English copyright laws, which said the content, if not the physical letters themselves, were owned by the sender. But this would not prevent them from being published in the United States, which was not then a signatory to international copyright agreements.

A temporary injunction could be secured—with a risk that it would become public knowledge—but if the King were to bring a full legal action to prevent publication of the letters in England and Daisy were to defend it, this would certainly result in publicity it was crucial to avoid. Moreover, such action would merely enhance their value when published in the United States. The first priority was to establish where the letters were and, if they still remained in England, then to devise a means of preventing them from leaving the country. The second was to silence Daisy.

The King wanted to know how much Daisy wanted. Neither Albemarle or Stamfordham knew precisely, although DuCros had told them the extent of her debts. That raised the issue of DuCros himself. Albemarle told the King he knew DuCros only as a parliamentarian and a member of his club. Lord Stamfordham knew him not at all but had no reason to suspect he was not a gentleman. Russell agreed that DuCros could serve as a useful go-between. None of them should deal with Daisy directly. Even so, it was decided to have the Metropolitan Police Special Branch, originally created to keep a watch on Irish nationalists, follow Daisy, DuCros, and Henry Paget, Daisy's attorney. Russell was also told to apply for a temporary injunction against Daisy but to keep it as discreet as possible.

Two days later, Russell met DuCros in Russell's offices in Norfolk Street and asked him to tell his story for the third time, from the beginning. Again, he was grilled about his own motives. Apparently satisfied, the lawyer told DuCros that "certain interested parties" might wish to purchase the letters and asked him to find out how much Daisy wanted. He told DuCros that it was important to keep the Palace as distant as possible from the situation and that he would be doing his King a service in acting as a negotiator, distasteful though it might be. DuCros agreed to go to Paris to meet with Frank Harris and Daisy. Russell did not tell DuCros he was being followed or about the injunction being sought.

Some days later, DuCros met with Harris in the Ritz Hotel in the Place Vendome. DuCros made no secret of his contempt for a man he already despised. As the two excoriated each other, Daisy arrived. Daisy and Frank Harris appear to have played an effective game of what law enforcement officials call "Mutt and Jeff." Daisy was compliant and reasonable; Frank Harris, contemptuous and belligerent. The key question was how much. Daisy started the bidding at £125,000. She said she had locked herself into a deal with Harris: five thousand pounds and a share of the royalties if the memoirs were published with the letters; ten thousand if they were published without the letters, because the royalties would be significantly less; fifteen thousand if there were to be no book at all. If she brought the price down to one hundred thousand pounds and agreed not to publish her memoirs, that left only eighty-five thousand pounds to cover her debts.

Desperate to lower the price to something he thought the palace would agree to pay, DuCros said the value of the letters was the value of the memoirs with the letters minus the value of the memoirs without them. The reasoning showed DuCros had a fine accountant's mind but knew little of the publishing world. The value of the memoirs without the letters was next to nothing. Harris, who knew this, began remonstrating with Daisy, telling her she could get at least £125,000 for the letters when all the royalties were counted, although this was probably part of the act. Harris feigned anger and walked out. Daisy told DuCros she wanted one hundred thousand pounds. The meeting broke up. Harris, who had waited in the lobby, walked Daisy over to the Hotel Avenida on the Champs-Élysées, leaving DuCros alone.

Two days later, Daisy made a point of running into DuCros on the Channel ferry to Folkestone. DuCros pleaded with her again to lower the price. This time, he asked her to write down all her outstanding debts, suggesting they could be reduced, beginning with her own debt to him. She wrote the list on the back of her hotel receipt and gave it to him. The discussions continued all the way back to London on the train from Folkestone.

DuCros reported back to Russell, but this time he had a concrete proposal. If Daisy Warwick were to be paid in cash, then there was no guarantee she would use the money to pay her debts and no guarantee she would not renege by publishing copies of the letters or simply publishing her memoirs in some other form. DuCros still knew nothing of the plans to seek an injunction. He proposed that he personally take over Daisy's debts but keep them active by making himself Daisy's only creditor. In this way he could probably reduce the amount owed. Many of her creditors had probably given up seeing their money again and would probably settle for a smaller amount. It would be more than they would get if she were to declare bankruptcy. Furthermore, some probably knew she had no head for figures and were overcharging her.

Russell asked DuCros to keep negotiating. But Daisy wasn't in a frame of mind to be patient. On July 21, DuCros was visited by a former British army officer, Bruce Logan, who brokered loans for aristocrats down on their luck and who had arranged loans for Daisy. He took the same tack Frank Harris had taken. He told DuCros he was now negotiating on Daisy's behalf and that the "friends" who wished to purchase the letters should make up their minds quickly. A deal with an American publisher was about to be concluded.

The Special Branch had already spotted Logan at a meeting with Daisy and were following him. She had given him a package, and he had taken it back to his office, which he shared with business partner Clarence Hatry. Russell concluded correctly that Logan and Hatry had the letters.

At that point, Buckingham Palace flexed its muscles. Russell applied for an injunction against Daisy, her long-suffering husband, the Earl of Warwick, who probably knew nothing of the plot, and Logan, Hatry, and Harris. The application was filed on behalf of Sir Dighton Probyn, former equerry to Edward VII and comptroller of Queen Alexandra's household; Lord Knollys, former private secretary of both Edward VII and George V and by 1914 a lord-in-waiting to Queen Alexandra; and Sir Arthur Davidson, also a lord-in-waiting to the dowager Queen. It was heard by Mr. Justice Low, of the King's Bench Division, in chambers rather than in open court.

The King's name was not mentioned in the application, only in an affidavit by Knollys. As an extra precaution, that affidavit was filed as an exhibit. Exhibits were not kept on file but were returned to the applicant. Elsewhere in the application, the King was referred to only as "the testator" and the letters only as "of a confidential character." The injunction was granted ex parte. Despite the precautions, anyone seeing the record of the cause of action would have recognized the names of Knollys, Probyn, and Davidson and concluded they were acting for the King. But it was so late in the court calendar—they were about to break for the long summer vacation—and attention was so focused on the deteriorating situation in Europe that nobody noticed.

The injunction could be contested, but Henry Paget would almost certainly have told Daisy she had little chance of winning. The application claimed that the proposed publication of the letters was both a breach of copyright—Daisy owned the letters as objects but not the rights to their contents—and a breach of confidence. But she would still be able to publish her memoirs in the United States, with the letters, if she was able to smuggle out copies.

Within a week, war had broken out. Daisy and her coconspirators were made aware through DuCros that they now faced prosecution under the virtual martial powers of the Defence of the Realm Act. Daisy, Hatry, Logan, and Harris—the latter suspected of being a German sympathizer—were still being followed, now conspicuously, partly to intimidate them and also to make certain they did not move the letters from Hatry's safe.

Meanwhile, a more public crisis had erupted. The opening weeks of the war brought only bad news, with reverses for Britain and her allies on land and at sea. In order to give the domestic war effort an additional boost, propaganda about German atrocities, much of it baseless, was being published everywhere, typically focusing on German troops raping Belgian women and mutilating and murdering their children.

A wave of anti-German feeling swept Britain. Businesses with German-sounding names—many of them actually owned by Eastern European Jews—were attacked. Some German families were interned as enemy aliens. German wines were poured into sewers, and those who persisted in their taste for hock were vilified at dinner parties. Even German breeds of dog were kicked in the streets and owners harassed into putting them to sleep. The anti-German hysteria may or may not have helped the war effort. But it did cause the Royal Family acute embarrassment, because they were Germans through and through.

The most notable of the German Princes in the Royal Family was Prince Louis of Battenberg. Battenberg was the son of Prince Alexander of Hesse, whose career reads like the life of a character from a Prokoviev opera. He had been sent to Russia in the train with his sister, who married the Czarevitch, the future Alexander II. He established himself so well at the Russian court that a marriage was arranged with the Czar's niece, Princess Olga. Already involved in a love affair with a minor Polish Countess, Julia von Haucke, he fled across the steppes in secret with his amour and married her, to the fury of the Czar, who stripped him of the numerous Russian honors and awards he had been given.

Prince Louis, born in Graz, Austria, was the product of this morganatic marriage. At fourteen, desperate to follow a naval career, he left Germany for England and joined the Royal Navy. European Royal Houses—indeed, the aristocracy generally—tended to frown on morganatic marriages and their offspring, but the Battenbergs were favored. Prince Henry of Battenberg married Queen Victoria's youngest daughter, Beatrice, after promising to live with the aging Queen.

Prince Louis had a distinguished and meteoric naval career. Most of his contemporaries agree it had more to do with his ability and industry than his background and position. He became director of naval intelligence from 1902 to 1905 and held various high admiralty posts. By the outbreak of the First World War, he was First Sea Lord, the key naval officer below the cabinet rank of First Lord of the Admiralty. He also made a brilliant marriage—to Princess Victoria of Hesse, Queen Victoria's granddaughter.

Louis had always regarded his ancestral land as his first home, although he claimed his greatest loyalty was to the navy. But in the period before World War I, national loyalties were not always easily defined. The first loyalty of any Prince was to his family. Prince Louis had suspended his naval career to fight for his brother, who had been nominated to the throne of Bulgaria, against the Russians. Another brother, a Prussian cavalry officer, had done the same. In the frenetic diplomacy of the conflict, they had solicited the support of the Turks. The Turks were now the enemy. The Russians were now England's ally against the Germans.

A number of naval reverses and what seemed to be a certain temerity on the part of the world's most powerful navy contributed to the belief that the senior service was being destroyed from within. A 23,000-ton

German battle cruiser, *Goeben,* had escaped when she appeared to be easy prey, and a number of British ships had been sunk with disturbing ease by German cruisers. Then there was spy fever. A Carl Lody was arrested and court-martialed in camera in the opening weeks of the war. Giving evidence while guarded at bayonet point by two soldiers, Lody admitted spying on fleet movements for the German Admiralty. He was executed by firing squad in the Tower of London a week later.

In the Commons and the Lords, government ministers were quizzed on German spy rings. The Earl of Crawford claimed that his home district of Fife was filled with German nationals signaling fleet movements to German spy ships off the coast. In this atmosphere, some of it whipped up by Lord Beresford, it seemed incongruous that the most important arm of the British forces should be led by a German princeling, particularly one with relatives in the German High Command. Soon suspicion of Prince Louis was transformed into suspicion of the whole Royal Family.

On October 29, 1914, at the insistence of the King, Prince Louis wrote to Winston Churchill, the First Lord of the Admiralty: "My birth and parentage have the effect of impairing in some respects my usefulness on the Board of Admiralty," and resigned. Churchill wrote back accepting the resignation, lamenting that this new kind of war "raises passions between races of the most terrible kind." The following day, he had a meeting with King George, who found Prince Louis a place on the Privy Council, the monarch's board of official advisers.

Ironically, the day Battenberg resigned, his nephew, Prince Maurice of Battenberg, was killed with the British forces at the Battle of Ypres. Prince Louis's son, Prince Louis Francis of Battenberg, attended naval college at the time of his father's resignation and was teased unmercifully, some boys telling him his entire family would end up in the Tower. What he saw as his father's disgrace fired the young man's ambition. As Lord Louis Mountbatten, he was to have his revenge.

The following spring, Daisy, Countess of Warwick, accepted DuCros's plan for the return of the letters and cut her losses. It was several more months before the application again came before Mr. Justice Low. Daisy handed the letters over, and they were destroyed. All records of the application were also destroyed, including the original record that any application had been made or any such case ever heard. Lord Stamfordham and Russell were able to report back to the King that the distasteful matter had been dealt with successfully. DuCros's role, the King was told, was particularly heroic. He was rewarded with a baronetcy and became Sir Arthur DuCros the following year.

It was as if nothing had happened. Daisy did write two versions of her memoirs some years later. Without the sensational letters, they made hardly a ripple. She referred to rumors that she had once been prepared to publish the King's letters to her, but she claimed she would never have stooped so low.

Nothing of the blackmail incident would ever have been known were it not for the fact that DuCros, worried that his part in the plot might one day be questioned, kept meticulous notes of all his meetings and all the messages and correspondence. They were discovered in Switzerland in 1963 by the author Theo Lang. Of the letters themselves and the secrets they contained, nothing is known. Daisy's memoirs are contradictory in details, but she recounts how Edward VII often told her court gossip and made disparaging remarks about the political figures of the day. It is very likely the letters contained similar material. For the palace, however, the fact that they were written and that they contained such explicit endearments as "My own wife" and "My only love" were more than enough for the King to do everything in his power to destroy them.

Six

The Windsors

World War I decimated an entire generation of European youth. As in all wars, it was the brightest and the best who were most readily sacrificed. Tactics had failed to keep up with technology, and the result was carnage on an unprecedented scale. King George V was among those wounded at the front. He was thrown from a chestnut mare while visiting members of the Royal Flying Corps at Hesdigneul, and the horse fell back on him. Had the ground not been so softened by rain, he would certainly have been killed. As it was, he broke three ribs, fractured his pelvis, tore muscles in his back and legs, and suffered severe bruising as well as acute shock. But the extent of his injuries was not immediately realized, and medical attention was neither adequate or prompt. As a result, he never fully recovered. "I was extremely lucky I was not killed," he wrote to the Duke of Connaught.

Both his eldest sons were also in the war. David, with the army general staff in Flanders, was kept, to his frustration, as far as possible from the action. He refused decorations awarded by his father on the grounds that he had not earned them in the trenches. Bertie, to his brother's envy, fought in the navy at the Battle of Jutland and distinguished himself.

By far the most alarming consequence of the war for the British Royals was the political and social upheaval throughout Europe. A tidal wave of change swept all before it—Kings, Emperors, political systems, social values. And no single event symbolized that upheaval more emphatically than the Russian Revolution, which came as a profound shock to the Czar's German and British cousins. Revolution did not seem far away in Paris, Berlin, or London. French and British troops mutinied, with the predictable consequences for those responsible, the firing squad.

In 1916, rebels arose in Dublin and elsewhere in Ireland, and the insurrection was put down with ferocity. One of the leaders of that rebellion, Sir Roger Casement, had tried to run German arms to the rebels and been hanged. Rebel leaders captured in the ruins of Dublin were court-martialed and hanged. For David, now the Prince of Wales, that punishment was not severe enough. He wrote to his father suggesting they be executed publicly in Hyde Park.

Sir John Fisher, who had replaced Prince Louis as First Sea Lord, only to resign seven months later, had enjoyed a close friendship with Edward VII but had a hostile relationship with George V. In 1916, he wrote to the *Manchester Guardian*: "I hear amongst the proletariat is a deep feeling that both Buckingham Palace and Sandringham should long ago been given up for our wounded and sick heroes. . . . Kings will be cheap soon!"

Perhaps if the British public had realized that George V's personal intervention had prolonged the suffering of British troops in the trenches, they would have taken Buckingham Palace and Sandringham themselves. The British army in France had been ill led from the outbreak of the war. Foremost among the incompetents was Field Marshal Sir John French, commander in chief. Ill prepared for the kind of war he was called on to fight, he indulged in trivial rivalries with his allies, failed to take advantage of his adversary's weaknesses, and worse, manufactured evidence that subordinates were to blame for his failings. After it became obvious that British troops had been needlessly sacrificed at the Battle of Loos in 1915, he was replaced by the King's intimate friend Douglas Haig.

Haig owed his career to his royal connections. His sister, Henrietta, had been an intimate, that is, a mistress, of Edward VII and through her he had been allowed to enter the Staff College despite having failed the entrance examination and to graduate despite the fact that he was color-blind. Edward VII, as Prince of Wales, used him as a spy against his own superior officers in a number of campaigns, and he never failed to criticize their conduct. This behavior won him a position of aide-de-camp, and his access to the Royal Family increased when he married Dorothy Vivian, one of Queen Alexandra's ladies-in-waiting. The ceremony was held at Buckingham Palace.

After the outbreak of war, George V employed Haig, as had his father, as a source of inside information from the front, particularly concerning French's conduct of the war. That Haig used his position to undermine French, his senior officer, would be considered disgraceful by normal standards of soldierly behavior. In his defense it should be noted that everything he said about French's incompetence and paranoia was true. On the basis of Haig's secret dispatches the King insisted that the prime minister fire French, awarding him the prize as often given for failure as for success in British public life: a noble title. The King's nominee for French's successor was the man who had helped bring him down.

Haig continued a futile policy of attrition, which Lloyd George described as unintelligent hammering against an impenetrable barrier. Losses at the Western Front were enormous—nearly fifty-seven thousand British casualties on the first day of the Battle of the Somme alone. No assault on the German lines seemed likely to break through to Belgian ports used by German U-boats to win a guerrilla war against British and allied merchant ships. Moreover, wrangling inside the coalition cabinet seemed to paralyze the government.

A new crisis struck when Lord Kitchener, secretary for war, was killed on the HMS *Hampshire*. The ship was sunk off the Orkney Islands on its way to Russia where he was to advise the Russian general staff, whose troops were being overrun. Immediately, Lloyd George, minister for munitions, made a bid for Kitchener's position. Within five months, he had plotted and maneuvered his way into 10 Downing Street as prime minister.

King George despised Lloyd George, and the prime minister felt nothing but contempt for the King. As had been done with Edward VII, he kept as much government business away from the monarch as possible and refused to send regular letters to the palace, where the King's fury reached a boiling point.

The King backed Haig throughout long months of wrangling in which Lloyd George and Churchill tried desperately to force Haig either to change strategy or resign. It was primarily because of the King's personal support of Haig against his political enemies that the appalling bloodshed in the trenches continued until America's entry finally tipped the scales against the Germans and their willingness to continue the senseless struggle evaporated.

On March 12, 1917, a sergeant of Russia's Volinsky Regiment shot and killed an officer while the rank and file were arguing over whether they should oppose St. Petersburg street mobs or join them in raiding granaries. As the result of the officer's death, the other officers fled from the barracks, and the rest of the regiment marched to join the insurrection. The mutiny spread with a momentum of its own, and by dawn, five other regiments, including the elite Preobrajensky Guards, founded by Peter the Great, had also mutinied. The following day, King George V wrote in his diary, "This rising is against the government, not the Czar." But within forty-eight hours news came of the collapse of the Imperial government, anarchy in St. Petersburg, Moscow, and Kronstadt, and the Czar's abdication. The King wrote to his friend and cousin: "My thoughts are constantly with you and I shall always remain your true and devoted friend, as I have been in the past."

Lloyd George, on the other hand, sent a message of support to the provisional government. The prime minister telegraphed to St. Petersburg: "The revolution, whereby the Russian people have placed their destinies on the sure foundation of freedom . . . reveals the fundamental truth that this war is at bottom a struggle for popular government as well as Liberty."

King George V was furious with Lloyd George for his support of the revolutionaries, but within days the King himself was sacrificing his "true and devoted friend" to save his own dynasty. On March 19, the provisional government, still in the hands of more moderate forces, contacted Sir George Buchanan, the British ambassador in St. Petersburg, and raised the possibility that the Czar and his family might find safety in Britain. The proposal had not even been discussed in London before Pavel Milyukov, the provisional government's foreign minister, urgently requested that the British give the Imperial Family asylum. Lloyd George, Lord Stamfordham, Chancellor of the Exchequer Andrew Bonar Law, and a senior Foreign Office civil servant, Charles Hardinge, discussed the request on March 22 at 10 Downing Street and agreed to accept the Czar in exile, provided he be allowed to leave with sufficient funds to support himself. Stamfordham went so far as to note that they all agreed that asylum "could not be refused."

It is inconceivable that the prime minister made the agreement without having had prior discussions with the King and that he did not speak for the King at the conference. But astonishingly, within the week, the King had changed his mind about supporting his cousin. Stamfordham, the King's private secretary, wrote to Arthur Balfour, the foreign secretary: "His Majesty cannot help doubting . . . on the general grounds of expediency, whether it is advisable that the Imperial Family should take up their residence in this country."

The letter was followed by another: "I do hope the whole question . . . will be reconsidered. It will be very hard on the King and arouse much public comment if not resentment."

And another: "Every day the King is becoming more and more concerned about the question of the Emperor and Empress coming to this country. . . ."

And yet another: "The residence in this country of the ex-Emperor and Empress would be strongly resented. . . ."

What had happened to cause King George to abandon his cousin? It was similar anti-German sentiments that had brought down Prince Louis of Battenberg. The Empress Alexandra was the German Princess Alix of Hesse, the same woman who years before had refused the hand of Prince Albert Victor. The Russians had proved to be weak allies, and that weakness could be laid at least as much at her feet as at her husband's. Lord Francis Bertie, the British ambassador to France, had dismissed any possibility that the French would accept them. "The Empress is not only a Boche by birth but in sentiment," he wrote.

The King had also been frightened and dismayed by the public support in Britain for the Revolution and the glee at the downfall of the Czar. He was afraid of standing side by side with his cousin in the face of public antipathy. The republican sentiment in England joined with the anti-German sentiment, and both were inseparable from the support for the Russian workers, at least in the early stages of the Revolution. In addition, the Czar himself was a near double of the King. It would have been inevitable that the image of a fallen Czar residing in Britain would have a negative effect on the image of the King himself.

The Russians knew nothing of the King's change of heart and believed the British would accept the Czar. But Buchanan, the British ambassador in Russia, had been instructed to do nothing further to encourage that view while not actually withdrawing the original agreement. The hatred of everything German had already begun to affect the public perception of the Royal Family by early 1917, and Lord Stamfordham had begun to persuade King George to change the dynastic name. Letters vilifying the King's British and German relatives as "Huns" had poured into 10 Downing Street, Buckingham Palace, and Fleet Street newspapers. Most were anonymous. Those sent to newspapers that were signed tended not to be published. One that was came from the writer H. G. Wells, who, writing in the *Times*, spoke of "an alien and uninspiring court" and called for like-minded Englishmen to set up republican societies.

Lord Stamfordham foresaw that the end of the war would bring down many of the Royal Houses. The Greek King Constantine had been deposed. Now the Czar. The Kaiser and the Austrian Emperor would be unlikely to survive defeat. The Ottoman Empire was finished; the future of the Italian and Spanish monarchies, uncertain. Stamfordham hoped to convince the King that the monarchy had to reinvent itself for the Brave New World following victory, albeit a victory which still seemed a long way off.

The College of Heralds, the ultimate authority of Royal and aristocratic titles, was consulted, and there was some disagreement on the dynastic name of the British Royal Family, since there were very few circumstances in which dynastic names were used. Some argued it could be that the British Royal Family was still the House of Hanover; possibly that it was Guelph. All were self-deceptions. The name was as German as could be: Wettin von Saxe-Coburg and Gotha. It had to go.

The choice of a new name proved more difficult. "England" was suggested, but the King's Scottish, Welsh, and Irish subjects would undoubtedly have been offended. Lancaster or York, ancient dynasties still retained in ducal titles, were put forward, but both were associated with civil war and rejected. Fitzroy was turned down because historically it had been a name taken by Royal bastards. Buckingham was also rejected because it rhymed with an obscenity. Cornwall and Kent were standbys. Lord Stamfordham ultimately suggested Windsor after the castle. It was an inspired choice—by no means a common name but with recognizably English connotations.

Stamfordham leaked the news to the *Times* on July 16, 1917, and a proclamation was readied for the next day. A small item said that the change of name would be "territorial in nature" but did not mention Windsor. On the eighteenth, the proclamation was published, relinquishing all German styles and titles, names and ranks, saying the King and his family and descendants wished to be known as "of the House and Family of Windsor."

A laudatory editorial also appeared in the *Times*, along with a convoluted account of the connections of Windsor with successive English Kings. The piece glossed over the King's German heritage, other than his descent from the Saxons, and made no mention of the reasons for the change of name. Instead, it pointed out that Windsor Castle had been home to Normans, Lancasters, Yorks, Plantagenets, Tudors, and Stuarts. The *Times* wrote somewhat archly: "For the first time in its long history Windsor becomes home to an eponymous House—the times are propitious to the innovation."

Other propitious innovations were announced in the next several days.

Prince Louis of Battenberg had been told to find himself an English-sounding name. He refused to go further than to anglicize his own name to Mountbatten, which to English ears sounded almost as alien as Battenberg. It mattered little, because the King had already decided that the Mountbatten name would rarely be heard. Prince Louis was to be given the new title Marquess of Milford Haven, another demotion, which he termed "cruel and unnecessary," and a title whose name he despised as long-winded and laborious. His wife, Princess Victoria, now Marchioness of Milford Haven, complained that her husband had been made a mere peer along with "bankers, brewers and lawyers." Prince Alexander of Battenberg became Marquess of Carisbrook. The Duke of Teck and Prince Alexander of Teck, the King's in-laws, became Duke of Cambridge and Earl of Athlone, respectively. The name Teck disappeared. Within a week, when many of the Royals gathered for a wedding, the *Times* and other newspapers were using the new names and titles without qualification, as if they were ancient titles known to everyone.

The King further decided, at Lord Stamfordham's urging, to limit the use of the title Prince so that there would not be a proliferation of Princes in subsequent generations of his children. At some stage, except for the Prince of Wales, all would take ducal and other subsidiary titles.

Equally important was the reinvention of the purpose of the monarchy. It was an infinitely more complex task. The political role of the monarchy had been gradually changing—indeed, diminishing. The value of the monarchy was now in question. The power of the Labour party had been growing steadily, and it was widely believed that once normal political life was restored, the Labour party would take office. What further inroads it might make on the position of the monarchy was anybody's guess. Clive Wigram, an assistant private secretary, appears to have fostered Stamfordham's belief that the monarchy would survive future upheavals only as a symbol of universally acceptable social virtues.

Wigram campaigned for the King's image to be buttressed by an endless public relations campaign and for palace receptions and court functions to be opened to schoolteachers, civil servants, and other ordinary people from walks of life divorced from the usual Buckingham Palace regulars of knights and baronets.

"The barriers have to be broken down if the monarchy is to live," he wrote in 1917. "I have been working very hard to get Their Majesties a good press."

Wigram complained that the King was surrounded by "duds" who regarded all changes as likely to lower the dignity of the monarchy. But Stamfordham, a man solidly rooted in the Victorian age, appears to have agreed with him.

The working classes would have to be induced, Stamfordham wrote to the King, "to regard the Crown . . . as a living power for good, with receptive faculties welcoming information affecting the interest and social well being of all classes." During visits to industrial centers, Private Secretary Stamfordham cautioned the King, he should affect an interest in the problems of employees.

A high-sounding but flawed concept. For centuries the Royal Family had been far removed from the realities of daily life, sheltered behind a wall of archaic court custom and obsolete manners. While the monarchy as an institution might be capable of reflecting universally acceptable virtues and principles—what today might be called family or middle-class values—unfortunately the Windsors themselves did not possess those virtues. In the coming years a phrase was to reappear constantly in the ever-expanding library of Royal hagiography: that the monarchy is the symbol of stability in a changing world. But the stability of the Windsors was confined to symbols. As George V's descendants were to discover, the new public relations–driven monarchy was a Pandora's box, which, once opened, would unleash destructive forces that could never be contained.

In April 1918, the Czar and his family were captured by the Bolsheviks and taken to Ekaterinburg, now Sverdlovsk, in the Urals. The Czar's mother and sister had escaped, but the rest of the Romanovs were doomed. Fearing that Ekaterinburg might be taken by the counterrevolutionaries, the local Bolsheviks massacred the entire family. It is possible, even likely, that they would have been prevented from leaving Russia even if the British had immediately moved to save them fifteen months earlier. But certainly King George's change of mind had sealed their fate.

After the murder of the Czar and his family, the King attempted to make it appear that his government's ineptitude and hesitation was the reason the Czar could not be saved, and he may even have convinced himself that that canard was true.

"Those buggers," he is said to have remarked of the British politicians who supposedly abandoned the Czar. "If he had been one of their own they would have acted fast enough, but just because the poor man was an Emperor!"

This fantasy was perpetuated by his son, then Prince of Wales and later Edward VIII. "My father had personally planned to rescue him with a

British cruiser but the plan was in some way blocked," he claimed as late as 1947, by which time he was Duke of Windsor. "There had been a very real bond between him and his cousin . . . it hurt him that Britain had not raised a hand to save his cousin Nicky."

Lloyd George, also not interested in telling the truth, laid the blame on the Russian provisional government for failing to act quickly enough to hustle the Czar out of the country. And it is true that at the time there was a standoff between the extremist St. Petersburg Soviet and the more moderate provisional government over the Czar's future.

In November that same year, the "indescribable mass carnage and slaughter," as the Prince of Wales described the war from the front, ended. The Kaiser was exiled to Holland, from where Lloyd George, violently opposed by the King, tried to have him extradited and tried. The trial of a grandson of Queen Victoria and cousin of the King for war crimes would have provoked republican disorder, and Lloyd George knew it. King George, unwilling to save the life of one cousin, apparently wanted to spare the life of another who had gone to war against him and his countrymen.

The Hapsburgs and their empire had also collapsed. But the social upheavals triggered by the war had only begun. The Prince of Wales summed up the reasons for discontent:

> The servicemen not yet discharged were angry over the clumsy demobilization program; those who had been demobilized were disgruntled over the lack of jobs and homes; the disabled were bitter . . . there were strikes and demonstrations disturbing in their frequency and prevalence.

It was not the "land fit for heroes" that the wartime propaganda had promised, but a nation of want amid plenty that was all too familiar to those lucky enough to return from the gray mud of Arras and Ypres and Passchendale. The four cornerstones of the Empire—India, South Africa, Australia, and Canada—seethed with radical independence and republican movements.

The King himself quickly discovered the discontent of his subjects. He rode on his horse with his two sons, the Prince of Wales and the Duke of York, all three in full uniform, to a parade of fifteen thousand disabled former servicemen in Hyde Park. The Prince of Wales recalled that as they drove to the front rank, "There was something in the air, a sullen unresponsiveness all three of us felt instinctively."

Agitators gave a prearranged signal followed by the unfurling of banners, some in red. There were shouts of "Where is this land fit for heroes?" The mass of men broke ranks and surrounded the King as his horse thrashed nervously. His two sons, who believed the crowd would pull the King from his mount, were unable to reach him. Police moved in, batons flailing, to extricate the King, and the three rode quickly away. Shaking his head, George V strode into the palace, saying to his sons, "Those buggers were in a bloody funny temper!"

Later the story would be changed so that the men whose arms reached up to the King did not seek to grab him but only wanted to shake his hand, or at worst, personally put their grievances before him. But there was no disguising the King's belief that the crowd's mood was ugly. Those close to the melee believed he was about to be assassinated. His confidence had been badly shaken. There was more to come. At a mass meeting of trade unionists at Albert Hall—named after the Prince Consort—there were thousands of hisses and boos when the King's name was mentioned. The House of Windsor had an inauspicious baptism.

Seven

Holding the Fort

D avid, Prince of Wales and later Edward VIII, was twenty-four
years old in 1918 when World War I ended. Like all the Royals,
he was short—George V and Queen Mary were so slight of build they
were nicknamed the "Four-Fifths"—but he cut a charismatic figure and
had a winning, naughty-boy grin. Men found him amiable; women
thought him handsome. His position as the youthful heir to the throne
wrapped him in an aura of romance. His exceptional popularity was
boosted by the fact that he had served in France and Belgium. The
perception was that he had shared the sufferings of the men at the
front. In fact, he had been kept away from much of the fighting, but he
had come close to being killed by "friendly fire." A French battery
accidentally shelled a detachment of the Welsh Guards for an hour
during the Battle of Passchendale, and he had been forced to crouch in a
dugout while shells exploded around him.

The war had left a deep emotional scar on him. He always looked
younger than his years, and he seemed little more than a child in
uniform among tall, burly Grenadier Guards in 1914. By 1918, his
physique was more manly, but there was a faraway sadness in his eyes
that stayed with him his entire life. Many years later he recalled that
memories of the nightmare of the battlefield were still never more than a
blink of the eye away:

"I have only to close my eyes to see those awful charred battlefields;
miles and miles of duck board winding across a sea of mud . . . the
ground gray with corpses."

As a result of his experiences he had been instilled with a contempt of
his own position as Prince. His Royal connection saved his life when
others his age were dying by the hundreds of thousands. Many of his

friends and acquaintances had been killed, and he never fully came to terms with the guilt of his own survival. He refused decorations because they had not been won in the heat of combat. Time and again he records praying as battles commenced, with him safely at the rear: "Oh, not to be a Prince. Oh, to have a real job."

The heir to the throne has always been the focus of more admiration and attention than the occupant. Extensive and grueling international tours in the years immediately following the war enhanced his reputation as a Prince of the people and able future king. The king himself acknowledged that his popularity amounted to worship but warned him that it was a fragile thing and could turn against him. No one was more amazed by his popularity in Britain and abroad than he was himself, and few outside his immediate circle guessed how much he resented being heir to the throne or how unsuitable for the job his personality made him. "Princing" is how he contemptuously referred to his official duties.

On one such trip to Australia, with his best friend Lord Louis Mountbatten in his entourage, he had a casual liaison with an Australian woman who is said to have had a child by him. It happened on the last day of a world tour on the battle cruiser HMS *Renown*. Several young women were smuggled aboard and kept out of sight of the farewell crowds until the *Renown* had sailed out into Sydney Harbor. They partied for several hours, then were taken back by launch. One of the women, Mollee Little, subsequently gave birth to a son whose likeness to the Prince of Wales ultimately earned him the nickname "the Duke."

It was during these years of frenetic traveling that he fell in love with the United States and with all things American. Stifled in Britain, he felt at home among Americans' easy manners. He even, for a time, affected what seemed to him to be an American accent, flavored by American-English usage and slang.

Almost as soon as he entered public life as the World's Most Eligible Bachelor, his mother, father, and the palace circle became preoccupied with finding him a wife and future Queen. Speculation about a possible bride had started at the age of seventeen, when reports circulated in London that he was to be betrothed to Kaiser Wilhelm's daughter Victoria Louise. That alliance was never seriously considered, but shortly before the war a suitable German bride had in fact been discovered. Queen Mary had promised him that he would never be forced into an arranged marriage with a woman he did not love, but it had been decided to gently push him toward Princess Caroline Matilda of Schleswig Holstein, who was related distantly to Queen Alexandra and by marriage to the Imperial Family. A possible engagement was still being discussed in June 1914, just weeks before war made the match impossible. "I could have done much worse," he would later remark.

The shortage of European princesses who could have been judged suitable for a future Queen became a drought once the Germans and those closely related to them had been eliminated from the running. Some years later, when the search turned desperate, Lord Louis Mountbatten drew up a list of some seventeen members of European Royal Families, the youngest of whom was only fifteen; the eldest, thirty-three. By 1917, King George V had made it clear to the Privy Council, though not, apparently, to his son, that there should be no objection to his marrying a well-born British woman if he chose to do so, even if she were a commoner.

War had brought David his first sexual experience. He had been taken to Calais to watch naked women cavorting in a brothel and found it, he wrote, "perfectly revolting." But after a visit to a prostitute named Paulette in Amiens, he was writing that he could think of nothing else but women and sex. He began visiting brothels at every opportunity. He wrote an embarrassing series of letters to one Paris prostitute and, as his grandfather Edward VII had done so many times, had to buy them back.

Shortly thereafter he began the series of love affairs with older, usually married women, who would continue to be his sexual preference. Throughout his life, he had an overwhelming desire to be mothered, and his choice of partners reflected this need. He became infatuated with Marion, Lady Coke, wife of the heir to the Earl of Leicester, some twelve years his senior. His letters to her were unmistakably those of a lover. He burned hers to him. Lord Coke warned the Prince to cease seeing his wife so often.

Tragically, the King and Queen opposed their son's desire to marry one woman who was single, his own age, and otherwise eligible. Rosemary Leveson-Gower was the youngest daughter of the fourth Duke of Sutherland and belonged to one of the most ancient families in the kingdom. She had been a Red Cross nurse at a French army hospital in 1916 when she met the Prince, and their love affair began the following year. In 1918, he had decided he wanted to marry her once the war ended. He asked her without first talking to his parents, and she accepted.

Queen Mary was bitterly opposed. The late Duke of Sutherland's widow, Millicent St. Clair Erskine, Rosemary's mother, had remarried Brig. Gen. Percy Desmond, only to run off with a lieutenant colonel, George Hawes, who had been embroiled in a homosexual scandal some years earlier. There was also scandal elsewhere in the family. Rosemary Leveson-Gower's uncle was the Earl of Rosslyn, a notorious professional gambler on whom the song "The Man Who Broke the Bank at Monte Carlo" was based. Harry Rosslyn was not always as successful as the man in the song. He had been bankrupt several times and lost fortunes of up to $1.3 million. He was almost as unlucky choosing brides and was twice divorced.

The Queen had concluded that there was "a taint of the blood" in the family as well as public scandals and would not permit a marital alliance. A distant mother when her children were young, she had become interfering and domineering once they were adults. In the coming decade, she was to forbid marriages or break up romances of all four of her sons.

The Prince broke the news to Rosemary that he could not marry her, lying that his father was insisting he marry a member of a European Royal House. He could not bring himself to tell his fiancée her family was not judged good enough. When she realized the truth, she pretended that she had never taken the proposal seriously. She subsequently married one of the Prince's closest friends, Eric, Viscount Ednam, and the three continued a close friendship for years.

In March 1918, David was at a house party in London given by Peter Kerr-Smiley and his wife, Maud, daughter of an American businessman, Ernest Simpson. An air-raid siren started to blare, and the drone of a German bomber, an R-39 Gotha, could be clearly heard. Two passersby ran to the Kerr-Smiley house and asked for shelter just as the guests were moving down to the basement. One of the uninvited guests was Winifred Dudley-Ward, wife of William Dudley-Ward, a prominent Liberal M.P.

The Gotha flew on beyond the Georgian terrace house where the heir to the throne was partying and dropped a ton of high explosives on a working-class district, killing several people and destroying dozens of homes. For the Windsors, however, the raid was to be destructive enough, for without it the Prince and Mrs. Dudley-Ward would most likely never have met. The Prince drove home "Freda" Dudley-Ward that night and soon afterward began a lengthy affair with her.

The daughter of a wealthy Nottingham lace manufacturer, she had married her husband, "Duddie" Ward, when she was still a teenager, and after less than five years they were living essentially separate lives. She had not contemplated divorce, but when she began her affair with the Prince, she already had a lover, Michael Herbert, whom she refused to give up. Even if her husband had helpfully died, the King and Queen would never for a moment have considered her a match. When the King spoke of the possibility of his son marrying a commoner, he meant someone who was not Royal. The younger daughter of a duke, perhaps, or even of an earl. But not the daughter of a man who owned a factory.

Possibly because the relationship had no future, the Prince became totally dependent on it, writing as many as three times a day when they were apart, constantly complaining, always depressed, and inevitably self-pitying. There was no secret in the affair. The whole of London society quickly knew that the heir to the throne was obsessed with a married woman. The King and Queen pleaded with him to let her go. He told them he wanted to marry her despite the fact that she would have to divorce. There is no documentary evidence, however, that he considered stepping out of the line of succession to do so and none that she had agreed to marry him if he did.

When she did divorce, he was panic-stricken that she would marry Herbert or another lover, a rich American polo player, Rodman Wanna-maker. His letters were filled with more cringing self-pity. The most destructive aspect of the affair was that it occupied him for several years and distracted him from seeking a more suitable bride. To be in love with a married woman in circumstances which make it impossible to divorce and remarry is one of the more exquisite tortures. It deeply increased his sense of loneliness and isolation by offering him a glimpse of happiness while emphasizing that happiness would never be his. When he did look elsewhere, it was to the least suitable women he could find.

In 1928, the Prince of Wales went on safari with a large party, including two of his younger brothers. Prince George, Duke of Kent, was a bisexual and a dissolute who had had an affair with, among others, the writer and actor Noel Coward. Prince Henry, Duke of Gloucester, was equally the playboy and womanizer. Kenya was in those days a colonial playground paradise of vast wealth and consummate decadence, dominated by a handful of white settlers. The colony was barely twenty-five years old, and vast tracts of land had been distributed to the first wave of colonists, an unlikely mix of aristocratic second sons, scoundrels, and adventurers. Wife swapping, morphine, and cocaine were accepted entertainments. The fulcrum of the white community was Happy Valley, an idyllic fertile region in the White Highlands, where the settlers had recreated England as they wished it to be, with compliant natives and elegant and obsequious servants. There they were a law unto themselves.

David soon found himself in the bed of Lady Gladys Delamere, who had been married to the settlers' leader, the third Baron Delamere, for only a few months. Prince George took up with a voluptuous American heiress, Kiki Preston, who, sporting a sterling-silver syringe, would revive herself from enervating revelries by injecting cocaine into a vein in full public view. She helped to get Prince George addicted to morphine and cocaine, and it was some years before he was able to give up the habit.

The sojourn in Kenya appears to have been a long, sodden, drug-laden debauch for all concerned, especially the Prince of Wales. There was no shortage of women, including the wives of colonial officials, who wished to claim they had slept with him, and he was only too willing to oblige. One who delighted in the opportunity was Idina, wife of the Earl of Erroll, whose sexual adventures were the talk of the colony and whose bed was known among the males of Happy Valley as "the battleground."

The center of social life was the Muthaiga Country Club, where drunken parties often ended with chairs being hurled through the windows, rowdy violent ball games in the dining room, or sexual athletics on the billiard tables. One dinner during the Prince of Wales's visit soon deteriorated into chaos, according to the writer Karen Blixen, better known as Isak Dinesen. She said that Lady Delamere pelted the Prince with large pieces of bread before rushing his chair, turning him out, and rolling him across the floor while the guests cheered. Another guest was ejected from dinner for pressing cocaine on the heir to the throne between courses. "I say," said one of the Prince's entourage. "There are limits."

Where precisely those limits lay neither the Prince nor his brothers seemed to learn. A Nairobi businessman, Sir Derek Erskine, reported that the Prince of Wales refused to go to bed before four in the morning and as the hours passed his behavior became more outrageous. One night he decided that the Muthaiga Club's collection of records was ill chosen and, aided by Sir Derek's wife, spun them through the windowpanes one by one. Sir Derek had to pay for both the records and the windows. Lady Grigg, the straitlaced wife of the colonial governor, complained that the Prince of Wales was "the most unpleasant and uncivil guest ever to visit government house."

"I was full of curiosity," David wrote of this period of his life, "and there were few experiences open to a young man of my day I did not savor. I used to say I liked to try everything once and there was plenty for me to try."

Before the scheduled end of the merrymaking, the Prince was recalled to London; the King was dangerously ill. At first, he claimed that the urgent message from London was either a ruse to spoil his fun and get him back to England or an election ploy by the prime minister. His private secretary, Alan Lascelles, had to insist on the Prince's immediate return, saying, "Sir, the King of England is dying and if that means nothing to you, it means a great deal to us."

The heir to the throne was so apparently unconcerned that he stalked off in search of a woman for the night, ending up, says Lascelles, in the bed of the wife of a government official. Upon the Prince's return, Lascelles and other members of his staff were so scandalized by his private life that they were dissuaded from resigning only with some difficulty. The King recovered.

Relations between the King and his son were now seriously strained. They rarely talked, and pleasant conversations between them seemed so unusual that when they occurred, they each noted the fact in their respective diaries. More often, King George only complained and criticized his son and made no secret of his belief that he would prove a disastrous monarch. "The boy" was how he usually referred to him. "That whore" is how he referred to Freda Dudley-Ward. Few escapades failed to be reported back to Buckingham Palace, and each fueled King George's worst fears. His son appeared to have enjoyed inspiring them.

The "boy" now had a new playpen, Fort Belvedere, a sprawling, ugly manse with wings, turrets, towers, and battlements, on the fringe of Windsor Great Park, near Sunningdale, outside London. It was a retreat from the rigors and stiff-necked protocol of official life and the recriminations of the palace and a ménage for David and his new mistress, the American socialite Thelma Furness. David would greet his weekend guests with an admonition: "I ought to tell you about the rules of the house. There are none."

Thelma, Lady Furness, was the twin sister of "Glorious Gloria"

Vanderbilt. Together they epitomized the fashionable, anorexic grace of
the twenties woman, with short, closely cropped hair, long, slender,
angular figures, and alabaster complexions. Together with their older
sister, Consuelo, the sisters had been known in the gossip columns of
the Hearst press as the "Magnificent Morgans." Their father, Harry
Morgan, was an American diplomat of limited means; their mother,
Laura Kilpatrick, an ambitious, grasping snob, whose own father was
one of General Sherman's most mercilessly rapacious cavalry officers.

The Magnificent Morgans had been pushed from their early teens to
find rich husbands, preferably with titles. Thelma had first married
James Vail "Junior" Converse, whose family had founded the Bell
Telephone empire. Often drunk and usually violent, Converse abused
his teenaged wife, once stripping her clothes from her body in a crowded
New York restaurant. They divorced after two years. Gloria had married the dissolute Reginald Vanderbilt, who quickly drank himself to
death, leaving her a widow at twenty-one. Laura personally arranged
Consuelo's short-lived marriage to Count Jean de Maupas de Juglart.
Thelma reentered the marital stakes and cantered away with the enormously wealthy shipping magnate Lord Marmaduke Furness and produced a son. But they were often apart, leaving each to pursue extra-
marital interests. The Prince of Wales met Thelma at, of all unlikely
places, an agricultural show at Leicester.

While David redecorated Fort Belvedere—"the Fort," he called it—
Thelma took a house nearby, Three Gables, with her sisters joining her
as cover. When the Fort was finished, Thelma moved in as hostess, and
David managed to have both twins presented at court. When Thelma
was not available, Gloria would step into her shoes and, it was rumored
but never confirmed, his bed. The twins shared everything. Sometimes
the Prince of Wales would be seen escorting both, one on either arm,
and few could tell the two apart. Later, Thelma was to write that their
lovemaking was a rapturous journey "into uncharted waters," with the
Prince at the helm, but she confided to friends that he was an unsatisfactory lover. Among them was a fellow American socialite whom
Consuelo had introduced to Thelma and whom Thelma in turn introduced to David. Her name was Wallis Simpson.

As Freda Dudley-Ward had done, Thelma tried to limit David's
drinking, which had become heavier each month. Thelma's innovative
cure was to teach him needlepoint, a somewhat incongruous hobby for
any male in those days but more so, perhaps, for a future king. He was,

however, already fond of knitting. Thelma told him he would never be able to master needlepoint with the unsteady hands of a habitual drunk, and he made an effort to cut back.

Her concern for his drinking was probably triggered by her belief that it was the root of his sexual inadequacy. Close though their relationship was, it was not monogamous. For several months David also slept with one of the most notorious women in Europe. Because it was one of the relationships that convinced the King that his son was a libertine, it is worth giving her background in some detail.

Marie Marguerite Alibert Laurent was an exotic, passionate, olive-skinned French woman who had befriended Blanche Auzello, the American wife of Claude Auzello, the colorful manager of the Ritz Hotel in Paris. Known as Maggy, she had divorced her husband, Guillaume Laurent, when he left France for the Far East and she refused to accompany him. She posed as a widow and lived on his generous allowance until she met a wealthy twenty-two-year-old Egyptian, Prince Ali Kamel Bey Fahmy, in Paris. She married him in Cairo in 1922 and spent the next seven months in Biarritz, Monaco, Paris, and London. On July 10, 1923, they were staying at the Savoy Hotel in London. At dinner that evening, the Princess told the leader of the restaurant orchestra and other hotel officials that her husband had been abusing her and she "would be dead by the end of the week." A violent summer thunderstorm raged outside and an almost equally violent argument was taking place inside their fourth-floor suite, the heated words almost drowned by loud claps of thunder while repeated flashes of lightning illuminated the two figures.

A night porter clearing trays in the corridor at one-thirty in the morning saw Prince Fahmy rush from Suite 41 shouting, "Look what she has done!" and pointing to a red fingernail mark on his cheek. She emerged almost immediately, screaming that her husband had punched her in the eye. The porter begged the pair not to wake up the other guests and retreated down the hallway. Moments later, he heard several shots amid the thunder.

Rushing back to the Prince's suite, he found Fahmy lying in a pool of blood, a bullet in his head and two in the abdomen, his wife standing over him with the revolver smoking in her hand, the foot of her white nightgown drenched in his blood. She was charged with murder.

Two months later, she appeared in the dock of No. 2 Court of the Old Bailey. She was defended by Sir Edward Marshall Hall, one of the most controversial barristers of the day. He was known for his fashionable clients, sensational cases, and dubious tactics. He filled the trial with racial overtones. Princess Fahmy was a beautiful French woman fatally attracted to, as he kept calling Prince Fahmy, "an Oriental," who kept his wife as a sex slave.

In a few months of marriage, Marshall Hall claimed, he had subjected her to the most bestial sexual depravities, and she had shot her husband in self-defense as he tried to force himself upon her once more.

For hours, the Princess testified that her husband had kept her in bondage, humiliated her, and forced her to participate in sadistic sexual practices with himself and others. She claimed that during one violent episode, he dislocated her jaw and, out of the sheer joy of terrorizing her, fired a gun over her head. She claimed he had wanted her to sleep with other men while he supervised, and when she told him that he might later dissolve their marriage if she complied, he signed a document promising not to divorce her for adultery. Marshall Hall repeatedly referred to the Princess being "at the mercy of Fahmy and his entourage of black servants," who intimidated her and her sole French maid. One black valet was portrayed as if he were a gigantic bodyguard when he was, in fact, only five feet tall and of slight build.

According to Marshall Hall, on the night of the shooting, the Prince was once again poised to sexually abuse his abject wife. They fought; then the Princess grabbed a gun which the Prince himself had loaded. As the Prince moved toward her, she fired twice through the open window to ward him off. The Princess, he said, was terrified of thunderstorms, and the storm raging outside added to the emotional strain she was under.

"He was crouching before her, crouching like an animal. Like an Oriental," Marshall Hall told the jury. So virulent was the attack by Marshall Hall and so strong were the racial overtones of the trial that the Egyptian government and Prince Fahmy's family made formal complaints to the foreign secretary. Mr. Justice Swift told the jury that the evidence they had heard was disgusting but directed the jury to acquit if they believed it. They did. Princess Fahmy went free that night and inherited everything her husband's family had been unable to secure.

Fahmy's family and friends believed that the Princess regretted her marriage within weeks and wanted a divorce. When she discovered she would be unable to secure any support if she left him, having given up a generous allowance from Laurent, she was afraid she would be destitute. On the other hand, Fahmy would be able to divorce her quite easily. The Princess, the family claimed, arranged the argument as an excuse to murder her husband, having spread malicious stories around the hotel that he intended to kill her.

The Prince of Wales met Princess Fahmy in Biarritz and could not fail to have known of her sensational widowhood. Yet he launched into an affair with her which she did not keep secret for very long. She confided to Blanche Auzello before a trip to London that she was the Prince's mistress, and some weeks later, the Prince took a suite at the Ritz; it remained empty for several days while he slept at Princess Fahmy's apartment. Auzello recounted that the Prince of Wales and an equerry would fly to Paris in a private plane piloted by the Prince himself. The four of them would then hit the Paris night spots incognito.

But they were not incognito to British intelligence agents based at the Paris embassy who watched them every minute. Details of the affair were reported to the prime minister and through him to the King, further straining relations between them.

Thelma also had other lovers. How unsatisfactory a sexual partner David was Thelma only fully realized when, on a transatlantic crossing, a somewhat firmer hand took the helm. She was wooed and won by Prince Aly Khan. Aly Khan had been schooled in the art of Imsak, a technique of prolonging sex more or less indefinitely. By the time their ship docked, Aly Khan had made the Prince's unchartered waters seem like the Sargasso Sea. Gossip of Thelma's affair reached England ahead of her. Several first-class passengers wired ahead the scandalous details to friends, and by the time she arrived in London, the affair was being whispered everywhere. David, who had also heard stories of Aly Khan's sexual prowess, was angry and humiliated. But by then, as Thelma discovered to her astonishment, she had already been displaced at the Fort.

Before leaving, she had asked her friend Wallis Simpson to "look after the Little Man" while she was away. "Hold the Fort for me," she joked. When she came back, she found that Wallis was in full possession. The "Little Man" and Wallis were lovers.

Eight

A Woman Named Wallis

The woman who now occupied the Fort and the attentions of the heir to the throne was an American socialite with a shadowy family background and a colorful sexual career. She is one of those rare characters of whom the more that is written the less is known. On one level she is simply a captivating divorcée, what used to be called a "woman with a past," with whom a King fell so deeply in love that he was prepared to give up his Crown, his scepter, his throne, and to a great extent, his duty and honor. On another level, she was a sometime spy and prostitute whose relationship with the King was, however, not the only nor indeed the prime factor in the events that led to the abdication crisis.

She was born Bessie Wallis Warfield in Baltimore in June 1895—out of wedlock. Later, records would be falsified to suggest that she had been born the following year, after her parents married. Her father, Teackle Warfield, died of tuberculosis in 1897, and her mother, Alice, was left to raise the child alone. Mother and child were rescued from penury by Alice's widowed sister, Bessie Merryman, who was a confidante and surrogate mother to Wallis until Merryman's death, at age 100, in 1964.

Wallis's childhood has been described as one of shabby gentility. They had no money, but they did have rich relatives, and life for Alice involved charity and dependence, on an uncle, on a sister, on lovers. There was enough, however, to send Wallis to private schools. For a time, her mother took in boarders, many of whom were young men. It has been suggested that, in fact, hers was a house of prostitution, but there is no evidence to support this claim.

Escape was Wallis's primary ambition, and in her time the only possible flight to freedom was through marriage. At twenty-one, she married Win Spencer, a young navy flier from a well-to-do Chicago family. It was a shaky marriage from the beginning. Spencer was an alcoholic on a slow downward spiral. His drinking made his career flounder, and so he drank more. His anger triggered violent arguments with Wallis, destroying their relationship, and his response was to drink even more. He also had numerous casual affairs.

Wallis was only prevented from discarding Spencer by her straitlaced Episcopalian relatives, for whom divorce was a social and spiritual disgrace. Then, in 1922, when they were living in Washington, Spencer announced he was leaving her for another woman. A few months later, he was sent to China, which enabled Wallis to pose as a navy wife with a husband posted abroad rather than as a woman whose marriage had collapsed and who had been abandoned.

Through her navy connections and her old private-school friends, Wallis had an entrée to the Washington power-party scene. She met Mussolini's ambassador, Prince Gelasio Caetani, descendant of a papal dynasty, who was nineteen years her senior, and had a short affair. There was a more serious relationship with Felipe Espil, an Argentine diplomat. Both were ardent, proselytizing Fascists. She also developed close contact with a number of American naval personnel in the American intelligence community in Washington, and it is possible—even likely—that she was used by them in some low-level espionage capacity. This world of Washington intrigue fascinated Wallis. She mixed gracefully among powerful men and found they responded to her directness and wit.

In 1924, after a lengthy trip to Europe, where she again made contact with known members of the American intelligence community, she agreed to join her husband in China, which was experiencing the chaos of civil war. No period of her life has been wrapped in more mystery and speculation than the two years she spent in Hong Kong, Shanghai, and Peking.

It is said she was so promiscuous on the voyage to China that ships' officers had to be ordered to stay away from her cabin. She had an affair with Count Ciano, Mussolini's son-in-law and later Italian foreign minister, and aborted a child by him. She had another affair with Alberto da Zara, then an Italian diplomat and later admiral of the fleet. She was a hostess in a fashionable brothel and the mistress of gangsters. It is claimed that she leaked American naval information to the Russians, that she learned sophisticated sexual techniques at Hong Kong's renowned "singing houses," and that she peddled drugs. Little time was spent with Win Spencer, and when she returned to the United States, it was to divorce him.

What is the truth of Wallis's China years? According to a confidential American intelligence source who has access to still-classified documents on the interwar years, she had been recruited as an American agent while in Washington by Capt. Luke McNamee, chief of naval intelligence, and sent to China in this capacity. Her reconciliation with Spencer, who had also joined naval intelligence and whose affairs were becoming more overt, was part of her cover.

Certainly, it seems unlikely that a woman who had just entered the glamorous world of men like Caetani and Espil would abandon it and go halfway around the world to seek the company of a man who had beaten, abused, and been notoriously unfaithful to her with both sexes and whom she wanted to divorce unless she was persuaded to do so for some ulterior motive. According to the source, she acted primarily as a courier, but her other duties were to insinuate herself into the foreign diplomatic community, which she did with aplomb. She identified a number of potential intelligence sources in the Russian and Italian legations and identified Americans whose gambling and sexual activities had made them vulnerable to the intelligence services of other nations.

Her chief coup turned out to be her affair with Ciano. That he had an affair with an American woman in China and, as a result, she had an abortion was later used by the U.S. government to blackmail Ciano, who leaked high-level foreign policy information to the United States from 1936 to 1941. When she came to be the cause of the abdication of Edward VIII, the United States was embarrassed by her role as a former American agent.

Christmas, 1926, saw her in New York at the Washington Square home of an old friend. There she met a wealthy Anglo-American businessman, Ernest Simpson. Simpson, a partner in a successful shipping brokerage business, was already married. She had an affair with him that ended because he showed no signs of getting a divorce. She managed to get herself a free trip to Europe with the help of her Aunt Bessie and a rich friend of her aunt's, Mary Adams, owner of the *Washington Star*. She even tried to get a job selling elevators. But her best hope of independence—inheritance—evaporated in 1927. A rich uncle died, and Wallis found she had been left only a few thousand dollars out of a $5 million estate.

It was 1928 before she again met Ernest Simpson and resumed the affair. This time, with Wallis's own divorce final, Ernest cabled his wife, Dorothea, who was in a hospital in Paris, with the news that he was divorcing her. Simpson and Wallis were married in London in July. Simpson was soon embroiled in saving the shipping brokerage business from destruction. The European end of the operation had been badly mismanaged before he arrived. In 1929, Wallis had decided to return to the United States for the funeral of her mother when the news of the Wall Street crash broke. Both her own small holdings and her husband's personal investments were wiped out.

Although Ernest Simpson's brokerage business remained intact, Wallis became obsessed with small economies and again dependent on occasional handouts from her aunt Bessie. They lived a relatively quiet life, on the periphery of the more glittering London social scene, until a chance event changed everything. Wallis had known Benny Thaw, scion of the wealthy Pittsburgh family, through her first husband. Thaw's brother had been a fellow officer. Now Benny Thaw was first secretary at the American embassy in London, and she became friendly with Thaw's wife, Consuelo. Consuelo, in turn, introduced Wallis to her twin sisters, Gloria Vanderbilt and Thelma Furness, the Prince of Wales's mistress. Thelma and Wallis had many traits in common and many risqué stories to share. They soon developed a lunch-at-the-Ritz friendship. Then, one weekend in January 1931, when the Thaws could not make it, Thelma invited the Simpsons to the Furness estate. Wallis was overjoyed. The Prince of Wales, Thelma told her, would be among the guests.

Wallis, then thirty-five, had once had a teenaged crush on the thirty-six-year-old Prince of Wales—as had countless other young women—and she kept a scrapbook of clippings and photographs of him. She had also glimpsed the Prince some years before. When Win Spencer was stationed in San Diego, the Prince and Lord Mountbatten had arrived at the port on the HMS *Renown*. She was a face in the crowd.

The weekend was a success. Wallis and the Prince had a somewhat banal conversation, but it served as an introduction to a new social level for the Simpsons. "I've had my mind made up to meet him ever since we were here. . . . I never expected to accomplish it in such an informal way," Wallis wrote to her aunt. Afterward, Wallis was fired by the ambition for what was then a social accolade: formal presentation at court. She used Thelma's influence to secure it.

That same year, 1931, a scandal surrounding Prince George, Duke of Kent, developed. For many years, it was covered up by Buckingham Palace. The Prince of Wales had successfully reduced his brother's dependence on drugs but had failed to impress on him the need for discretion in other aspects of his social life. Prince George had had a homosexual affair with a youth in Paris and had given him expensive, personally inscribed mementos. Prince George was being blackmailed by the youth and some demimonde associates. The Prince of Wales found himself buying the mementos back. It was deemed wise to get Prince George out of the country for a while to ensure that he did not revert to his old addiction, and so the two Princes went to South America for an official visit.

On their return, Thelma threw a party for them, and Wallis was invited. The Prince of Wales remembered his meeting with her and this time chatted amiably. They met again weeks later when Wallis was presented at court. It was all leading, casually but inexorably, to a closer friendship, and Wallis, judging by her letters home, already envisioned the possibilities of an affair despite the fact that Thelma was now one of her closest friends in England.

Meanwhile, Wallis set out on another adventure. She was invited to Cannes in a party that included Gloria Vanderbilt, Nadeja, Marchioness of Milford Haven, the sister-in-law of Lord Louis Mountbatten, and Consuelo Thaw. When she arrived at the Hotel Miramar, she found Gloria and Nadeja paired off in one suite, while she shared a bedroom with Consuelo. Thelma and the Prince of Wales, staying in Biarritz, came to visit. The relationship between Gloria and Nadeja would explode in a further scandal before long, and the Prince of Wales and Wallis were almost dragged into it.

The casual friendship between the Prince of Wales and the Simpsons continued to develop slowly. Consuelo had a birthday party at which the Prince and Wallis met again, and this led to the Simpsons inviting the Prince to their home. In return, the Simpsons were invited to the sanctum sanctorum, Fort Belvedere, where Wallis and the Prince of Wales danced together and played parlor games. The Simpsons became regulars. When Wallis left England for a visit to the United States on the *Mauretania* in March 1933, the Prince of Wales paid her the unusual compliment of a bon voyage telegram, news of which instantaneously made her a shipboard VIP. Upon her return she began seeing him alone for the first time.

Standards of beauty change rapidly, and it is not always easy to appreciate the allure of women of an earlier generation. The voluptuous women in vogue in the late-mid-nineteenth century are fat by the standards of a generation later. The reedlike forms of the twenties seem asexual by the standards of the fifties. Wallis was not beautiful—still less pretty—by the custom of her own day, and she seems less so from this distance. But she did have a commanding presence. She possessed an attractive, slender figure, a bold personal style of great panache, and a riveting personality. She had always competed successfully against women more physically attractive than herself.

She was intelligent, she read the newspapers assiduously each day and so had a grasp of issues the Prince usually discussed only with men, and she never hesitated to air her views with directness and force. She had a disrespectful razor wit from whom, to the Prince's delight, no one was immune. She was an accomplished mimic, and her repertoire broadened to include members of the Royal Family. She exuded self-confidence and an indefinable gift which enabled her to make ordinary mortals feel like Princes and a Prince feel like an ordinary mortal. There was no fawning from Wallis Simpson. The Prince of Wales lapped it up.

Thelma left England late in December 1933 and was away for four months. Shortly before Christmas that year, the Prince and Wallis consummated their relationship—in a bubble bath. It was as an eye-opening experience for the Prince, as the tryst with Aly Khan was to be for Thelma. Wallis Simpson's sexual techniques, presumedly honed in Hong Kong's singing houses, enabled him to prolong sex beyond the frantic self-conscious coupling which had hitherto been his modus operandi. It has been suggested that if it were true that the Prince of Wales had really been an unsatisfactory lover, subject to premature ejaculation, he would hardly have sought so many lovers.

The opposite is actually true. Sex cannot be compared to playing the piano or bridge, which a man might give up if he is no good at it. Some men who have severe doubts about their sexuality often seek numerous lovers, desperate to find one who can be satisfied or at least someone who has not yet witnessed the humiliating debacle of sexual failure. Certainly the Prince of Wales had more opportunity than most men to find them. Later, intimates of both suggested there was an even more bizarre sexual magnet which kept the Prince of Wales bonded to Wallis Simpson. A sexual extrovert, she was willing to indulge the Prince in practices he was unable to suggest to other lovers. These included sex games which cast Wallis in the role of dominatrix and him in the role of submissive, a foot and shoe fetish, and infantilism.

Even outside the bedroom, there was much in his behavior toward Wallis Simpson that was submissive, even self-abasing. One intimate of the Prince's described him as "Mrs. Simpson's absolute slave." And "Poots" van Ralte, wife of the Duke of Kent's equerry, Humphrey Butler, recounted an incident at her home. The Prince asked Wallis for a light for his cigarette, calling her "darling."

"Have you done your duty?" Wallis asked.

The Prince hunkered down, put his hands up like paws, his tongue out, and begged like a dog. It was, van Ralte said, "horrible to see."

There were many similar anecdotes being told in the drawing rooms of London in the months to come.

On Thelma's return, the Prince had already become aware of the Olympic liaison with Aly Khan and confronted her. It offended his sense of propriety. Thelma was, after all, widely known as the Prince's mistress; it played on his sense of sexual inferiority. He was only too aware of Aly Khan's reputation for sexual gymnastics, and it played on his innate racism. He later referred to Thelma as "a beast." She denied the affair. She fled to Wallis to cry on her shoulder, unaware that the latter had become her rival. While she remained at the Simpsons' apartment, in Bryanston Court, the Prince of Wales telephoned.

Thelma suspected but did not realize what had happened until the following weekend, when the Prince of Wales's regulars, Thelma and Wallis included, gathered at Fort Belvedere. She saw little domestic intimacies between them that were as unmistakable as finding two people in bed together. Among them was an incident at dinner. The Prince leaned across the table to eat something with his hands. Wallis playfully slapped his wrist. That night, Thelma lay in her pink bedroom at the Fort waiting for her Prince to arrive. He did not appear. The next morning, she left and returned to Aly Khan's bed, abandoning the field to her former friend.

At this time, Ernest Simpson had fallen into serious financial difficulties. His wife's social strivings cost him large amounts of money and time that should have been applied to business. He must have realized that it was not for his company that the Prince invited him and his wife to the Fort. But because the relationship developed slowly and since the reflected glory of Royal intimacy is sometimes blinding, he allowed himself to assume that the three of them were friends. Business was so bad that Wallis and Simpson argued about trivial amounts of money, such as a five-dollar bill for a masseuse.

Wallis found herself faced with a choice between a glamorous life of a Royal mistress and the pedestrian realities of life with a businessman whose trade had failed, whose bank balance had shrunk, and whose charm had turned to pomposity. Less grasping women than she would not have found the choice difficult. Her life up to then had taught her to look out for number one. Her temperament impelled her to go on the adventure. But for several months at least, Wallis did not regard it as a choice between the two men. "I shall try and be clever enough to keep them both," she confided to her aunt.

Nine

Ladyships and Lesbians

O n the other side of the Atlantic a quite different drama threatened to draw members of the Royal Family into a sensational scandal of lesbian sex and adultery, one that ironically, had it been allowed to become public knowledge, might have ended the Prince's affair with Wallis. It was the courtroom custody battle between Gloria Vanderbilt and her sister-in-law, Gertrude Vanderbilt Whitney, over ten-year-old Gloria Laura, Reginald Vanderbilt's daughter.

Gloria Morgan had married Reginald Vanderbilt in 1923, when he was forty-three and she was eighteen. Although it seemed unlikely that he could give her children, Gloria gave birth to little Gloria the following year. Reginald Vanderbilt was old well before his time: a degenerate, hopeless alcoholic; an inveterate and unskilled gambler whose friends were paid a cut of his losses for bringing him to the casino; a roué set firmly on the course to an early grave. He reached his destination in 1925 in the most grotesque manner. He refused to stop drinking despite the fact that the functions of his enormously enlarged liver had all but been destroyed and his blood pressure was dangerously high. The end came when the varicose veins in his throat ruptured. He drowned in his own blood.

He had long since spent his inheritance of $7.5 million and was living off the income of an inviolable $5 million trust. At the time of his death he had $100,000 and debts well in excess of that sum. But while he left nothing to his wife, his daughter inherited the income from the trust—some $112,000—and on her twenty-first birthday, she would inherit a principal of $2.5 million. Gloria Laura Vanderbilt was a very wealthy ten-year-old. Her mother, little more than a child herself, was almost destitute, her daughter the key to her future security.

While Gloria had custody of her daughter, her daughter's money remained with the Vanderbilt lawyers and the courts. A complex series of events, rivalries, and alliances brought Gloria's aunt, Gertrude Vanderbilt Whitney, and her mother, Gloria Morgan Vanderbilt, into court in the Matter of Vanderbilt. It is unnecessary to discuss them all here. But at the heart of the case was the extravagant and allegedly immoral lifestyle of Gloria herself.

Gloria was somewhat justified in believing she could do nothing right in a situation in which she was her own infant daughter's dependent. At first, she lived off $130,000 she was able to grab from the sale of her husband's property, before creditors closed in, then became dependent on a $4,000-a-month allowance from her daughter's income. When Gloria came to the United States, she was treated as an outsider by the other Vanderbilts. When she went to Europe, she was criticized for not giving her American daughter an American upbringing. When she took little Gloria on her resort-hopping jaunts, she was accused of exposing the child to an inappropriate lifestyle; when she left her behind, she was accused of neglecting her; and when she left her with her Vanderbilt relations, she risked having her allowance cut off.

Three years after Reginald Vanderbilt's death, Gloria met Prince Gottfried von Hohenloe-Langenberg on the transatlantic liner *Leviathan*. He was accompanying his aunt, Queen Marie of Rumania. A cousin of the former German Empress, he was also a closer blood relative of the Windsors. His maternal grandfather had been Queen Victoria's son, Alfred. He had little money, and Gloria's mother, Laura Morgan, campaigned to break up the affair, partly by claiming he planned to murder little Gloria so that her mother would inherit her money, a plot Prince Gottfried claimed and which probably was a figment of Laura's warped imagination.

In the summer of 1929, the relationship between Prince Gottfried and Gloria had cooled, but they were still officially engaged. That summer, Gloria met Nadeja, Marchioness of Milford Haven, at a party in Cannes for the Grand Duke Boris. Nadeja introduced herself. A childhood friend of Gottfried's, she wanted to meet the woman he planned to marry. Two women could hardly be less alike. Nadeja was thirty-three, Gloria twenty-four. Nadeja was independent, wild, rich, and adventurous. Gloria was a beautiful wallflower, childlike, willful, and with no income of her own beyond her child's fortune.

Nadeja was the daughter of the Russian Grand Duke Michael Mikailovich and Sophie Merenberg. Unable to win the approval of successive Czars for their morganatic marriage, they had moved to England. The Grand Duke had immense wealth despite having to forfeit his Russian estates. His deposit in gold in the Bank of England on his arrival was said to be the largest made by a single individual. Nadeja's mother was a descendant of Alexander Pushkin, the Russian classic poet, and Nadeja herself had the dark, sultry, exotic beauty that emanated from the genes of an Ethiopian who had been a favorite at the seventeenth-century court of Peter the Great.

Nadeja married Prince George of Battenberg, eldest son of Prince Louis of Battenberg, in 1916. When the German names in the Royal Family were dropped and English-sounding names took their place the following year, Prince Louis became Marquis of Milford Haven, and George and his brother, Louis, lost their titles as Princes and changed their names to Mountbatten. Their father died in 1921, and George became second Marquis of Milford Haven, and his wife became Marchioness. Technically, they were on the periphery of the Royal Family. But Royal Family relationships are not always a simple matter of blood. King George and Prince Louis were related by marriage, but they were as close as brothers. Toward Prince Louis's children His Highness felt the responsibilities of an uncle.

In the twenties, Nadeja had a notorious reputation within the closed confines of London society and the international set, of which she and her husband were the undisputed leaders. In Cannes, after she and Prince George—not her husband but the Prince of Wales's bisexual younger brother—had won a Charleston competition, she soaked her aching feet in a bath of champagne and had the bill sent to her hostess. Cannes in those days was a wild playground. It had once been a winter resort, but in the twenties the chic month was July. It was a magnet for the wealthy, for the bored, for the titled, for the adventurous, and for the courtesan and the gigolo. It was sex and romance. It was gambling and cocaine. It was the taste of champagne and the sounds of jazz. The twin domes of the Carlton Hotel, it was said, were representations of the breasts of a famous courtesan.

For the next several years Nadeja and Gloria remained close. Gloria was a frequent guest at the Milford Havens' English home, Lynden Manor. Nadeja stayed close at Gloria's Paris triplex on the Avenue Charles Floquet. Nadeja had taken Gloria to meet her mother-in-law, Princess Victoria, now the dowager marchioness. Nadeja, Gloria, and

Lord Louis Mountbatten's wife, Edwina, also took trips together, including one to California to stay at William Randolph Hearst's San Simeon ranch with Fred Astaire, Douglas Fairbanks, and Mary Pickford.

The battles over little Gloria's upbringing reached a climax in 1934, when Gloria and her sister-in-law Gertrude clashed in court in New York over custody of the child Gloria. The Vanderbilts had the child's nurse, Emma Keislich, and Gloria's own mother, Laura Morgan, on their side, each because of a personal, selfish agenda. Laura Morgan always went where the money was and believed she would have more control over her grandchild if she was in the hands of the Vanderbilt Whitneys. Keislich had testified that Prince Gottfried had shared Gloria's bed in the Charles Floquet apartment. But the most sensational testimony against Gloria was brought out unintentionally by Gloria's own attorney, Nathan Burkan. He was cross-examining Maria Caillot, Gloria's French maid who had served her in Paris, London, Cannes, New York, and at San Simeon. She claimed Gloria had been repeatedly drunk. Burkan tried to make the point that a long procession of respectable guests had passed through Gloria's Paris home.

He raised the name of the Marchioness of Milford Haven. Yes, Maria Caillot agreed, they were often together and had both stayed at the Hotel Miramar in Cannes for two months. Burkan had plunged on, trying to show that these two ladies were not persistently drunk when in Cannes, nor did they run around with men. Maria Caillot agreed. They did not run around with men. Burkan might have left it there, but he continued, looking for a new line of attack.

"You saw nothing improper in her conduct in that entire two months, isn't that true?"

"Yes, I remember something. It seems to me very funny."

"Tell us if you can the thing you saw."

Caillot said she had taken some of Gloria's clothes from her closet to her own room to press them. That done, she returned to put the clothes in Gloria's closet and serve breakfast.

She told the court: "Mrs. Vanderbilt was in bed reading the paper, and there was Lady Milford Haven beside the bed with her arm around Mrs. Vanderbilt's neck and kissing her just like a lover."

The revelation brought pandemonium to the courtroom, and Manhattan Supreme Court justice John Carew cleared the court. Shaken by his own fundamental error—asking a question to which he did not know the answer—Burkan had all but destroyed his client's case. He announced he would call the Marchioness of Milford Haven to testify. While American papers reported the story in lurid detail, the British journals gave sketchy accounts of the allegations about Nadeja. The *London Daily Express* mentioned only that the witness had described "a kissing incident" between Gloria and "a titled English lady."

Such discretion was unlikely to last very long. Mobbed by reporters as she arrived in London from Paris by plane, Nadeja appeared almost hysterical. Her lips were quivering, and tears were streaming down her face. She said the allegations were "disgusting, malicious lies." She told the reporters she was going to see her husband and then a lawyer. "I shall stand by Mrs. Vanderbilt to the bitter end," she said.

But there was more at stake than their friendship. Nadeja's name had already been blackened, and there was a risk others would become involved. Wallis Simpson had been Gloria's friend. She had shared a room with Gloria's sister, Consuelo, at the time Maria Caillot said she saw evidence of the lesbian affair between Gloria and Nadeja. She had even made a guarded reference to the absence of men on the vacation in her letters.

Mrs. Simpson, now the Prince of Wales's mistress, could be called to give evidence. The Prince of Wales had visited the hotel to see Gloria and Nadeja with Gloria's twin sister, Thelma, when she had been his mistress, and she would certainly be called. The Prince of Wales had also loaned or given Gloria large sums of money when he and Thelma had been together. If there was a further probe into Nadeja's relationship with Gloria, the Prince of Wales's name was almost certain to be mentioned.

Any further inquiry into what went on behind the bedroom doors in the Hotel Miramar would also raise issues about the lifestyle of Edwina, Lord Louis Mountbatten's wife, who had gone on long trips alone with Nadeja, her sister-in-law. Edwina and Mountbatten had just recently been involved in a scandal and did not need another. The *People* newspaper had claimed that a titled Englishwoman had been given an order "from a quarter that cannot be ignored" to stay out of England for a protracted period because of an illicit affair with a black entertainer. Edwina's penchant for black males was an open secret in aristocratic and society circles. The titled woman was Edwina; the entertainer, Paul Robeson. Neither had actually been mentioned by name in the newspaper, but the inference was so clear that the Mountbattens successfully sued for libel.

A further complication involved Gloria's relationship with Prince Gottfried. Gottfried's family connections with the Windsors had been severed by the war, but the round of Royal intermarriage cemented them again. Prince Gottfried had known Nadeja since they were children, and now, years after his relationship with Gloria had ended, he was married into the Mountbatten clan, to Princess Margarita of Greece. Princess Margarita was the Milford Havens' niece. And Princess Margarita's cousin, Princess Marina, was engaged to marry even closer to the Windsors, to Prince George, the bisexual drug-addicted Duke of Kent, King George V's son, and one of Nadeja's fellow travelers in Cannes.

Nadeja was in a difficult position. There were others who were able to testify to Gloria Vanderbilt's lesbian activities. She was said to have been seen drinking champagne in the wood-paneled library of an East Seventy-second Street townhouse with an American socialite, both of them naked. If Nadeja denied the allegations in person, it was conceivable that others would be called to testify that she had perjured herself. And there was no telling whose name or which incident might be mentioned in court next.

And then there was the little matter of the family pornography collection.

The Marquis of Milford Haven kept a vast and eclectic collection of pornography at his home in Lynden Manor, much of it dealing with rape, sadomasochism, sexual torture, bondage, and flagellation. Some pornography of a similar kind had been found by servants at Gloria's Paris apartment. Furthermore, the child had been exposed to it. If Nadeja testified, she might be asked if she had seen any pornography. She could have no way of knowing for certain whether the Vanderbilt Whitney lawyers knew that the pornography belonged to her and her husband.

It is unclear how deeply King George and Queen Mary involved themselves in the case. But it was soon clear to Nadeja and her husband that she could not afford to testify on Gloria's behalf. Prince Gottfried, however, testified, with aristocratic hauteur, that his three-year relationship with Gloria had been as chaste as the day is long. And nobody seemed to believe it. Keislich claimed that she had seen the two in bed.

Prince Gottfried was not used to a culture in which servants were expected to testify against their masters, and worse, be believed. He later said that the atmosphere in court had been so hostile that he wanted to get out of America "before I am accused of complicity in the Lindbergh kidnapping."

At this point a subtle, resourceful British lawyer named Theobald Mathew entered the picture. Precisely who Mathew represented was not quite clear. Ostensibly, he was sent to New York to look after Nadeja's interests. He had been recommended, it appeared, by Nadeja's sister-in-law, Edwina, who had admired his work—against her side—in her libel suit against the *People* newspaper. But his law firm had quite another Royal connection. Charles Russell & Co. had acted for George V in his case against Daisy, Countess of Warwick, when the Countess had tried to blackmail him with her love letters from Edward VII. Whenever Burkan referred to Mathew, it was as "the King's solicitor." His brief was to keep not only Nadeja's name out of court and the newspapers but that of the Prince of Wales and Mrs. Simpson as well.

Mathew's first task was to win Thelma Furness over to his side despite the fact that she was still bristling over the way she had been supplanted by Wallis. She may have had few reasons to do anything for the Prince of Wales and Mrs. Simpson, but her discretion would help her twin sister, Gloria, and keep her own name out of a scandal. Mathew traveled with her to New York and in the course of the journey persuaded her that her best interests lay in helping him. She also filled him in on the subtleties of the case.

It was clear to Mathew that the worst possible development from his point of view would be if Burkan tried to destroy Gertrude Vanderbilt's reputation as efficiently as he had inadvertently destroyed his client's. In some ways Gertrude Vanderbilt's downtown bohemian life was as potentially outrageous as Gloria's champagne-drenched partying. Burkan had compiled a list of witnesses, including artists she had sponsored and a woman who had posed nude for her while she sculpted. But if Burkan went for Gertrude's moral jugular, her attorneys would be compelled to broaden the investigation into Gloria. And that would lead to Royal name-dropping from the witness stand—precisely what Mathew was being paid to avoid.

Mathew met separately with the two opposing groups of attorneys— Gertrude Vanderbilt Whitney's, led by Herbert Smyth; and Gloria's, headed by Burkan—and with Justice Carew. He obtained from Smyth an agreement that if Burkan did not call evidence of Gertrude's sexual impropriety, he would not pursue further evidence of Gloria's. He then had himself invited to Burkan's home overlooking Long Island Sound for dinner. Over brandy, he played his trump card. Burkan admitted he was planning to call evidence against Gertrude Vanderbilt's character and blacken her reputation, as Gloria's had been blackened. Mathew told him that would not be wise. He mentioned Smyth's promise and produced a list of witnesses that could be called against Gloria and the allegations they could make.

The inference was clear. If Burkan did not agree to leave Gertrude's character intact, the list would be handed over to Smyth. Burkan had no choice but to agree. For the remainder of the trial, whenever a mention of a member of the Royal Family seemed unavoidable, the name was written on a piece of paper and handed to the judge. In a case from which Gloria Vanderbilt, Gertrude Vanderbilt Whitney, and particularly the child Gloria all emerged to varying degrees losers, the British Royals were the only participants that achieved everything they wanted.

That a scandal had been avoided was an immense relief to King George and Queen Mary, who continued to be deeply concerned by the private lives of the Royal Family. They could afford to turn a blind eye to the behavior of the Marquis Milford Haven and his wife, to be complacent about the womanizing of Prince Henry, Duke of Gloucester, even sympathetic to the sufferings of the drug addict Prince George. But there was no sympathy for the Prince of Wales, whose duty was to marry and beget an heir.

The wedding of Prince George and Princess Marina of Greece was set for November 29, 1934. The Prince of Wales told his brother to include Wallis Simpson among the guests or he would not come. In recent months he had become obsessively sensitive about her acceptance among his family, friends, and staff and would brook no criticism of their relationship. Her presence at a family wedding, he believed, would be one step on the way to her acceptance by his parents. He pressured Prince George to include her. The King saw her name on the invitation list and crossed it off. The Prince of Wales brought her, anyway. The King was livid, but like any parents at any wedding, King George and Queen Mary were anxious to avoid a scene. They were scrupulously polite but no more. "That woman! In my house!" the King railed later to his private secretary, Lord Wigram.

So concerned was King George V by this time that in bouts of depression over the future of the Empire over which he had presided for a quarter of a century, he would voice prescient doubts about his son's fitness for the throne. "What's the use," he once said to Prime Minister Baldwin. "After I am dead the boy will ruin himself in twelve months." On another occasion he is reported to have remarked that he hoped "nothing would stand in the way" of his second son, Bertie, Duke of York, taking the throne.

Although friends noted that the Prince had become increasingly dependent on Mrs. Simpson—he had twice taken her on secret vacations—he does not appear to have been entirely faithful. It now seems that by the time he introduced her to the family circle at his brother's wedding, another woman was carrying his child.

Vera Seely was the younger sister of Freda Dudley-Ward, and in the way that many younger sisters have crushes on their older sister's male friends, she had had yearnings for the handsome prince when she was a teenager and was aware of her sister's relationship with him. In September 1934, with Wallis Simpson in France, the Prince of Wales tried to rekindle his relationship with Freda, but she refused to see him. Instead, he met with Vera, who had married a friend of the Prince's, Frank "Jimmy" Seely.

The following year she had a son, Timothy, and Jimmy Seely's name appears on his birth certificate as father. But not only is there a striking resemblance to the Prince; Seely has admitted that rumors about his Royal parentage have followed him his whole life. He has been quoted as saying that he simply does not know the truth.

At about the same time there was another affair, with a Swedish woman who has never been identified. It is possible that the Prince had had a resurgence of sexual confidence brought about by his satisfying relationship with Wallis. However, within a few months, friends could see that he was totally dependent on her, and there is no evidence of his having strayed after 1935.

Their letters to each other that year reflect his emotional dependence on Wallis and betray something of the mother-son nature of their relationship. His are filled with childish slang and cloying sentimentality. He is "a boy" and she "a girl," and there are indecipherable words such as "eanum." The word WE in capitals substitutes for the word "us" and is an abbreviation of Wallis-Edward. Her replies to him contain an occasional rebuke for demanding too much of her time.

In 1935, the Prince first conceived the possibility that they would one day marry. "Presently and imperceptibly," the King later recalled, "the hope formed that one day I might be able to share my life with her, just how I did not know." Most couples locked in a relationship in which one or both are married to other people fantasize about the possibility of being free to marry. In May of that year, King George V celebrated his Silver Jubilee. He had been on the throne for twenty-five years.

But when, that same month, he had a protracted private talk with his son about his personal life and the urgent need for him to marry, the Prince of Wales did not reveal any wish to wed Mrs. Simpson. He did tell his father, however, that she made him "supremely happy" and asked for her to be included in invitations to Ascot and to Buckingham Palace as his friend. The King then asked his son directly if he was sleeping with Mrs. Simpson: "If you will give your word of honor that your relationship with Mrs. Simpson is an absolutely clean one, I shall of course believe you," he told his son. The Prince of Wales gave his word.

A gentleman's word of honor, even as late as 1935, was as serious as an oath, and those who were aware of the conversation, including Lord Wigram, were shocked by this lie. The Prince's own staff had seen them in bed together and had what Wigram recalled was "positive proof" that he was having a sexual relationship with her.

Precisely when he fixed his intention to marry her has never been clear. There is no record of a specific proposal. His own memoirs refer only to his "hopes" rather than to an intention, until the abdication crisis was actually under way.

Late in 1935, the Prince of Wales is said by some sources to have talked of stepping out of the line of succession and retiring to land he had bought in Canada. But in light of the life they later led, a retirement to a Canadian estate could hardly have interested Wallis. It is believed that the Prince wanted to confront his father with his wish to marry Mrs. Simpson in the New Year. He would, by law, have needed the sovereign's permission. But he must have had few doubts about what his father would have said.

In the last weeks of 1935, he made an attempt to buy Fort Belvedere, the estate near Windsor that had been given him by his father for his private use but which was still state property. Edward Savill, who administered Windsor Great Park and adjacent lands belonging to the Crown, brought up the matter with Lord Wigram. According to Wigram, the Prince had said that the day would come when a republic would be declared and he would have nowhere to live unless he bought the estate he had already spent so much on developing. It was pointed out to him that in the unlikely event that a republic was declared, the Royal Family would probably be exiled, as had happened in other European states, and owning Fort Belvedere would be of little help to him.

It is unlikely that the Prince of Wales was so worried by the prospect of becoming homeless when a republic was declared. It is more probable that he was already thinking of a day when he might step out of the line of succession or be forced to.

Then, in the first weeks of 1936, King George V died, or more precisely, was murdered.

Bertie, Prince of Wales, at the time
of his visit to the United States in
1860. (Courtesy *New York Post*)

Bertie and his bride, Alexandra of Schleswig-
Holstein, on their wedding day in 1863.
(Author's collection)

A caricature of Bertie that appeared during the Tranby Croft Scandal.

Prince Louis of Battenberg.
(Author's collection)

Four generations of monarchy pictured in 1894. Queen Victoria with her son, Bertie, later Edward VII, (left) her grandson, the Duke of York, later George V, (right) and her great grandson, David, later Edward VIII. (Author's collection)

King Edward VII (seated), his son, the Duke of York (left), later George V, and David, Prince of Wales, later Edward VIII, all in naval uniform at the Cowes Regatta in 1909. (Author's collection)

King George V and Queen
Mary. (Author's collection)

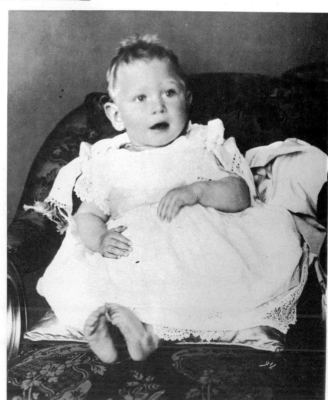

King George VI as an infant
in 1897.

The sultry Nadeja,
Marchioness of Milford
Haven. (Author's collection)

Queen Alexandra as dowager
Queen in 1919. (Courtesy
New York Post)

An official coronation portrait of Queen Mary in 1911. (Author's collection)

Edward VIII and the Duke of York in 1936. (Courtesy *New York Post*)

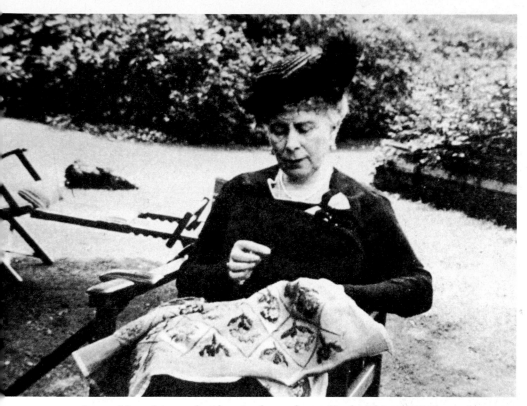

Queen Mary doing embroidery in the garden at Sandringham in 1935.
(Author's collection)

Edward VIII and Mrs. Simpson frolic near Cannes in 1935. From a frame of
Movietone Newsreel. (Courtesy Movietone News)

Edward VIII and Mrs. Simpson in the garden at Fort Belvedere in 1936.
(Courtesy ABC News)

Wallis Warfield Simpson.

Ten

To Kill a King

K ing George V was in his seventy-first year when he celebrated the New Year at Sandringham for the last time. He had had recurrent bronchial problems, but he continued to smoke in spite of them. For several months since the Silver Jubilee celebrations in May 1935 he had slept restlessly, breathed with difficulty when he did sleep, and was repeatedly given oxygen in the middle of the night from a tank kept behind the bed. He may not have been aware that the end could not be long delayed, but those around him clearly were. Palace officials had been meeting secretly for weeks to ease the coming transition, and Stanley Baldwin, the prime minister, remarked that the King "looked like a man with his bags packed." Shortly before Christmas, 1935, his sister, Princess Victoria, had died, and his distress weakened his constitution even further.

Lord Dawson of Penn, a year older than his patient, had been the Royal physician extraordinary since 1907. Apart from his prestigious Royal appointment, he was the most prominent physician of his day and a campaigner for socialized medicine—a controversial figure.

In 1928, when the King lay gravely ill from a chest infection and was almost given up for lost, Dawson refused, apparently because of professional jealousy, to bring in the leading thoracic specialist in the face of advice from ten other consulting physicians and the threat by medical students to demonstrate in protest outside Dawson's house. He nevertheless saved the King by lancing a large abcess behind the diaphragm after several earlier attempts had failed.

He believed medicine was as much an art as a science and relied on his instinct and experience over observation. His instincts were not always correct, according to his critics, who were numerous and vocal.

121

One story about Dawson, presumably apocryphal but nevertheless telling, is that he treated a patient for jaundice for six weeks before discovering he was Chinese.

Lord Moynihan, a leading surgeon of the day, taunted Dawson with a bitter quatrain that is extraordinary even in a profession notorious for the vicious feuds among its leading minds.

> Lord Dawson of Penn
> Has killed lots of men
> And that's why we sing
> God Save the King

Dawson visited the King three times in the first two weeks of January 1936 and found that his health and vitality were deteriorating. Not only had the bronchial infection returned, but his heart had become weak, and the blood vessels to the brain had narrowed.

The Prince of Wales, now in his forty-second year, was out shooting in Windsor Great Park on January 16 when a note from Queen Mary was delivered to him. It said that Dawson "was not too pleased with Papa's state" and asked him to come up for the weekend, but to make it appear a casual visit so as not to alarm the King. The Prince recalls flying to Sandringham the next morning. Lord Dawson remembers having a lengthy conversation with the Prince on the train from London. Either way, the Prince arrived for the weekend, as did his brother Prince Albert, the Duke of York, whose own daughter, Elizabeth, was seriously ill with pneumonia, and other members of the family, plus Lord Wigram, the King's private secretary.

A bitter family argument erupted between the Queen and her eldest son when the Prince of Wales somehow let it be known that he hated Sandringham, regarded its various farms, stables, and stud as one of his father's more expensive hobbies rather than a Royal residence, and that he would sell it when he was King. Queen Mary was so upset by the proposal that she had to be comforted by Lord Wigram, who told her he would do his best to prevent it. Recovering, she secretly distributed Princess Victoria's jewelry among her daughters-in-law, reserving nothing for the Prince of Wales, apparently determined that Wallis Simpson would not get any.

The archbishop of Canterbury, Cosmo Lang, later known for his role in the abdication crisis as "Old Lang Swine," arrived on Sunday, swiftly followed by a quorum of privy councilors. By this time the King must surely have suspected that his condition was very grave. The Prince of Wales returned to London to tell the prime minister that the King was dying. Before doing so, he called on Mrs. Simpson to inform her.

On Monday morning, Dawson found that the King was unable to concentrate and that his mind was wandering. He examined his heart and discovered an irregular beat in the left ventricle. Lord Wigram had a conversation with the King and found him only intermittently lucid. "I feel very tired," the King said eventually. "Go and carry on with your work and I will see you later." It was their last conversation.

That afternoon, the Privy Council was summoned to the King's room to request formal approval for a council of state to act in his stead during his illness. The King, who sat supported in a chair, assented in a strong voice but took several agonizing minutes to scratch something approaching a signature "G.R." on the order-in-council, refusing any assistance. At one point, Dawson had to kneel down to turn the pen around for him because he was trying to sign with the wrong end. He was put back to bed, lapsed into sleep, and stayed unconscious while Dawson examined him again. He concluded he was unlikely to survive the night, and the Prince of Wales was summoned back.

It is usual for the King's physician to issue bulletins when the monarch is ill. So far, no news of the true gravity of the King's condition had been given to the public, only that it was causing "some disquiet." Over dinner, Dawson and other palace officials tried to compose a dignified statement. The last bulletin on King Edward VII was retrieved, but Dawson, conscious of the historic nature of the occasion, found it to be "too commonplace." At last, Dawson wrote on the back of the menu: "The King's life is moving peacefully to its close." It was issued to the BBC by Wigram a short time later and was broadcast on the radio at 9:00 P.M., Monday, January 20.

That night, Mrs. Simpson was at a movie premiere of *The Amateur Gentleman* starring Douglas Fairbanks, Jr. With her were several friends, including Nadeja, Marchioness of Milford Haven, and Edwina Ashley, wife of Lord Mountbatten. In a scene repeated in theaters, cinemas, concert halls, and other public places across the country, the performance stopped suddenly, the lights came up, and the manager stepped up to read the bulletin just heard on the radio. The audience stood and sang "God Save the King."

At Sandringham, Wigram was already making plans for the funeral as the King struggled to rouse himself from unconsciousness. His attempt to do so was interpreted as a sign of pain by another of the King's doctors, Sir Stanley Hewett, who gave the King an injection of morphia. As the narcotic began to take effect, the King roused himself enough to snarl, "God damn you!" at Hewett, which made the Queen laugh.

At 11:00 P.M., while the King slept peacefully, Lord Dawson held a family conference. He told Queen Mary that the King would die soon, though death might not occur for several hours. Both the Queen and the Prince of Wales agreed that they had no wish for his life to be uselessly and perhaps painfully prolonged. Having said that, they told Dawson all decisions were his.

There had been a running debate in medical and legal circles over euthanasia, or mercy killing. The ethics of prolonging the painful end of a terminally ill patient is still a perennial controversy. In 1936, the debate was somewhat different from today's. At that time, doctors had fewer means of artificially prolonging mechanical life as well as fewer drugs for alleviating pain, and there were in those days less subtle definitions of what constituted death.

Euthanasia had some very prominent supporters. Dr. Killick Millard, president of the Society of Medical Officers of Health, had founded the Euthanasia Society to lobby for legal approval of euthanasia under stringent controls. Legislation was expected to come before Parliament later in the year. Doctors in the House of Commons and the House of Lords were aware that many of their fellow medical practitioners had already declined to take heroic measures to prolong life when it was clear it could only be extended for a limited time and to the detriment of the patient. Some doctors prescribed drugs to ease the pain of the terminally ill in doses coincidentally large enough to prove fatal.

But collusion with the family—and indeed, with the patient—to end a life was, and still is, a crime. A notation by Dawson, which remained secret for half a century, is therefore remarkable:

> It was evident that the last stage might endure for many hours unknown to the Patient but little comporting with that dignity and serenity which he so richly merited and which demanded a brief final scene. . . . I therefore decided to determine the end.

The key words here are "unknown to the Patient." Clearly, in Dawson's opinion the King was not in any pain. Nevertheless, there was another reason to hasten the King's end that Dawson thought equally pressing. He had composed the bulletin which suggested that death was imminent. If the King were to linger for many hours, it would seem to some that either he, Dawson, had given up too soon or that an unseemly struggle was taking place. The deadline for the morning edition of the *Times* loomed, and it now appeared likely that the King would linger until well into the morning. Dawson's notes make it clear that he was concerned that the death should be announced in the *Times* and the *Daily Telegraph* "rather than the less appropriate evening journals."

At 11:40 P.M. Dawson told Sister Catherine Black, who had been nursing the King for eight years, to prepare two syringes—one a quarter of a gram of morphine and another a gram of cocaine—and administer them. She refused, but whether it was because of the emotional intensity of the moment or because she found it morally objectionable is unclear. "It was obvious," Dawson's notes say, "that she was disturbed by the procedure." Alone in the room, Dawson distended the jugular vein and gave the King the lethal injections himself.

Queen Mary, the Prince of Wales, and the King's other sons were brought in and witnessed his death fifteen minutes later. Queen Mary kissed her son's hand and curtsied the moment George V had breathed his last and the Prince of Wales had become King. Prince George also bent and kissed his brother's hand. The new King walked from the room weeping aloud, according to Dawson—hysterically, according to Lord Wigram—returning when he was more composed.

The loss of a close relative, especially a parent, is an emotionally turbulent experience, even when it is expected. The Prince of Wales's loud wailing came in sharp contrast to the quiet composure of the rest of the family, a contrast which made his behavior seem "frantic and unreasonable," according to one witness. But for the Prince of Wales it was an especially poignant and disturbing moment. If he really had harbored plans to step out of the line of succession, it was now too late. As has been suggested, if he had expected his father to live several more years and hoped to win his approval, that fantasy had been shattered. In one sense, he was free: King, head of state, head of the church, head of the family. In another, he was imprisoned by his duty and by his subservience to the will of the government. His first act as King was a petty one, but perhaps symbolic of his desire to assert himself.

Even as Dawson and Wigram were fixing the official time of death at 11:55 P.M., the new King looked at the clock. It said 12:25 P.M. For a moment he was confused, then remembered that the clocks at Sandringham were always half an hour fast. It had been that way since Edward VII's day. It was said to encourage Queen Alexandra to be punctual but probably was done to squeeze an extra half hour's shooting into the day. It was an eccentricity masquerading as a tradition and always rankled the Prince. Now head of the house, he strode away from his father's deathbed and loudly ordered all the clocks put right. He then called Mrs. Simpson and told her the news, once more breaking down and weeping.

The precise details of the death of George V were not released, and accounts stressed the swiftness of his deterioration, the comfort in which he made his exit, the placid imperceptibility of the moment of death, and the courage and dignity of the distressed witnesses. In fact, Dawson had taken it upon himself to kill his patient. Had his actions become known, there would have been many who would have called it murder. Indeed, as the law stood then and as it stands now, it *was* murder.

There was no medical reason to administer such a large dose of pure cocaine and morphine—enough in fact, to kill a younger, healthy man—other than to achieve death. Even many of those who support the concept of euthanasia to limit a patient's suffering would have been appalled by the banality of Dawson's motives.

During the following months, the public debate over the ethics of euthanasia increased in intensity as the legislation to codify it progressed through Parliament. None of those taking part except Dawson were aware that it had already been practiced on the King. The Church of England opposed it. Public feeling generally ran against it, and the Voluntary Euthanasia Bill was defeated in both Houses. Remarkably, Dawson was among those who voted against it in the House of Lords. He supported the practice but said he believed that life and death were not a matter for lawyers but "for the wisdom and conscience of the medical profession." It does not seem to have occurred to Lord Dawson that this decision might be a matter for a higher authority.

George V had reigned during the most tumultuous period in his people's history: world war, economic catastrophe, social unrest and upheaval. The endurance of his reign through unprecedented turmoil had become a symbol of stability and continuity; indeed, stability amid change is the often-stated justification for the British monarchy. Less than eight months earlier there had been an outpouring of affection for the King at the Silver Jubilee celebrations, and the fresh memory of that occasion increased the public grief at his death. At one point during the Silver Jubilee, the King had seemed amazed by the warmth of his reception—not merely at the official events but by crowds that gathered spontaneously in the thousands every night for a week to sing outside Buckingham Palace.

"But I'm an ordinary sort of fellow," the King remarked to the archbishop of Canterbury.

"Yes, sir," Lang told him, "that's just it."

He was, in many ways, an ordinary sort of fellow. He had not been trained from childhood to be King. He had had the mantle of heir apparent thrust upon him as an adult. He was also the first British monarch whose voice had become familiar to his subjects. He had begun a tradition of Christmas radio broadcasts to the nation which enhanced the image that the monarchy was now trying to promote, that of patriarch rather than ruler, head of an extended family rather than of state.

A monarchy that was above party politics had been the concept of George V's grandfather, Queen Victoria's consort, Prince Albert. George V was the embodiment of that ideal. He would have preferred to have followed his naval career rather than become King, but the qualities honed by his period in the navy were those that made him a successful monarch: self-discipline, conscientiousness, and an acute sense of fairness. A Victorian by nature and upbringing, he was ill at ease in the world of social upheaval after World War I, and he hankered for the more stable world he had known in his youth. He retreated into the background in the later years of his reign, finding solace in his hobbies: stamp collecting, sailing, and shooting.

Tragically, though he was a beloved patriarch of his people, he was incapable of being as successful a parent to his children.

Part Three

EDWARD VIII
(January 1936 to December 1936)

Eleven

Who Is King Here?

Queen Mary—and George V himself—would have preferred a quiet cremation and entombment at Sandringham, but funerals had become part of the curriculum of Royal pageantry, and the monarch is invariably buried at Windsor. The body of the King was embalmed early on January 21, 1936, and the coffin was taken on a handcart that evening in an eerie, torchlight procession led by a single Scottish piper, to lie in state at Sandringham. The new forty-one-year-old King, Edward VIII, was not present. He had flown that day to London to meet with the Accession Council. He asked Lord Wigram to stay on as his private secretary, but Wigram did so reluctantly, asking the monarch "not to keep me too long."

The new King made it clear that he wished to be known as Edward VIII. Wigram and family members tried to talk him out of it, telling him pointedly that his private life already bore too close a resemblance to that of his grandfather, Edward VII. The following day, January 22, the new reign was proclaimed by heralds at four sites across London: St. James Palace, Charing Cross, Temple Bar, and the Royal Exchange.

Monarchs are normally not present at their own proclamations, usually because they are in mourning. But Edward VIII had arranged for several friends to watch from a window at St. James Palace and at the last minute broke tradition and joined them. A keen-eyed photographer caught him looking from the window, a woman's angular face next to his. It was Wallis Simpson. The general public did not know her. She was not identified in the caption when the photograph appeared in newspapers. But his family and palace officials were deeply offended.

But that controversy did not compare to the scenes back at Sandringham when the late King's will was read by his private attorney, Sir

Bernard Halsey Bircham. All the ranks and titles of George V passed to Edward VIII automatically under the law of accession, but the will was the disbursement of his large private fortune. The property at Balmoral and Sandringham went to the new King, but there was no money for him. His mother, brothers, and sister were left large undisclosed sums.

Edward VIII was aghast at what he called being "left out" of his father's will. He kept interrupting the proceedings, saying "Where do I come in?" Bircham, Wigram, and his brothers tried to explain that the late King had assumed that as Prince of Wales his eldest son had a large income from the estates of the Duchy of Cornwall, which included some of the most expensive and profitable properties in England, and that he had already amassed a large fortune. Indeed, he had saved between $4 and $5 million from his Duchy of Cornwall properties. He would also be amply supported by the Civil List, the parliamentary grant to the Crown. But he would not be consoled.

"My brothers and sister have got large sums, but I have been left out," he said repeatedly, and wanted to challenge the will. Wigram told him his father would turn in his grave if that happened. Alan Lascelles, the former private secretary to the Prince of Wales, saw the new King striding out of the room where the will had been read, his face black with anger.

The world stage on which King Edward VIII took his place in January 1936 presented a tragedy of violence and strife. The Treaty of Versailles that followed World War I was meant to be the foundation of peace in Europe. It was in tatters. The League of Nations, created to guarantee that peace, had been discredited. Much of Europe was already in the thrall of dictators: Hitler in Germany, Mussolini in Italy, Stalin in the Soviet Union, von Schuschnigg in Austria, Horthy in Hungary, Kemal Ataturk in Turkey, Salazar in Portugal. Right-wing coups had taken place in Bulgaria and Greece.

Italy, bent on colonial adventure, had invaded Ethiopia, aided by the impotence and vacillation of the European democracies. In contemptuous violation of the Treaty of Versailles, Germany had openly rearmed, building an air force, the Luftwaffe, and introducing conscription. The French government of Pierre Laval had fallen the week of the accession. Spain was already spiraling into a bloody civil war that would erupt that year and become a proving ground for the weapons and tactics used in World War II. Japan, its government dominated by militarists, had conquered Manchuria, created a puppet state, and proclaimed Japanese domination of eastern nations as its manifest destiny.

Britain had its own potential dictator in Sir Oswald Mosley. Educated at Winchester and the army staff college at Sandhurst, he had been a Conservative Member of Parliament, then an independent, then a member of the Labour government of 1929. When he found himself in opposition to Labour orthodoxy, he formed the New party, whose twenty-one candidates were all defeated in the 1931 election. With financial help from Mussolini, he formed the street-fighting British Union of Fascists and National Socialists, known as the Blackshirts, with a creed of violence, extremism, and anti-Semitism. He was a friend of both Edward VIII and Wallis Simpson, and in 1936 he married Diana Guinness, sister of Unity Mitford, one of Hitler's mistresses, in Dr. Goebbels's home in Berlin.

By 1936, British foreign policy toward Italy and Germany, begun under the national coalition government of Ramsay MacDonald and continued under Baldwin's Conservative government, was well established. The term used to describe it, appeasement, later took on an odious connotation, particularly when it was continued under Prime Minister Neville Chamberlain in the face of growing German aggression. But the policy grew out of a frank realization that the Treaty of Versailles had been self-defeating; disastrously harsh on Germany— economically, socially, and politically—and the only alternative to appeasement was a renewed war that Britain was ill equipped to fight. Moreover, a powerful peace movement existed in Britain that would have made rearmament difficult to carry through. The appeasement policy was also encouraged by the erroneous assumption that Hitler and Mussolini could be bargained with on the same basis as other heads of state and that agreements made were likely to be kept.

But there were also many in influential positions in Britain in the thirties who frankly admired Mussolini and Hitler, sympathized with their territorial ambitions, and saw a future alliance in which the Western democracies joined the dictatorships in a crusade against Soviet communism.

There were those, other than Mosley, who sought to bring Nazi-style fascism to Britain. The sentiment was not so extensive as to be described as a movement, but it was more than a cabal. The two most prominent sympathizers were the new King, Edward VIII, and his brother, Prince George, Duke of Kent.

One factor that drew them to the Nazis was their hatred of, and contempt for, the Communists in the Soviet Union and their belief that Hitler had saved Germany from communism. The Windsors regarded all members of the Soviet government as personally responsible for the murder of their Russian relatives, notwithstanding George V's own guilt in refusing his Russian cousins asylum in Britain. Edward VIII refused to seat Russian diplomats at a dinner the night of George V's funeral, and when he met Maxim Litvinoff, the Russian envoy, at a separate reception to receive condolences, he asked him point-blank: "Why did you kill my cousin Czar Nicholas?"

"It wasn't me. I was among the conservatives," Litvinoff replied.

George V had a similar exchange and had berated Prime Minister Ramsay MacDonald for forcing him to speak to Russian diplomats.

They were also drawn to Nazism because of the Windsors' own family connection to Germany. Edward VIII once announced that "every drop in my blood is German." While he wrote disparagingly of Germany shortly after World War I, he was soon reconciled with his surviving German relatives, a number of whom were to play secret roles in the events leading to the abdication, and both he and Queen Mary were still in touch with the Kaiser in exile and other members of the Hohenzollern house.

But Nazism also had a strong ideological appeal to both Edward VIII and the Duke of Kent. Genuinely concerned with the economic hardships of the working class in Britain, without, however, letting that concern interfere with their own extravagance, and skeptical about the laborious and often divisive processes of parliamentary democracy, they saw in Nazism a solution to social and economic problems that undercut socialists, disciplined the trade unions, and maintained power in the hands of the elite. Their own passive anti-Semitism, rife throughout the British upper classes and indeed throughout European society to varying degrees, allowed them to ignore the virulent anti-Semitism of the Nazis with no pangs of conscience.

This was the world scene in January 1936 and the stage on which the traumatic events of the next eleven months would be played out.

But the events which led to the abdication crisis and their connection to the influential pockets of support in Britain for the Nazis cannot be fully appreciated without an understanding of the role of the monarchy and of the power structure in British society known as the Establishment. There is no written British constitution akin to that of the United States, no Bill of Rights, and no court of final constitutional appeal like the Supreme Court. Rather, there is a series of accepted traditions, many of which have evolved over a comparatively short period of time, by which the political game is played rather than the solid surface provided by a written document. The British "constitution" has always depended for its success on a well-defined social structure, economic stability, politically and militarily secure borders, and the correct behavior of the political players.

In the mid-thirties these assumptions were being challenged. Economic stability had evaporated. It was widely accepted that even if Britain's natural defenses were not breached in a future war, air power would bring the conflict into the heart of the nation's ports and cities. *The Shape of Things to Come* by H. G. Wells, one of the most popular novels of the day, was made into a movie released in 1936. It portrayed a war in which the great cities of Europe were destroyed from the air. Winston Churchill had predicted that another great war would be "the end of the world." There was a strong Communist groundswell not only within the trade unions but among the literati and intellectual elite in the universities, particularly Cambridge. Although the first Labour government of 1929–31 had not been a success, the growth of the Labour movement and the desperate conditions of the working class in many regions challenged the accepted social structure.

The monarchy's role had been diminished by successive governments that had sought not just the supremacy of Parliament as a legislative body but that of the cabinet as an executive body. The monarch still had the right to be consulted and informed; he could advise his ministers, and they would at least consider his advice. Theoretically, the monarch had the right to appoint anyone to be prime minister, but in practice he could only choose someone who he knew commanded the support of Parliament. Theoretically, he had the power to dissolve Parliament and cause an election, but in practice he could do so only at the will of the government of the day.

A power structure subject to no democratic controls underpinned the processes of government. What was later to be called the Establishment consisted of the upper reaches of the civil service, the mandarins of Whitehall, who keep their positions regardless of changes in government; the palace circle of advisers to the monarch; the leading members of the judiciary; the handful of key Church of England bishops; the editors and proprietors of what used to be called "quality" newspapers; the most senior officers of the armed services; the governors and directors of the British Broadcasting Corporation (BBC) and the Bank of England, and a sprinking of other bodies.

Their education at the leading private schools, Eton, Harrow, Winchester, and Marlborough, and at Oxford and Cambridge, and their
membership in a handful of gentlemen's clubs, produced an orthodoxy
which is the foundation of British institutions and life. It also produced
an intimate network in which the leading members of one institution
might well have known the leading members of several others from
school or university days or through long-standing family relationships.
Their existence caused the Conservative prime minister, Lord Balfour,
to remark that no matter which party is in office, the Conservatives are
always in power. In a crisis, particularly a constitutional impasse, the
ability of the Establishment to communicate through a shared set of
experiences and relationships is of paramount importance to the out-
come.

These subtler aspects of British political life, particularly the limits
on the power of the monarchy, were not adequately understood by the
Nazis, who believed that they could conduct a separate foreign policy
with Edward VIII and that he could either impose his view on the
government of the day or replace that government with one that would
accept it. The Russians also believed it, for they kept a fearful eye on
developments through their network of spies in Whitehall and in the
German embassy. The Russian experience of absolute monarchy had
prejudiced their view. But what is most astonishing is that, for a time at
least, Edward VIII believed it.

The King had in fact been pursuing a foreign policy separate from the
government's even when he was Prince of Wales. He was, for example,
in regular contact with his cousin Charles, Duke of Saxe-Coburg
Gotha, one of Hitler's diplomats and a senior officer in the S.S. Coburg,
a grandson of Queen Victoria, was born in Britain and educated at Eton
and had been heir to the English title Duke of Albany. While still a
teenager, he had been sent to secure the succession of the dukedom
which had been held by the Prince Consort's family. When the Saxe-
Coburgs became the Windsors, Coburg had been stripped of his British
titles. Vicissitudes following World War I had made Coburg—and the
handful of remaining members of the German Royal Family—fervent
Nazis.

He used his frequent visits abroad to espouse personal views to heads
of state at variance with those of the British government, particularly on
relations with Germany and Italy and on the usefulness of the League of
Nations. He supported an alliance with Hitler, advocated a free hand

for Mussolini in Africa, and opposed sanctions against Italy over its invasion of Ethiopia. He despised the League of Nations.

Personal contacts in London show a bias toward pro-Nazi elements in British society. They included Lord Londonderry, an immensely wealthy land and mine owner, and the Duke of Westminster, who owned vast stretches of London's most expensive districts, including much of Belgravia and Mayfair, as well as large estates in the north of England, Ireland, and Canada. Both were supporters of the Nazis. Lord Londonderry particularly wrote admiring missives to the Führer. The King was encouraged in his pursuit of a German alliance by two British lobbying organizations: the Anglo German Fellowship, run by Lord Mount Temple, and the Imperial Policy Group (IPG), founded by Sir Reginald Mitchell Bank. Kenneth de Courcy, who was to remain a close friend of the King's, was a principal officer of the IPG.

Personal contacts of Wallis Simpson's also betray a pro-Nazi influence. She was close to the German ambassador Leopold von Hoesch and a frequent guest at German embassy receptions because of her husband's business dealings with Germany. She was a friend of French attorney Armand Gregoire, who served as a conduit for German subsidies to Oswald Mosley's Blackshirts. She regularly saw Beatrice Cartwright, the Standard Oil heiress and Nazi collaborator, and Emerald Cunard, a rich pro-Nazi social climber who gave lavish parties in London for a pro-German circle.

Joachim von Ribbentrop, one of Hitler's special envoys, later ambassador to London and ultimately foreign minister, soon became aware of Wallis Simpson's hold on Edward VIII. Ribbentrop acted quickly to win her friendship and was so successful that it has been claimed, though without much evidence, that they were having an affair. It is incontestable that one of the key reasons for Hitler's appointment of Ribbentrop was his relationship with Wallis Simpson and hers with the King. Prince Otto von Bismarck, grandson of the former German chancellor, became another regular contact of the King and Mrs. Simpson. It was this group of Nazis and Nazi sympathizers that the British satirist Osbert Sitwell referred to when he wrote that the King's circle included "the riff-raff of two continents."

At the time of George V's Silver Jubilee in 1935 celebrating twenty-five years on the throne, Hitler had sent the Duke of Saxe-Coburg Gotha, Princess Cecilie, the Kaiser's daughter-in-law, and her son, Prince Frederick, to London. Princess Cecilie had urged the then

Prince of Wales, who would be King in another eight months, to call publicly for closer ties with Germany. Wallis, prompted by Ribbentrop, supported the idea. A month later, the Prince of Wales addressed the British Legion, Britain's veteran organization, and called for the old hostility toward Germany to be buried and new links forged. His words were greeted with a standing ovation. A swastika-waving delegation of German veterans was received in Brighton with a warm message from the Prince.

A month later, Hitler greeted a British delegation of veterans, sponsored by the Prince of Wales, in Berlin. Both the British government and King George V were outraged by the Prince's interference.

Months before his accession, he had made it known to both British and German confidants that he believed his immense popularity among the British public would allow him more personal power than any constitutional monarch before him and that he was prepared to use it. He had often spoken of the illogic of a monarchy in which the rhetoric suggested that the ministers were subservient to the Crown but practicalities made the King subordinate to his ministers. If he did not, as King, like their advice, he was said to have remarked, he would not accept it. His views had made their way back to Berlin via the Duke of Saxe-Coburg Gotha, with whom he had many private conversations. Within a week of the accession, Coburg wrote a secret report on the implications of having a pro-Nazi on the British throne:

> The King is resolved to concentrate the business of government on himself. For England, not so easy. The general political situation, especially the situation of England herself, will perhaps give him a chance.

The Duke reported a conversation with King Edward in his first days on the throne in which Edward VIII stated frankly that he wanted a dialogue with Hitler which excluded Prime Minister Baldwin. "Who is King here, Baldwin or I? I myself wish to talk to Hitler, here or in Germany. Tell him that, please!"

As a result of his conversation with the King, Coburg agreed to a private diplomacy with frequent meetings with the new King.

Coburg's secret report did not remain secret for very long. A spy in the German embassy had placed it in the hands of British intelligence and the Russian NKVD, probably before it had been read by Hitler. He was Baron Wolfgang zu Putlitz. He worked for the Russians but with their approval passed selected information about German intentions to Robert Vansittart, the senior civil servant at the Foreign Office and effective head of British intelligence. Alarmed by Edward VIII's Nazi sympathies, Vansittart had already begun monitoring his private diplomacy and had the King and Wallis Simpson under secret surveillance. He lost no time in bringing this startling new intelligence to the prime minister.

Much of the documentation on the political aspects of the abdication either remain secret or have been destroyed. Many of those in German hands after the war were captured and have never been released. As we shall see, some were recovered from Germany by Anthony Blunt, the celebrated Russian spy who not only recruited moles for the Russians but personally penetrated MI5 and the palace. Blunt had become a Soviet agent in 1934. He may also have been a source for the Russians on Edward VIII's pro-Nazi leanings. Blunt had an impeccable source in the Royal Family because he himself had had a homosexual affair with the King's brother, Prince George, Duke of Kent.

Both the Russian intelligence services and Vansittart came to believe that the King was prepared to subvert the processes of democracy in Britain, using as an excuse some future political crisis, such as a general strike, an indecisive election result, or a paralyzing constitutional stalemate, which had occurred during Edward VII's reign.

In such a scenario, the King would take the reins of power himself. With many parliamentarians unlikely to serve in such an administration, key positions would go to the King's personal circle, including Sir Oswald Mosley.

Edward VIII's conversations with the Duke of Coburg became an open invitation to Hitler to provoke, by covert subversion, the crisis which would enable the King to seize extraconstitutional powers. Whether the King actually intended to do this is less important than the fact that the British government was disposed to believe that he would.

Alarm intensified when it was discovered that intelligence from the King's red dispatch boxes was being leaked to the Nazis. These dispatch boxes contain official information for the King's private attention. Robert Vansittart, the head of British intelligence, had begun to screen the information supplied to the King in the dispatch boxes. He learned that highly critical reports from the British embassy in Berlin were making their way back to Berlin via Wallis Simpson and Ribbentrop. This discovery gave rise to speculation that Wallis Simpson was herself a spy. But Vansittart concluded that the King was using her as a courier for his personal diplomacy. It was a role she knew well from the days when she served as a courier for American naval intelligence.

To counter suspicion and widen the circle of potential suspects, the King went out of his way to be careless with the dispatch boxes. On one occasion, he asked an American diplomat, who also happened to be an intelligence agent, to deliver the boxes and their secrets to Buckingham Palace on his way home from visiting the King at Fort Belvedere, his retreat near Windsor.

At the end of February 1936, just six weeks after the Prince had become King, Vansittart and Prime Minister Baldwin summoned Lord Wigram, the acting private secretary, and broke the news that the King himself was leaking information to the Germans. It was a crucial period in relations with Germany. Hitler was about to make his boldest stroke to date.

After World War I, the French had insisted on a secure border on the Rhine by creating an occupied zone in the heart of German territory. The British had opposed the occupation, claiming it would be a thorn in Germany's side over which a future generation would go to war. A compromise produced a zone on the western banks of the Rhine from which German forces were excluded. On March 7, Hitler sent artillery and infantry units into the zone, the Rhineland, fully aware that if Britain and France responded with military force, he would be forced into an ignominious withdrawal.

Communications between the German envoy, Leopold von Hoesch, and Hitler at the time the Germans marched into the Rhineland suggest that Edward VIII had had advance notice of the move. Von Hoesch offered the opinion that the French would not oppose Hitler without British backing and promised to help defuse any attempt by the British to defy him. Four tense days after the Germans marched, von Hoesch reported to Hitler that he had spoken to Edward VIII on the Rhineland situation and that the King had played a forceful role in subduing the British response.

It should be noted that Edward VIII probably exaggerated his role and that von Hoesch expanded it further. But Albert Speer claims that upon hearing the news that the British and French would take no military action against him, Hitler said, "The King of England has kept his promise." Von Hoesch reported to Hitler that King Edward VIII was someone who "understood the *Führerprinzip* [authoritarian principle] and wants to introduce it into his own country."

At what stage Prime Minister Baldwin and Vansittart, the effective head of British intelligence, decided to take the extraordinary step of moving to oust the King is not known. It may have started with an attempt to isolate the King from Mrs. Simpson and the circle around her. But the first step was almost certainly to plant Alec Hardinge, an Establishment figure, as Edward VIII's new private secretary. The private secretary is the most senior palace official—chief administrator, chief of staff, senior aide, counselor, and often confidant. Lord Wigram had served as private secretary to George V and did not wish to serve under Edward VIII, for whom he had scant regard. It was Wigram who first recommended Hardinge. Edward VIII offered the post to Godfrey Thomas, who had served as his private secretary as Prince of Wales. He had been on the Prince's staff for seventeen years. Thomas turned it down and took a more junior position. Thomas also recommended Hardinge, and the King relented.

It was a fateful choice. Hardinge saw a distinction between his allegiance to the Crown as an institution, which was his first loyalty, and his loyalty to the King in person. Although Hardinge and Stanley Baldwin had very different backgrounds, they had been to Harrow and Trinity College, Cambridge, together.

Throughout the crisis to come, Hardinge acted with the King's political enemies, met Baldwin privately to discuss the crisis with no brief from the King to do so, and was a fount of information for Baldwin as well as a source of pressure on the King. After the crisis, he was one of the few officials who had served under Edward VIII to keep their positions under his successor, George VI. Hardinge received numerous honors from George VI, while Winston Churchill, by contrast, who supported Edward VIII throughout the crisis, was never fully forgiven by Edward's successor.

That summer of 1936, Edward VIII took a five-week vacation with Wallis Simpson and his personal circle, spending much of the time cruising the Mediterranean on the luxury yacht *Nahlin*. The King and Mrs. Simpson had adjoining suites. They were seen walking hand in hand, sunbathing, and sightseeing together. Photographs made the front pages of European and American newspapers. British newspapers eliminated Mrs. Simpson from the pictures.

Anthony Eden, the foreign secretary, had persuaded the King to stay out of Italy and away from Mussolini. Nevertheless, the King did meet with a number of heads of state, including his cousin, George II of Greece. King George had been an exile in London for four years, living at the sedate Brown's Hotel until a right-wing coup in Greece brought him back to the throne.

"I'm King in name only," George II told Edward VIII, lamenting that the real power lay with the military. "I may as well be back at Brown's."

Edward VIII returned to Britain convinced he should not remain a puppet monarch. He was equally determined to have Wallis at his side.

Back in Britain, the conspiracy to oust King Edward VIII gathered momentum. Prime Minister Baldwin, Foreign Secretary Eden, intelligence chief Vansittart, the outgoing private secretary, Lord Wigram, and his successor, Alec Hardinge, were joined by the archbishop of Canterbury, Cosmo Lang.

Archbishop Lang had his own agenda. British monarchs are traditionally crowned by the archbishop of Canterbury, the leading Church of England cleric, in Westminster Abbey, in a ritual which symbolizes the belief that the monarch is God's anointed. The Coronation service is part state occasion, part religious ceremony. The new monarch, who is also head of the Church of England and "Defender of the Faith," takes an oath of office and swears to uphold the Protestant religion. Prayers are offered for the new reign.

Archbishop Lang had been hoping to use the religious aspects of the Coronation, set for May 1937, to trigger a spiritual revival. Edward VIII, however, regarded the oath to uphold Protestantism as "repugnant." He believed in God, but he was dubious about the trappings of organized religion and his own role as head of the church. There was also personal animosity between Edward VIII and Archbishop Lang. The archbishop had had numerous conversations with George V about his son's private life, and Edward VIII had resented his interference.

In the fall of 1936, Foreign Secretary Eden began secretly preparing foreign heads of state for the impending crisis. He told Czech leader Jan Masaryk that the British government was increasingly concerned with the King's interference in foreign policy and that he believed he would abdicate. Eden was not a man given to indiscretion. He could only have told Masaryk such a startling piece of information if he wanted the word to go out on the diplomatic grapevine.

Geoffrey Dawson, the editor of the *Times*, also appears to have gained some inside knowledge. The next in line to the throne was Edward

VIII's forty-year-old brother, Prince Albert, Duke of York. He was a shy, retiring man who had kept a low profile most of his life and had few public engagements. Positive profiles of the Duke and Duchess of York began to appear in the *Times* for no apparent reason.

The conspirators had their motive. Mrs. Simpson's divorce was to give them the means and opportunity.

Twelve

A Very British Coup

I t was Ernest Simpson, rather than Wallis, who wanted a divorce. He had been having an affair with Mary Raffray, a friend of Wallis's, for several months. Their affair and the King's with Mrs. Simpson were so open that the four had stayed together at the King's home at Fort Belvedere outside London and at the Simpsons' London home in Bryanston Court. Ernest Simpson told the King of his decision and in at least three conversations asked Edward VIII about his intentions toward Wallis. In one of those discussions, the King is said to have remarked that he would not be crowned "without Wallis at my side."

If Edward VIII ever made this remark, and it has been challenged, he may not have meant it literally. He had been King since January 1936. If he intended Wallis to be his wife and Queen before the Coronation, planned for May 1937, he had done nothing to bring this state about when he returned to England from his five-week summer cruise aboard the *Nahlin* in September. Precisely when the King and Mrs. Simpson made a decision to wed has never been clear. That Edward VIII wanted to spend the rest of his life with Mrs. Simpson is indisputable, but he seems to have given little thought to how that wish might be achieved.

He had toasted the first moments of 1936, when he was still Prince of Wales, as the year "when we will be one." It was reported to MI5 in March that the King had inscribed a gift to Wallis with the words "to our marriage." An inscription on another item of jewelry suggests that it was during the *Nahlin* cruise in the summer of 1936 that the two agreed to marry someday. But there is a world of difference between wanting to marry and arranging a wedding. By the fall of 1936, it appears their "plans" were simply a hope and a wish and not fully formed.

Divorces were usually granted in those days on the grounds of adultery. There was no catchall of irretrievable breakdown as there is today. Although Ernest Simpson wanted the divorce, it was agreed that Wallis should divorce him and he would provide evidence of his adultery. This was a common, although illicit, arrangement undertaken to prevent the woman in a divorce case from suffering the ignominy of being the guilty party. A hearing was set for October 27, 1936.

A few days before the hearing, the King met with the newspaper proprietor Lord Beaverbrook and asked him to arrange with other newspaper owners to be discreet in their coverage. In sharp contrast to their later sensationalism, the British press was circumspect in stories regarding Royalty.

The next move belonged to Prime Minister Baldwin. He knew his best chance of ousting the King would come before the Coronation had triggered a resurgence of Edward VIII's popularity and that the King's intention to marry a divorced woman would provide perfect grounds. MI5 had had the King and Mrs. Simpson under surveillance. The intelligence branch of the government had discovered evidence that the King hoped to marry Mrs. Simpson, but the King had said nothing definite to anyone, including his own family, about his intention to do so by a particular date. Probably prompted by Vansittart, Baldwin resolved to bring the matter to a head and trigger the crisis himself.

In order to do so, he had to maneuver the King into seeking the prime minister's advice on his marriage.

Four days before the scheduled hearing, Hardinge, Edward VIII's private secretary, called the King, who was at Sandringham, and told him the prime minister urgently wished to see him. The King was surprised, for the two had met only a few days before and nothing seemed amiss. Hardinge went on to say that Baldwin would not come to Sandringham because his presence there on a weekend would cause comment and speculation. The King agreed to go back to Fort Belvedere, some twenty-five miles from Central London.

It was a tense first meeting concerning a subject about which Edward VIII was notoriously sensitive. Baldwin sipped whiskey throughout the discussion, although it was midmorning and the King had pointedly refused a drink. The King declined to be drawn into a discussion of his future plans, what he called in his memoirs eleven years later "my hopes"—another indication that there was then no definite decision to marry. Finally, Baldwin asked if the divorce petition could be postponed. The King said disingenuously that he had no right to interfere in

Mrs. Simpson's affairs just because she was his friend. Her marital problems were her private business, and she had a right to divorce like anyone else.

On the surface, the meeting seems to have achieved nothing. But it was important, because it established for the first time that the King's relationship with Mrs. Simpson was an affair of state. Baldwin could proceed with secret meetings to prepare the groundwork for abdication, stating truthfully he had discussed the relationship with the King. It was no longer a private matter.

The divorce hearing took place on October 27, 1936. Mrs. Simpson arrived at the courthouse in the Norfolk town of Felixstowe in the Royal Buick. Ernest Simpson did not appear. As the judge, Mr. Justice Hawke, sneered at her from the bench, she claimed under oath that she had had a happy marriage until she discovered evidence of her husband's affair with another woman. She said she had found letters from Simpson's lover suggesting a relationship and produced one letter, a thank-you note for a gift of roses. Two waiters who worked in a hotel gave evidence that they had served breakfast in bed to Ernest Simpson and a woman in July. The judge, with some apparent reluctance, granted a decree nisi. Under English divorce law at the time, the divorce would not become fully valid, leaving the parties free to remarry, until a decree absolute six months later.

On November 13, the King returned to his estate at Fort Belvedere, near Windsor, after a two-day naval inspection. He found a letter from his private secretary, Hardinge, marked "urgent." It was, in effect, an ultimatum from the government, via Hardinge, to send Mrs. Simpson out of England. The cabinet was meeting that day to discuss his relationship with Mrs. Simpson, prompted to do so by speculation in the foreign press and by the likelihood that British newspapers would not remain silent much longer. The government was prepared to resign, Hardinge said, if Mrs. Simpson was not sent abroad. "I have reason to know," the King's private secretary wrote ominously, that in such circumstances none of the major parties would form another. Mrs. Simpson should go "without further delay."

It is now clear from the letter that a conspiracy was afoot. Baldwin and Hardinge had had secret meetings, and Baldwin had won the agreement of other party leaders and members of his own party not to form a new government if Baldwin resigned. But why? The King had still given no indication that he wished to marry Mrs. Simpson.

After a sleepless night, the King decided that Hardinge was Baldwin's agent and cut him out as his channel of communication with the prime minister. He turned instead to Walter Monckton, who had been acting as a legal adviser to the Duchy of Cornwall. An Establishment figure, Monckton was another Harrow and Trinity alumnus whose actions throughout show more loyalty to the Crown than to the King. The best advice Monckton could offer was to meet the prime minister and put his cards on the table. This was precisely what Baldwin wanted. The best advice would have been to do nothing.

The King told Wallis of the development that evening. She gave him better advice than Monckton, which was to say and do nothing impetuous. But on November 16, the King met with Baldwin at Buckingham Palace, which had just recently been vacated by Queen Mary. He played directly into Baldwin's hands.

He said, "I understand you and several members of the cabinet have some fear of a constitutional crisis over my friendship with Mrs. Simpson."

"Yes, sir, that is correct. I am personally disturbed, and I know many members of the cabinet are disturbed over the prospect of Your Majesty marrying a woman whose former marriages have been dissolved by divorce."

It was the first time marriage had been mentioned.

Prime Minister Baldwin continued: "I believe I know what the people will tolerate and what they will not, sir. Even my enemies would grant me that. They would not tolerate a twice-divorced woman becoming Queen."

As the King listened to Prime Minister Baldwin, he felt he heard the words of the archbishop of Canterbury, who was then leading a campaign for a "Recall to Religion" and what today might be called family values. It was a concept Edward VIII's closest friend would not pretend he embodied. Throughout the crisis, Edward VIII was to write later, while he never once saw the archbishop, he believed he could feel his presence "hovering noiselessly about."

Drawing on his omnipresent pipe, Prime Minister Baldwin seemed to suggest that it was the King's duty to marry a woman suitable for the title of Queen of England and that while he might marry out of duty, there could be no objection to a more private dalliance. It was a polite version of a remark he had made earlier to a cabinet colleague: "If she was just a respectable whore, I wouldn't mind."

It was a homily designed to provoke. The King rounded on him. "If I were to take your argument to its conclusion, then I should take a mistress, a discreet house nearby, a key to a garden door. But I do not have a sinful wish, only to marry like other men."

Rising to the bait, he went on: "I intend to marry Mrs. Simpson as soon as she is free to marry. If I can marry her as King, well and good. I would be happy, and therefore I would be a better King. But if the government opposes the marriage, then I am prepared to go."

It was an impetuous remark and a fateful one. "I carried on the process a good deal further than I had expected," the King recalled later. After he had chivalrously shown Baldwin out of the palace, he seems to have thought better of it. He had said nothing to his mother and decided to break the news that night. He arranged to be invited to dinner at Marlborough House, where Queen Mary now lived.

The Queen, however, already knew—probably from Hardinge, the private secretary, and the former private secretary, Lord Wigram—of the conversation with the prime minister. That was evident when, at the close of a somewhat tense dinner, the King's sister-in-law, the Duchess of Gloucester, retired early, leaving the King alone with Queen Mary and her daughter, Princess Mary.

The King told her he was determined to marry Mrs. Simpson. He begged his mother to meet Wallis so she could understand why he wished to marry her. "The iron grip of royal convention," the King later wrote, would not allow her to unbend. But significantly, no attempt was made to persuade him to change his mind.

A possible solution to the crisis came a short time later from Lord Rothermere, a powerful newspaper magnate, admirer of both Hitler and Mussolini, and a supporter of Mosley's Blackshirts. He sent his son, Esmond, to suggest to Wallis a morganatic marriage, one in which she would not take the title of Queen and her children could not inherit their father's titles. Children were in any case irrelevant. But even if Wallis had not been made sterile by her infection following her abortion, she was forty-one years old, and the likelihood of her having a first child at that time were severely reduced. Morganatic marriages, although accepted among some European houses, were frowned upon. But as we have seen, the Mountbatten line, at the very center of the Windsor circle, was the product of a morganatic marriage, and there was a morganatic alliance in Queen Mary's family.

Wallis rushed to the King with the idea. Monckton, his attorney, was predictably dubious, but the King asked him to look into the legal precedents and told Esmond Harmsworth to put the idea to the prime minister. It was the last thing Baldwin wanted to hear, but he said he would discuss the matter with his cabinet. Two days later, the King asked for a meeting with Baldwin on the possibility of a morganatic marriage. He was clearly stepping back from his offer to quietly abdicate. Baldwin told him he had not even considered it yet. "It would take an act of Parliament, and Parliament would never pass it," he said.

"Are you sure?" the King asked him.

"Sir, would you like me to examine the proposition formally?" Baldwin said, turning the situation to his own advantage.

"Yes, please do."

"This would mean not only submitting the plan to Parliament but to the cabinets of the dominions, too. Do you really wish that?"

"Yes I do."

Baldwin hurried off before the King could change his mind. As the King soon realized, he had once again played into Baldwin's hands. He had allowed the prime minister to frame the question to the cabinets of Australia, New Zealand, Canada, South Africa, and other British colonies and could be relied on to pose it in such a way as to elicit the answer he wanted. And by asking the prime minister to consult the dominion governments on his marriage, he had implicitly agreed to follow their advice. Baldwin had already begun secretly consulting with the dominions to prepare the groundwork for the abdication.

One of the King's strongest supporters, Lord Beaverbrook, had been in the United States during these crucial few days. When he returned and the King told him what had happened, Beaverbrook was aghast. He saw through the plot and advised the King to withdraw the proposal for a morganatic marriage before it could be discussed in detail. The best course, Beaverbrook proposed, was to delay. Baldwin was trying to trigger a crisis, and the King was allowing it to happen. He told the King, "We have to delay things until we can find a way to put your case before the people."

Over the next twenty-four hours Beaverbrook was joined in this advice by several more influential supporters of the King, but by the time Edward VIII was persuaded, it was too late. Baldwin called a secret cabinet meeting to discuss the King's marriage. Realizing that the morganatic marriage was a possible solution, he quickly dismissed it as impractical and undesirable. He put two choices before the cabinet:

approve the King's marriage to Mrs. Simpson and welcome her as Queen or accept his abdication as King.

Duff Cooper, secretary of state for war and the King's close friend, was the only dissenting voice. He knew there were no hard plans for a marriage and told the cabinet so. There was no need to put the question. He proposed that the matter be dropped for a year. The prime minister wanted Edward VIII ousted before the scheduled Coronation in May 1937. He would have none of it.

The reason why Baldwin wanted Edward VIII to abdicate had more to do with the King's relationship with Hitler than his relationship with Mrs. Simpson. The crisis over his supposed intention to marry Mrs. Simpson had been engineered by the prime minister.

Meanwhile, secret cables had gone out to the cabinets of the dominions of Australia, South Africa, Canada, and New Zealand, whose members knew very little of the intrigues that had been taking place in London. The cables began with a lengthy précis of the meetings that had taken place with the King. Baldwin claimed there was no possibility of dissuading the King from marrying Mrs. Simpson. In fact, not only had no attempt been made to do so; the question of marriage had originally been raised by Baldwin. The cables stated that the question of a morganatic marriage had been discussed and there was "not in my view any chance" of the British Parliament passing the necessary legislation. Such legislation, Baldwin said, would bar any issue from inheriting the throne, implying there would be a family of pretenders to the throne; even though Wallis knew she could never have any children.

Baldwin's final dismissal of the morganatic marriage proposal was to suggest that even if it were arranged, at some point in the future the King would demand legislation for his wife to be made Queen, a proposal that came exclusively from Baldwin's imagination.

The cables ended by giving the dominions three options: approval of marriage to Mrs. Simpson and her acceptance as Queen; a morganatic marriage; abdication. It was not surprising that when the cables came in they heavily favored abdication. As the responses arrived, Baldwin moved to maintain the initiative. Worried that the newspaper magnates, Lord Beaverbrook and Lord Rothermere, were about to break the news blackout with a campaign favorable to the King, the prime minister briefed the editors of newspapers friendly to the Conservative government. Friends of Edward VIII had described the situation to Kingsley Martin, editor of the respected news weekly the *New Statesman*. He had prepared a positive story proposing the morganatic marriage and showed it to the King for his approval.

Coincidentally, on December 1, 1936, the bishop of Bradford, who had been at a convocation, published an address calling on the King to devote himself to what the bishop called "his Christian duties." It was primarily meant as a criticism of Edward VIII's frequent absence from church on Sundays, but when it was published in the archconservative regional daily the *Yorkshire Post*, it was the signal for the deluge.

Geoffrey Dawson, editor of the *London Times*, led the charge with a stinging denunciation of the King's plans to marry Mrs. Simpson. Only a few days before, in an editorial on the King's opening of Parliament, the same newspaper had praised the King for qualities even he had never claimed. The *Times* was joined by the *Daily Telegraph* and several other influential newspapers. Their chorus of disapproval stunned the King, who had believed that his personal popularity would carry the day.

The Beaverbrook and Rothermere press, which had mass circulations but less influence in public life, countered with attempts to present the King's case. The Liberal newspaper *News Chronicle* advocated a morganatic marriage, as did several regional newspapers. The news weeklies, including the *New Statesman* and *Nation*, supported the King. Remarkably, the Roman Catholic weekly the *Tablet* concluded that there was no constitutional reason why the King should not marry Mrs. Simpson. Of newspapers that took a position, those supporting the government had combined circulations of 8.5 million; those supporting the King, 12.5 million.

With the affair now public, crowds began to gather at Buckingham Palace and 10 Downing Street. Oswald Mosley, sensing the crisis might be the moment to seize power, organized street demonstrations in favor of the King. MI5 stepped up surveillance of Blackshirt agitators. On December 3, 1936, the King held a number of meetings with his lawyer, Walter Monckton, leaving Buckingham Palace for Fort Belvedere late that night. There was a crowd of several thousand waiting, and they gave the King a rousing cheer. When Baldwin had appeared in public earlier in the day, he had been booed. There were a number of street demonstrations in London in favor of the King, some of which had been dispersed by baton-wielding mounted police.

The King proposed to broadcast directly to the people, after which he planned to remove himself to Belgium to await a decision. Baldwin refused to allow Edward VIII to go on the air, for the obvious reason that he might succeed. It would have been useless to try to sidestep the cabinet on this issue. The BBC director general, Sir John Reith, a ruthless and puritanical Calvinist, would never have allowed the King to make a radio address without the government's approval. Even so, Baldwin still feared that the King might make some public statement calling for support, then withdraw to await events. He arranged for Edward VIII to be prevented from leaving the country should he attempt to do so without abdicating.

The crisis now erupted in the House of Commons, and again the prime minister was in command of the situation. He told the House that the government would not sponsor legislation proposing a morganatic marriage and that such a proposal was pointless, since the dominions had effectively vetoed it. As we have seen, he had used the unwillingness of the government to propose the legislation to win that veto and now offered the dominions' view to justify the government's unwillingness. He went on to say that the crisis had come about because "the lady whom he marries . . . necessarily becomes Queen." This was not entirely true. Kings who marry do not pass on their rank to their spouse.

That night, Baldwin called at the King's country home, Fort Belvedere, again. He was a little shaken by the vocal support for the King in the streets and the activities of the Blackshirts. He wanted the crisis to end as soon as possible before Edward VIII could rally more support. Loudspeaker vans cruised London and other cities calling for the public to back the King. Graffiti began to appear on walls in London, Birmingham, Manchester, and Liverpool, with such slogans as "God Save the King from Stanley Baldwin" and "Stand by the King." The prime minister pressed him for a decision: to abdicate or declare his intention not to marry Mrs. Simpson. The King demanded more time.

Time was something the prime minister no longer had. The longer the crisis continued, the more the King's supporters would rally public opinion. The real source of the crisis, the King's interference in foreign policy and his dealings with Hitler, could not be made public. It would have politicized a quarrel that Baldwin believed had to be kept on a moral and constitutional plane not only for the prime minister's purposes but in the nation's interest as well. Archbishop Lang warned Baldwin that more sympathy would be generated for the King the longer the crisis continued. The younger generation believed Edward VIII should marry whom he pleased.

Amid the gatherings and conclaves, Baldwin held a series of secret

Crowds keep a vigil outside Buckingham Palace the night before the Abdication of Edward VIII December 10th 1936. (Courtesy *New York Post*)

Edward VIII inspecting housing in South Wales in November 1936. His remark, that "something must be done" angered Prime Minister Baldwin. It was to be one of his last official duties as King. (Courtesy *New York Post*)

The three sheets attached hereto are the original
script from which His Royal Highness The Duke of
Windsor broadcast his Farewell Message from Windsor
Castle at 10 p.m. on December 11th 1936.

They have remained in my possession from that moment
until I restored them to His Royal Highness in
October 1948.

Walter Monckton.

April 12th 1949.

---

1. At long last I am able to say a few words of my own.
I have never wanted to withhold anything, / but until
now it has not been constitutionally possible / for me to speak.

2. A few hours ago I discharged my last duty as King and
Emperor, / and now that I have been succeeded by my brother / the
Duke of York, | my first words must be to declare my allegiance
to him. || This I do with all my heart. ||

3. You all know the reasons which have impelled me to
renounce the Throne, / but I want you to understand that in
making up my mind / I did not forget the Country or the Empire, /
which, as Prince of Wales and lately as King, / I have for 25
years tried to serve.

4. But you must believe me when I tell you / that I have
found it impossible to carry the heavy burden of responsibility /
and to discharge my duties as King, as I would wish to do, /
without the help and support / of the woman I love, / and I want
you to know that the decision I have made / has been mine, and
mine alone. || This was a thing I had to judge for myself. ||
The other person most nearly concerned has tried, / up to the
last, / to persuade me to take a different course, / I have made
this, / the most serious decision of my life, / only upon the
single thought / of what would in the end be best for all.

2.

5. This decision has been made less difficult to me / by
the sure knowledge that my brother, / with his long training in
the public affairs of this Country / and with his fine qualities, /
will be able to take my place forthwith / without interruption or
injury to the life and progress of the Empire, / and he has one
matchless blessing, / enjoyed by so many of you, / and not bestowed
on me, / a happy home with his wife and children.

6. During these hard days I have been comforted by / my
Mother and by my Family. *and in particular Mr Baldwin*
The Ministers of the Crown / have always treated me
with full consideration.   There has never been any constitutional
difference between me and them / and between me and Parliament. /
Bred in the constitutional tradition by my Father / I should never
have allowed any such issue to arise. ||
Ever since I was Prince of Wales, / and later on when I
occupied the Throne / I have been treated with the greatest
kindness by all classes wherever I have lived or journeyed
throughout the Empire. // *For that I am very grateful*

7. I now quit altogether public affairs / and I lay down
my burden. || It may be some time before I return to my native
land, / but I shall always follow the fortunes of the British
race and Empire with profound interest, / and if, at any time in
the future, / I can be found of service to His Majesty in a
private station, / I shall not fail. /

3.

And now we all have a new King. //
I wish Him and you, His people, / happiness and
prosperity with all my heart.
God bless you all.
God save the King.

The Instrument of Abdication. (Courtesy *New York Post*)

INSTRUMENT OF ABDICATION

I, Edward the Eighth, of Great
Britain, Ireland, and the British Dominions
beyond the Seas, King, Emperor of India, do
hereby declare My irrevocable determination
to renounce the Throne for Myself and for
My descendants, and My desire that effect
should be given to this Instrument of
Abdication immediately.

In token whereof I have hereunto set
My hand this tenth day of December, nineteen
hundred and thirty six, in the presence of
the witnesses whose signatures are subscribed.

SIGNED AT
FORT BELVEDERE
IN THE PRESENCE
OF

Edward VIII's farewell speech to the
nation. Originally an intemperate
tirade, Winston Churchill re-wrote
it to produce a speech of poignant
dignity. (Courtesy *New York Post*)

Edward VIII and Wallis Simpson
after the wedding in June 1937.
(Courtesy *New York Post*)

Official portrait of the new Queen Elizabeth, 1937. A 12 ft. by 18 ft. copy was installed at the New York World's Fair in 1939. (Courtesy *New York Post*)

King George VI and Queen Elizabeth visit troops in Scotland in 1941.

Official family group photo at Prince Charles's christening in 1948. Seated left to right: Dowager Marchioness of Milford Haven; Princess Elizabeth, holding the infant Prince Charles; the Dowager Queen Mary. Rear left to right: Lady Brabourne, daughter of Lord Mountbatten; Prince Philip, the Duke of Edinburgh; King George VI; David Bowes Lyon, brother of Queen Elizabeth; the Earl of Athlone; and Princess Margaret. (Courtesy *New York Post*)

Princess Elizabeth in 1949. She has just christened a British Overseas Airways airliner "Elizabeth of England."

Princess Margaret in 1965.
(Courtesy *New York Post*)

Princess Margaret and Lord
Snowdon in the first official
portrait after their wedding
in 1960. (Courtesy *New York
Post*)

The wedding day portrait of
Lord Snowdon and Princess
Margaret in May 1960.
(Courtesy *New York Post*)

Princess Margaret and the
Queen Mother in 1958.
(Courtesy *New York Post*)

One of the few official photographs of the Royal Family showing them in a relaxed mood. Queen Elizabeth and Prince Philip enjoy a joke with Prince Andrew, fourteen, and Prince Edward, ten, in 1974. (Courtesy British Information Services)

Princess Anne was awarded the Sportswoman of the Year trophy in 1971. (Courtesy *New York Post*)

meetings with Prince Albert, the Duke of York, Edward VIII's younger brother by nineteen months, to prepare him for the succession. It was an eventuality the Duke dreaded. He was a few days from his forty-first birthday, was painfully shy, and suffered from a serious stammer. He had had little public life, no training to be King, and no enthusiasm for its burdens and restrictions. Baldwin and the Duke even chose the name by which he would be known as King, well in advance of Edward VIII's departure. All his life he had been known as Bertie, but King Albert was judged by Baldwin to be too German. It was agreed he would take the throne as George VI.

The King's most vocal supporter in the Commons, Winston Churchill, advised the King to fight on, to retreat to Windsor Castle, refuse to see the prime minister, and wait for public support to build while he, Churchill, lobbied political support. Churchill was out of the government and still in the political wilderness in 1936. He had only contempt for Baldwin and was not aware of the extent of Edward VIII's intrigues with Hitler.

The supporters of the King, both in the streets and in Parliament, became known as the "King's party." But it was not a political party in the true sense. Rather, it was a groundswell of opinion, loosely organized at best, with no policy other than not to lose a figure who had been popular with the masses for over twenty years. By retiring behind the castle walls, so the theory went, the King might prod the government to resign. With the leaders of the opposition parties unwilling to enter another administration, the King would call on Churchill to form a government. He would inevitably fail. A general election would be called on the divisive issue of the King's personal life.

Edward VIII now faced the crossroads. He could encourage Churchill and allow a King's party to be organized. It was a recipe, if not for civil war, then for the kind of constitutional impasse from which civil wars were created. Blackshirts were regularly parading in the streets and fighting with police and their political opponents. Unemployment was high. Trade unions were restive, and grass-roots opinion in the Labour movement backed the King. There was no telling what forces might be released once the Pandora's box of a constitutional crisis was opened. In a cable to the viceroy of India, the Marquess of Zetland, secretary of state for India, wrote: "Therein lies the danger . . . there might arise in this country a situation not far short of civil strife."

At this moment of truth, Edward VIII had no stomach for the fight.

Victory was by no means certain, and if he were to be defeated, he would be forced off the throne. It could be the end of the monarchy itself. Even victory was likely to be hollow, for it would have torn at the fabric of British society.

If he was to take power into his hands, as he had told the Duke of Coburg he wished to do, he wanted to appear as the savior from, rather than the focus of, a crisis. That he might have carried the people was not enough. Not only was the government against him; so was the invisible power structure, the Establishment. And he could draw no support from his own family. He summoned his lawyer, Walter Monckton, and told him he was resolved to abdicate.

The details were thrashed out, incongruously, over lunch at the Windham Club in St. James Square on Saturday, December 5, 1936, five days after the crisis had become public and only three weeks since Baldwin had confronted the King. Monckton and another lawyer, George Allen, acted for the King, and the prime minister was represented by his parliamentary private secretary, Thomas Dugdale, M.P., and an aide, Sir Horace Wilson. The King had only one important demand: If he were to abdicate, the six-month wait for a decree absolute should be waived. It would take an act of Parliament, but so eager was Baldwin to see the King off, he promised to resign if he could not steer the bill through the House. It was a rash promise and one he subsequently broke.

The crisis might have ended there, but Churchill and Beaverbrook would not give up. Churchill, a Member of Parliament but with no government position, sent an eloquent and dignified letter to the cabinet arguing that the government had acted unconstitutionally by pressuring the King to abdicate. There was as yet, he argued, no conflict between the King and Parliament. The marriage, which was the ostensible cause of the crisis, could not happen for several more months because Mrs. Simpson's divorce would not be final until April 1937. Indeed, it might never happen.

Churchill wrote:

> The question is whether the King is to abdicate upon the advice of the Ministry of the day. No such advice has ever been tendered to the sovereign in Parliamentary times. If the King refuses to take the advice of his ministers they are, of course, free to resign. They have no right whatever to put pressure on him to accept . . . thus confronting him with an ultimatum.

The prime minister knew that he already had the King where he wanted him and ignored Churchill's letter.

Independently, the newspaper magnate Lord Beaverbrook tried to fend off the crisis by pressuring Wallis to withdraw. She had fled to Cannes with one of the King's entourage, Perry Brownlow, who also happened to be a friend of Beaverbrook's. Wallis Simpson was under intense emotional pressure, and Beaverbrook sought to have her issue a statement saying she had no wish to cause the King's abdication and that she would offer to withdraw. This turn of events threw Baldwin into a last-minute panic. Sir Horace Wilson, one of Baldwin's aides and one of the men who had brokered the abdication agreement at the Windham Club, sought out Mrs. Simpson's London lawyer, Theodore Goddard, for confirmation that this was his client's intention. Goddard went to Fort Belvedere to ask the King, who, not surprisingly, told him to stay out of it.

But Baldwin did not want it to appear that he had ignored Wallis Simpson's offer. He had Sir Horace Wilson send Goddard to Cannes to verify that Mrs. Simpson was willing to give up the King. Now it was Baldwin who was buying time. When the King discovered that Goddard had been sent to Cannes, he called Mrs. Simpson—which Baldwin could easily have done himself—and warned her to promise him nothing. Meanwhile, Baldwin hurried to have the abdication instrument drawn up.

Wallis Simpson did agree to withdraw. She called the King after a breakfast meeting with Goddard and said she was willing to end their relationship. It was one of several conversations between them which, according to witnesses, brought the King to tears. There was an emotional discussion during which the King begged her to change her mind. They had been deprived of each other's emotional support for several days. Wallis Simpson had set out on her course with no intent other than adventure. She did not realize that implacable forces would be ranged against them or foresee the drastic consequences of their relationship. She was now in a desperate panic. The King, who knew the strength of those forces only too well, was incapable of facing them alone. Suspicious of all who were around him, he was bent on surrender. He persuaded Wallis that he was determined to abdicate and that no plea on her part would change his mind.

At the same time, she threatened to end their relationship and urged the King not to abdicate, Wallis also pressed him to make the best financial arrangement possible. By abdicating he would forgo a gigantic fortune in property and income, heirlooms and jewelry, art and antiques. Individual paintings in Buckingham Palace and Windsor Castle alone were worth several million dollars. Balmoral and Sandringham were arguably his personal property on or off the throne.

Although he had a good argument for securing a handsome financial settlement, the King lied when he told his brother that he had very little personal fortune saved. He had, in fact, at least $4 million. The Duke of York agreed to give him about $100,000 a year for life—a very considerable sum in 1936—in return for allowing Balmoral and Sandringham to pass to the new monarch. When the lie was discovered some months later, George VI was so horrified that his brother had deceived him that it soured their relationship for the rest of their lives. Churchill, who had also been misled about the money, and had helped argue Edward VIII's case, was similarly displeased.

The matter of money having been dealt with, King Edward VIII signed the instrument of abdication on December 10, 1936, with his three brothers as witnesses. After it was done and the Duke of York, as next in line, had become King George VI, he asked his brother if he had given any thought to what he would now like to be called. He was still, technically, a Royal Prince, but after some discussion it was agreed that the new King would make him a Duke the next day. He suggested Duke of Windsor. It was also agreed that he should quit Britain for a time to allow wounds to heal and prevent the reemergence of any Edwardian faction. The Duke of Windsor believed it would be a short period. It was, in effect, to be a lifetime's exile.

But the ex-King had one last demand. He wanted at last to have his say. He was now a private citizen, and the cabinet could not prevent him broadcasting a dignified farewell to the nation. Baldwin had qualms, but he agreed. It was Churchill who rewrote key passages and phrases after the departing King had composed a first draft. That the dignity of the farewell was due to Churchill's genius is evidenced by the elimination of the original first line: "I now wish to tell you how I was jockeyed off the throne." It became "At long last I am able to say a few words of my own."

Churchill, recognizing defeat, persuaded him to prefer dignity to rancor. His rewrite was a masterpiece which was to go a long way toward creating the legend of the King who, torn between love of a woman and a Royal Crown, chose love but remained loyal to his people, his country, and his new King. The broadcast that night was indeed a dignified exit, reducing millions of Britons who heard it to tears. Wallis Simpson, listening from Cannes, sobbed hysterically, a scene her companion, Perry Brownlow, described as harrowing.

The former monarch told the nation:

> You must believe me when I tell you that I have found it impossible to carry out the heavy burden of responsibility and to discharge my duties as King, as I would wish to do so, without the help and support of the woman I love. . . .

He put a heavy emphasis on the "I" in "as I would wish to do"—his only reference to the pressure placed on him to conform to the constitutional restrictions on the monarch or step down from the throne. He ended with a statement of loyalty to his brother and the words "God save the King!"

Immediately after the broadcast the Duke of Windsor and Monckton drove to Portsmouth, where a naval destroyer, *Fury*, waited to take him to France and exile. Behind him he left a country confused and divided, with no idea of the subterranean political intrigues that had led to the abdication.

The broadcast by the King, however, was not to be the last word. It was followed some days later by a broadcast by Archbishop Lang. He had remained silent throughout the crisis—which was surprising, for the furor was ostensibly about the intended marriage of the head of the Church of England and a divorced woman. He had offered no public counsel but had conspired against the King behind the scenes. Now that the victory had been won, he rounded on his prey, fulminating against the circle that had surrounded the former sovereign and brought about his downfall. It was in unseemly contrast to the dignity of Edward VIII's farewell, and there was widespread criticism of the archbishop. Kingsley Martin quotes a quatrain that made the rounds:

> My Lord Archbishop, what a scold you are!
> And when your man is down, how bold you are!
> Of Charity, how oddly scant you are
> Old Lang Swine, how full of Cantuar!

. . . Cantuar being Latin for Canterbury.

All great historical events have a tapestry of causes. It is simplistic and futile to pull at a single thread. The myth that the relationship with Mrs. Simpson and the King's determination to marry her was the primary, indeed the only, cause of the abdication crisis persists. Not even King Edward himself was fully aware of the extent to which he had been forced to abdicate. But Mrs. Simpson was never more than the opportunity to remove the King. She was not the motive. The prime minister created the crisis in order to oust the King. It was, in effect, a coup d'état by the Establishment, a very gentlemanly, very British coup.

Others involved had a variety of motives. The archbishop of Canterbury believed the King was an ungodly, irreligious man. Wigram and Hardinge believed he was not cut from his father's mold. Baldwin was undoubtedly aided in his enterprise by the King's own ambivalence about his rank and role. When he did abdicate, it was in the belief that at some time in the future he would still play a prominent role in British life, and with the woman he loved by his side. He never envisioned the wandering exile that was ultimately to be his. Had Baldwin genuinely wanted Edward VIII to remain on the throne, he had only to turn to the man who had the solution in his hands, Ernest Simpson.

Ernest Simpson was horrified by the consequences of his wife's relationship with the King and the crisis into which the nation had been plunged. When the crisis became public, he agonized about the situation for days; then, on December 7, three days before the abdication document was signed, he contacted Lord Wigram and offered to nullify the divorce. It was the product of collusion, and if he confessed, the courts would invalidate it. The King would not be able to marry her. Wigram, who knew more than anyone the real reason for the crisis, told Simpson to do nothing and let events take their course.

Part Four

GEORGE VI
(1936–52)

Thirteen

Out of the Shadows

A lbert, Duke of York, ascended the throne as George VI the moment
the instrument of abdication was signed on December 10, 1936,
four days before his forty-first birthday. He was utterly unprepared for
the spiral of events that had brought him to the throne. Like all the
Windsors, he was short, but he possessed sharp, handsome, manly
features and piercing china-blue eyes. He had a history of frail health
and had had three major surgical procedures. He suffered from poor
digestion and stomach ulcers. His speech impediment seemed so serious
that it was considered doubtful he could struggle through the Coronation ceremony without embarrassing himself.

He suffered from muscle spasms and twitches in the face which
would make it necessary to edit newsreels of his public appearances. In
fact, he blinked so often that those forced to make eye contact with him
found it disconcerting to do so. He was painfully shy. Like others in his
family, he drank too much and was given to manic extremes of emotion,
including clinical depression, tearful outbursts, and violent fits of temper. He was no better educated than his father and ranked sixty-first
out of sixty-seven in his graduating class at Dartmouth Naval College.
He read very little and preferred gossip sheets to serious newspapers.
Edouard Daladier, later premier of France, described him unequivocally
as "a moron."

He was panic-stricken at the thought of being King, an ordeal made
particularly difficult by the fact that he had lived his entire life in his
glamorous brother's shadow and had been consistently compared with
him in an unfavorable light. The turmoil of the abdication crisis had
taken a tremendous emotional toll on him. At the height of the crisis, he

had put his head on his mother Queen Mary's shoulder and wept for a solid hour.

But given the trauma of the abdication, he did have an attribute that was priceless. In his farewell broadcast, his brother had called it his "matchless blessing." That was a solid marriage to an aristocratic and thoroughly conventional woman, and two attractive daughters, Princess Elizabeth, ten, who now became heir apparent, and Princess Margaret, her younger sister, then six. Throughout his married life he leaned heavily on his astute and fiercely loyal wife.

Elizabeth Bowes-Lyon, who at thirty-five years old now became Queen Elizabeth, was the first commoner to marry an English Prince since the middle of the seventeenth century and the first to become Queen since the sixteenth.

Commoner sums up images of a grocer or a baker, but the highest-ranking aristocrat in Britain ranks as a commoner in relation to the Royal Family. Although she could not claim Royal lineage, Elizabeth Bowes-Lyon was born into one of the most prominent and wealthiest families in Britain, whose ancestors included the eleventh-century Scottish warrior chieftain Robert the Bruce. Her father was Earl of Strathmore and had half a dozen lesser titles in Scotland and England as well as an ancestral seat at Glamis, the oldest continuously inhabited castle in Britain.

She had grown up in regal splendor, but without the restrictions of the Royal court and certainly with none of the child abuse that Prince Albert had experienced and which produced the emotional and physical impediments, the twitches, stammer, ulcers, and other problems from which he suffered so acutely. When Elizabeth met Prince Albert, the future George VI, at a Jockey Club ball at Buckingham Palace in 1920, she was an attractive, outgoing, independent, and accomplished debutante, as opposite to him in character as it is possible to be.

She also had a string of other suitors, millionaires and landowners among them. The most favored among them was the rakish James Stuart, an equerry to Prince Albert. When his master eventually triumphed, Stuart emigrated to the United States. It proved a difficult courtship. Prince Albert fell desperately in love with her soon after their first meeting and pursued her shamelessly, while she showed no signs of returning his love. When he proposed in the spring of 1921, she turned him down flat. He continued to pursue her and proposed again the following year. Again, she refused. In July 1922 he was so distraught that she would not marry him that he was close to an emotional breakdown. He was on the destroyer HMS *Versatile*, returning from a Royal engagement in France, when he unburdened himself to a Member of Parliament, John Davidson, private secretary to Andrew Bonar Law, then prime minister. He told him he was in despair because he had given up hope of marrying the only woman he loved and would never marry anyone else.

Prince Albert had had only two previous attachments, one to Phyllis Monkman, an actress and dancer and star of the London stage in the twenties, and another with Lady Maureen Vane-Tempest-Stewart, daughter of the Marquess of Londonderry. The romance with Phyllis Monkman appears to have been a full-blown affair, with secret meetings in rooms in London's Half Moon Street. It was not a romance that could have ended in marriage, given Prince Albert's social position, but he sent her gifts on her birthday each year for the rest of his life, and a photograph of the young Prince, in a scuffed leather frame, sat near her bedside until her death in 1976. The romance with Lady Maureen came to nothing. She married Oliver Stanley, brother of the Edward Stanley who had married the Prince of Wales's former love, Portia Cadogan.

Elizabeth Bowes-Lyon had hesitated because she feared the restricted life and confining protocol inside the Royal Family. She already had wealth, social position, and independence. She could only lose it by marrying into the Royal House. But she was pressured by a series of emissaries and go-betweens who laid the groundwork for a third and, it was agreed, final proposal in January 1923. This time, she accepted. She had been comforted by the knowledge that although she would be joining the Royals, she would never have the responsibilities of being Queen. She and Prince Albert were married amid glittering pomp in Westminster Abbey on April 26, 1923. The ceremony was filmed but not broadcast on radio because it was feared ordinary people might sully the occasion by listening to it in public bars.

Even at his own wedding, Prince Albert was overshadowed by his older brother, the Prince of Wales. The *London Times* observed that the public looked forward to another wedding with "still deeper interest— the wedding that will give a wife to the heir to the throne and in the due course of nature, a future Queen to England. . . ."

Prince Albert, who had been created Duke of York in 1920, had been judged unfit for public life in 1925 when he made a speech at the Empire Stadium at Wembley, outside London, closing the yearlong

British Empire Exhibition. He stammered, amid long pauses, through his prepared speech, which had a worldwide radio audience of 10 million people. It was an ordeal, described by one witness as "horrifying," that must have been almost as difficult to witness as for the Prince to undergo.

Among the onlookers was a speech therapist, Lionel Logue, who had built a practice treating soldiers suffering from post-traumatic stress syndrome, then known as shell shock. Speech therapy was a relatively infant branch of rehabilitative medicine, and the Society of Speech Therapists saw the Duke's difficulties as a challenge. They recommended that Logue treat him. He initially concluded that his stammer had been caused by the abuse he endured as a child and by being forced by his father and successive tutors to use his right hand when he was naturally left-handed. He was, Logue said, too old to cure. Logue did agree to help him disguise his stammer for public appearances and treated him for his chronic impediment for the rest of his life.

The primary task of the new King was to re-create the now-tarnished monarchy in the image of his father, George V, which was one reason why the new King took his father's name. In a family in which one brother was bisexual and a drug addict, another an inveterate womanizer, and a third a disgraced and exiled adulterer and with in-laws who included a lesbian and an avid collector of sadomasochistic pornography, the image of wholesome family life might have been difficult to maintain.

But little was known, and even less was spoken, of the Windsors' real private life. Almost within minutes of the accession, a welter of self-congratulation erupted over the apparent sangfroid with which the transition had been achieved. All the forces of the Establishment moved to laud the new King with the same determination with which it had unloaded his predecessor. The first problem which greeted George VI on his accession was a whispering campaign, mounted by King Edward's remaining supporters in influential positions, to the effect that he was incapable of performing his duties as King.

Rumors surfaced that he was epileptic, like his late brother, Prince John, and had suffered a number of seizures soon after the accession and henceforth would rarely appear in public. Another suggested that the Coronation ceremony would have to be canceled or heavily abbreviated. The rumors were fueled by the fact that the 1936 Christmas address, which would have been broadcast only two weeks after the abdication, was called off and the Durbar, the Coronation as Emperor in India, postponed. Part of the campaign was pique. The new King fired some of King Edward's staff and blacklisted people who had been King Edward and Mrs. Simpson's friends, particularly those, like Lady Emerald Cunard, who were judged to have encouraged the relationship. Monckton, Edward's lawyer, was not only retained but knighted, and Alec Hardinge stayed on as private secretary.

Baldwin and the circle of palace advisers knew that a lavish display of pomp and pageantry at the Coronation would enhance the new King's image and cement his relationship with the people. The Duke and Duchess had a rather drab image, and it was hoped that the more glittering the Coronation, the more effectively that Banquo's ghost at the banquet, Edward VIII, would be exorcised.

Some two hundred thousand extra visitors crowded London's hotels for the occasion, set for May 12, 1937. At least twenty thousand came from the United States alone, making the event a bonanza for London businesses. Some 3 million people lined the route to Westminster Abbey to witness the procession, some paying up to one thousand dollars for prized positions in upper windows.

The ceremony itself, based on medieval traditions, was an extraordinary spectacle. Two crimson and gold thrones stood on the triforium, where the chancel, nave, and transept meet and which was itself carpeted in gold cloth. The dresses of the queens, princesses, ladies-in-waiting, and other women taking part in the ceremony found their origin in bosomy early Victorian designs. All the women were ablaze in diamonds, sapphires, and emeralds. Queen Mary, breaking a tradition that the dowager queen never attended a successor's coronation, wore jewelry valued at $2 million in 1936 money. Queen Elizabeth had a special crown made from a Victorian ringlet and the fabled and priceless Kohinoor diamond.

By inserting three-word pauses into his responses and oaths, the King, who had had extra training from Logue, managed to disguise his speech impediment to everyone's satisfaction. But there were other hitches. A piece of thread had been tied to St. Edward's Crown to show which was the right way around, but moments before the ceremony, some officious courtier removed it. The archbishop of Canterbury, who was in ill health, had Lord Dawson waiting nearby with a syringe filled with amphetamines should he need it to complete the ceremony. Two bishops, charged with holding the oath for the King to read, obscured a key section with their thumbs. The Lord Chamberlain accidentally struck the King with the hilt of the sword of state, and a bishop stood on the King's train as he was leaving the throne and pulled him up short.

Television was in its infancy in 1936, with only a handful of sets and with reception possible only within a twenty-five-mile radius of central London. Sir John Reith, director general of the BBC, had hoped televising the Coronation would help increase popularity of the medium. But the plan to do so was shelved. The official reason given was that there were not enough television sets in existence to make it worthwhile. The real reason was that live television pictures could not be edited. Newsreel of the Coronation was to be censored to eliminate close-up shots of twitches, blinks, and spasms.

A little over two weeks after the Coronation a ceremony of significantly less pomp took place at the Château de Cande at Tours, France. The Duke of Windsor had spent a miserable several months in Austria, while Wallis Warfield—she had reverted to her maiden name—remained in near isolation at a villa near Cannes. He had begun to realize for the first time how deftly he had been railroaded off the throne. His nemesis, Baldwin, had resigned as premier two weeks after the Coronation in favor of Neville Chamberlain, his Chancellor of the Exchequer, and the Duke had begun to wonder if he should have played for time. What had been relief at the moment of the abdication turned to bitterness.

On June 3, 1937, with only a handful of guests present, the Duke and Wallis were married. The Duke had hoped until the very last moment that at least one of his brothers, the Duke of Kent and the Duke of Gloucester, would attend. Both were told not to do so by King George VI. A number of Anglican clergymen were forbidden to perform a religious ceremony to bless the union. The Reverend Anderson Jardine, the vicar of St. Paul's Church, Darlington, defied the ban, and his career was ruined by it. Relations between the Duke and King George had become strained a few weeks earlier when the Duke's title was gazetted, or made official.

As the wife of a Royal Duke, the Duchess of Windsor would have been entitled to the regal title "Her Royal Highness," but the cabinet had advised the King to specifically forbid her from using it. There was no legal basis for doing so. It did, however, provide a bone of contention between the Duke and his family which lasted until the end of his life.

The Windsors remained under close surveillance by the British intelligence services. (MI5 is the domestic counterintelligence agency; MI6 is the foreign intelligence agency.) MI6 had a number of agents among the Duke's personal staff. After an incident in Austria, the American authorities also began to view the couple with suspicion. An American embassy official in Vienna had indiscreetly allowed the Duke to know information from the Austrian government that exposed secret Nazi arms shipments to Italy. At the time it was sensational intelligence of the close collaboration between the two totalitarian regimes. The Duke almost immediately leaked the information back to the Italians, which embarrassed the Americans. In August 1937, conversations between the Duke and various friends in which he discussed the possibility of a return to Britain to enter politics were reported back to intelligence chief Robert Vansittart via MI6 agents.

The Duke had been led to believe that his exile would be temporary, that he would marry abroad, stay away for a decent interval, and once the new King was established and old wounds healed, return to Britain. Opinion polls showed that the Duke continued to be immensely popular. It was estimated that 61 percent of his countrymen wanted the Duke to come back home. George VI had no intention of having his brother return to England. He had attorneys look into the feasibility of making his exile legally enforceable but discovered there was no constitutional mechanism by which that could be achieved. He had an absolute right to return. The King then made it clear to his brother that his financial settlement was dependent on his staying away from Britain indefinitely.

In the fall of 1937, the rift between George VI and the Duke of Windsor widened with the Duke and Duchess's visit to Nazi Germany. The German press had been virtually silent during the crisis and circumspect about the abdication itself. When the Duke arrived in Germany, he was given the rights and privileges normally accorded a visiting head of state. He inspected a factory bedecked with Nazi swastika banners, stood for the Nazi anthem, the *"Horst Wessel,"* inspected a training school for the Death's Head battalion of the S.S., and gave the Hitler salute. He was entertained at Karinhall, the palatial estate of leading Nazi Hermann Goering, by Rudolf Hess, at that time Hitler's deputy, and by Joseph Goebbels, the Nazi's chief propagandist. Wherever they went, crowds shouted "Heil Windsor," and the Duke repeatedly returned the Nazi's stiff-armed salute.

The Duke even visited a concentration camp, although no prisoners were evident. When he asked what was inside a long, low, gray, concrete building, he was told, with Bavarian black humor: "That is where they store the cold meat!"

The highlight of the visit was a personal meeting with Hitler at the Führer's country estate at Obersalzburg. The visit included a twenty-minute private talk. Accounts of the conversation vary, but there is no reason to doubt that they agreed that Britain and Germany were natural allies, that the common enemy was Russia, and that European civilization depended on an alliance against the Bolshevik giant. The Duke is also reported to have described his brother King George VI as a pawn of an anti-German clique at the Foreign Office. Hitler left the meeting more convinced than ever that Germany had lost a firm and powerful friend but one who, in the right circumstances, could still be useful to the Third Reich.

In England, newsreels were shown of the Duke's visit to Germany, but clever editing eliminated his Nazi salutes. In cinemas all over Britain, where the weekly newsreels filled something of the function of television's nightly news, the Duke was loudly cheered. But while a sentimental attachment still existed for the former King, the Coronation had fulfilled its function of rallying support for, and loyalty to, George VI. Bad relations with his brother dominated the first year of his reign, however, reaching its lowest point in the autumn of 1937.

The Duke gave an interview to a correspondent from the *Daily Herald*, the only daily newspaper that espoused the views of the opposition Labour party. In the interview, the Duke remarked that if a future Labour government wished to eliminate the monarchy and create a republic, he would be ready to serve as its first president.

It is no longer possible to discover the context of this inflammatory statement. It was not official Labour party policy to create a republic, and there was no reason for either the Duke or his interviewer to suggest that it might happen. When news of his remarks filtered back to the Palace, it was taken as evidence that the Duke wished to enter politics on his return to Britain. But the British public discovered nothing of the controversy. Arthur Greenwood, the deputy leader of the party and editor in chief of the newspaper, suppressed the interview under pressure from Vansittart.

Vansittart's own days as the senior Foreign Office official were numbered. As the policy of appeasement reached its nadir under Prime Minister Neville Chamberlain, the most vocal anti-German voice in

British government conclaves was silenced. Chamberlain forced Vansittart's retirement in 1938.

The image of the whole Royal Family was enhanced by a grueling schedule of public appearances in many parts of Britain and by two successful state visits abroad. The first was to France, in 1938, meant to shore up the shaky alliance by recalling the sacrifices and victories of the Great War. The second was to Canada and the United States in 1939, during which the King and President Franklin D. Roosevelt discussed a future military alliance against Germany. The latter visit greatly increased the King's standing at home, and there were vast chanting crowds along the Mall, the wide avenue leading from Buckingham Palace, to greet the King and Queen upon their return. It was June 23, 1939. Ten weeks later, Britain, France, and Germany were at war.

Fourteen

Peace at Any Price

G ermany invaded Poland with fifty-two divisions, some 1.5 million men, on September 1, 1939. Britain and France, committed to Poland's security by treaty, declared war on Germany two days later. In reality there was little the British or the French could do to help the beleaguered Poles. The German Luftwaffe destroyed the Polish air force in the first twenty-four hours of the war. Although Polish ground forces put up a gallant defense, Panzer divisions closed inexorably on Warsaw. The night that war was declared, King George VI began the daily diary he was to keep for the rest of his reign. His first entry recalled how, almost exactly twenty-five years earlier, war had been declared when he was on active service in the North Sea as a midshipman aboard the HMS *Collingwood.*

"We thought we were prepared for it," he wrote. "We were not prepared for what we found a modern war really was and those of us who had been through the Great War never wanted another."

The Duke of Windsor was swimming at his villa, La Croe, at Cap d'Antibes in the south of France when he was informed of the outbreak of war in a telephone call from the British ambassador. He returned to the pool and told Wallis, predicting that the war would end in the final triumph of Soviet communism.

The Duke's position caused an immediate problem for the British government. After some petty negotiations over where he might live, he was briefly recalled to England on a destroyer. The Queen refused to meet the Duchess and the King, and his brother had an awkward, desultory reunion at a house in Wilton Place, London, owned by the Duke's friend "Fruity" Metcalfe. Over the objections of the British commander in chief, Gen. Sir Edmond "Tiny" Ironside, who knew the

170

Duke had become a security risk, the former monarch was given the rank of major general and attached to the British Expeditionary Force (BEF) staff in France.

That a man who could not be trusted was given a sensitive post seems ludicrous, and indeed, it may have had catastrophic consequences. But it was deemed preferable to a position in England where he and the *non grata* Duchess would have a higher profile. George VI was irritated by his brother's presence in Britain. Despite the succession, he still felt overshadowed by the Duke and wanted him out of the way. His brother's company did nothing for his speech impediment, which worsened whenever the Duke was near. Leslie Hore-Belisha, the minister for war, came up with the solution and persuaded the Duke to take up his post in France immediately. The Duke and Duchess had a palatial Paris home at 24, Boulevard Suchet, but for the time stayed at a hotel in Versailles. Their exile had resumed just days after it had seemed to have ended.

Within weeks, George VI was firmly in the center of a crisis in his government which was to rob him of one of his most able ministers, and for the most disgraceful of reasons. Hore-Belisha had headed the war ministry since 1937. A rising star in the Conservative party, he was considered a possible future prime minister. Believing the policy of appeasement must ultimately fail, he had made drastic efforts to reform, modernize, and rearm the British army for the war he knew would be inevitable.

He had improved the conditions of ordinary soldiers in barracks, increased recruitment, and retired a number of senior officers. Inevitably, he made implacable enemies on the General Staff and at the War Office, the most powerful of whom were Sir James Grigg, senior War Office civil servant, and Field Marshal Lord Gort, who commanded the expeditionary force in France.

His struggle with the most senior army officers came to a head in November 1939 when Hore-Belisha visited the BEF in France. He was severely critical of Lord Gort, whose army was ultimately routed, and of the lack of any strong concrete defenses. Gort was outraged, the more so because, as Gort time and again pointed out, Hore-Belisha was a Jew. The British officer class was notoriously anti-Semitic and would have resented being placed under the control of a Jewish politician even if he had lacked Hore-Belisha's reforming zeal. Gort was given to referring to Hore-Belisha as "Hor-ebrew," and Lt. Gen. Henry Pownall, his chief of staff, consistently referred to the war minister as "Ikey." That Hore-Belisha was aware of the anti-Semitism among the senior officers undoubtedly contributed to the tension.

Gort had a number of friends and contacts at the Palace who shared his anti-Semitism. He decided to use them. One was the Duke of Gloucester, the King's younger brother, a liaison officer between the BEF in France and the French General Staff. In November 1939, he returned to Britain to visit the King at Sandringham, complaining about Hore-Belisha over a day's shooting. General Pownall came back from France within a few days and briefed Hardinge on the King's scheduled visit to the front, again using the opportunity to criticize Hore-Belisha and intimate that Lord Gort, in command of British forces in France, and other senior officers might resign if Hore-Belisha was not forced out.

In the first week of December 1939, the King and the Duke of Gloucester visited the troops, and Lord Gort and General Pownall renewed their campaign against Hore-Belisha. General Pownall later noted that he sat next to the King and regaled him with criticism of the war minister. "There's no doubt," he wrote, "we have the Palace on our side. His Majesty . . . went so far as to ask me who in my view should replace H.B. at the War Office."

Upon his return, George VI met Prime Minister Chamberlain and insisted that Hore-Belisha be fired. He was supported by two of Whitehall's most powerful civil servants, Sir Edward Bridges and Sir Horace Wilson, who themselves had heard a litany of complaints. Chamberlain admired the war minister, wanted to keep him in the cabinet, and resolved to offer him the job of secretary of state for information. Lord Halifax, the foreign secretary, opposed it, according to Chamberlain, "because H.B. is a Jew . . . his methods would let down British prestige." Caught off guard by Halifax, Chamberlain offered Hore-Belisha a more junior post outside the cabinet. He turned it down, and unable to instigate a public debate because the controversy involved defense secrets, he was forced to accept his ouster.

Within a few weeks there was more trouble with the General Staff in France, this time involving the Duke of Windsor. Part of the Duke's mission was to study the French defenses and report on them. The French were notoriously unforthcoming about their military secrets, even to their own allies, but the Duke of Windsor's unique social status gave him access to French positions which would have been denied other British officers. Astonishing though it may seem, no British army officer had been allowed to visit the Maginot Line, the chain of fortresses that formed the keystone of French defense. The Duke visited the line and reported that its reputation as an impregnable barrier was grossly overestimated, predicting enterprising German infantry and armor would penetrate it. Unfortunately, he expressed the same views over lunch at the Ritz to almost anyone who would listen, including known German collaborators and agents.

Although the British were eager for the Duke to visit French positions, they were alarmed at the prospect of the former King viewing British defenses. George VI was aware that the Duke had built his glamorous image and a great deal of his popularity in World War I on his appearances among British soldiers. So the decision was made to keep him away from all British units except General Headquarters.

The Duke may have thought the reasons were more sinister. Indeed, they may have had more to do with security considerations than his brother's concern with the ex-King's personal popularity. Either way, he was deeply offended when he realized he was not allowed to visit British units and repeatedly threatened to return home and confront his brother the King. He even wrote letters to George VI, accusing him of hating him and conducting a campaign to humiliate him.

Shortly after this dispute, in January 1940, the German ambassador to Holland, Julius Graf von Zech-Burkesroda, cabled Baron Ernst von Weizsacker, the Nazi under secretary of state for foreign affairs, claiming to have begun a channel of communication to the Duke of Windsor. He reported that the Duke was disillusioned with his posting and with the British conduct of the war. This channel is likely to have opened through Charles Bedaux, an American with French business interests who was arrested later in the war by the Americans as a Nazi agent. Bedaux had loaned the Duke and Duchess the Château de Cande for their wedding and continued to be a close friend. He also traveled frequently to Holland on business.

A month later, on February 19, the German ambassador to Holland, Zech-Burkesroda, reported to Weizacker, the under secretary of state, on the disposition of French forces and plans for the French response to an invasion of Belgium. He attributed the information to the Duke and to an Allied War Council that he claimed had discussed the plan. Possibly the Duke of Windsor was being used as a conduit for disinformation. Many of the communications from the German embassy in

Holland were sent back to London by Wolfgang zu Putlitz, the spy in the German embassy in London who was now in the German delegation in The Hague. The plan Ambassador Zech-Burkesroda sent to Berlin was only one of several contingencies and not the one which ultimately was employed. However, when the German invasion of France occurred, it took place in precisely the weak positions that had been identified by the Duke.

The period between the declaration of war in September 1939 and the German invasion of Denmark and Norway in 1940 became known as the Phony War. It was not only a period of stalemate. The British made repeated efforts to continue the policy of appeasement, even in the midst of war, and find some means of accommodation with Hitler. They ranged from the well-intentioned but misguided projects of pacifists to the intrigues of defeatists and outright Nazi collaborators.

A number of right-wing, pro-Nazi, or anti-Semitic organizations with members prominent in British life remained active until they were suppressed shortly before the fall of France in June 1940. They included the Blackshirts of Sir Oswald Mosley; the Anglo-German Fellowship, which had connections to the palace through the Duke of Windsor and the Duke of Kent; Link, a right-wing fringe organization, favoring an alliance with Germany, that had been founded by Adm. Sir Barry Domville; and the Right Club, founded by an ultra-right-wing Member of Parliament, Archibald Ramsay. These pro-Nazi lobbies, heavily penetrated by MI5, boasted of hundreds of members drawn from the military, both Houses of Parliament, financial institutions, and the Establishment, as well as numerous connections to the Royal Family. Some fifteen hundred Britons who were known or suspected to be pro-Nazi activists were ultimately detained in British prisons in 1940.

The urge to strike a deal with Hitler was particularly strong among a powerful cabal linked directly to the palace. Chief among them was the foreign secretary, Lord Halifax, encouraged by George VI and aided by the under secretary for foreign affairs, R. A. "Rab" Butler. The King's brothers, the Duke of Kent and the Duke of Windsor, were also in touch with Hitler through their cousins Prince Philip of Hesse and Charles, Duke of Saxe-Coburg.

There is nothing discreditable in itself in trying to find peaceful solutions to political problems that will otherwise lead to war. But Hitler's unshakable belief that Britain would not oppose him and his confidence that this lack of fortitude reached to the palace guided his policy with tragic consequences. It was not all self-deception.

Something of the views being expressed by the Duke of Kent and the Duke of Windsor at this time can be gathered from the latter's comments on parliamentary democracy—which Hitler had made an endangered species—in a letter Windsor sent to his friend the historian Philip Guedalla on May 3, 1940. He told Guedalla that the war was starting to go badly for the Allies, and "they can't possibly go any better until we have purged ourselves of . . . much of our out-of-date system of government." He said the parliamentary machine was "cumbersome" and "strangles us."

In May 1940, Germany mounted a lightning invasion of Norway and Denmark. Anglo-French efforts to oppose them ended in confusion, defeat, and ultimately, evacuation. The conquest of Norway cost the Germans some of their finest capital ships, but the failure of British troops to prevent supplies of strategic raw materials from falling into enemy hands brought demands for Chamberlain's resignation. He was so badly bloodied in a debate in the House of Commons on his government's prosecution of the war that though he survived a no-confidence vote, it was clear from the number of rebels in his party's ranks that he could not last as prime minister.

The most obvious heir apparent was Lord Halifax, the foreign minister, favored by the King, the Conservative old guard, and key elements of the Establishment. Winston Churchill, the underdog, who had been brought into the government at the outbreak of war as minister responsible for the navy and who therefore bore a measure of responsibility for the Norway debacle, was favored by the younger bloods in the Commons. At the time, the Conservative party had no internal democratic means of electing a leader. It would be up to Chamberlain to recommend a successor to the King.

Lord Halifax, fifty-nine, became a member of the House of Commons at twenty-nine, fought with distinction in the Great War, had been Minister of Education and Viceroy of India, Chancellor of Oxford University, and finally foreign secretary. By that time, he had succeeded to his father's title and was in the House of Lords. A devout churchgoer, he used to pray for guidance before taking political decisions, but as one critic has pointed out, "At times it would appear he misinterpreted the counsel thus revealed to him." It was his inconsistency and mishandling of affairs in India that led directly to Gandhi's civil-disobedience campaign.

In his dealings with Hitler he was also misguided, describing him in 1937 as "very sincere." In January and February 1940, Halifax still encouraged peace feelers to Germany, and there can be no doubt that, faced with the ultimate crisis in June 1940, he would have, as prime minister, negotiated a surrender. Churchill described Halifax's policy as "grovel, grovel, grovel."

Halifax had unique access to and the unflinching support ôf King George VI. It was his rare privilege to be allowed to take regular strolls through the gardens of Buckingham Palace, and he would often chance upon the King, who regarded him as a close friend.

It could have been no secret to the King—indeed, it was no secret to anyone in the political inner circle—that Halifax believed even in 1940 that a peace agreement with Hitler had to be obtained at almost any cost and that further support for Poland, now overrun by the Nazis, would prove futile.

When Chamberlain's government staggered into a crisis over Norway, Halifax, somewhat typically, believed it was a storm in a teacup and nothing would come of it. Only when Chamberlain had been savaged by his own side in the Commons debate did he realize that the prime minister was going to resign. Chamberlain offered Halifax the premiership on the condition that he, Chamberlain, retain the key position of leader in the House of Commons. Halifax was in the Lords, and the Commons was the fulcrum of political activity. The arrangement would leave Halifax prime minister in name only. The real power would remain with Chamberlain. Halifax refused and told Chamberlain he would not take the premiership if it meant serving only as a figurehead in the House of Lords.

There is some evidence that Halifax met secretly with the King—it may have been on one of his spring walks through the grounds of Buckingham Palace—and told him he wanted his viscountcy set aside so that he could take a seat in the Commons. The last person the King wanted as prime minister was Churchill. He had not forgiven him for supporting his brother Edward VIII so vocally in the abdication crisis.

There followed a complex series of negotiations, comparable to the power broking that once marked American political party conventions, from which Churchill emerged as Chamberlain's nominee. But when Chamberlain went to Buckingham Palace to recommend his successor, the King was still convinced he was going to name Halifax. Chamberlain began his meeting with an account of his reasons for resigning, which the King already knew. Finally, George VI became impatient and proposed Halifax himself. Chamberlain pointed out that Halifax was unwilling to be prime minister from the Lords. The King, already aware of that, quickly suggested that the title be set aside, although there was no legal mechanism for doing so.

Before he could be backed into a corner, Chamberlain formally recommended Churchill. The King flew into a temper, made it clear he was bitterly opposed to Churchill, and insisted that Chamberlain was making a tragic error. "Halifax," the King protested, "he's the obvious man." But faced with an unequivocal recommendation, there was nothing the King could do. Realizing his man had been outmaneuvered, he summoned Churchill and told him coldly: "I suppose you have no idea why I have sent for you?"

He expressed his bitterness to Chamberlain in a time-honored Royal manner, with a petty slight. He refused to write the customary note of thanks and farewell to the outgoing prime minister, which, trivial though it may seem, deeply hurt Chamberlain.

It has been suggested that Chamberlain had always wanted Churchill to succeed him and had tricked Halifax into turning down the premiership so he could take his refusal to the King. The King's anger at Chamberlain suggests that he, too, suspected that to be the case.

Churchill patched together a government that included, for unity, Chamberlain, with the title Lord President of the Council, and with Lord Halifax as foreign secretary. Halifax told friends, including the King, that Churchill's supporters were "rabble" and "gangsters" and that his government would last only weeks or months. There is every indication that George VI shared this view, for his opinion of Churchill remained low, especially when Churchill insisted on appointing Lord Beaverbrook, the newspaper proprietor, to the cabinet as minister for information. The King despised Beaverbrook for his outspoken support of Edward VIII during the abdication crisis.

May and June 1940 brought a series of reverses. Holland fell. German forces broke through in Belgium. French forces were routed at Sedan. Half of the British fighter planes based in France were lost in a grim seventy-two-hour period. Some 380,000 men of the BEF were trapped in a sixty-square-mile area around Dunkirk. By mid-June, France had surrendered, and the forces that were left from Britain's defense were ill equipped to meet a German invasion.

Churchill insisted, in a series of eloquent speeches that have now become legendary, that Britain would never surrender. Nevertheless, Lord Halifax continued to seek a means of giving up the battle. He was encouraged to do so by the King, with whom he continued to have private meetings. When British forces were being evacuated from Dunkirk, the cabinet held a three-day secret debate over whether to seek an immediate peace. The King's favorite, Halifax, led the calls for an armistice.

Even though Churchill's determination to fight on prevailed, Foreign Secretary Halifax made secret efforts to get Italy, not yet in the war, to negotiate peace terms. When France fell and the crisis deepened, he approached Sweden, again on his own and with the encouragement of the King. Referring disparagingly to Churchill's efforts to sustain public morale at this supreme moment of crisis, Halifax told the Swedish ambassador, Bjorn Prytz, through Butler: "Common sense and not bravado will dictate the British government's policy."

It is evident that that phrase was reported directly to Hitler because of his reference to it in his "*Friedensrede*," a speech he made from the Kroll Opera House calling on Britain to surrender on generous terms. He said he was addressing those people in Britain who displayed "reason and common sense." In an attempt to signal that he had prevailed over the defeatists, Churchill ordered Halifax himself to reply in a radio and newsreel address that Churchill himself had framed. The efforts of Lord Halifax to negotiate a surrender only ceased when he was removed from office at the end of 1940 and sent to Washington as ambassador.

After the war it was in Churchill's and the nation's interest to perpetuate the myth that there had been an iron unity in the face of the Nazi threat; that Britain's sovereign and political leadership had recognized what Churchill called the "tragic simplicity and grandeur of the times." The wrangling in the cabinet over possible peace terms, the King's bitter opposition to Churchill, his support for Halifax, and his encouragement of Halifax's search for an ignominious armistice were buried as deeply as possible as the victors exercised their right to rewrite history.

Fifteen

The Windsor Plot

B y May 15, 1940, one week after Winston Churchill had assumed the premiership, the French and British forces in France and Belgium were in headlong retreat. The French army was routed at Sedan; German armor pierced the Maginot Line even more easily than the Duke of Windsor had predicted. Some forty-five thousand German vehicles had flooded into a forty-eight-mile-wide gap in the French lines. British forces were retreating west of Brussels, while the Germans closed in on Antwerp. The strategic towns of Amiens, Cambrai, and St. Quentin were about to fall. There was panic in Paris.

On May 16, 1940, the Duke of Windsor left his post to evacuate the Duchess and his household to Biarritz along roads choked with refugees fleeing Paris with any personal effects they were able to carry. There is a dispute, as with so much else involving the Duke, whether he went AWOL or had permission to do so.

He returned—according to some sources, to a reprimand from Lord Gort—but his role inspecting French positions had become meaningless. By the end of May he was back in the south, ostensibly to view French defenses near the Italian border. Instead, he used the opportunity to pack up the family silver at La Croe, his villa at Cap d'Antibes. On Saturday, June 9, the French government abandoned Paris, and an arm of the invading German army reached down into the Rhone Valley. The following day, the Italians invaded the Riviera, the assault pitiably ineffective. The following Thursday, the Germans marched into Paris. On the advice of the British consul in Nice, Hugh Dodds, the forty-five-year-old Duke and his forty-four-year-old Duchess headed for the Spanish border on the nineteenth with a small household entourage.

The short overland trip was clearly less dangerous than crossing the

Mediterranean to French North Africa. As a refugee soldier of a belligerent, however, the Duke was very likely to be interned in neutral Spain. Interestingly, General Vignon, the Spanish ambassador to Berlin, had been advised by Ribbentrop of the Duke's likely arrival in Spain nine days before. After tortuous negotiations at the border at Perpignan, the Duke and Duchess entered Spain and reached Barcelona just hours before the French formally surrendered and days before German troops reached the Pyrenees. He cabled Churchill that he had fled "to avoid capture" and was heading for Madrid, for some reason signing his name "Edward" rather than the usual David.

Madrid had become a diplomatically strategic location at this crucial moment. Spain was officially neutral and exhausted by civil war, but Francisco Franco, the Spanish dictator, owed his victory in the civil war to military aid from Germany and Italy. He was under pressure to join the war on the Axis side. The Spanish capital crawled with German agents, and pro-Nazi Spanish diplomats were in ready contact with their German counterparts. Samuel Hoare, appointed British ambassador to Spain with the prime directive of encouraging its neutrality, had been a leading appeaser. He was an old friend of the Duke's. The Duke fled to Spain, rather than to French North Africa, and risked internment there so that he could be in a better position to play a role during and after what he believed would be Britain's inevitable capitulation.

Within minutes of the Duke's arrival in Madrid, Eberhard von Stohrer, the German ambassador, cabled Joachim von Ribbentrop, now the Nazi foreign minister, that the Duke was in their midst. Ribbentrop, who had been foiled in his mission to win an alliance with Britain four years before, now saw another opportunity to suborn the former King.

Ribbentrop ordered his ambassador to keep the Duke in Madrid as long as possible. It was at this time that the Germans were sending out and picking up peace feelers from Lord Halifax, the British foreign secretary. Hoare, who had greeted the Duke at Madrid's Ritz Hotel, received a telegram from Churchill ordering the former King to return to Britain as soon as possible. But the Duke first wanted to know what job he would be given and where he would live. He felt he had been humiliated on his last visit to Britain after war broke out, and subsequent events had made him more bitter. He implied through Hoare that unless he was given a favorable response, he wouldn't return.

Hoare backed him up, cabling Churchill that the Duke would be a nuisance and possibly an embarrassment if he did not return. "I shall never get him away from here unless you can find something for him," he wrote. The King and his private secretary, Alec Hardinge, preferred that the Duke stay away from Britain but understood why the war cabinet thought it wise that he should return. But they strongly objected to his being given any responsible position.

There followed an increasingly acrimonious exchange of telegrams between the Duke, who was entirely wrapped up in his personal future, and Churchill, who was up to his cigar ash in the more pressing problems of the war.

The full text of the cables will remain secret until well into the twenty-first century, but it is possible to glean some information as to their contents from indexes to classified Foreign Office documents, which paraphrase them. The Duke kept escalating demands he must have known would not be met, including Royal status for the Duchess. He also wanted to know in advance what post he would have and insisted that both he and the Duchess be received by the King and Queen and that the event be published in the *London Times*. At the height of the exchanges, Churchill told the Duke he was still under military command, implying he could be court-martialed if he refused a direct order to return unconditionally.

Although there is no record of any immediate contact with the Germans, the Duke met with Miguel Primo de Rivera, the civil governor of Madrid, who acted as an emissary of the German government via the Spanish foreign ministry. It seems from the correspondence with Churchill that the Duke was playing for time, delaying his departure from Madrid, precisely as Ribbentrop wished.

One reason the Duke and Duchess contacted the Germans through Primo de Rivera was that they were worried about their property in Paris. They actually received assurances that the Boulevard Suchet house would be guarded by German troops, and a servant was allowed to return to Paris under safe conduct and remove some prized possessions. The Duchess even proposed, at one point, going herself.

The Duke expressed defeatist views during his stay in Madrid while volunteering his admiration for the German way of doing things. He told an official at the American embassy in Spain that the ordinary French soldiers had been let down by their officers and that is why they had been defeated. The Germans, on the other hand, "totally reorganized the order of its society in preparation for war. Countries which were unwilling to accept such reorganization and concomitant sacrifices should avoid dangerous adventures."

The Duchess chimed in that France was "internally diseased" and should never have declared war because she was in no position to fight it. The views were similar to those expressed in the Duke's letter to the historian Philip Guedalla a few weeks earlier, when he called for the old, "cumbersome" democratic system to be "purged."

The Duke and Duchess's remarks were relayed to the State Department by A. W. Weddell, the American ambassador, with the observation that they reflected the attitude of "an element in England which . . . hopes to come into its own in the event of world peace." Sumner Welles, the American secretary of state, channeled the report back to Whitehall. Similar reports about the Duke's views were being sent by Stohrer to Berlin and were echoed in cables from Baron von Hoyningen-Huene, the German ambassador to Portugal.

Hoare not only had been told to persuade the Duke to return to Britain via Lisbon but to keep the Duke out of Lisbon until after the Duke of Kent, who was on an official visit there, had left on July 2. The official reason for keeping them apart was that there was no wish for the Duke of Windsor's arrival to overshadow his brother's visit. This seems a somewhat lame excuse. The reality was that the two Dukes both had defeatist tendencies and it was judged there would be greater mischief if the two were to meet. The Portuguese dictator, Antonio Salazar, was as pro-British as Franco was pro-German, and the Nazis were busy plotting a putsch in Portugal to replace him.

The cable traffic between Madrid and London was being read by the Germans, and the confirmation that the Duke was returning to London disappointed Ribbentrop. The Nazis were eager to keep the Duke within reach to act either as an intermediary for peace or as the head of a puppet British government. The Duke arrived in Lisbon on July 3, 1940, and met with Sir Walford Selby, the British ambassador. Arrangements were made for the Duke and Duchess to fly back to Britain on two RAF flying boats the following night. At the last moment, Churchill sent a new directive. The Duke was offered the post of governor of the Bahamas and was to proceed there without returning to Britain.

The war cabinet had second thoughts about the Duke's future. The palace believed it was too dangerous to bring him to Britain, where he could still attract allies, while the war cabinet believed it too dangerous to allow him to remain in Europe, where he was the focus of Nazi intrigue. But the report sent back to London by Sumner Welles helped to persuade Churchill that some safe job had to be found for him. The archbishop of Canterbury, the Duke's old enemy, suggested the governorship of the Falkland Islands, the remote British colony in the South Atlantic. Churchill, believing the Duke would turn down the appointment as godforsaken, came up with the Bahamas.

The post did not please the Duke. He called it "this wretched appointment," while the Duchess called the Bahamas "the St. Helena of 1940," a reference to the island in the Atlantic where Napoleon had been exiled in 1815. But the Duke had little choice but to accept. At least the posting had the advantage of being close to the United States, which the Duke had not visited for fourteen years and the Duchess had not seen in three. But the Duke's further delay in Lisbon while he arranged to take up his new posting gave Ribbentrop a fresh opportunity. After consultations with Hitler, it was decided to try to persuade the Duke to return to Spain, where he could more easily be brought under German control.

Ribbentrop, aware of the Duke's reaction to the Bahamas posting, cabled his ambassador in Madrid, von Stohrer, to try to approach the Duke through a Spanish emissary and persuade him to return to Spain. Once in Spain, he was to be offered a large sum of money, at least $35 million in Swiss francs, and "any wish," including the throne once the British surrendered. In return he had only to "hold himself in readiness," as Ribbentrop put it. Von Stohrer consulted Ramón Serrano Suner, Franco's brother-in-law, and Suner sent Primo de Rivera to persuade the Duke to return to Spain. It is uncertain whether Primo de Rivera realized that the mission originated with the Germans.

Primo de Rivera traveled to Baco do Inferno, outside Lisbon, where the Duke was staying at a villa owned by a pro-German bank owner. It was the same villa to which the Duke of Kent had come days before. It had the advantage that it was already under constant surveillance by MI6. Rivera told the Duke and Duchess that an important message concerning their personal security waited for them if they returned to Spain. At the same time, he hinted it was dangerous for them to stay in Lisbon. Precisely from whom this alleged danger came is unclear.

The message from Rivera came at the right psychological moment, for the Duke was again in the midst of a furious battle over the Bahamas appointment. He wanted to go via the United States, while the British

feared indiscreet public statements there might encourage the isolation-
ists in an election year. So intent was the British government on keeping
the Duke out of the United States that it was prepared to divert his ship,
the *Excalibur*, to Bermuda, where he could take another to the
Bahamas, at considerable cost. There were other, more trivial difficulties, including the recurrent question of the Duchess's rank. Getting
nowhere with his complaints and demands, the Duke claimed he was
"sorely tempted . . . to retire from the contest."

Rivera also seems to have sounded him out about a return to British
politics, but the Duke, on this occasion at least, said he believed that
would never happen. Rivera reported to Suner that the Duke was depressed, saw his appointment as a form of exile, and believed he was
surrounded by spies.

Word of the Duke's state of mind reached Ribbentrop at a crucial
moment. It was July 23, the day Churchill forced Halifax to reply to
Hitler's "peace speech." Hitler had gotten the message that Churchill
had prevailed over defeatists in Britain and decided the Duke was more
important than ever.

Walter Schellenberg, Nazi Germany's counterintelligence and
covert-operations chief, had been sent to Madrid to help von Stohrer
detain the Duke. Having failed, he moved on to Lisbon. Schellenberg
was skeptical about the operation, but Hitler had personally told him to
use any means at his disposal, including force "and at the risk of your
life," to bring the Duke under German control. Hitler particularly
pointed to the Duchess of Windsor's sympathies and her influence over
the Duke as potentially decisive to the success of the plan.

Schellenberg and a German agent, a high-ranking Spanish civil servant named Angel de Velasco, arrived in Lisbon on July 26, 1940, with a
plan to abduct the Duke. Velasco was to arrange for the Duke to be
invited on a hunting trip near the Portuguese border with Spain. Once
there, German commandos would spirit him across the frontier. Schellenberg abandoned the idea when he realized there were eighteen
British agents watching the Duke at all times. Meanwhile, Walter
Monckton, who had acted as the Duke's legal adviser during the abdication crisis, arrived with instructions from Churchill to ensure that the
Duke left for the Bahamas as scheduled.

One last attempt was made by the Germans to get the Duke to go to
Spain. Velasco tried to convince him that Britain was about to surrender
and that he, the Duke, could be the nation's savior by negotiating fa-

The wedding of Princess Anne and Captain Mark Phillips in November 1973. (Courtesy *New York Post*)

Five generations of Royals pictured in 1977 at the christening of Princess Anne's son Peter Phillips. Rear: Peter Phillips and his wife, Anne, parents of Captain Mark Phillips; Queen Elizabeth II; Captain Mark Phillips; the Queen Mother; Prince Philip. In the front are Princess Anne and her infant son with Princess Alice, the last surviving grandchild of Queen Victoria and the infant's great-great-great-aunt. (Courtesy *New York Post*)

The Duke of Windsor shortly before his death in 1972, aged seventy-eight.

The Queen and Prince Philip at an exhibition in 1954. After seeing a potato peeler demonstrated, Prince Philip remarked, "Just the thing for the wife!" On this occasion the Queen was amused. (Courtesy *New York Post*)

Queen Elizabeth II and Prince Philip with Prince Charles and Princess Anne on the balcony of Buckingham Palace in 1954. (Courtesy *New York Post*)

Lord Mountbatten in one of the last pictures taken before his assassination by the Provisional I.R.A. in 1979. (Courtesy *New York Post*)

The wedding cake designed for Prince Charles and Princess Diana. (Courtesy *New York Post*)

By the time Prince Charles and Princess Diana married, royal weddings had become an economic bonanza as well as a royal pageant. Millions bought British stamps issued on the wedding day. (Courtesy British Post Office)

Prince Charles and Princess Diana walk down the steps of St. Paul's after the wedding ceremony in July 1981. (Courtesy *New York Post*)

The marriage register.

The official group photo following the wedding. Back row, left to right: Mark Phillips, Prince Andrew, Viscount Linley, Prince Philip, Prince Edward, Princess Diana, Prince Charles, Ruth, Lady Fermoy, Lady Jane Fellowes, Viscount Althorp, Robert Fellowes. Center row, left to right: Princess Anne, Princess Maragaret, the Queen Mother, Queen Elizabeth II, India Hicks, Lady Sarah Armstrong-Jones, the Hon. Mrs. Shand Kydd, Earl Spencer, Lady Sarah McCorquodale, Neil McCorquodale. Front row: Edward van Cutsem, Clementine Hambro, Catherine Cameron, Sarah Jane Gaselee and Lord Nicholas Windsor. (AP/Wide World photo)

Prince Charles and Princess Diana on vacation together at Balmoral. (Courtesy *New York Post*)

Queen Elizabeth II and Prince Philip in full regalia at the state opening of Parliament in 1981. (AP/Wide World photo)

Princess Diana only two years after her wedding. Her eating disorder has already begun to affect her and she has become thin and angular. (Courtesy *New York Post*)

Princess Diana and Prince Charles cut short a vacation at Lech in Austria after the death of Princess Diana's father. Prince Charles's lack of compassion for his wife over the next several days heightened speculation that their marriage was unsalvagable. (AP/Wide World photo)

Queen Elizabeth II moments before making the "Annus Horribilis" speech at the Guildhall, November 1992. (AP/Wide World photo)

vorable terms. But Monckton persuaded him that Churchill had won the upper hand against the defeatists and appeasers, at least for the moment.

The Duke told Velasco he would return from the Bahamas to act as intermediary or otherwise step into the breach once Britain surrendered. He even agreed to a contact code with Velasco for use at some time in the future. He left Lisbon on the *Excalibur* on August 1, 1940. Two Scotland Yard detectives were on board for the couple's protection, and at least three agents of MI6 traveled on the ship to ensure that the Duke and Duchess arrived in Bermuda and proceeded directly to the Bahamas.

The British government and the Royal Family went to extraordinary lengths to bury the details of the so-called Windsor plot after the war, but copies of some of the German documents relating to the event eventually surfaced in the United States. There are still many aspects of the affair that remain secret. Apologists for the Duke of Windsor have consistently claimed that the plot existed primarily in the fertile imagination of Ribbentrop and Schellenberg, that the Duke can hardly be blamed for their flights of fancy, and that he did board the first available ship to take up a post that he did not relish.

It is true that the plot appears disjointed and ill conceived, but that is because the documentation that describes the plot is fragmentary. Missing from all accounts is the Duke's responses to the various approaches that he must have realized were being made on Hitler's behalf. The Duke vacillated throughout the period, from the day France surrendered on June 21 to the day he boarded the *Excalibur* on August 1. He fully expected Britain to be defeated and surrender within weeks. He wanted to return to England as the man who would rebuild the nation after its humiliation. On the other hand, he feared throwing in his lot with Hitler too early and that he would be perceived as at best a defeatist and at worst a traitor.

He could not decide whether the Bahamas furthered his ambition— he could not possibly be associated with Britain's defeat from so isolated a post—or stifled his aims by moving him too far from the crucible of the action.

On August 1, 1940, the Duke gazed wistfully from the deck of the *Excalibur* as the last view of Europe, the Cap de São Vicente in southern Portugal, disappeared over the horizon. There were parties in progress throughout the ship. Many of the passengers were refugees; some of them had suffered nightmarish experiences as they fled from Holland, Belgium, and France ahead of the advancing German armies. Most were headed for the United States. The Duke was deluded enough to believe that he might yet play a leading role in the great drama about to be played out. In fact, he was never again to rise above the role of supernumerary.

Sixteen

Windsors at War

B ack in Britain, the next phase of the war, the climactic battle between the German air force, the Luftwaffe, and the Royal Air Force, had begun. The plans for the German invasion of Britain, known as Operation Sealion, called for the Luftwaffe to establish air superiority by September 1940, before a massive invasion of southern England. Hitler had good reason to believe that an invasion would not be necessary and that a negotiated peace would leave him free to turn his attention to, and his firepower on, the Soviet Union.

Ordinary British citizens braced for the holocaust to come. There was severe rationing, desperate shortages, widespread fear that a German attack was imminent, and few resources with which to meet the threat. Children were evacuated to rural areas, further dividing families who had breadwinners in the armed forces. Women joined the depleted work force in key industries. At night, waves of German bombers destroyed homes, factories, entire neighborhoods. The heart of British defense consisted of a few thousand fighter pilots, many of whom were too young even to vote. They were greatly outnumbered and outgunned.

In this atmosphere, people looked anxiously to Winston Churchill for political and military leadership, although they were unaware of the degree of defeatism inside his own cabinet. For moral leadership, they looked to the King and the Royal Family. Churchill called this period of the war Britain's "finest hour." That was, of course, not a judgment after the fact but a prediction, and at the time a very optimistic one. But it became reality. It was also the Royal Family's finest hour, for the public came to perceive that the King was in fact sharing the hardships of the people.

To a very large extent, this was more than just perception. The Royal

187

Family did rise to the occasion. The first impulse of palace officials was to have the two Royal Princesses, Elizabeth, fourteen, and Margaret, ten, sent to Canada and out of danger. It was George VI's consort, Queen Elizabeth, who vetoed the idea. She had a keen awareness of public relations and realized the chasm this would create between the Royal Family and virtually every other family in the nation. She also had no wish to be separated from her daughters. So the public was told that Princess Elizabeth and Princess Margaret had been evacuated to "somewhere in England," like many thousands of other children. In fact, they continued to live at Windsor.

Other branches of the Royal Family, however, availed themselves of the chance to get their children out of danger. Lord Mountbatten sent his daughters to the United States to live with the Vanderbilt family. He may have felt that as some of their mother's family were Jewish, they would be in greater danger if the Nazis were to invade. His letters to his daughters reveal an unexpected, condescending anti-Americanism. The Mountbattens could not quite decide which was worse, having to live with American ill manners and poor taste or face the threat of Nazi panzer divisions.

At first, the air war went badly for the British. While the Luftwaffe concentrated on air bases, landing strips, and other military targets, even at enormous expense in men and machines, it seemed that the greater resources of the Luftwaffe would prove decisive. The RAF's light Spitfire and Hurricane fighters were downing many enemy aircraft, but it seemed inevitable that steady attrition would ultimately wear down Britain's resources.

The first German bomber shot down—a Heinkel—spiraled out of an iron-gray sky and crashed in a fireball on a hillside near the town of Whitby, in North Yorkshire in the north of England, on February 3, 1940. It had been gunned into flames from the cockpit of a Spitfire of the RAF 43 Squadron, piloted by a young man who was to play a pivotal role in the life of Princess Margaret, at that time only ten years old. He was Squadron Leader, later Group Captain, Peter Townsend. His action in drawing the first blood of the air war was to bring him into the center of the Palace Circle and set in motion a chain of events that was to have a profound effect on the entire Royal Family.

On August 8, 1940, the Luftwaffe launched a massive offensive against Britain's air bases, designed to draw the RAF into open battle in large numbers and destroy hundreds of aircraft. It failed. Then, in a strategic blunder, Luftwaffe marshal Hermann Goering switched the offensive to London and other important cities. Despite the dangers, the King, prodded by Queen Elizabeth, insisted on living at Windsor outside London and traveling to Buckingham Palace in the heart of the capital every day. It was the residential East End of London, near the docks, that took the brunt of the blitz on London, as well as, of course, industrial areas of cities like Liverpool, Manchester, Birmingham, and Coventry.

Although specifically designed to attack industrial production and commerce, the raids had a terrifying and demoralizing effect. Churchill and the King and Queen were booed on some visits to bombed-out areas, and hostile crowds were held back by police. The hostility was born of frustration that working-class districts were being destroyed while the neighborhoods of the rich were intact. In some instances, newsreels showing the visits to bombed neighborhoods had to be doctored so that only cheering could be heard. Close-ups of the friendly faces of stalwart East Enders had actually been taken from peacetime events and edited into newsreel accounts.

But the Luftwaffe inadvertently assuaged the bitterness of working-class Londoners by bombing ritzier sections of central London, including Bond Street and Park Lane. The legend of the Blitz—as the bombing came to be known after the German word *Blitzkrieg* ("lightning war")—is that adversity drew people together. While it is generally true, there was also a grimmer reality. There was widespread looting, even of dead bodies, for jewelry, money, ration books, anything of value, from overcoats to silk stockings.

The King and Queen were aware of some of the horror stories of looting and of the bitterness and unrest in severely damaged working-class areas, so it was with some feeling that after Buckingham Palace itself was bombed, the Queen remarked that she was glad to have been bombed: "We can now look the East End in the face."

The palace was bombed twice, the first by accident, the second time in a deliberate assassination attempt. On September 9, 1940, a stray bomb fell on the north side of the palace but failed to explode until the next day. For several hours, the King had continued to work in his study close by. When it did explode, it shattered many windows in the palace and destroyed the palace swimming pool.

But two days later, a German bomber was seen to dive out of the clouds, fly directly above the Mall, the long avenue leading to the palace, and drop six bombs on the palace while the King was there. The King wrote that night in his diary: "We all wondered why we weren't dead . . . two bombs in the forecourt, two in the quadrangle, one in the Chapel and one in the garden. There is no doubt it was a direct attack on the Palace."

He was particularly bitter about the attack, not just because he suffered a severe, delayed shock reaction but because he was convinced it was the work of one of the many Royal relatives fighting with the Nazis. Although Buckingham Palace is easily recognizable from the air, the bombing of a specific building in an air raid was extremely difficult in an era without "smart" bombs and guiding devices.

The King believed the attack showed detailed knowledge of the palace. His chief suspect was a son of the Infante Alfonso of Spain, Prince Juan, and Princess Beatrice who had been with the Italian air force. Another suspect was Prince Christoph von Hesse, who was a *Standartenführer* in the S.S. before the war and who had since joined the Luftwaffe. He was the brother-in-law of Prince Philip of Greece, later to marry King George VI's daughter, Princess Elizabeth.

The assassination attempt was another example of German misunderstanding of the role of the monarch in British political life. Hitler and Goering believed that if George VI could be eliminated, either the Duke of Kent, who exhibited Nazi sympathies before the war, would become Regent and insist on a negotiated peace, or the Duke of Windsor would be reinstalled. But Hitler was not alone in overestimating the power of the Crown. Whenever Roosevelt disagreed with Churchill on the conduct of the war, he would threaten to appeal to the King.

The bombing of Buckingham Palace proved to be excellent propaganda from the British point of view, although the extent of the damage to the palace remained a secret. The King and Queen were portrayed as just another British family whose home had been struck by bombs. Crowds that gathered when the King and Queen visited bombed-out districts were now altogether more friendly. In a well-received gesture, the Queen sent sixty suites of furniture from Windsor Castle, where they had been kept unused, in storage, to deserving families in the East End.

Both the King and Queen worked tirelessly during the war. They covered fifty-three thousand miles by railroad, visiting bomb sites, military installations, and other places. The King himself visited battle zones from North Africa to France. He took a night shift at a munitions factory and worked side by side with ordinary workers. He displayed great personal courage to carry out these duties because he had to overcome all his phobias, secret from the public, to do so. He feared crowds but faced them genially. He was claustrophobic but shared packed civilian shelters with ordinary people. He was afraid of heights but never showed his fear. He particularly feared flying but traveled to the front. These things do not seem much when men were facing death daily in combat, but what one individual does with ease another needs all his courage to do.

The Queen insisted that the whole family participate in both public duties and domestic hardships. Princess Elizabeth joined the Auxiliary Territorial Service and learned to service motor engines. She also gave up her German-language lessons and learned American history instead. Rationing of food and utilities was strictly adhered to at the palace, Windsor, Sandringham, and Balmoral. Red lines were drawn inside all the bathtubs to indicate the maximum-permitted amount of water—just a few inches—to bathe in. While ordinary citizens spent their spare time converting every spare corner to vegetable gardens to combat food shortages, the King ordered all but a few of his herds of deer slaughtered and turned over thousands of acres of his personal property for cultivation. Both the King and Queen learned to use handguns, and the King carried a revolver and a rifle with him throughout the war.

The Royal Family also suffered the loss of a loved one, as did so many thousands of other families. In 1943 the Duke of Kent was killed when a plane taking him on a Royal visit to an RAF base in Iceland crashed on a Scottish hillside. It was an accident, but there was speculation that the Duke had been at the controls, somewhat the worse for drink. The King liked to think, however, that his beloved younger brother had been killed on active service.

As a result, while many European Royal Families had questionable records during the war—King Leopold of Belgium was regarded as a collaborator, and King Carol of Rumania openly allied himself with the Germans—the British Royal Family emerged from the darkest days of the conflict more popular than ever. The King was seen as a leader who had shown his people a brilliant moral example; the Queen was regarded with warm affection; their children were viewed as model youths.

But there was another side to the behavior of the Royal Family during the war that was kept secret and would have damaged this heroic image. The various members of the British Royal Family, including the King but most notably Lord Mountbatten and his nephew, Prince Philip of Greece, were in regular contact with dozens of German relatives throughout the war, many of whom were ardent Nazis. They did so through diplomatic contacts in Sweden. When Prince Christoph von Hesse, suspected of having bombed the palace, was shot down and killed in Italy, the Mountbattens sent their condolences to his wife, Princess Sophie.

The King was also deeply concerned about British and American bombing of Germany and sought to spare those towns and cities where Royal palaces and the estates of relatives existed from Allied bombing. He was particularly outraged by the destruction of the historic German city of Dresden, which was totally destroyed by Allied bombing for no strategic reason during the last months of the war. It was the King's personal opposition to terror bombing of German cities that led him to refuse to significantly honor the man chiefly responsible for the planning and organization of the raids, Air Chief Marshal Sir Arthur "Bomber" Harris, one of the few leading military figures so ignored.

No doubt George VI felt a moral objection to civilian bombing, but there was also a more practical concern. He firmly believed that a Germany without Hitler was a future ally against the Soviet Union. He was also horrified at the prospect of the destruction of Germany from the west while the Russians fell on her from the east. Like a number of other leading figures in British and American political and military circles, the King wanted the war with the Reich to segue into a war against communism.

But the most bizarre wartime secret of the Royal Family is the mission—actually several missions—undertaken between 1945 and 1948 to scour Germany for documents and other material, some of which could discredit the Windsors, and to prevent them from falling into the hands of both the American occupying forces and the new West German civil power.

The man in charge of this mission was Sir Anthony Blunt, later unmasked as a Soviet spy, who was in 1945 a major and an agent of MI5. A leading European art historian and specialist in Poussin, he spoke fluent German, and had extensive Royal connections. He was admired by Queen Mary, had been the homosexual lover of both the Duke of Kent, and, it has been suggested, David Bowes-Lyon, brother of Queen Elizabeth. He was appointed surveyor of the King's pictures in April 1945.

The Germans had looted an enormous number of art treasures, from France to the Soviet Union, some officially confiscated, some simply stolen by individual officers. As the Allies pressed into Germany, a massive search began to find some of these treasures and restore them to the countries and individuals from whom they had been stolen. Blunt's mission was partly undertaken under this guise, but he was never attached, according to Allied records, to any of the groups officially charged with recovering the art treasures.

Owen Morshead, the Windsor Castle royal librarian, accompanied Blunt on a number of these missions. They made one of their first raids on the palace of the Hesse family at Schloss Friedrichshof near Frankfurt. The region had been occupied by General Patton's Third Army, and the palace and its grounds were being used as an American military camp. The Hesse family had fallen on hard times in the last month of the war. Following the July 1944 plot on Hitler's life, the Führer had become convinced that most, if not all, members of the former German Royal Family had plotted against him. Many were purged from the military and sent to concentration camps.

Prince Phillip von Hesse, the head of the family and at one time an S.S. *Obersturmbannführer* and Nazi governor of the region, had been dispatched to Dachau, although this experience did not save him from being detained by the Americans as one of the most-wanted war criminals. His wife had died in Buchenwald during an American air raid. Prince Christoph von Hesse had been shot down over Italy. His widow, Princess Sophie, had remarried Prince George of Hanover, grandson of the Kaiser. Prince Wolfgang von Hesse, Phillip's twin, had been evicted from the palace and was living in somewhat reduced circumstances nearby. Morshead showed Prince Wolfgang a letter signed by King George VI asking for numerous Hesse family files and documents. Prince Wolfgang revealed where many documents were stored in the palace but suggested that the Americans would not allow them to be removed.

This prediction turned out to be the case. The senior American officer at the palace told Morshead that they were technically on American soil and had no authority to take anything, even if the Hesse family agreed. So Blunt began to argue, negotiate, and placate. While he kept the officer occupied, Morshead and a small party of British soldiers explored the palace, found the documents they wanted, and took them away.

After the British party had left, Capt. Kathleen Nash of the Women's Army Corps and Col. Jack Durant searched for more items the British might have missed or ignored. They stumbled across $3 million worth of Hesse family jewels, including solid gold swastika brooches, and smuggled them back to the United States. Prince Wolfgang complained to King George VI that his palace had been looted, and a U.S. Army investigation resulted in Nash and Durant being court-martialed after the war. The court-martial came close to blowing the Blunt-Morshead operation.

This was only one of several similar missions across occupied Germany undertaken by Blunt and Morshead over the next two and a half years. Another was to Blankenburg Castle, home of Prince George of Hanover, where more documents were removed, this time with considerably more ease because the region was occupied by British troops.

Prince George of Hanover had fought on the Russian front as a General Staff officer with the Second Panzer Group under General Guderian. He and his mother, Princess Victoria, had been detained by the British on arms-hoarding charges. Princess Victoria haughtily informed British officers that her son was a member of the British as well as the German Royal Family and insisted on being treated accordingly. The British officers were at first contemptuous of the two Royal Germans. Word came from London to show them respect, and in May 1945, Blunt and Morshead arrived and removed a number of boxes.

The purpose of these missions remains a closely guarded secret—so secret that, over twenty years later, when Blunt was being questioned after it was confirmed that he was a Russian spy, his interrogators were specifically ordered not to inquire into the series of assignments he carried out for the King. The warning came to MI5's interrogator, Peter Wright, directly from Michael Adeane, the Queen's private secretary, in a briefing on Blunt's work for the palace.

"From time to time," Adeane told Wright, "you may find Blunt referring to an assignment he undertook on behalf of the Palace—a visit to Germany after the war. Please do not pursue this matter. Strictly speaking, it is not relevant to considerations of national security."

Wright recalled the meeting with Adeane in his memoir *Spycatcher*, and it was one of the anecdotes that the British government went to considerable lengths—unsuccessfully—to suppress.

Wright never discovered the details of the missions. But some conclusions can be drawn. According to British intelligence sources, a number of the missions were to recover relatively mundane items—letters from Queen Victoria, King Edward VII, and George V to their German relatives to prevent them going on the open market in the hard times that would inevitably follow the war. Some of the letters contained material of a personal nature, mirrored by the correspondence and documents that had been expurgated after Queen Victoria's death. There were also many decorations the King wanted recovered for similar reasons. He was an avid collector and did not want medals that had been given to his German relatives to be sold.

There was jewelry that had been given to the Kaiser's family and other German Royals which the Windsors regarded as rightfully theirs. But the sources say there were also other items that would have been seriously embarrassing to the Royal Family. Among them was the correspondence between Royals and their German cousins and in-laws before and during the war. Some proved embarrassing because of their very existence, having been delivered during wartime, a prima facie breach of the various laws against trading and communicating with the enemy; others, because they betrayed the Nazi sympathies of the Duke of Windsor and the Duke of Kent, called for German and British action against Russia, and were critical of British political life.

There were also the war records of German relatives of the Royal Family—among them the Hesses, the Hanovers, the Hohenloe-Langenbergs, the Margrave of Baden, and the Duke of Saxe-Coburg's family, which the British Royal Family wanted expunged. German archives today contain few references to the wartime activity of the many relatives of the British Royal Family. None of the Royal relatives were tried as war criminals, although a number of them, like Prince Phillip von Hesse and the Duke of Saxe-Coburg, were among the United States's top fifty wanted Nazis to be rounded up in the arrest operation known as "Ashcan."

And there were also documents relating to the intrigue surrounding the Duke of Windsor during the war. The King wanted German Foreign Office documents on the secret foreign policy of Edward VIII, Germany's use of the former King after the abdication, and other material confiscated.

But there was much about the Blunt-Morshead mission that we don't know and which remains a closely guarded secret in the archives of MI5 and Windsor Castle. That after many years Blunt's MI5 interrogators were told that the information was off limits even to them suggests that there are good reasons for the British Royal Family to remain so remarkably sensitive on the subject. One man who knew all the details was, of course, Blunt himself. It was this knowledge that helped him retain his post as surveyor of pictures, his knighthood, and his social standing for fifteen years after he was unmasked as a Soviet mole.

Of course, nothing was known of all this when the Windsors and the British people celebrated the end of the war in Europe in May 1945. There were spontaneous celebrations throughout London, and crowds descended on the Mall to demand an appearance by the family that had come to symbolize all families at war. The King accepted unrestrained jubilation and the accolades with modesty, voluntarily sharing the balcony with Churchill and at one point stepping aside to join the crowds in lauding his wartime prime minister.

Princess Elizabeth and Princess Margaret, who had little contact with people their own age, having been educated exclusively by tutors, were allowed to join the celebrating crowd incognito—a spontaneous, exciting, fun-filled night they were to remember all their lives. Four months later, the atom bomb brought a sudden end to the war with Japan. The only disappointment for the King was the defeat of Churchill in an election shortly after the German surrender.

The nation had survived a long, terrible ordeal, and there was a widespread feeling among the populace that the Royals had endured it with them in equal share. But there was one member of the Royal Family who had every right to regard himself as a greater hero than the King himself. And he had the battle scars to prove it.

Seventeen

The Royal Warrior

N o other member of the Royal Family was as active during the war as Lord Louis Mountbatten. Few warriors in World War II enjoyed such rapid promotion; none of the leading Allied commanders were so controversial or so heavily criticized or so lavishly acclaimed. His critics, and they were legion, claimed he was promoted too fast, that he enjoyed too much undue influence in high places, that he was irresponsible and headstrong in command.

The key to Lord Mountbatten's character, the root of his boundless ambition, was the dishonor and shame he felt when his father, Prince Louis of Battenberg, was forced to resign from the Admiralty during the first months of World War I. His resignation came about primarily because of his German birth and a vicious campaign of vilification by two London newspapers, *John Bull* and the *Globe*. The change of name from Battenberg to Mountbatten that had been forced on his family and the reduced status to plain Lord from Prince and Serene Highness that he and his brother had to accept emphasized the blow. His determination to settle those scores would ultimately lead him to set his sights on placing a Mountbatten on the throne of England. Along the way, hundreds, perhaps thousands, of lives were sacrificed in the cause of establishing him as a warrior and statesman.

Mountbatten had something of a playboy image in the twenties and thirties. In 1922 he had married Edwina Ashley, the immensely wealthy and very beautiful daughter of Lord Mount Temple and granddaughter of Edward VII's old friend the financier Sir Ernest Cassel. Her money and his Royal status made it in every way a spectacular match. The then-Prince of Wales had been best man. King George V, Queen Mary, and the aging Queen Alexandra were all at the lavish wedding. They traveled widely, and their social circle ranged from European Kings and Queens to the royalty of Hollywood, including Mary Pickford, Marion Davies, Douglas Fairbanks, and Charles Chaplin, all of whom they regarded as close friends.

They had a rather unusual marital relationship in which neither was monogamous, and both were more or less open about their infidelities. They spent long periods apart, he in the navy, she on long, adventurous journeys. Either despite these absences or because of them, the marriage survived, but there were periods of enormous strain, particularly for him.

The outbreak of World War II found Lord Mountbatten, age thirty-nine, in command of the destroyer *Kelly* and the Royal Navy's Fifth Flotilla of K-Class destroyers. It was the *Kelly* that took the Duke of Windsor back to England soon after war was declared. Mountbatten and the Duke had at one time been very close. But Mountbatten realized that his own interests lay in distancing himself from his old friend so as to avoid being "purged" by the new palace clique, and he took every opportunity to do so. On the short journey from France, he even tried to keep the Duke away from the officers and crew as much as possible so that there would be no unwelcome demonstrations of loyalty and support that would upset George VI.

Mountbatten's handling of the *Kelly* in the first months of the war created a pattern of controversy that persisted throughout his career. Typically, he turned to his advantage behavior that had brought him intense criticism and censure. If he was not always able to snatch victory from the jaws of defeat, he was usually able to grab some personal aggrandizement.

He was eager for early action and days after war began claimed to have sunk a U-boat following two near misses from torpedoes. The Admiralty appears to have not even listed the claim as probable, and later German records showed no U-boat within fifty miles of Mountbatten's position. But such errors were common in the early days of the conflict.

After ferrying the Duke of Windsor to England, his first wartime task in the *Kelly* was to intercept a British merchant ship, *City of Flint*, which had been captured with its crew and cargo by a German battleship. A German crew was trying to reach a German port, hugging the Norwegian coast. Mountbatten made a headlong dash to intercept the ship at a point which, all of his officers told him, she must already have passed. He ignored their advice, only to find they were correct. Racing back to home port in heavy seas, he was going far too fast at twenty-eight knots when the ship was hit by a wave that almost capsized her. She was badly damaged, one crew member was lost, and she was forced into dry dock for repairs.

Just hours after repairs were completed, the *Kelly* sailed into the Tyne estuary, where an oil tanker was on fire and sinking. The *Kelly*'s propeller was blown off and her stern twisted by a mine. Once more she sat in dry dock, this time for nearly three months. Soon after the *Kelly* went to sea again, the ship again found itself in more trouble. She collided with a destroyer from another flotilla and suffered a serious gash in her side.

Mountbatten had ordered his wireless operators to send out a standard, preliminary emergency message immediately on hearing an explosion aboard ship: "Hit by mine or torpedo. Uncertain which." The purpose was to ensure that the ship would not go down without a Mayday message. When the *Kelly* collided with the HMS *Ghurka*, the wireless operators heard an explosion and sent their message. The captain of the *Ghurka*, which had sustained little damage, wired back: "Not mine but me."

The *Kelly* had become a joke in the navy, and Mountbatten with it, which may account for some of the later events which were to overtake the ship. After six more weeks in dry dock the *Kelly* was sent to Norway to evacuate hapless Allied soldiers who had been pinned down at Namsos by superior German forces. It was a successful operation, brought off with great daring despite heavy air attacks on Mountbatten's flotilla.

But days later, the *Kelly* and the flotilla were in pursuit of German minelayers off the Dutch coast when Mountbatten learned that a submarine was in the vicinity and set off with two other destroyers in pursuit. The U-boat was nowhere to be found. Mountbatten soon found himself out of visual contact with the main body of his flotilla, at night, diverted from his mission, and a sitting target should the submarine be lurking nearby, all at odds with accepted naval procedure at the time. Mountbatten would not be persuaded to call off the hunt, however. Then, for no apparent reason, he ordered a childish and unnecessary message sent by Aldis lamp to one of his accompanying destroyers, which betrayed his position. Moments later, a torpedo struck, and there was an enormous explosion on the starboard side. Twenty-seven men were killed, and scores more were wounded.

Irresponsible as Mountbatten's actions might have been up to that point, his subsequent handling of the situation was impeccable. The *Kelly* limped back to port under tow, with Mountbatten ignoring advice to allow her to sink, surviving attacks by German aircraft, the attentions of more submarines, and a collision with a German gunboat—a masterly display of seamanship and iron determination.

But though he won glory for this exploit in the eyes of Churchill and the public, his senior officers realized he had been the architect of the original disaster. This view was reflected in their decision not to recommend Mountbatten for a Distinguished Service Order despite campaigns on his behalf by Churchill and the Duke of Kent.

While the *Kelly* was again undergoing repairs, Mountbatten took command of another flotilla led by the destroyer the *Javelin*. Again he met with disaster. The flotilla had been searching for a group of German destroyers when the two flotillas suddenly encountered each other at night. The Germans heard the British coming from some distance away, for Mountbatten was pressing on at full speed, as usual. But the British flotilla had little warning. Closing at less than one thousand yards, Mountbatten was faced with three possible modes of attack and chose the one which presented the most risk. He was hit by two torpedoes. Forty-six men were killed instantly, dozens more were wounded, and the *Javelin*'s bow and stern were blown off. An inquiry later found that Mountbatten had made elementary errors in his handling of the battle. But once again, in the eyes of Churchill and the general public, Mountbatten had proved himself a courageous and intrepid commander, willing to chase the enemy, take him on, and to hell with the consequences.

When the *Kelly* was once again ready for action, the Fifth Flotilla was sent to the Mediterranean to reinforce the defense of Malta and to take part in the Battle of Crete. The Germans had established air supremacy, and the *Kelly* and the other K-Class destroyers under Mountbatten's command came under repeated air bombardment. Again Mountbatten was accused of near incompetence during a failed attempt to blockade Benghazi, the port which supplied Rommel's troops in North Africa.

Then, in May 1941, came Mountbatten's worst and finest hour. The *Kelly* and two other ships in the flotilla were sent to bombard the German-held airfield of Maleme in Crete. Larger ships originally designated to accompany them were withdrawn, which made the fate of the flotilla almost certain. After a successful bombardment the flotilla was racing back to port when it was attacked by dive bombers. A sister ship, the *Kashmir*, was sunk in two minutes; then the *Kelly*, struck by a number of bombs, capsized.

Mountbatten stayed on the bridge until the last possible moment, then found himself clinging to debris with other survivors. He and another officer showed consummate courage in helping weaker swimmers and injured men reach rafts and floats and maintaining morale despite strafing runs by German aircraft on the men in the water. They were eventually rescued by another destroyer, the *Kipling*. More than half the company of 270 aboard the *Kelly* were killed.

The saga of the *Kelly* was made into the wartime propaganda movie *In Which We Serve*, with Noel Coward, Mountbatten's friend and the Duke of Kent's sometime lover, in the title role. Although the captain portrayed in the movie was decidedly middle class, he was unmistakably based on Mountbatten, and the addresses to his crew were taken verbatim from Mountbatten's talks to the crew of the *Kelly*. Mountbatten also had a say in casting, and he demolished obstacles that were placed in Coward's way to ensure that the movie was made. Among them was the government's reluctance to produce a film in which a British ship went down. Another was the casting of Noel Coward, a homosexual, as the British navy captain.

Lord Beaverbrook waged a particularly nasty campaign against the film. In revenge, Coward aimed a blow at Beaverbrook by showing in the movie a scene with a copy of the *Daily Express*, in which the newspaper predicted there would be no war, floating amid the wreckage of a British ship. Beaverbrook blamed Mountbatten, and the feud between the two former friends continued for the rest of their lives. Mountbatten never tired of watching *In Which We Serve*. It turned out to be excellent propaganda for the Royal Navy and for Britain's struggle after Dunkirk. It was also excellent propaganda for Mountbatten personally, enhancing his public image further but increasing the jealousy of him among more senior officers.

After the demise of the *Kelly*, Mountbatten was given command of the aircraft carrier *Illustrious*. George VI's reaction to the news was unusually blunt. "That," he said, "is the end of the *Illustrious*." But before he could take up that command, he was given a new post. From commanding a flotilla at sea he became chief of combined operations. And it was in that role that he was to suffer his greatest setback, an operation that remains the subject of much acrimonious debate even today.

Almost all modern warfare is a combined operation, with air, sea, and land forces acting in concert, often under a single command. Before World War II, individual services acted independently. But the nature of war had changed. Clearly, if the Allies were ever to achieve victory as opposed to merely avoiding defeat, Europe would have to be invaded. To do that, all three services would be called on to act as a cohesive force.

Initially, Mountbatten's task was· to mount small operations against the Germans, combining elements from the navy, army, and RAF, but ultimately he was charged with laying the groundwork for the invasion of Europe. It was also in the role of chief of combined operations that Mountbatten indulged his obsession with gadgetry and off-the-wall inventions. Some worked; others now seem ridiculous. One of the more expensive and ineffective plans called for the creation of enormous artificial icebergs as floating landing strips.

By 1942, with the United States and Russia in the war, the pressure was brought to bear on the British to take the offensive. The Russians desperately needed the Germans to be drawn to the west to relieve pressure on the Russian armies in the east. The Americans needed evidence that it was worth pursuing an offensive against the Germans at the expense of the war in the Pacific against the Japanese.

There were a number of small raids mounted to harass the Germans, some suicidal for those involved. There was a plan for a small-scale invasion—code-named Sledgehammer—which might gain a toehold for a larger-scale invasion later in the war. But Sledgehammer was shelved, and the Dieppe raid was planned instead, partly to appease the Americans, who wanted to see some action from the British forces, and partly as a somewhat grotesque experiment.

No invasion of Europe from the sea had been attempted before, and it was established military dogma that a large-scale invasion of France would demand the initial capture of at least two ports from which the invading army could be supplied; without these ports the invasion would ultimately fail. Just as important, the ports would have to be captured intact. The only way to discover if that could be achieved was to attempt to do it. The channel port of Dieppe was chosen as the site of the experiment. It was believed to be poorly defended. It was militarily irrelevant, as the full invasion would probably not take place near there. And it was just close enough to the English coast to allow a force to cross the Channel in darkness at the height of summer.

The battle was lost before the first landing craft set out. Disagreements on basic matters of strategy were settled by compromise. General, later Field Marshal, Bernard Montgomery, also involved in the planning of the operation, insisted on a frontal attack on the port, believing there would be effective air support. But when the air support was canceled because it was feared that shattered buildings would block roads into the town, the plan for a frontal attack went ahead, anyway.

Two other elements were to be landed several miles east and west of Dieppe, too far away to reach the port in the time allowed for the operation, which was less than a single day. Artillery support for the operation from the sea was known in advance to be too weak to be effective. Perhaps worst of all, there was no clear military objective other than to land, penetrate the town, and stay ashore for some fifteen hours. The German defenses at Dieppe were greatly underestimated.

On August 19, 1942, six thousand troops, most of them untried Canadian units, were sent ashore. The main frontal assault on the port was repulsed, many men dying without even reaching the beaches. Two other landing parties enjoyed minor successes to the east and west but sustained heavy losses before withdrawing. Three thousand were killed or captured in a few hours, and many of those who survived did so because they had been unable to leave their landing craft. One of the Canadian battalions sent in lost all but 65 out of 528 men. In short, it was a debacle.

There remain many unanswered questions about Dieppe. It has been speculated that the Germans knew in advance some of the details of the attack and stepped up their defenses accordingly, but this view is not supported by captured German documents. It is true, however, that a postponement of the original operation from July 4 to August 19 compromised the security of the operation. Several thousand men knew that Dieppe was the target of an attack for several weeks, and word could have reached the Germans. It remains a mystery why a port of no great military value was so heavily defended unless an attack was expected.

Another unanswered question is why Mountbatten allowed the operation to go ahead knowing—as he must have—that artillery support from destroyers off shore was neither accurate nor powerful enough to take out German batteries. It has been suggested that Dieppe was a learning experience, but almost all the lessons had already been learned at some cost elsewhere and should not have needed to be relearned.

There is a strong argument to suggest that Mountbatten and some other Allied commanders knew the raid would fail. Apart from the deficiencies inherent in the operation, a full rehearsal for the assault had taken place at Bridgeport some weeks before and had turned into a disaster. Why, then, did the operation go ahead? One theory is that Mountbatten and Churchill were trying to convince the Germans that the full invasion of France would center on specific ports, and it is true that the Dieppe raid did persuade the Germans to concentrate their defenses around ports that the Allies later avoided.

Many decisions taken in World War II, when civilization itself was under threat, appear callous years later in an altogether different world. Entire nations were engaged in mortal combat. Few in the armed forces, or indeed in civilian life, had the right to expect to survive. If a massive intelligence deception was the reason for the apparent incompetence of the planning for Dieppe, then it can only be said that events ultimately justified it. Mountbatten claimed after the war that for every life lost at Dieppe ten were saved in the invasion of Normandy in 1944.

Arguments raged years later. Montgomery and Mountbatten publicly blamed each other for the catastrophe. On Mountbatten's side, a number of the decisions which led to the raiders being inadequately supported were taken by Montgomery. But the ultimate responsibility for the failure rests with Mountbatten. Lord Beaverbrook, a Canadian, and already an enemy of Mountbatten's, never forgave him for what he saw as the senseless sacrifice of his countrymen's lives. Churchill never blamed Mountbatten and continued to have confidence in him, however. His next promotion was even more spectacular than the last. He was created supreme commander, Southeast Asia.

The British defeat in Burma and Malaya—and particularly in Singapore—had stripped away the aura of invincibility that all Imperial armies must maintain to overawe subject peoples. In 1943, the Far East was a sideshow. The British Fourteenth Army had been called "the Forgotten Army." It was plagued by malaria. For every wounded soldier in the hospital more than one hundred could not fight because they had been afflicted by a tropical disease. The monsoon interrupted every offensive for six months of the year. Morale was low among the ranks. Mountbatten was quick to recognize the three problems—the "3Ms": Monsoon, Malaria, and Morale—and attacked them.

He ordered that the campaign against the Japanese be conducted throughout the monsoon, which was easier to demand than carry out. He launched a health and hygiene campaign that did much to eliminate malaria among British troops, and his flamboyant style helped improve morale. But he was in constant conflict with his commanders. Ultimately, he faced one insuperable problem. The Americans had little interest in helping Britain reconquer her colonies in the Far East as a prologue to the defeat of Japan itself. And Britain needed to physically repossess the colonies in order to retain them after the war.

Mountbatten was the antithesis of a front-line commander. Although he traveled extensively, he conducted the campaign from headquarters first in Delhi, fifteen hundred miles away from the front, then from Kandy, in Ceylon, two thousand miles from the actual battles themselves. His headquarters in Kandy was unashamedly lavish, with a staff of ten thousand, the men drawn mostly from field units where they might have been more useful. His ability to promote himself and his ideas enabled him to claim the ultimate victory of his field commanders as his own victory despite the fact that the defeat of the Japanese in Burma was brought about in precisely the opposite way Mountbatten had intended: by land rather than by sea. His personal plan for a combined maritime offensive never took place. The Japanese, having attempted to break out of Burma to threaten India, were repulsed, pursued, encircled, and destroyed.

After Rangoon had fallen, Mountbatten mounted an operation to invade Malaya, but the Japanese surrender following the bombing of Hiroshima and Nagasaki made that operation irrelevant. Despite Japan's formal surrender on September 2, 1945, Operation Zipper, the invasion of the Malay Peninsula, went ahead one week later. Mountbatten insisted that the Japanese units there would disobey the surrender order. The real point was for Britain to reestablish her pre-Imperial control before partisan organizations claimed independence.

Had it met armed resistance, it turned out, the invasion would have been a debacle. The landing force was bogged down on the beaches that had been inadequately reconnoitered and could have been massacred had a strong Japanese contingent offered resistance. Except for some isolated pockets, the war was already over.

Despite the decorations, honors, and titles, Mountbatten was unhappy. He threatened to refuse the offer of a barony—his noble title from birth already outranked that title—and insisted on a viscountcy, a somewhat greater honor. Other leading commanders had been offered viscountcies, and he felt discriminated against. The title he chose was Lord Mountbatten of Burma, which he did to match his old rival Lord Montgomery of Alamein. For all practical purposes he was still known as Lord Louis Mountbatten. He had to lobby hard to get the coveted

Order of the Garter, an effort which ought to have diminished its worth. Well before the end of the war he had his eyes on a much greater prize, the throne itself. Not for himself, certainly, but for his family. He had for some time set his heart on a Mountbatten dynasty, and his instrument for this purpose was to be his nephew, Prince Philip.

Eighteen

Eyes on the Prize

T he Greek Royal Family was perhaps the most degenerate, certainly the most unstable, arguably the most bizarre, of all the European dynasties. They were not Greek but German-Danish: Schleswig-Holstein-Sonderburg-Glucksburg, of the same line as Edward VII's long-suffering wife, Queen Alexandra. They reigned at the whim of a succession of unstable and often incompetent national governments.

Prince Philip of Greece and Denmark was born on June 10, 1921, on the dining-room table at his parents' dilapidated home in Corfu, a Greek island in the Mediterranean. His father, Prince Andrew, was away fighting the Turks in an action in which his troops were routed and, during a disgraceful retreat, raped, pillaged, and burned villages in their path. His mother, Princess Alice of Battenberg, was the profoundly deaf, thoroughly neurotic older sister of Lord Louis Mountbatten. The labor was a lengthy, agonizing nightmare made more traumatic by the incompetent interventions of the Corfu doctors in attendance. The Prince, the fifth child of the marriage and the only son, was a robust baby but was born into a dynasty that was in its death throes.

Greece had been a dependent of Britain's for years. George I of Greece was Queen Alexandra's brother. In 1913, he was assassinated and succeeded by his eldest son, Constantine. Constantine's wife was Princess Sophie of Prussia, a sister of the Kaiser's, and when World War I broke out, Greece had divided loyalties. Officially neutral, Constantine favored Germany but gave the British and French permission to land troops on Greek territory to attack Greece's old enemy, Turkey. In 1916, however, Constantine and his younger brother, Prince Andrew, ordered the army to attack Allied forces in Greece.

Britain responded by subverting the Greek throne and having Con-

207

stantine deposed. His younger brother, Alexander, utterly uninterested in government or politics, assumed the throne as a puppet of the Greek government. In 1920, Alexander was bitten by a rabid monkey and died, and Constantine was invited back.

Soon after Prince Philip's birth, Prince Andrew became involved in an incident that almost got him executed for cowardice. He was fighting the Turkish army on the Sakharia River when he asked to be allowed to order a retreat. His commander in chief refused. Prince Andrew asked to be replaced. He was told to obey orders and fight on. He disregarded his orders and fell back, returning to Corfu to await events.

When Prince Philip was fourteen months old, in August 1922, the monarchy in Greece finally collapsed. Constantine abdicated in favor of his son, George, and the army staged a coup. The Greek Royals appealed to the British for asylum in Malta but were refused because King Constantine and Prince Andrew were still despised for their attack on the Allies in 1916. But King George V still regarded the Greek Royals as his family. George I had been his uncle, so Constantine and the other Greek Princes were his cousins. He had no wish to see them all executed, as the Czar's family had been. So while the British overtly refused to help, they covertly had the Greeks shipped to Sicily with the connivance of Mussolini.

For reasons best known to himself, Prince Andrew refused to go with the other Royals and stayed in Corfu. He was arrested and taken to Athens to be tried for treason for his ignominious behavior some months earlier. While he was in custody, the prime minister and former cabinet of King Constantine were ordered by a revolutionary junta to dress in full diplomatic uniforms of morning coats, top hats, and breeches and to be taken to a wall and shot.

It seemed only a matter of time before Prince Andrew himself would be executed, but British officials, on the orders of King George V, sent an emissary from the Vickers Munitions Company to bribe the members of the junta. Prince Andrew was tried and made a cringing confession, but instead of being killed, he was exiled with his entire household. A British ship took them to Italy in December 1922. Prince Philip was then eighteen months old.

Life turned into an aimless, wandering exile for the Greek Royals. Philip was raised by his nurse to speak English as his first language, German as a second, and to use sign language to communicate with his deaf mother. He spoke no Greek. During the years of exile, much of it in Paris, his mother drifted into a neurotic religious obsession and became a recluse. His father left for Monaco, financially supported by the wealthier branches of the family. His sisters were sent to Darmstadt to be raised by the family's German relatives. Philip lived variously with his uncle Prince Christopher and his American wife, Anastasia; his nymphomaniacal aunt, Princess Marie Bonaparte; his English uncle, the pornography collector, the Marquess of Milford Haven and his wife, Nadeja; and most significantly, with Lord Mountbatten.

There are many paths through life and many crossroads. For Philip, one route might have taken him back to Greece and the throne. He was still a serious contender as late as 1947. Another might have taken him to Germany, where his sisters were to marry men who were to become leading Nazis. Princess Margarita had married Prince Gottfried von Hohenloe-Langenberg; Princess Theodora married Gottfried, Margrave of Baden; Princess Cecelia married Georg Donatus, Grand Duke of Hesse; and Princess Sophie had married Prince Christoph von Hesse. That path would certainly have taken him into the Nazi armed forces. But the route he eventually took, guided by Mountbatten, led him to Buckingham Palace as the husband of Queen Elizabeth.

Philip was educated at an American school in Paris and at an English preparatory school at Cheam, Surrey, but in 1934, for his secondary education, he was sent to Schloss Salem, a German school founded by Kurt Hahn. Hahn was a German intellectual whose intelligence work in World War I had led the German navy to believe that the American transatlantic liner *Lusitania* was carrying munitions. The sinking of the *Lusitania* in 1916 was one of the events that led America into the war.

Hahn's curriculum emphasized physical education at the expense of academic achievement. A Jew, Hahn left Germany before Prince Philip's arrival there, but his grueling curriculum of sexual repression, meditation, cross-country runs, and forced marches survived. Ironically Hahn's program became the inspiration of the Strength Through Joy regimen, the keystone of Nazi education. It has been claimed that Prince Philip refused to give the Nazi salute while at the school, but this seems unlikely. While he was there, he was close to his brother-in-law Prince Gottfried, who had become an ardent Nazi.

After one year at the school, Prince Philip transferred to Gordonstoun, the sister institution Hahn founded in Scotland. It was a mirror image of Schloss Salem, but without the Nazi banners and Hitler salutes. Clearly Philip came to believe in Hahn's Strength Through Joy principles. He ultimately sent his own sons to the school. Prince Philip emerged from Gordonstoun a striking young man with perfect Nordic looks and physique, emphasized by his blond hair and piercing blue eyes. He had a love of all outdoor—what were then called "manly"— pursuits and a contempt for anything that smacked of intellectualism.

His character was honed by tragedy. Apart from his father's disgrace and his mother's neurotic eccentricity, his sister Cecilia and brother-in-law Grand Duke Georg Donatus von Hesse had been killed in a plane crash. His uncle, the Marquess of Milford Haven, had died from cancer.

His princely title and his uncertain future made him a target of wealthy parents looking to improve the bloodstock. He enjoyed relationships with the American heiress and debutante Cobina Wright and with Princess Alexandra, a cousin. But as early as 1937, Mountbatten, who had no sons, was scheming to marry him to the then Princess Elizabeth, whose father, King George VI, had then been on the throne for only a few months. Princess Elizabeth was then only eleven years old; Prince Philip, sixteen.

Princess Elizabeth's secure childhood contrasts sharply with the upheaval, insecurity, and insanity that permeated Prince Philip's upbringing. Princess Elizabeth—known to her family as Lilibet—was born in 1926 to the then Duke and Duchess of York. It was a year of civil strife in Britain, caused by widespread industrial unrest culminating in a general strike.

When she was only two months old, Scotland Yard was informed of a plot to kidnap the Princess and murder her mother. Detectives stepped up security at their home at 17 Bruton Street, off Berkeley Square in London, a house owned by the Duchess's family. Some days later, a man was arrested on the grounds of Buckingham Palace uttering various threats against the Princess.

Almost all those who have attempted violence against the Royal Family have been dismissed as madmen, and James Burke was no exception. He was committed to an insane asylum. But Scotland Yard believed there was a serious plot against the future Queen. There were a million unemployed, millions more living in foul, unsanitary, and hopeless conditions, and active anarchist cells operated in London. Scores were secretly arrested and questioned, but no one was charged.

When Elizabeth was four, her mother gave birth to another daughter, Margaret Rose. The two became very close, although they had very different personalities. Princess Elizabeth was the more serious of the two; Margaret was boisterous and *méchant*. Princess Elizabeth was precocious and self-consciously Royal. Princess Margaret was rather more informal and playful.

Little reality was allowed to enter their closeted world of privilege. They rarely mixed with other children and were educated by tutors. In the normal course of events, they might have looked forward to a life of continued wealth and privilege, devoid of responsibility, on the comfortable periphery of the Royal Family. But when the abdication crisis thrust the Duke of York onto the throne, Princess Elizabeth suddenly became heir presumptive. And with the Duchess of York unable to bear more children—a younger brother would have taken precedence—for all practical purposes she was heir apparent. The knowledge made her more self-conscious and precocious than ever.

The prospect of a future Queen Regnant meant that the dynastic name of Windsor would one day change with her marriage and accession. Mountbatten was fired by the idea that the new dynastic name would be his own almost from the moment the Duke of York became King George VI. And he took immediate steps to bring it about by seeing to it that his Greek nephew became an English officer and gentleman.

Mountbatten encouraged Prince Philip to join the Royal Navy over the objections of his father, Prince Andrew, and other Greek relatives who insisted he join the Greek navy. Although he was a foreign national, at the request of Mountbatten, the King asked the Royal Naval College at Dartmouth to accept him. In 1939, Prince Philip met Princess Elizabeth for the first time during a Royal visit to Dartmouth. They had both been present at a number of earlier functions but had not been formally introduced. Again urged by Mountbatten, he continued to write to her throughout the war.

There was nothing casual about his correspondence. Lord Mountbatten made it clear to him that the Princess would one day be Queen and that there were only a handful of men on the planet she would be allowed to even consider marrying. One was Prince Charles of Luxembourg. There were two Danish Princes, Olaf and Gorn, who were practical possibilities. And there was the teenaged grandson of the Kaiser and a clutch of other German Princes, but looming war with Germany would make that impossible.

Prince Philip was the front-runner, and Mountbatten told him he should make himself her friend. Even before their first meeting in 1939,

Mountbatten had discussed the match with Philip's uncle, King George II of Greece, who had been restored to the throne. George II had spent much of his exile in London. His enthusiasm was enhanced in the years to come when Prince Philip became a potential rival claimant to his throne, a rank he would have to give up if he became the consort. Mountbatten had only to overcome George VI's likely objections and the fix would be on.

On several occasions during the war, well before the idea was presented either to King George VI or Princess Elizabeth, Prince Philip told intimates that he would marry the next Queen of England. Nobody at that stage considered the Princess's aspirations in a husband.

Prince Philip's war record was commendable without being exceptional. Mountbatten was torn between trying to guarantee his nephew's survival while at the same time offering him a chance to win laurels. In 1940 he was assigned to troop convoys from Australia aboard the HMS *Ramillies*. While in Australia he and other officers of the *Ramillies* visited a notorious house of prostitution. When the *Ramillies* later entered the Mediterranean, he was forced to leave the ship, since he was a citizen of a neutral country.

A few months later, Greece was invaded, and Lord Mountbatten pulled strings to allow his nephew to stay in the Royal Navy rather than have to join the Greek armed forces. He was assigned to the battleship HMS *Valiant* and saw action against the Italian navy in the Battle of Matapan. Lt. Prince Philip R.N., as he was known, was mentioned in dispatches. His granddaughter, Zara, is named after one of the Italian ships sunk in that action.

The HMS *Valiant* fought again in the Battle of Crete and was badly damaged by a bomb. Prince Philip was unhurt. In 1942 he was second in command of the destroyer HMS *Wallace*, the youngest second in command in the Royal Navy. At Christmas the following year he had an opportunity to renew his friendship with Princess Elizabeth. When he had last met her, she was little more than a child, Now, at seventeen, she was a young woman and he a young and daring warrior. Just about every British woman at that time had a husband or a lover in combat, and to have Philip to write to and worry about made her feel more a part of the war and more adult than her years.

In 1944, Prince Philip and Princess Elizabeth began to see each other often. He was regularly invited for weekends to Windsor Castle and to numerous other functions and special occasions which demanded that

Princess Elizabeth have an escort. Her access to other escorts was strictly limited by protocol, and this dashing, handsome, and somewhat wayward man, a Prince in his own right, into whose company she was thrown, inevitably attracted her. Exactly what his feelings were for her are uncertain. When he was not at the palace or at Windsor, he was availing himself of the nightlife in London with a variety of other young women.

War had actually done very little to damage the social life of the elite in London. If anything, the threat of air raids, death in combat, and the shortage of eligible men had made wealthy Londoners more promiscuous, more intent on having a good time when there was a good time to be had. It was eat, drink, and be merry, for tomorrow, perhaps even tonight, we die. The band always played on.

In 1944, British intelligence agents began keeping Prince Philip under surveillance. As a foreign national in British uniform, he would have deserved some attention. As a man whose family still had extensive German relatives and contacts, he merited further watching. But as a possible husband of a future Queen, it was deemed crucial that his every move be noted. An extensive file began to be compiled, noting other girlfriends, visits to their apartments, and appearances at nightclubs and the theater.

Regular reports were made to the Foreign Office and, through their senior civil servants, to the King. He did not like what he read and did not consider Prince Philip, whom he regarded as something of a playboy, even a libertine, a suitable husband for his daughter. At first, Mountbatten did not seem worried. Princess Elizabeth was only eighteen in 1944, and it was unlikely she would marry before she was twenty-one. George II of Greece, guest of the King one night at Buckingham Palace, unwisely mentioned how fond Princess Elizabeth and Prince Philip had become of each other. He began to speculate whimsically as to the benefits of a further marital alliance between their two already related families. King George VI cut him off. "Philip had better not think about it anymore at present. They're both too young."

George II was upset and told Mountbatten about the exchange. Mountbatten admonished him for speaking up too soon and told him to let him handle the future negotiations. Meanwhile, the romance at least was still on, and Prince Philip was still the front-runner.

Mountbatten did not underestimate the problems ahead, however. The British public was only vaguely aware of Prince Philip's past and his Nazi connections through his sisters. It would take some subtle diplomacy to prevent newspapers from making the matter an issue. Then there was Philip's relatives, among them his mother, Princess Alice, who wanted her son to claim the Greek throne. That would make marriage impossible.

There was also the issue of citizenship. Prince Philip was still a Greek, although he was carrying a Danish diplomatic passport. He would have to take British citizenship, but neither he nor Mountbatten wanted to trigger speculation about the reasons for doing so too soon.

Even Prince Philip's name was a problem. After nearly six exhausting years of war against Germany, the British people were not likely to be overjoyed by the prospect of a new dynasty named Schleswig-Holstein-Sonderburg-Glucksburg.

Prince Philip was starting to get worried, too. His father, Prince Andrew, had died in Monaco at the end of 1944, leaving his only son a handful of mementos. Prince Philip had few close relatives left. He was as keenly aware as Mountbatten of the problems in securing the marriage over the objections of the King. But he also knew that his uncle's interest in him would diminish considerably if he failed to win the Princess. He had never been to the university. He despised the Greeks and Greek government and had no interest in claiming the Greek throne, as his mother wished him to do.

Even if he had, there would have been almost insurmountable problems, for there were others with more substantial claims than he. His only career was in the Royal Navy. He would lose that career if he remained a Greek citizen because foreign nationals would be asked to resign the service once peace came. His prospects depended almost entirely on a good marriage. All he could do now was wait.

Nineteen

Walking With Death

T he long war years had strained the King's health. He tired easily. His speeches were more halting than ever. He battled fits of depression. He was shocked by the Conservative defeat in the general election of 1945 and pessimistic about the prospects for the future. With his depression came more uncontrollable fits of temper. His pessimism was well founded. The celebrations that greeted the end of the war gave way to a troubled reality. Economically exhausted, Britain by 1947 faced an economic crisis, with more than 2 million unemployed and its citizens experiencing desperate fuel, food, clothing, and housing shortages. Bread was rationed, and taxes were punitive. The situation was made all the more miserable by a bitterly cruel winter.

Peace had brought a sense of victory and security to Britain that disguised the process of steady political and economic decline that lay ahead. Millions lived in nineteenth-century homes with no bathrooms. Hundreds of thousands of homes had been destroyed or severely damaged by German air raids. In a desperate bid to create housing for 5 million people, factories churned out temporary homes, known as "pre fabs." Some were still occupied as late as the mid-1980s. The victors took much longer to recover from the war than the vanquished. While the industrial base and urban infrastructure of Germany had been totally destroyed and had to be entirely rebuilt with American and British help, Britain's infrastructure had only been damaged and was patched up as inexpensively as possible. Children born years after the war ended could still see the evidence of the savage conflict around them—shells of buildings, water-filled craters, and sealed air-raid shelters.

Britain entered the postwar world with a prewar outlook as well as antiquated housing and machinery. Part of that prewar outlook was the attitude concerning Empire. Conservatives in Britain believed that the nations of the Empire and Commonwealth would continue to live in thrall of British supremacy. But the war had only sharpened the determination of nationalist forces to secure independence. As a result, a series of unsuccessful police actions took place in Africa, the Mediterranean, the Middle East, India, and the Far East. The first to go was India. In 1947, Lord Mountbatten was sent to India as viceroy, charged with arranging for the independence of India within a year. His wife, Edwina, was soon having an affair with Nehru, one of the leading opponents of Britain in Gandhi's Congress party, while Mountbatten himself struggled to reconcile the rival religious sects, his own position as representative of King and Emperor, his practical task of bringing peaceful independence, and the turmoil in his marriage.

King George VI had always been aware that peace would bring serious social and political problems to Britain and the empire. He realized that the peace had been lost after World War I and was interested in any plans to ensure peace and prosperity following World War II. In this endeavor, he was more forward looking than his ministers. He had distrusted the Russians and opposed the refusal of Britain and the United States to consider a separate peace with Germany in the closing months of the war. He believed the readiness of Britain and the United States to trust Russia had led to the enslavement of Eastern Europe.

The King was only fifty-two in 1947, but he was prematurely old. He undertook a grueling state visit to South Africa that year and returned seventeen pounds lighter. He looked tired and emaciated. During a speech at a state banquet that May he broke down in a fit of coughing to the consternation of witnesses. Always frail, a heavily addicted smoker, as his father and grandfather had been, he and others believed he was dying. His wife, Queen Elizabeth, who had always been the driving force behind the frail, shy King, increasingly bore his responsibilities, advising him on matters of state, interpreting his wishes, keeping his schedule as undemanding as she could, and to all intents and purposes, ruling in his name.

It was time to give some thought to the succession. Princess Elizabeth would one day be Queen; very soon she would be one of the youngest in history. There were, of course, no male heirs, and if some tragedy were to befall Princess Elizabeth, Princess Margaret was only sixteen. After Margaret, the next in line to the throne would be Prince Henry, Duke of Gloucester. The King's youngest brother was a man of few talents and limited intellect, someone who the Duke of Windsor said could only recognize the national anthem because everybody stood up. It would be better for Princess Elizabeth to marry and hopefully have an heir herself as soon as possible, preferably before she became Queen.

Mountbatten and Prince Philip had met with the King several times in 1946, and King George VI listened to Prince Philip's case. Mountbatten said that Princess Elizabeth had shown little interest in anyone other than Prince Philip and apparently loved him. The Prince, Mountbatten added, was in love with Princess Elizabeth. He had proposed to her, and she had accepted, subject to her parents' consent. The King expressed his fears about Prince Philip's character and said he was not certain he could be faithful. Mountbatten tried to reassure him.

When the King persisted in his reluctance, Mountbatten coolly went over the other candidates, some of whom the Princess had never met and was unlikely to meet. The list was even shorter than at the start of the war. Among them was Prince Rainier of Monaco, a Catholic, who would have to renounce his faith and possibly his own throne. There were a clutch of German Princes that King George VI did not need to be told were out of the question so soon after the war. Some of the German Princes were already subjects of the King: Viscount Althorp, the Earl of Airlie, the Duke of Rutland, and Lord Euston.

The King had no objection to the Princess marrying a subject and a non-Royal. He had done so himself and never regretted it for an instant. But he knew that he had only been able to do so without objection because at the time of his marriage he had never been expected to succeed to the throne. He was very close to his eldest daughter, an unusually healthy emotion for a member of the Royal Family, in which parent-child relationships—particularly with the eldest child—are almost invariably stormy.

The King was heartbroken at the thought of "losing" his daughter to another man. But the last thing he wanted was for the Princess to be unhappy or for her marriage to become the focus of political controversy, which was likely to happen if she waited until she became Queen to get married. And once she was Queen, meeting a man and developing a relationship would be even more difficult than it had been as a Princess.

Prince Philip was himself controversial. The marriage would mean that the next Queen of England would have marital ties to a gaggle of former Nazis. Mountbatten countered that Prince Philip could hardly help who his sisters had married. He believed the press, with the possible exception of Lord Beaverbrook, would cooperate by not making too much of Prince Philip's in-laws, any more than they pointed out which Nazis were related to the King by blood, as the Duke of Coburg had been.

There is no doubt that Princess Elizabeth was enraptured by Prince Philip, who was of the right age and rank, whom she knew well, and who had no other political ties, as another foreign Prince might have had. He was an assertive and charismatic figure, and she admired him. They had interests in common, particularly horses, although the Princess's tastes ran to horse racing and the Prince's to polo and equestrianism. But she was also a pragmatic person. She knew that Philip knew how to adapt to his future role, that he understood what was expected of him and had no outside interests likely to clash with her future role as monarch. It was neither a passionate love match nor an arranged marriage. Rather, it was a marriage that fell between the two and had some of the characteristics of both. Princess Elizabeth told her father she was determined to marry him.

The King still had concerns, not the least of which included the fact that the Princess and Prince Philip were blood relatives—third cousins to be precise. The question of inbreeding in the Royal Family had been on the King's mind because of the shame and embarrassment felt in the family over two relatives of Queen Elizabeth, his wife. They were Nerissa and Katherine Bowes-Lyon, daughters of the Queen's brother, John Bowes-Lyon, and his wife, Fenella Trefusis. Both mentally handicapped, they had been placed in a Victorian-era mental institution, Royal Earlswood Hospital, in Surrey, in 1941, when they were in their teens. It was a private family tragedy for the Bowes-Lyons, but it had been kept secret because the King and Queen feared there would be talk of bad blood and recessive genes in the Royal Family. For similar reasons, the King's own brother, John, suffered from epilepsy and had been shut away until his early death. Many years later, the treatment of the sisters would become a scandal of sizable proportions.

After some reassurance that there was no question of any genetic difficulties ahead, the King agreed that if Princess Elizabeth still wanted to marry Prince Philip when the Royal Family returned from South Africa, she could do so. Mountbatten was delighted. He then played his trump card. Prince Philip would need to become a British citizen, and obviously Princess Elizabeth would take his name after the wedding.

Schleswig-Holstein-Sonderburg-Glucksburg, Philip's legal surname, was clearly unsuitable. He should change his name to something more appropriate. One name suggested was Oldcastle, an Anglicized version of Oldenburg, an ancient German ducal title to which Prince Philip was distantly related. Oldcastle had also been put forward to George V during the debate over the change of name from Saxe-Coburg Gotha.

Behind the scenes, Mountbatten, Philip's uncle, subtly began to lobby in the College of Heralds for something with a little more panache. His mother's maiden name was suggested. Princess Alice had never changed her name from Battenberg, so that was ruled out. But clearly Lord Mountbatten believed they were on the right track. He had a friend at the College of Heralds suggest the name Mountbatten to the home secretary, Chuter Ede, which gave Mountbatten the opportunity to say modestly that it had not been his idea. The King agreed.

Mountbatten was naturally overjoyed, since that was the name he had wanted all along. Prince Philip was not as enthusiastic as his uncle with the suggestion. He had not used his old surname, preferring simply "Philip," and the name Mountbatten meant very little to him. But he could not think of anything better, and so he agreed.

The citizenship and name change had been accomplished by the time the Royal Family returned from South Africa. With the citizenship change, Prince Philip lost his Greek Royal title and rank, though not, incidentally, his place in the Greek line of succession.

One hitch remained: Widespread speculation about a future husband for Princess Elizabeth appeared in the press, and an opinion poll suggested that a large minority of Britons did not want a Prince from a foreign power to marry the future Queen. Mountbatten and his nephew met with the editors of the fiercely patriotic Beaverbrook newspapers and persuaded them to carry features stressing "Lt. Philip Mountbatten's" British background, his service in the navy, and his war record in return for leaks on various matters of social and political gossip. Despite Lord Beaverbrook's personal enmity toward Mountbatten, stories singing his virtues were published.

The announcement of the wedding of the future Queen, twenty-one, and the Prince, twenty-six, was made on June 10, 1947, but with no proposed wedding date. The King wanted another year to pass, but the Princess, asserting herself finally, insisted that they had waited long enough. If the wedding was going to take place, it should do so the following November.

Not all Britons greeted the prospect of the future Queen's marriage to Prince Philip with joy. Many possessed a xenophobic distaste for the Greeks, which, ironically, Prince Philip shared. Something, but not much, was known of his German associations. A compliant press had suppressed the extent of his Nazi connections. If the attention and unrestrained criticism leveled against the Royal Family today had been prevalent then, the marriage would not have taken place. Prince Philip never shook off the nickname "Phil the Greek," regardless of how British he had become.

As the date neared, the first Royal wedding of such historic significance generated intense excitement. Because of the gloomy atmosphere of austerity and restraint, the public needed a public celebration. There was surprisingly little resentment of the enormous expense involved. The wedding dress, designed by Norman Hartnell, was studded with ten thousand pearls. The cake consisted of a vast structure decorated with significant events in the lives of both the bride and groom and included a depiction of the Battle of Matapan, in which Prince Philip had fought. The couple were showered with priceless jewels: a hoard of rubies from Burma; emeralds and diamonds from British Columbia; uncut diamonds from South Africa; and similar presents from all over the Commonwealth. Individual admirers also sent lavish gifts of jewelry, among them a single 54-carat uncut diamond.

Queen Mary gave the couple the gifts she had herself been given fifty-five years before, including a diamond tiara of inestimable worth from Queen Victoria and priceless diamond brooches that had been given to her by a Maharajah. The King gave them hundred-year-old earrings that featured every cut of diamond and flawless antique pearls once worn by Queen Anne.

There was much wrangling over the invitation list. Those not included were as significant as those who were. Prince Philip was forbidden to invite his sisters, because they were married to former Nazis, or his former Gordonstoun tutor Kurt Hahn, who had reclaimed Schloss Salem and installed Prince Philip's brother-in-law, Prince George of Hanover, as principal. The Queen Mother refused to have the Duchess of Windsor at the wedding, and that meant that the Duke of Windsor could not be invited. But there was to be no shortage of European Royalty present: Kings, Queens, and Princes from Denmark, Norway, Rumania, Greece, Holland, Sweden, Yugoslavia, and Iraq.

On the wedding day itself, November 20, 1947, Prince Philip suffered from an acute hangover, which he attempted to quash with gin. He and Lord Mountbatten, and many of the Prince's friends, had been at a riotous stag party at the Dorchester Hotel until close to dawn. The public was informed that morning that Philip had been awarded a string of titles and honors. He became His Royal Highness, Duke of Edinburgh, Earl of Merioneth, and Baron Greenwich—Scottish, Welsh, and English titles, respectively.

A series of petty catastrophes, which seem to dog royal occasions despite months of preparation, occurred on the morning of the wedding. Shortly before Princess Elizabeth was scheduled to leave Buckingham Palace, she decided to wear the priceless pearl necklace her parents had given her, but it was on display, along with other gifts, some distance away, at St. James Palace. John Colville, her private secretary, rushed from the palace and commandeered the state limousine of King Haakon of Norway. The car soon slowed to a crawl in the crowds on the Mall, and Colville had to push his way through on foot. At St. James's, officials refused to hand over the pearls. Detectives finally agreed to allow three police officers to take them to the palace.

Back at the palace, Princess Elizabeth's tiara broke while she was putting it on—an incident taken as a bad omen—and a substitute had to be found. And finally, the bridal bouquet was feared lost until, after a frantic search, it turned up in a refrigerator.

The aging dowager Queen Mary led the procession of Royals from Buckingham Palace down the Mall amid roaring crowds to Westminster Abbey. They were accompanied by Life Guards and Horse Guards in dress uniforms, plumed headdresses, and flashing swords and spurs that had not been worn for years. Although some economies had been observed, the British could enjoy the most magnificent Royal display anyone had seen since the Coronation—only ten years before, now a world away for millions of Britons. There were street parties and festivities across the nation, and millions heard the wedding service, conducted by the archbishop of Canterbury, Geoffrey Fisher, live on radio, the first live broadcast of a Royal event. Bells pealed across London and in every city, town, and village of the kingdom.

The celebrations reached a crescendo after the bride and groom left Westminster Abbey. The crowds broke through the police cordon after the procession had passed on the return to the palace. As the last coach and the final phalanx of red-uniformed guards passed through the palace gates, the crowds surged around the iron fence of the palace, thousands deep, and roared, cheered, sang, and chanted until the whole Royal Family appeared—the Princess in her magnificent wedding dress, Prince Philip in his naval uniform and wearing his grandfather's, Prince Louis of Battenberg's, ceremonial sword. Both were flanked by the King in full admiral's uniform, the Queen, Lord Mountbatten, and scores of relatives bearing the premier Royal and Ducal titles of Britain and Europe.

The short honeymoon was spent at Lord Mountbatten's estate, Broadlands, but there was little privacy. Press photographers and reporters camped outside the walls, tried to follow them on horseback, and climbed into trees to catch a glimpse of them and snap an exclusive picture. They filled the pews of a local church where the honeymoon couple were expected to attend services. There were some angry exchanges between some photographers and the Prince. The age of the paparazzi was dawning. Relations between the press and the Royal Family had started to change, from compliant admiration and respectful distance to intrusion and frustration.

The couple began their domestic life in apartments in Clarence House, an immense mansion just yards down the Mall from Buckingham Palace; it is something of a Royal Family apartment building with a variety of palatial suites. By February 1948, within three months of the wedding, the Princess was pregnant, although the public was not informed until June. With the King's health steadily deteriorating and Princess Elizabeth's condition delicate, many Royal duties fell upon Prince Philip or seventeen-year-old Princess Margaret. Princess Margaret handled them with aplomb; Prince Philip, with less grace. Formal occasions made him bad-tempered. He hated speeches, had contempt for the general public, and despised the press.

On November 12, 1948, just a week short of her first wedding anniversary, Princess Elizabeth, twenty-two, gave birth to a golden-haired seven-pound-six-ounce son in the Buhl Suite of Buckingham Palace, temporarily converted for the occasion into a labor room and nursery. It was a mercifully short labor, just two hours. Princess Elizabeth, like others in her family, believes strongly in homeopathic medicine, and she was assisted by a homeopathic physician, herbal remedies for pain, and relaxation techniques. One tradition attached to Royal births that had been a source of irritation and humiliation for some years was broken in the case of the newborn Prince.

The home secretary, the British minister responsible for internal security, traditionally attended the birth of Royal children. The King had been annoyed by the custom when his own children were born. In the case of his daughter's firstborn he insisted that the tradition be dropped. The child was to be named Charles Philip Arthur George— Philip after his father and Arthur after a beloved uncle, the Duke of Connaught, Queen Victoria's last surviving son, who had died in 1942. George was, of course, a traditional family name as well as England's patron saint.

David was omitted so as not to give the impression that another David—Duke of Windsor—was being honored. But the choice of Charles was also unusual. The name Charles had not been used in the family for generations. Charles I had been executed. Charles, Duke of Albany and Saxe-Coburg Gotha had been a prominent Nazi. Furthermore, the word "Charley" connotes idiocy in colloquial English.

The stated explanation was that Charles was simply Princess Elizabeth's favorite name. But there is another explanation. Philip's favorite nephew, son of his sister Sophie and her first husband, Christoph von Hesse, was named Charles Adolph, the latter name after Hitler. Despite the rapidly changing relationship between the Royal Family and the press, no one pointed out this connection.

The unusual choice of names did nothing to diminish the national jubilation at the first birth of a male direct heir to the throne in the twentieth century. A massed artillery salute in Hyde Park echoed off the façades of buildings across London; the fountains in Trafalgar Square spurted blue-dyed water; bonfires were lit on hilltops across the country to carry the news in medieval tradition; the bells of St. Paul's Cathedral, Westminster Cathedral, and Westminster Abbey pealed continuously for hours. The stability of the Royal Family, it seemed, was assured for another generation. Symbolic of this enduring stability was the present the eighty-two-year-old Queen Mary gave to the new Prince. It was a silver goblet, a gift, she pointed out, bought by her great-grandfather George III, which she happily passed on to her own great-grandson.

Prince Philip felt confined by palace life and bored by his desk job at the Admiralty. He demanded an overseas naval posting and an eventual command. Princess Elizabeth, for the time being the dutiful wife, went with him to Malta, where she became pregnant with her second child. Anne Elizabeth Alice Louise was born on August 15, 1950. Anne was chosen because Philip, hoping for a boy, had wanted to name him Andrew. Elizabeth and Alice were for the child's maternal grandparents and Louise for Louis Mountbatten.

It was an idyllic period for both Prince Philip and Princess Elizabeth. Ordinary people dream of being celebrities, even Royal. Royalty fantasize about being ordinary people. Away from Britain and the constraints of palace life, they could live more as ordinary people do. Princess Elizabeth, as far as she could, shared the lives of other navy wives. Prince Philip, in command of his own vessel at last, pursued his naval career. But it was a short-lived idyll. In 1951, realizing the King had not long to live, they returned to Britain.

That spring, King George VI developed a harsh, hacking cough and the symptoms of influenza. He looked so ill that there was widespread public concern, but surprisingly, efforts to treat him proceeded at what today would be regarded as a leisurely pace. His favorite homeopathic remedies were tried with little result, and antibiotics also failed. It was not until September that a radiologist, Dr. George Cordiner, discovered a growth on his left lung and suggested a bronchoscopy. The bronchoscopy confirmed a malignant tumor.

A leading thoracic surgeon, Dr. Clement Price-Thomas, performed the operation to remove the tumor on September 23, 1951, in the same suite at Buckingham Palace where Princess Elizabeth had given birth to Prince Charles. He found he had to remove the lung and part of the larynx. It was clear that the cancer had already spread to the King's right lung, too.

The surgery took place as a crowd of some five thousand people gathered at the gates of Buckingham Palace awaiting the bulletin on the King's health. When it was posted on the gates, the anxious crowd pushed through the police cordon, and it took forty-five minutes to restore order. They filed by in twos until late into the night, peering at the terse notice, which said very little, only that his condition was "satisfactory." The Queen and other members of the Royal Family, some leading courtiers, the prime minister, Clement Attlee, and Winston Churchill, then the leader of the opposition Conservative party, were told the truth—that the King was terminally ill and was unlikely to live more than a year. Apart from his inevitable death from lung cancer, there was the strong likelihood of a heart attack, which could occur at any moment. The King was not told of either prognosis.

The public was given the impression that the operation had proved a success and that the King would get well. A national day of thanksgiving was proclaimed to celebrate a recovery which, of course, had never taken place, with the key participants, the archbishop of Canterbury, the prime minister, and several members of the Royal Family, going through the pretense that the King was not dying. The Christmas broadcast that year, at the insistence of the Queen, was prerecorded for the first time. The King could barely speak above a whisper and had to force himself to disguise the weakness of his voice. For hours the BBC engineers taped a few words at a time until the broadcast of just a few minutes in length could be edited together from dozens of takes. Even then, the King's voice sounded husky, his breath short.

By the New Year of 1952, spent, as usual, at Sandringham, the King was making plans for a visit to South Africa to convalesce. He appeared to believe he was recovering and insisted that Princess Elizabeth and Prince Philip proceed with plans to visit East Africa, Australia, and New Zealand in February. On January 30, the King, Queen, Princess Elizabeth, Prince Philip, and Princess Margaret went to a performance of *South Pacific* in the West End, and the following day they drove to Heathrow Airport to bid farewell to Princess Elizabeth and Prince Philip.

Returning to Sandringham, the King spent several active days shooting on his private estate. On February 5 he and several other hunters shot 280 hares. He spent a quiet evening with the Queen and Princess Margaret and went to bed at 10:30 P.M. His valet, James MacDonald, found him dead the next day, He had had a heart attack during the night. The Queen and King George VI had separate bedroom suites, and she ran down the corridor to his room in tears when she was told the news. Princess Margaret locked herself in her own room and refused to come out for hours.

Palace and government officials have a prearranged code word for the sudden death of the monarch so that the news can be spread quickly and secretly to all corners of the Establishment. That morning, telephones rang all over London's Whitehall, in government offices, at the home of the prime minister, and elsewhere, and voices declared: "Hyde Park Corner! Hyde Park Corner!" Winston Churchill, who had become prime minister again a few weeks earlier, broke down and wept when he was told.

In the streets of London, people openly expressed their grief, an unusual response for the reserved British. Traffic stopped as the news spread. People climbed out of taxis and off buses to stand in the street and weep, and a somber crowd gathered outside Buckingham Palace. The Queen, his widow, was inconsolable. Despite knowing that his death could not be long delayed, she had convinced herself in his last weeks that he was growing stronger and that they would have several more months together at least before the end came.

A newspaper reporter gave the word to palace officials who were with Princess Elizabeth and Prince Philip. They were staying at the exotic Treetops Hotel in the Aberdare Forest game reserve. Michael Parker, Prince Philip's equerry, told him, and the Prince broke the news to his wife. However she may have received the news in private, in public she appeared calm and composed. And she was now Queen, at twenty-five. Arrangements were made to fly home immediately.

Her plane was met at Heathrow by her uncles the Duke of Gloucester and Lord Mountbatten and by Sir Alan Lascelles, who had been the King's private secretary and was now hers. She descended from the plane alone and was greeted by Sir Winston Churchill, who was weeping, and by representatives of each of the three major political parties—the Conservative, Labour, and Liberal.

Given the personal handicaps under which he had labored, George VI had been exceptionally successful. He had taken the Crown reluctantly and under difficult conditions following the abdication crisis. He became a symbol of national strength, unity, and purpose during the war years and was just reaching that point in his life when wisdom and maturity might have been of value to a struggling nation. It has become virtually a slogan of the British Royal Family that they are the symbols of stability in a changing world; it is a phrase often repeated by monarchists when asked about the purpose of the Crown in an age of democracy. George VI was probably more capable of symbolizing that stability than any of his descendants.

The death of the King plunged Britain into the deepest mourning. The King's coffin was placed in the chapel at Sandringham on Saturday, February 9, 1952. Nearly one thousand estate workers, gamekeepers, foresters, and servants filed past in tears. The tears were as much for a vanished era as for the King himself. The last monarch of the Victorian generation, he had actually stood at the old Queen's knee.

The new Queen and Prince Philip arrived the next day and joined the King's mother, Queen Mary, his widow, Queen Elizabeth, to be known as the Queen Mother, Princess Margaret, and other family members for a private service. The following Monday, the coffin was brought by train to London, and in an echo of the funeral of Queen Victoria, thousands solemnly watched the train crawl slowly by on its sad journey.

Hundreds of thousands more filed by the coffin at Westminster Hall in London before the final funeral procession. For once, family rivalries and the bitterness over the abdication crisis were set aside, and the Duke of Windsor was allowed to attend. Windsor, Prince Philip, the dead King's surviving brother, the Duke of Gloucester, and his nephew the Duke of Kent walked behind the gun carriage containing the coffin in the driving rain and sleet and biting cold. The new Queen and the Queen Mother rode in a state coach, their faces heavily veiled. Queen Mary was too ill to attend her son's funeral.

Europe's surviving royalty, now a greatly diminished band, also came: from Norway, Sweden, the Netherlands, Denmark, and Greece. They were a drab and meager bunch compared to the full flower of European Princes who had attended earlier state funerals in what seemed now to be another world. Only the British Crown had retained the full measure of pomp and pageantry, majesty and awe, in their regal displays. In the Royal Family, the continuity of monarchy is paramount. So even as the sleet was forming a white shroud over the coffin of George VI, preparations were being made for the most extravagant and spectacular Royal event in history—the Coronation of Elizabeth II.

Part Five

ELIZABETH II
(1952 to the Present)

Twenty

The Year
of Three Queens

T he reign of Elizabeth II began with an unseemly row over the
family dynastic name, Windsor. Almost no attention had been paid
to Princess Elizabeth's surname after her marriage to Prince Philip. It
was popularly supposed that legally it must be Mountbatten. But as
neither Princess Elizabeth nor Prince Philip had any practical use for a
surname—she signed her name Elizabeth; he signed his Edinburgh—
the question attracted little if any concern inside the family or among
the general public.

But once King George VI died and Princess Elizabeth became Queen,
the issue was raised unwisely by Lord Mountbatten. Had he realized
the opposition such a change in the dynastic name would produce, he
most likely would have been more devious. It did not occur to him that
the surname of the Queen was anything other than her husband's—
Mountbatten. Common sense dictated it. So when, at a party on his
estate, Broadlands, Mountbatten gave a toast, saying "The House of
Mountbatten now reigns," he did not realize he was giving offense or
igniting a fuse.

But when the eighty-five-year-old dowager Queen Mary heard about
the toast, she was furious. She had not acquiesced in the destruction
of the Royal dynasty of Saxe-Coburg Gotha in order to live to see it
replaced by what she continued to refer to scornfully as "the Battenbergs." She wrote to her granddaughter, to the prime minister, and to
the Lord Chancellor insisting that her husband, George V, had proclaimed that the name of the ruling dynasty would be "the House of

Windsor" in perpetuity and could not be changed by what she called "the Battenberg marriage." She poured scorn on what she believed was Mountbatten's upstart aspirations.

Winston Churchill had been Mountbatten's ally throughout the war years, but he had bitterly opposed independence in India and was outraged by Mountbatten's enthusiastic surrender of sovereignty while he was the Labour government's viceroy in India after the war. Churchill saw the issue of the dynastic name as one way to even the score. He supported Queen Mary wholeheartedly.

Lord Mountbatten had to fight a rearguard action. Realizing that it would be out of place to argue for the House of Mountbatten himself, he encouraged Prince Philip to press for it. Philip then wrote to the prime minister, insisting that he had changed his name from Schleswig-Holstein-Sonderburg-Glucksburg specifically because the name would be inconvenient when his wife became Queen. His legal name was Mountbatten; his wife's legal name was therefore Mountbatten, and so was his children's. But, he suggested, to satisfy all parties, the dynastic name of Mountbatten-Windsor might be adopted.

He was supported by Edward Iwi, a leading genealogist, who argued that unless the family formally changed its name to Windsor for a second time, the name of the Royal House must be Mountbatten.

Lord Beaverbrook, Mountbatten's old enemy, learned of the developing battle and warned that his newspapers would mount a no-holds-barred campaign against the use of Mountbatten's name for a new dynasty. Churchill called a cabinet meeting to advise the Queen which name to adopt. But he opted out of the meeting himself, allowing Sir John Colville, the senior civil servant, to preside. The cabinet decided that the name Windsor should be retained.

Queen Elizabeth, with her uncle and husband insisting on Mountbatten and her grandmother, mother, and more important, her government insisting on Windsor, issued a proclamation two months after her accession, in April 1952, announcing that the name of the dynasty would continue to be Windsor for both herself and her heirs. Prince Philip remained angry and felt insulted. There is no record of the arguments that must have taken place between the two other than one telling remark by the Prince: "I'm just a bloody amoeba! That's all!" There's no doubt that the Royal row caused a serious strain on the couple's marriage for several months.

Lord Mountbatten was disappointed by the decision and blamed

Churchill and Beaverbrook's antipathy toward him. He accepted it with grace, however, and bided his time, hoping he might yet get the decision reversed. Meanwhile, he comforted himself with the advice of Iwi and other genealogists that, for a few weeks, anyway, the legal name of the dynasty had been the House of Mountbatten.

Meanwhile, preparations for the Coronation, scheduled for June 2, 1953, continued. At twenty-five, the young Queen was the same age as the sixteenth-century Elizabeth I when she acceded to the throne. Palace officials turned that coincidence into a theme and mounted a campaign to promote the concept of the "New Elizabethans." The Elizabethan era had been a heroic period in British history—the era of Drake and Raleigh and Shakespeare—at least in the popular view. So the new reign was meant to herald a British renaissance in a wide range of endeavors and lift the prevailing atmosphere of postwar despondency. It was short-lived. Britain's economic and political decline was everywhere evident, and no public relations effort could change that reality.

One other event threatened to cast a shadow over the Coronation. Queen Mary's health had been deteriorating for some years. She now had colon cancer and heart problems. The death of her most beloved son, the King, had shattered her morale. Parents never expect to have to bury their children; she had lost three and virtually disowned one. Her age and her weak heart prevented surgeons from operating on her colon, and it was felt she would die before the Coronation or soon after. The question was when. The death of a dowager Queen who represented the last living link with Queen Victoria and who had outlived four monarchs would demand a significant period of official mourning, possibly six months.

As the months dragged on, it was feared that her imminent passing might cause the postponement of the Coronation. If she died a week or two before, her death would have been more than an inconvenience and a disappointment. The Coronation was timed for June to create the maximum revenue for London's tourist industry. A year's schedule had been built around it not only in Britain but in several nations whose heads of state were expected to attend. The last postponement of a Coronation had been in 1902, due to Edward VII's appendicitis. Queen Mary could remember the chaos that delay had caused.

There is circumstantial evidence to suggest that Queen Mary dutifully had herself killed with a drug overdose as the deadline for a postponement drew near. Several times she told cancer specialist Lord

Webb-Johnson and physician Dr. Horace Evans, the doctors who were attending her, that she had no wish to go on living indefinitely and was particularly concerned that any period of mourning for her should not force the postponement of the Coronation. She believed in euthanasia; in fact, as we have seen, she had sanctioned it in the case of her husband, George V.

The drugs prescribed in increasing doses to control her pain were becoming less effective and more dangerous as the amount necessary to relieve her suffering neared the level of fatal overdose. On February 28, 1953, Dr. Evans wrote the Duke of Windsor in the United States that his mother was seriously ill. Evans said that the Queen had told him on numerous occasions that she "had no wish to go on living as an old crock." Evans wrote, "I cannot help feeling that she wants to see you, though she has not said so." The Duke left for Britain on March 6 aboard the transatlantic liner *Queen Elizabeth*—named for the Queen Mother—and arrived five days later.

During the journey, the Duke wrote his wife, Wallis, that his mother had stayed alive this long because "ice in the place of blood in the veins must be a fine preservative." The Duke visited his mother almost every day and was regularly briefed by Dr. Evans on her condition. On March 14, the Duke wrote to Wallis: "It drags on, agonizing for Mama and for all concerned." Several days later, he wrote to her that "there could be absolutely no hope" for recovery, and while she could linger for several more weeks, the only question was how soon she would die.

Queen Mary realized better than anyone the predicament in which her imminent death placed the entire family. She knew she would never be well enough to see her favorite granddaughter crowned and had no wish to ruin the occasion by dying shortly before. Around the middle of March, according to a number of sources, a remarkable and macabre scene took place at Queen Mary's London home, Marlborough House. Queen Elizabeth II visited Queen Mary's deathbed with some of her ceremonial garb and with the Crown of St. Edward, which was to be used in the Coronation. She modeled for her in her regalia so that the old queen would, after all, see her granddaughter wear the Crown of England.

Gordon Winter, a writer and former MI5 field intelligence agent, claimed in 1990 that he had been informed by a member of the Duke of Windsor's staff two days beforehand of the precise time of death of Queen Mary—between ten and eleven o'clock at night on March 24,

1953. He was so convinced that he tried—unsuccessfully—to place a bet on the time of death of the dowager Queen. She did, in fact, die at 10:15 that night. None of the Royal Family were at her side, having taken their leave some hours before. No death certificate was made public, nor was an official cause of death issued. The Duke of Windsor was brought to her bedside a few minutes after her death. It was a death scene similar to that of George V.

The Queen declared two months of mourning, just enough to ensure that the Coronation took place as scheduled. Had Queen Mary lingered just a few days more, a postponement would have been inevitable. There is no hard evidence that Queen Mary was euthanized, as her husband had been. But a family that can sanction a King's mercy killing so his death can make the morning papers can certainly do so when a Coronation is at stake.

It is perhaps telling that the official biographies of Queen Mary contain no details of the circumstances of her death. The palace routinely demanded the right to censor any material from an author who has direct access to the archives at Buckingham Palace and Windsor. When James Pope-Hennessy wrote his biography of Queen Mary, published in 1959, he agreed to allow Queen Elizabeth II's private secretary, Alan Lascelles, to censor it and agreed that even if something scandalous should turn up in the archives, he would not write about it. He devoted only a single line to the death of Queen Mary, recording only the time and date.

The Coronation of Queen Elizabeth II was the most extravagant ever staged. The Queen rehearsed the ceremony repeatedly, determined it would not be marred by mistakes. George V's Coronation service had been preserved on 78 rpm discs, and she listened to them over and over for weeks. A partial film record was viewed by palace officials to make sure that every slip and near mishap would not be repeated.

When it was discovered that the supply of holy oil for the anointing of the monarch by the archbishop of Canterbury had been destroyed in a German air raid in 1940, Prince Philip was given the job of finding the original recipe. Tiny silver stars were affixed to the Crown of St. Edward and the Imperial Crown of state so that they could not be placed back to front. In order to get used to the heavy crowns, Queen Elizabeth began wearing them at her desk.

Norman Hartnell, who had designed the Queen's bridal gown, produced eight different designs for the dress the Queen would wear. She chose a white-and-silver satin gown bearing the diamond-encrusted emblems of Great Britain and all of the Commonwealth dominions. Hartnell also designed the spectacular gowns of every female member of the Royal Family participating in the ceremony.

For the first time, the Coronation would be broadcast live on television. Churchill's government and several advisers to the Queen, including the archbishop of Canterbury, had at first opposed allowing TV cameras in Westminster Abbey. But the Queen, who had more tolerance of the new medium, insisted that television would allow millions who had no concept of what a Coronation looked like to witness the spectacle not only in Britain but throughout the Commonwealth.

In 1953 relatively few families in Britain had television sets, and the BBC broadcast for only a few hours a day. The decision to televise such a historic event brought an immediate social change. Every family who could possibly afford one, and many who could not, bought a TV set and had a better view of the Coronation ceremony than many of the invited guests in Westminster Abbey. The Coronation of Elizabeth II heralded the dawn of the armchair society in Britain.

The presence of cameras also affected the participants. The likelihood that cameras and microphones would magnify any slip increased the pressure to ensure that everything went ahead smoothly. Meticulous attention was even paid to the length of the pile on the carpet used for the aisle of Westminster Abbey. Queen Alexandra's heels had become embedded in the carpet used for the Coronation of Edward VII. The robed peers had caught their hems on the carpet pile in the Coronation of George VI. Such incidents before television cameras would have brought public ridicule. As the television broadcasts of 1953 were in monochrome, the Queen brought in specialists to design makeup that would look attractive in black and white. As a result, the lipstick she wore looked pale blue in the Abbey but natural on television.

The Queen personally signed off on the four-thousand-name guest list. Among them, at Prince Philip's insistence, were his three sisters, but not their former Nazi husbands. That these three women attended the ceremony was discreetly kept from the British public at the time. There was no mention of them or their connections in the newspaper reports of the Coronation.

June is usually a month of bright, sunny weather interrupted by showers in Britain, but on June 2, 1953, a cold, heavy rain persisted. Despite the daunting prospect of being drenched, hundreds of thousands began to gather along the processional route several hours before the scheduled start. Some had camped out along the route all night, singing songs to pass the time and keep up their spirits.

The procession was led by the lord mayor of London in a state coach drawn by six grays and with an honor guard of pikemen. The coaches and open carriages of various heads of state followed. Sir Winston Churchill led a carriage procession of Commonwealth prime ministers. Then came the carriages of the members of the Royal Family: Princess Margaret, looking radiant; the widowed Queen Elizabeth, who now took the title Queen Mother, in charge of Prince Charles; and finally, the gold state coach carrying Prince Philip and Queen Elizabeth II. Nearly twenty-nine thousand soldiers in full dress uniform either rode or marched in the procession or lined sections of the route.

The Abbey was an explosion of red, white, and gold—banners, gowns, and ermine-trimmed robes. A shaft of light fell on the ceremonial throne through the vast stained-glass windows. A four-hundred-voice choir sang, apart from traditional works, new works by six prominent British composers.

At last, when everyone had taken their place, the queen entered the Abbey with Prince Philip. She strode purposefully down the aisle, wearing a long, flowing crimson robe trimmed in ermine and gold lace and a diamond-encrusted tiara that had been worn by Queen Mary at the coronation of George V. The choir of four hundred roared, "*Vivat! Vivat Regina!*"—Latin for "Long Live the Queen." At the altar, seated on the throne of St. Edward, she was stripped of the robe, and a simple white garment was placed over her diamond-encrusted gown. She then removed all of her jewelry. A Coronation robe and a ceremonial stole were placed over her shoulders, and she was given the various symbols of her Royal authority—ring, bracelets, orb, rod, and scepter.

The archbishop of Canterbury recited an admonition: "Be so merciful that you be not too remiss; so execute justice that you forget not mercy; punish the wicked, protect and cherish the just and lead your people in the way wherein they should go."

A deathly silence fell inside the Abbey for the solemn moment of the crowning. The archbishop placed the gold Crown of St. Edward, with its 275 diamonds, rubies, sapphires, and emeralds, on the Queen's head and administered the oath. A roar of "God Save the Queen" shook the roof.

Outside, the rain continued to pelt the thousands lining the route back to the palace, and the procession from the Abbey seemed subdued. But when the Queen and the other Royals appeared on the balcony at Buckingham Palace, they were cheered by sixty thousand people. Unlike George VI and the Queen Mother, who had found the day of the Coronation exhausting, Queen Elizabeth II thought it invigorating. She insisted on being seen by as many people as possible, appearing on the balcony several times, waving to the enthusiastic crowds, and during the following two days being driven in an open car around parts of London off the processional route.

Hers was an enthusiasm for contact with her subjects that has continued throughout her reign; indeed, it has become her trademark. Realizing that the Crown had become a symbol of nationhood rather than a source of authority, she accepted more quickly than any in her circle that symbols had to be seen to be of value. That was the reason she had insisted that television crews be permitted to record the triumphant opening of her reign. That also explains why she insisted on driving past her subjects in a Royal coach and eventually walking among them, shaking hands, greeting and talking with them. This accessibility was to be a Pandora's box. In the years to come, the monarchy was to become public property; and public property was media property. In the future, the Royal Family was to be subject to a scrutiny never imagined by Queen Elizabeth's predecessors.

The Coronation of 1953 was the most expensive in history. The money was spent on detail that was lost on those who watched the event. The ornate, rococo gold state coach was completely restored inside and out with the care and precision given the restoration of an old master. Buckingham Palace was lavishly redecorated; the two ceremonial crowns were rebuilt to fit the new Royal head. In all, the ceremony cost £4 million, which is equivalent to about $55 million today, and all of it came from the taxpayer. Apologists for Royal extravagance say that there was a net profit. More than a million tourists crammed London's hotels and restaurants, spending much more money than the Exchequer.

Across the country there were simultaneous celebrations of all kinds—community street parties, firework displays, and other spectacles. Every school student was given a Coronation mug. For the first time in over a century the nation had a monarch who was younger than most of her subjects. Perhaps few working-class Britons would have analyzed their feelings, but the Queen's youth seemed to symbolize hope. That hope for the future of declining Britain seemed to be buoyed by the news that a Commonwealth mountain climber, Sir Edmund Hillary, had conquered Mount Everest. For a short time it seemed that the theme of the new reign—the New Elizabethans—was more than just a public relations concept.

But unknown to the public, a scandal was developing inside the Royal Family that was to set an altogether different theme for the reign of Queen Elizabeth II. It was the first of a saga of sex scandals that would plague the Royal family for the next thirty years and more. It had been simmering for months, even years, and the details were known to a few inside the government and the intimate circle at the palace. It might have remained a secret for many more months, perhaps forever, but for a simple but intimate, telling gesture at the Coronation.

After the Coronation ceremony, hundreds of VIP guests from the Royal Family and the ranks of the nobility milled about in the great hall of the Abbey. Among them were several senior Royal staff administrators, including Group Capt. Peter Townsend, who had been equerry to King George VI and was now comptroller over the Queen Mother's household. He was in his full dress Royal Air Force uniform, and as he stood in the crowd, Princess Margaret approached him. Both were in high spirits and laughed gaily. The Princess noticed a hair on the group captain's lapel, and she reached up and brushed it off with proprietary care. Their eyes met, and they smiled.

Twenty-one

The Tortured Princess

P rincess Margaret, younger sister of Queen Elizabeth II, was a beautiful and voluptuous young woman of twenty-two and the belle of the Coronation ball. She was petite, like all the Royals, but with an attractive figure, almost Mediterranean features, and large, liquid violet eyes. Despite the isolation of her upbringing, she had developed a fun-loving, outgoing, passionate personality, devoid of the self-conscious reserve and the many restraints her elder sister had imposed on herself because of her future role.

By 1950, the births of Prince Charles and Princess Anne had pushed back even further the likelihood of Princess Margaret's ever succeeding to the throne. So this enchanting teenage princess found herself with privilege and wealth without the burden of future responsibilities. It was a time when the world self-consciously tried to slough off the cares and memories of the war.

In her parents' minds and probably in her own, her destiny was set. In the next several years she would undoubtedly marry a high-ranking member of the nobility. Since her sister, Queen Elizabeth II, had married a foreign prince, King George VI and her mother were eager for her to marry a British citizen—a duke, possibly, or the heir to a Dukedom. There seemed to be plenty of time for her to find the right candidate. In the meantime, she was free to taste the social delights of London, which, despite the leaden austerity of postwar Britain, were for a rich few considerable.

Princess Margaret had the zest for life of Edward VII, her great-grandfather. She was an accomplished pianist and singer; she drank and smoked, which was daring for her age and rank; she loved dancing and late nights and theater. She was surrounded by young, elegant, rich,

240

and attractive men and women, many of the men potential suitors. But sophisticated in her tastes and more mature than her years, the Princess had an eye for older men.

One of those men was Danny Kaye, the comedian and actor, who became the hit of London's West End in 1948 with his show at the London Palladium. The Marquis of Milford Haven befriended him and brought Princess Elizabeth and Princess Margaret backstage to meet him. Princess Margaret was dazzled by him and induced the King and Queen to see his performance. They, too, met him later in his dressing room and, in a surprising break with the protocol of the times, invited him to Buckingham Palace for dinner.

It was the beginning of a remarkable, intermittent romance between the teenaged Princess and a married American entertainer twice her age. Perhaps because it was such an unlikely match, the King and Queen let down their guard when the Princess and Danny Kaye began seeing each other more frequently. But when they realized that the friendship had become intimate, the King and Queen insisted that their daughter end the relationship. In order to decrease the risk of the friendship's being resumed, Kaye was told by British theatrical friends not to pursue further stage success in London. Almost as remarkable as the relationship itself is that it never became a public scandal.

Another beau of Princess Margaret's later became a symbol of scandal in Britain—John Profumo. The wealthy descendant of a Lombard banking family and a rising star in the Conservative party, Profumo had a relationship with Princess Margaret in 1949. Their favorite hangout was the Cafe de Paris, where they shared champagne, caviar, dancing, and late, late nights. Profumo loved her; she admired him. But there was another man to whom Princess Margaret compared all others, a man she had known since her first pubescent stirrings, a man with whom she had fallen in love by the time of the Coronation.

As previously noted, Group Capt. Peter Townsend had first come to the attention of the King in February 1940, when as the leader of 43 Squadron, RAF, based in North Yorkshire, he had shot down the first German bomber of the war. He had endured almost two years of combat, forcing himself time and again to scramble into the cockpit of his fighter to fly into the loneliest of all forms of warfare. He had twice been shot down, once in the North Sea, when he had the astonishing good fortune to be rescued by a ship that was way off course. Along the way he had won a Distinguished Service Order and a Distinguished

Flying Cross and Bar. Combat fatigue had ultimately grounded him, and 1944 found him training other young men to fly and die.

In the midst of the war, the King had decided to draw his personal administrative staff from the ranks of decorated officers who were no longer in combat. Until then, the posts were given to members of a few prominent families. Peter Townsend was the first to be offered the position of equerry, a sort of aide-de-camp in March 1944. Townsend was delighted at the prospect, as was his wife, Rosemary, whom he had married in 1941.

Townsend has sometimes been portrayed as being lower middle class—almost an upstart—little more than a servant. But he had impeccable credentials. His father had been a high-ranking member of the Colonial Service and served as a commissioner, or colonial administrator, in Burma. Townsend's wife, Rosemary, was the daughter of a brigadier, one of the highest ranks in the army.

Princess Margaret met Townsend on his first day in his new post and formed an immediate friendship, although she was only fourteen years old and he was thirty, with a child of his own. At that time, those young men who had fought their lonely battles in the skies against insuperable odds and saved Britain were regarded as larger-than-life heroes. As she struggled through adolescence, watching her sister's relationship with Prince Philip blossom, she formed a crush on Townsend.

The King and Queen were also very much taken with Townsend and treated him more like the son they never had than as an equerry. King George VI agreed to become godfather to Townsend's second child, gave the couple a handsome grace-and-favor home, and took an avuncular interest in him. He even asked Townsend's opinion of Prince Philip, who, learning about the inquiry, resented it. Townsend was a more senior officer in his service than Prince Philip was in his, yet Townsend was clearly the Prince's social inferior. When Townsend accompanied the Royal Family to Balmoral and made a point of getting to know Princess Elizabeth's suitor, the Prince realized what was afoot. He may have suspected that Townsend voiced objections to the King about his proposed marriage.

After the war, tensions in Townsend's marriage surfaced. It had been a typical wartime marriage, contracted at a time when few could afford to look more than a few days ahead, let alone a lifetime. Tens of thousands of wartime marriages broke up in the immediate postwar years, and although the Townsends struggled to maintain a home for their children, their marriage was effectively over by the time Princess Elizabeth married Prince Philip in 1947.

Princess Elizabeth's absence, first from the Palace, then from England, her two successive pregnancies, and the deteriorating health of the King brought Princess Margaret a larger share of Royal responsibilities. These duties increased her contact with Townsend, who helped to guide her. The two became good friends and confidants, close enough for Townsend to confide in Princess Margaret the true state of his marriage. The affection for each other grew, but at this stage there was no question of the relationship being consummated. He was married; she was off limits.

After the death of George VI in February 1952, Townsend became comptroller of the Queen Mother's household, which kept him in close daily contact with Princess Margaret. At the end of the year, Townsend and his wife were divorced, citing her adultery with John de Lazslo, son of a Royal portrait painter, Philip de Lazslo. She married her lover within weeks of the decree, and Townsend retained custody of their two children. It was at the New Year celebrations at Sandringham that Townsend confessed the depth of his feelings to Princess Margaret. She reciprocated.

The pair had known each other for several years, and the release of their unspoken feelings for each other forced the pace of the relationship over the next several weeks. Although they had waited until he was divorced before acting on their desire for one another, their romance still had an illicit quality. And illicit relationships feed upon themselves. By the end of February 1953, they were deeply in love. Queen Elizabeth, Prince Philip, and the Queen Mother were aware of their growing affection but perhaps underestimated how intense the relationship had become. In early March the two closeted themselves in a drawing room in Windsor Castle and talked the issue out. Both were aware that there would be obstacles placed in their path. They did not know how yet, but they both agreed that they wanted to be together always.

Townsend told Sir Alan Lascelles, the Queen's private secretary, that he was in love with Princess Margaret. Lascelles's reaction was one of outrage, but he kept the true depth of his opposition to himself. Townsend offered to resign, but Lascelles feared that such a move would give rise to speculation immediately before the Coronation. Meanwhile, Princess Margaret told her sister. She was more understanding but not encouraging. The Queen consulted Prime Minister Churchill about the affair, and both agreed that nothing should be said or done until the Coronation was safely accomplished.

Ostensibly, the problem concerned divorce. The Anglican church neither recognized divorce nor permitted remarriage in a church. The Queen was head of the Anglican church and therefore could not sanction the marriage. And as Princess Margaret was under the age of twenty-five, under an eighteenth-century law she needed the sovereign's permission to marry. Both Townsend and Princess Margaret believed that if they waited until she was over twenty-five, she would be able to marry whom she pleased. Meanwhile, they expected to be free to see each other as any other two adults.

A good deal of hypocrisy and cant has colored accounts of the Townsend affair. Just as the abdication crisis in 1936 had more to do with politics than romance, the Townsend affair was more concerned with money and class than divorce. Townsend's position in the Royal household had to do with service. Except for the war and King George VI's decision to reward distinguished military service, he would never have come within a hundred miles of the post of equerry. To use that position to—as Lascelles seems to have seen it—seduce the youngest daughter of the Royal Family, someone he had known as a child, reflected scandal and dishonor.

Rumors about the affair had already begun to circulate when Princess Margaret made that unmistakably intimate and proprietary gesture at the Coronation. Newspapers in New York carried stories that Princess Margaret was in love with a divorced man seventeen years her senior. European newspapers were quick to pick up the reports. Such stories could not be suppressed today, but in the Britain of 1953 newspapers were more in awe of the Royal Family. The Buckingham Palace press office managed to prevent any British newspaper from reporting the sensation for nearly two weeks, when at last the storm broke.

The *People*, a popular Sunday newspaper specializing in self-righteous reportage of usually petty scandal, asserted that foreign newspapers were carrying reports of an affair between Princess Margaret and a divorced man. Reassuring its readers that the reports could not be true—unthinkable, in fact—the newspaper demanded that the palace end the rumor.

Lascelles, the Queen's private secretary, arranged for Townsend to be hurriedly exiled. He could become an air attaché in Brussels, Belgium, Johannesburg, South Africa, or Singapore, but he must leave the country. Townsend chose the nearest post to London—Brussels. Princess Margaret was preparing for an official visit to Rhodesia (now Zimbabwe) when news of the posting came. Both were led to believe that there would be enough time to say their good-byes and that Townsend would not be forced to take up his new position until Princess Margaret returned to London. But while she was thousands of miles from home, Townsend was ordered to Brussels without seeing her.

It was like a plot from a Henry James novel, the two lovers parted in the hope that time would change their feelings for each other. Churchill, Lascelles, and the archbishop of Canterbury, Dr. Geoffrey Fisher, appear to have been among the conspirators. The couple were allowed to make telephone calls and to exchange poignant, sometimes steamy letters. According to a British intelligence source, the telephone calls were monitored and the letters intercepted and read. But it was close to a year before the couple were able to see each other again.

The year proved emotionally exhausting, particularly for Townsend. He was besieged by reporters and photographers wherever he went and was afforded little protection by officials at the British embassy in Brussels. Princess Margaret flung herself back into a hectic social life in a desperate attempt to deflect attention from her relationship with Townsend and to disguise her own feelings of loss.

In the meantime, Churchill had resigned the premiership as the result of a strike, and Sir Anthony Eden had succeeded him. Eden might have been expected to take a more lenient view of the affair, since he and a number of other members of his cabinet were also divorced and had remarried. But there was a cruel shock awaiting the couple when Princess Margaret became old enough to marry without the sovereign's consent in 1955. The Princess met with Sir Anthony at Balmoral on October 1, six weeks after her twenty-fifth birthday, and was told that nothing, in fact, had changed since 1953.

Eden—he must have squirmed when he explained it—told the Princess that the government could not countenance her marriage to a divorced man and that the lord president of the Privy Council and leader of the House, the Marquess of Salisbury, had threatened to resign if the marriage was permitted. She would, in any case, lose her place in the line of succession if she contracted a civil marriage to Townsend, and the government had prepared a bill to remove her from the Civil List, the funds from which the Royal Family derive their state incomes.

Princess Margaret and Townsend met on October 13 at Clarence House as a crowd of reporters and photographers waited outside. They talked the matter out and, in these elegant and peaceful surroundings, decided they still wanted to marry, come what may. But Townsend returned that evening to Allanbay Park, a sprawling Georgian mansion where the Queen Mother had arranged for him to stay. He found the place again besieged by press reporters and photographers, this time kept out of the sixty acres of grounds by teams of police officers with dogs. For Townsend, this was a vision of a future very different from that conjured up a few hours earlier in the embrace of the beautiful young Princess.

The Princess and Townsend met every day for a week while speculation about the marriage mounted in the press and the public debate became heated. For those few days it seemed that the marriage was on; that Princess Margaret was prepared to sacrifice her income, her line in the succession, and virtually all of her public functions. Clearly the government and the Establishment felt they had lost the battle. So the pressure on the couple, already under enormous strain, was stepped up. Princess Margaret was informed that she and Townsend would be expected to be married and live abroad for at least several years. It would mean a life of aimless exile, possibly for ten years or more. Then the *London Times*, the oracle of Establishment orthodoxy, publicly denounced the proposed marriage in a lengthy, stinging, and self-righteous editorial that had all the hallmarks of having been inspired by a Buckingham Palace briefing.

The *Times* said, "The princess will be entering into a union, which vast numbers of her sister's subjects, all sincerely anxious for her lifelong happiness, cannot in conscience regard as a marriage."

The threat of exile and the public denunciation in the press ended their dreams. They would not have been left penniless, for the Queen would certainly have provided her sister with an income out of her own considerable resources. But Townsend would have been placed in an invidious position, dependent on his young wife's fortune, probably unable to earn his own living, even to support his own children, and responsible for their unhappy separation from friends, relatives, and places they knew and loved. It would also be an exile in which they were constantly pursued by reporters. Townsend had already had a taste of what that was like. He no longer believed he could make Princess Margaret happy as his wife, and, honorably, he refused to try, even in the face of her own protests that all would be well.

The same day the *Times* editorial appeared, Townsend wrote a statement for Princess Margaret to read, one which made it appear that it was she who had decided to put honor and duty before personal happiness. Some years later she told friends she would still have been willing to try to make the marriage work in spite of all the obstacles.

The statement said in part:

> I would like it to be known that I have decided not to marry Group Captain Peter Townsend. I have been aware that, subject to my renouncing my rights of succession, it might have been possible for me to contract a civil marriage. But mindful of the Church's teaching that Christian marriage is indissoluble and conscious to my duty to the Commonwealth, I have resolved to put these considerations before any others.

The statement disguised the truth of the pressure under which the couple had been put and the real reasons for it. Had Townsend been of aristocratic birth and with a significant income, no great constitutional issues would have been raised to prevent the couple from marrying, although the Princess would still have been required to give up her place in the line of succession. The government would not have been able to place them under such serious financial pressure. The shame of having to live off his wife's family could not have been used as leverage.

That Prime Minister Eden continued to object to the marriage even after Princess Margaret no longer needed her sister's permission exposes the fact that this was a matter of class, not religious scruples or constitutional issues. The Marquis of Salisbury, Local President of the Privy Council, so eager to resign from the government and the Privy Council if Princess Margaret were to marry a divorced Townsend, served enthusiastically under a divorced Eden. And the Church of England had no moral objections to a divorced Eden choosing and appointing its bishops. It is far more likely that the Marquess and others in the Establishment objected to Townsend because he was not of their number. Far from being reluctant to recognize such a marriage, as the *Times* asserted, most ordinary British people wanted Princess Margaret to be happily married to the man she loved, and there was widespread sympathy for their plight.

There was another issue, however, which ultimately turned the Queen and Queen Mother against the proposed marriage to Townsend, although neither harbored the animosity toward him that Churchill, Eden, and other Establishment figures did. That issue concerned

Princess Margaret's willingness to remove herself from the line of succession, which touches a sensitive nerve with the Royals. The monarch may reign by consent and rule constitutionally, but the heart of the institution is birthright. The head that wears the Crown does so because he or she is descended from a long line of others who have done so. To the members of the Royal Family, for someone to abdicate in favor of a substitute, as Edward VIII had done, or step out of the succession, as Princess Margaret proposed to do, made the position of monarch or of heir more like a job that could be resigned like any other rather than a rank that came with Royal birth.

Townsend and Princess Margaret continued to see each other inter-mittently and secretly over the next several years. But for the next year or more, they went their separate ways: Townsend on an extended trip around the world in search of both peace and obscurity; Princess Margaret on an equally arduous quest for fun to anesthetize her emo-tional anguish. Both harbored, for a time, the hope—perhaps the fantasy—that one day they would be allowed to marry without inter-ference. Most thwarted lovers do. Princess Margaret had several other romances in the following five years but continued to compare her suitors unfavorably with Townsend. The affair cast a long shadow over her emotional life for many years.

By the standards of the mid-fifties, an unmarried woman was justi-fied in feeling the first twinges of panic as she approached thirty. Princess Margaret began to consider her options. A number of the aristocratic suitors she had once dallied with in her late teens were now married or engaged. Those who were left began to look slightly more attractive than before. Among them was Billy Wallace, son of a former Conservative government minister and the super-rich but rudderless heir to a series of fortunes through a complex web of spectacular mar-riages and untimely deaths.

Wallace had proposed to Princess Margaret on several occasions, and in 1956, worrying that she might never marry, she accepted. It was still a secret engagement when Billy Wallace was found to have been un-faithful during a bachelor weekend in the Bahamas and the Princess broke it off. That same year, the Princess was a guest at the wedding of another former flame, wealthy landowner Colin Tennant. The photo-grapher at the wedding was a man rapidly making a reputation for himself with glossy magazines and newspapers—Antony Armstrong-Jones.

Armstrong-Jones was the twenty-six-year-old son of a barrister. His parents divorced when he was a child, and his mother, Anne Messel, daughter of a millionaire stockbroker, then married the immensely wealthy Earl of Rosse, making her Countess of Rosse. Armstrong-Jones had suffered from poliomyelitis when he was a child—polio was a scourge of British children until the fifties—and although he had made a good recovery, his growth had been severely stunted.

An innovative photographer with spectacular social connections, he had been commissioned to take photographs for the Duke and Duchess of Kent, which led to his taking official portraits of Prince Charles. Part bohemian, part social climber, he monopolized Princess Margaret over dinner. The two were soon enjoying an intimate, but casual, relationship.

No member of the Royal Family is able to pursue a love affair without the knowledge of the phalanx of bodyguards and detectives who protect their persons or the intelligence services that routinely investigate their friends, and we shall see later, bug homes and monitor telephone conversations.

The profile of Armstrong-Jones drawn up by the Royal Protection Squad of the Metropolitan Police with the help of the Special Branch and MI5 revealed that he was already involved with an exotic-looking model and actress, Jacqui Chan, who was half Chinese, half Caribbean. For a long time he was seeing both women. Investigators also found he had several homosexual friends, a matter which was to cause a behind-the-scenes scandal later. And according to one source, it was discovered that a darkroom assistant employed by Armstrong-Jones had resigned from his studio after she found pornographic photographs he had apparently taken showing another exotic girlfriend with an inanimate object.

The Queen, Prince Philip, and the Queen Mother had serious reservations about Armstrong-Jones, and Prince Philip thought him effete. They hoped the affair would burn itself out. But it only intensified. Armstrong-Jones rented a romantic retreat in the London district of Rotherhithe, today a rather fashionable riverside neighborhood but in the late fifties a most unlikely place to find a Princess and her lover. They savored each other's worlds, his upper-class bohemian, hers the Royal stratosphere of privilege. For both, their affair soon turned into an urgent physical relationship.

In October 1959, Princess Margaret finally realized that there was no hope of ever marrying Townsend. He wrote to tell her, before she read about it in the newspapers, that he would wed a tobacco company heiress, Marie-Luce Jamagne, a woman half his age. The same evening, Armstrong-Jones, who was staying at Balmoral, asked the Princess to marry him. She told friends later that his timing was perfect. Still reeling from Townsend's news, she accepted.

The wedding plans were not announced for another four months, until after Queen Elizabeth had given birth to her third child, Prince Andrew, on February 19, 1960. The child was named for Prince Philip's ill-fated Greek father. The announcement that the Princess and Armstrong-Jones would marry in May came as a complete surprise. Fleet Street had not heard a whisper about the affair. Antony Armstong-Jones's presence at Balmoral and Sandringham in the preceding months had generated no gossip because most observers believed his visits were connected to his many Royal assignments as a photographer. His friends, many of whom were journalists themselves, had kept quiet.

Not everything went smoothly, however. Antony Armstrong-Jones asked his friend Jeremy Fry, scion of a wealthy chocolate-manufac-turing dynasty, to be his best man. Palace officials objected because it was discovered during routine screening that he was a homosexual. Homosexual practices were illegal at that time. Armstrong-Jones then asked another close friend, Jeremy Thorpe, a Liberal party politician, to serve as best man. The Metropolitan Police Special Branch discovered that he, too, was a homosexual, and the palace once more told the groom to choose someone else.

The discovery of Thorpe's sexual preference in 1960 was kept from the British public for another sixteen years, when, as leader of the Liberal party, he was responsible for a revival of the party's political fortunes. He was toppled by a scandal generated by a deranged former lover. Conveniently for the Conservative establishment, the affair helped to derail the Liberal revival.

The spectacular Royal wedding, the first of such significance for thirteen years, became a live television extravaganza. Flags bearing the monograph "M + A" fluttered across London. Tens of thousands of well-wishers lined the Mall between the palace and Westminster Ab-bey, and as with the Coronation seven years before, many had slept on the sidewalks to secure the best places in the crowd. For once, Princess Margaret was the center of attention in the Royal procession, with Prince Philip, who was to give the bride away, at her side rather than at her sister's. There were chants of "We want Margaret! We want

Margaret!" and full-voiced cheers for the Princess as she went by in her gold-and-glass state coach. Millions who had sympathized with Princess Margaret during the Townsend affair now poured out their feelings of joy that she had at last found happiness. And when, at the end of the day, the Princess and her husband sailed off on the superb Royal yacht *Britannia*, there seemed to be a fairy-tale ending to the tragic tale.

Princess Margaret had passed through a harrowing and public ordeal to find apparent happiness. Her sister, Queen Elizabeth, had been through an equally harrowing, though secret, crisis of her own. There had been a rift in her marriage.

Twenty-two

A Divided Union

The Royal rift in the marriage of Queen Elizabeth and Prince Philip had been developing since the battle over the Queen's refusal to incorporate her husband's name into the House of Windsor. Prince Philip had quickly become impatient with his subservient public role in relation to the Queen; he was crass in his dealings with the media and the public and wistful about his career in the Royal Navy, which he had effectively lost when his wife took the throne. A man of action, he desperately sought a fulfilling role and could find none.

He became moody, restless, and difficult to live with. The Queen and Prince Philip were supposed to embody the ideal British family. However, they kept separate apartments at Buckingham Palace and at Windsor. Prince Philip was indiscreet in his private life, and rumors of illicit liaisons surfaced. Stories were published in the Italian and German press that the Prince kept a private London apartment as a "love nest"; that one of his closest friends, the photographer Baron Nahum, known as Baron, acted as a "beard" for the Prince and that women Baron was seen with actually had relationships with the Prince.

By 1956, the Queen's relationship with her husband seemed so distant that when their schedules kept them apart for several months, it was widely believed that they both wished to be as far away from one another as possible: the Queen home in Britain and Prince Philip on a tour of Southeast Asia, Australia, and Antarctica. There could be no question of a divorce or even a formal separation, but there was much public speculation about the real nature of their relationship. It was even suggested that their marriage was a sham and they were leading essentially separate lives. For several months in 1955 they barely spoke, and in 1956 they were happy to be separated while the Prince traveled and the Queen remained in Britain.

King George VI had always been skeptical about Prince Philip as a potential son-in-law and told Lord Mountbatten that he believed him incapable of being faithful. Like all Royal suitors, Prince Philip had been under surveillance by the British intelligence services prior to his marriage. Among the matters that interested agents investigating the Prince was his membership in an organization called the Thursday Club and his friendship with the beautiful Helene Foufounis, by whom he was once rumored to have had a child out of wedlock.

Prince Philip had been a childhood guest in the Foufounis home in St. Cloud, France. They were wealthy, influential expatriate Greek Royalists, and Prince Philip became close friends of the three children of the house: Jean, Helene, and Ria. Their mother, Anna Foufounis, had hoped that Prince Philip and Helene would marry. Through the years, Prince Philip and Helene had remained on intimate terms and visited each other often, sometimes for weeks at a time. By the end of World War II, Helene had endured two unhappy marriages and had two children. The intelligence service compiled a secret report on Prince Philip's relationship with her.

Prince Philip had stood godfather to the children and took a personal, avuncular interest in their welfare. He directed their education and acted as a surrogate father during family crises. In 1951, Helene Foufounis came to live in London, changed her name to Helene Cordet, and became a popular nightclub performer and one of the queens of London's nightlife. And it was around this time that gossip surfaced in London society that Prince Philip was the father of at least one of her children.

Helene and Prince Philip remained close despite Queen Elizabeth's evident disapproval. She was often Prince Philip's guest at social functions, such as polo games, but was never invited to more formal Royal events and ceremonies at which the Queen would be present, an unequivocal sign that Her Majesty felt the relationship was not entirely appropriate.

The Queen's view of Philip's relationship with the beautiful and exotic actress Merle Oberon can only be imagined. Merle Oberon, who died in 1979 at sixty-eight, appeared in more than fifty movies between 1930 and 1973, including the classic *Scarlet Pimpernel, The Divorce of*

Lady X, and *Wuthering Heights*. An affectionate, intimate friendship between Philip and the actress began in the mid-fifties and was renewed intermittently until the late sixties, according to a variety of sources. Merle Oberon's friends are convinced that the actress was in love with Prince Philip, and she at least gave them the impression they were having an affair, although she was fifteen years older than him. He visited her at her home in Acapulco, Mexico, several times and once reportedly had a naval salute fired beneath her windows in Acapulco Bay.

Another aspect of Prince Philip's private life that the Queen did not feel was entirely appropriate was his continued membership in the Thursday Club. Prince Philip had joined the all-male club in 1946, pressed to do so by his cousin, David, the Marquess of Milford Haven. Reports of its activities had been made to the King soon after Prince Philip became a member.

The club members met once a week in a private room in a seafood restaurant, Wheelers, at 21 Old Compton Street in Soho, London's nightclub district. On the surface, it was simply a group of men dedicated to having a riotous good time. One of the founders was Vasco Lazzolo, a socially well connected photographer and portrait painter. Others included minor members of the aristocracy, a sprinkling of politicians, including Iain Macleod, who was to become chairman of the Conservative party, a number of political journalists, and several show-business personalities, including the American musician Larry Adler and the actor James Robertson Justice.

The group exchanged high-powered gossip, drank heavily, ate abundantly despite the food shortages, and engaged in juvenile games, vulgar banter, and what today would be regarded as sexist humor of the most demeaning sort. The atmosphere among the members was self-consciously informal. Larry Adler remembered: "We never called him anything but Philip, and one wasn't expected to. It was just a group of men, good fellows, out for a good time, drinking, telling jokes—some of them dirty jokes"—hardly an edifying association for a man who aspired to be a consort of the Queen of England. Yet Prince Philip continued to be a member of the Thursday Club following his marriage and even after his wife became Queen.

For most of its members the Thursday Club was doubtless no more than just a place where heavy burdens of responsibility might be set down for an hour or two amid convivial company. For some, it was an anteroom to a more shadowy world of illicit, even orgiastic, sex. And a complex web of social and sexual connections linked Prince Philip and some members of the Thursday Club with one of the most serious and far reaching scandals in modern British history.

There were, for instance, sex orgies conducted by Prince Philip's cousin, David, the third Marquess of Milford Haven, son of the equally notorious and exotic Nadeja, Marchioness of Milford Haven. The Marquess, who had been a close childhood friend of Prince Philip's as well as a blood relative, organized bizarre parties for his male friends at his home close to the U.S. embassy in fashionable Grosvenor Square. It is claimed that the guests played cards and parlor games in which the sexual services of high-class prostitutes were offered as prizes.

A regular at the Thursday club and the Grosvenor Square parties was Dr. Stephen Ward, an osteopath and amateur portrait painter who insinuated himself into the inner circles of London society. He gave lavish parties at his home in Cavendish Square at which prostitutes rubbed shoulders with politicians, wealthy businessmen, and aristocrats. Among the guests was Prince Philip, reportedly accompanied by a beautiful Canadian-born model, Maxie Taylor.

One of Prince Philip's friends whom the Queen believed led him astray was Michael Parker, an old comrade in arms. Parker was an Australian serving in the Royal Navy when he and Prince Philip became friends. After the war they met again. Parker, somewhat down on his luck, worked for his father-in-law selling rope. In 1948, Prince Philip, bored by the Buckingham Palace bureaucrats who ran his and his wife's lives, appointed Parker as his equerry, or aide.

It was Parker's job, among other things, to keep Prince Philip entertained, and this was an area in which the fun-loving Australian excelled. Perhaps Parker did his job too well. By 1956, Parker's own marriage was in tatters, and his wife sued for divorce. She cited Parker's presence at wild parties in fashionable London homes that Prince Philip had also attended and sexual escapades on a tour of Southeast Asia and Australia, also with Prince Philip. She even threatened to call Prince Philip as a witness in the divorce case.

The palace bureaucrats whom Prince Philip so despised quickly moved to suppress what might have become a nasty scandal. With the public already speculating about the Queen and Prince Philip's long separations, each performing Royal duties thousands of miles from one another, Parker was forced to resign, quietly settle the divorce case, and keep the Royal Family out of the scandal.

In a vain attempt to end rumors of an irrevocable split, the Queen named Prince Philip a Prince of the United Kingdom shortly after Parker's dismissal. His official title hitherto had been Duke of Edinburgh; his only princely title had been Greek. She even flew out to visit him in Gibraltar on his return from the Far East, indicating she couldn't bear to be separated for the few more days it would take for him to reach England. But speculation continued unabated for many months. The long separation did assist in bringing about a reconciliation, however. There could be no question of a formal separation, let alone a divorce, and this reality forced them to try again. The birth of their third child, Prince Andrew, in February 1960, ten years after the arrival of their second, was an emblem of their rekindled union.

But even as their marriage healed, a fresh crisis loomed—a series of interrelated scandals that would rock the government, the Royal Family, and the nation. At the center were two men well known to the Royal Family: one of Prince Philip's friends from the Thursday Club, Dr. Stephen Ward, and Princess Margaret's former suitor, John Profumo.

Twenty-three

Affairs of State

T he Profumo Scandal was to the Britain of the sixties what the
Watergate scandal was to the America of the seventies. It cut to
the quick of British government and society, exposing a diseased and
corrupt subderma, affecting forever the way the British view their
elected representatives and social superiors. But while Watergate was
exposed in the full glare of television lights, some of the details of the
Profumo scandal remain half-hidden to this day.

In brief, it was discovered that John Profumo, the minister of war and
an ambitious politician, with every expectation of one day becoming
prime minister, had had an adulterous affair with Christine Keeler,
a prostitute who, during approximately the same period, had a sexual encounter with Yevgeny Ivanov, a high-ranking Soviet agent. Two
elements seasoned the mix. One was a matter of honor. Profumo lied
about his relationship in a public statement to the House of Commons,
enough in itself to ensure the destruction of his political career. The
other concerned a matter of security. Keeler was said to have been asked
by Ivanov to obtain military secrets from Profumo.

But the Profumo scandal was infinitely more complex than that, for it
embodied a web of lies, deceit, betrayal, and decadence, with many
strands, some of which reached from KGB headquarters in Moscow to
the ornate corridors of Buckingham Palace.

The early sixties marked the height of the Cold War, the tense, bitter
conflict between the Communist bloc, dominated by the Soviet Union,
and the Western democracies, led by the United States. The visible
elements of the conflict were the steady buildup and deployment of
nuclear arms on both sides, a number of bloody but limited conflicts in
Central America, Africa, and Southeast Asia, and a series of flash-point

257

crises, such as those in Berlin and Cuba. The invisible element of the conflict involved the struggle between the intelligence agencies, the through-the-looking-glass war of subversion, espionage, and counter-espionage in which nothing was as it seemed. Britain had become one strategic battleground where a class-ridden society was in its death throes and a thriving and vocal left wing challenged the Conservative Establishment.

Britain's Conservative government had been in office almost a decade and seemed unlikely to have to call an election for another four years. In 1956, Britain had invaded Egypt in a shabby deal with France and Israel to recover the Suez Canal. Sir Anthony Eden, the prime minister, had to resign, but the party remained in power under Harold Macmillan. Macmillan had repaired the crack in the alliance with the United States caused by the Suez crisis, accelerated the British withdrawal from its old Imperial dominions, taken a hard line against the Soviet Union, and supported the deployment of American nuclear missiles in West Germany.

The KGB had successfully penetrated several British institutions and had many agents in place—in the Labour party, the trade unions, the intelligence services, the Civil Service and even in Buckingham Palace. Despite the handicaps under which the British intelligence services worked, there were numerous successful counterstrikes against the Soviet Union, and a number of Soviet spies had been unmasked. One successful operation in the spring of 1961 had been to induce Oleg Penkovsky, a Soviet spy, to act as a double agent. Among his first acts had been to identify a number of his fellow Soviet agents. One was the assistant naval attaché at the Soviet embassy in London, Yevgeny Ivanov.

Penkovsky claimed that Ivanov was a high-ranking agent of Soviet military intelligence, GRU, and that his taste for the seedier pleasures of life in the West made him a potential defector. He also had family connections in the Soviet Union that went to the highest levels of the Party bureaucracy. The intelligence chiefs had already noticed that Ivanov had cut a swath through a fashionable and somewhat decadent set in London society almost from the moment he had taken up his post in March 1960. The embassy had made a great fuss over Ivanov when he first took up his post, ensuring that MI5 would sit up and take notice of him.

Part of Ivanov's mission in Britain was to ensure that the opposition

Labour party won the next election by undermining confidence in the Conservative government. New evidence suggests that this was to be done in conjunction with the secret assassination of Hugh Gaitskell, the moderate leader of the Labour party, who, the Russians expected, would be replaced by someone further to the Left. There is no evidence that Ivanov was himself involved in that part of the plot. Ivanov had a number of possible "targets of opportunity" in the Conservative Establishment.

Other help may have been available. For years it was suspected, but never proved, that the Russians had a deep-penetration agent at the highest levels of the intelligence services. One of the chief suspects was Sir Roger Hollis, the MI5 director general. Hollis played a pivotal role in the events that were to become known as the Profumo Affair. Ivanov failed to trigger the Royal scandal he had hoped for, but the one he did engineer had serious implications for the Crown.

Ivanov's entrée into London's high life, low life, and nightlife was Dr. Stephen Ward, Prince Philip's old friend from the Thursday Club. Ward had developed a thriving practice as an osteopath, manipulating the backs of the rich and famous. His patients were actors, politicians, diplomats, and aristocrats and ranged from Elizabeth Taylor and Mike Todd to Sir Winston Churchill and Joseph Kennedy; from Frank Sinatra and Ava Gardner to Mahatma Gandhi. His social contacts were equally impressive. He knew both Prince Philip and the Marquess of Milford Haven well and Lord Mountbatten distantly. He had become a close friend of Lord "Bill" Astor's, son of Nancy Astor and scion of the English branch of the immensely wealthy Anglo-American business dynasty. Another of Ward's friends in those days was a man then obscure—he was a personal assistant to the world's richest man, Paul Getty—who was to become notorious in the United States in the 1980s: Claus von Bulow. A talented osteopath, Ward also had become a gifted amateur artist and managed to persuade many celebrities of his day to sit for him, including Sophia Loren, Douglas Fairbanks, Jr., Paul Getty, a posse of British politicians, and several members of the Royal Family, among them Prince Philip, Princess Margaret, the Duchess of Kent, and the Duke and Duchess of Gloucester.

But Ward had a dark side that drew him into a more shadowy world. He was obsessed with prostitutes and women who catered to unusual sexual preferences. He had only a limited interest in sex for himself, but he enjoyed sexual pleasures vicariously. He liked to watch. He liked to matchmake. He enjoyed the gossip and company of prostitutes, pimps, and drug dealers as much as he took pleasure in the friendship and small talk of Royalty. His wide contacts among the demimondaine enhanced his popularity. He could always be relied on to introduce his friends to women of easy virtue.

Among Ward's patients was Sir Colin Coote, editor of the ultraconservative newspaper the *Daily Telegraph*. Coote had been a former field agent for British intelligence and later served as a propaganda agent. Coote had met Ivanov among a group of foreign diplomats touring the Daily Telegraph Building in Fleet Street. He invited Ward and Ivanov to lunch at the Garrick Club, ostensibly—and just as improbably—so that Ward could ask Ivanov to help him sort out some problems he had in obtaining a visa to visit the Soviet Union.

Ward and Ivanov struck up a solid friendship. Ward introduced Ivanov to his rich and famous friends and clients, and Ivanov, an entertaining drinking companion, took Ward to diplomatic events. Ward also told Ivanov all the gossip that Ivanov loved to hear and relate—who was sleeping with whom, who had slept with whom, who wanted to sleep with whom. It is likely that Ward, who knew Ivanov was an intelligence agent, found the friendship stimulating because he became an entrée to yet another shadowy world.

Ivanov would have been under surveillance as a possible agent even before he was identified by Penkovsky, and his friendship with Ward had been observed and noted. It is possible, given the origin of the friendship—the luncheon table of a known intelligence agent—that the relationship was deliberately encouraged by MI5 from the beginning. In June 1961, Ward was contacted by an MI5 case officer using a cover name. British intelligence sources who have contributed information for this chapter have asked that he not be identified.

The mission was simple and classic: to sexually compromise Ivanov either to the point where he was vulnerable to blackmail or so addicted to his lifestyle that he was willing to defect to maintain it rather than one day return to Russia. MI5 was well aware of both sides of Ward's character—the side that mixed easily and gracefully with the Royal Family and his penchant for cultivating more dubious connections. Given that the operation was of some importance, it seems likely that Ward had been used by MI5 before in some capacity. Interestingly, after the first meeting with Ward in the early summer of 1961, the MI5 case officer expressed reservations about Ward's usefulness.

It was Hollis, the suspected mole, who insisted he be employed in the key role of baiting the trap for Ivanov. But Ivanov had only been playing the role of the potential defector. He had assumed from the start that Ward was either an MI5 agent or was likely to be approached by one of the intelligence services. So clearly he would not fall into the trap that MI5 was setting for him. But by cultivating Ward's friendship, he believed he could turn the tables and bait a trip of his own.

In the summer of 1961, Ward was occupying, at some ludicrously low rent, a secluded, picturesque cottage on the grounds of Cliveden, the magnificent, sprawling Astor family estate overlooking the Thames at Taplow. Cliveden had been famous in the thirties as the fulcrum of the appeasement movement. The influential mongers of peace at any price had been known as the Cliveden set. But in the fifties and sixties, Cliveden had become famous for the Astors' lavish hospitality and riotous weekend parties. Ward, who always filled the cottage with his own eclectic group, would wander over to the main house to mingle with Astor's weekenders.

Prince Philip and Princess Margaret were among their guests. So was Lord Mountbatten. There would be, on any given weekend, cabinet ministers, a movie star or two, a brace of Dukes. The Duchess of Westminster might find herself seated next to a singer whose record had just edged into the Top Ten. Billionaire Nubar Gulbenkian might have as his dining partner a left-wing Labour MP. When Douglas Fairbanks, Jr., wanted to throw a coming-out party for his daughter Daphne in 1957, Lord Astor offered him Cliveden. It was one of the social events of the decade. The Queen, Prince Philip, Lord Mountbatten, Princess Margaret, and the Duke of Kent were among five hundred glitterati who watched a spectacular fireworks display that spelled out DAPHNE in letters ten feet high. The more sedate Cliveden weekends saw Astor's friends spreading out across the estate for picnics, boating, swimming, tennis, riding, or for the more adventurous, al fresco lovemaking.

The first weekend in July 1961 proved oppressively hot for a British summer. The group that assembled at Ward's cottage included Christine Keeler, a nineteen-year-old member of a coterie of promiscuous women in Ward's circle. She has been described as a prostitute, but this appellation deserves qualification. She was not a full-time working girl but a showgirl at a topless club and an aspiring legitimate model. She was, however, available under the right circumstances, which usually involved gifts or money. Peter Rachman, a disreputable London slumlord whose scandalous harassment of tenants brought a new word to the English language—"Rachmanism"—was one of her more profitable adventures. He gave Keeler and her friend Mandy Rice-Davies, a prostitute, expensive clothes, a sports car, and occasional small gifts of cash in exchange for a series of desultory sexual encounters.

Keeler was not beautiful, but she had a waiflike form that men found sexually stimulating. She had large, dark, widely spaced, oval eyes and sharp, high cheekbones that gave her a somewhat exotic appearance. She was uninhibited sexually but derived little enjoyment from the sexual act. Rather, she had found from childhood that sex was her only means of social communication. At sixteen, she had had a child by an American serviceman, but the baby had not survived a week. She had met Ward on one of his regular forays to the topless club where she worked and she was staying at his London apartment, but their relationship was not sexual. He delighted in the stories of her sexual adventures; she, in his impressive circle.

The group that assembled at the main house in Cliveden that weekend included Lord Mountbatten; Ayub Khan, the then president of Pakistan; a high-ranking British diplomat, Sir Gilbert Laithwaite; and the British secretary of state for war, John Profumo, and his actress wife, Valerie Hobson. Profumo's career had advanced considerably since the days when he had dated Princess Margaret. He had been, in rapid succession, under secretary at the Foreign Office and minister of state for foreign affairs and now held the top defense post in the Macmillan government. Macmillan was grooming him as a possible successor.

Ward and Keeler dropped by the main house for a swim on Saturday evening and found Profumo and Lord Astor by the pool. Both were taken with Keeler, and soon there were childish games being played. Ward dared Keeler to strip off her black one-piece bathing suit and swim naked. When she did, he hid the bathing suit. Astor and Profumo, both of them wearing dinner jackets, chased Keeler around the pool as she giggled and tried to cover herself with a small towel, visibly inadequate for the purpose. The laughter subsided when other guests, including Mountbatten and Profumo's wife, Valerie, came out to investigate. But Ward and Keeler were invited to stay, and there were more antics. Profumo showed her around the enormous house. At one point, Keeler was helped into a suit of armor and staggered around to the delight of the celebrated guests.

On Sunday, Ivanov arrived at Ward's cottage, and there were more games by the Astors' pool. The women climbed onto the shoulders of male partners and descended into the water, each woman trying to unseat another from the shoulders of her partner. Keeler rode Profumo. Ivanov noticed the interest Profumo was developing in Keeler, and his judgment was confirmed when Ward revealed that Profumo had asked Ward for her telephone number. That same afternoon, Ward asked Ivanov to take Keeler back to London and promised to meet them later at Ward's apartment.

Ivanov brought Keeler to Ward's home at 17 Wimpole Mews, but Ward never turned up. Ivanov and Keeler, doubtless with little else to do, ended up in bed. It was, as Ivanov himself described it thirty years later, a ferocious coupling. Ivanov left in the middle of the night. It was the only time they slept together, but because of Ward's continuing friendship with Ivanov, she still saw him on numerous occasions. It was not lust that drove Ivanov to Keeler's bed. It was too obvious a setup. He had to have been confident that either Profumo and Keeler would sleep together or that there was evidence she had already slept with other high-placed individuals.

Profumo knew nothing of Ivanov's wild night with Keeler when he called her the following Tuesday and took her for a drive around London in his official car. There was a second date the same week. This time, Profumo took her to his house in Regent's Park, and they went to bed. Astonishingly, the MI5 case officer working with Ward was told that week both that Ivanov had slept with Keeler and that Profumo was chasing her. MI5 appears to have done nothing to break it up other than to let Profumo know that Ivanov had become a target and he should steer clear of Ward for a while. The affair continued for months, until Profumo broke it off at the end of the year. He was, however, foolish enough to have written to her in familiar terms so that Keeler was able to prove there had been an intimate relationship.

In the months that followed there were more trips to Cliveden for both Christine Keeler and her friend Mandy Rice-Davies. How many other members of the sixties version of the Cliveden set came to share the beds of Christine Keeler and Mandy Rice-Davies is not known. Mandy Rice-Davies claimed under oath that she had an affair with Lord Astor. It was widely believed that at least two other government ministers slept with Christine Keeler. And there was a persistent rumor—probably fueled by the Russians—that a member of the Royal Family found his way into her bed.

It was not until January 1963 that Keeler began to talk to newspapers about her affairs with Ivanov and Profumo. She added some spice by claiming that Ivanov had asked her, through Ward, to discover from Profumo the delivery date of atomic weapons to West Germany. British libel laws are stringent, and the charges could not at first be published without enormous risk. But they became common knowledge at Westminster. Russian diplomats spread rumors that Keeler had slept with a number of government figures. Ivanov, meanwhile, had returned to Moscow. A newsletter, *Westminster Confidential*, carried the allegations of Keeler's affairs with Profumo and Ivanov. The sources were two journalists from Tass, the Russian news agency. Labour M.P.s eventually asked questions in the House of Commons about Keeler under the protection of privilege. Profumo, cornered, denied that there had been any impropriety between them.

In the midst of all this, Hugh Gaitskell, the moderate leader of the Labour party, died suddenly from a rare disease, disseminated erythematosus lupus. Harold Wilson, his deputy, became leader after a party election. Gaitskell's death was taken as an untimely and tragic end to a promising political career, one that would almost inevitably have seen him prime minister of a future Labour government. But in total secrecy MI5 began investigating his death as a Russian-inspired political assassination. Circumstantial evidence suggested that he had been infected with the disease deliberately, but nothing was proved.

Meanwhile, Ward now found himself under investigation on vice charges. It was a transparent attempt to either keep him silent or destroy his credibility, but it backfired. He told Labour M.P.s that Profumo had lied to the House of Commons and that he, Ward, was being set up as a scapegoat for the failure of the operation against Ivanov. It is a convention of the House of Commons that being caught in a public lie to legislative colleagues is an offense that demands a member's resignation. When it became obvious that members in all parties knew that Profumo had lied, he admitted it and resigned, his political career over forever.

But the stories about Keeler continued to circulate. One suggested she had been introduced by Ward to Prince Philip and slept with him. Photographs confiscated in a police raid at Ward's apartment were alleged to show Prince Philip in a compromising position. A Conservative M.P. tried to raise the question of Prince Philip's rumored connections to the Profumo Affair and was prevented from doing so. The rumors were strong enough for Lord Denning, who conducted an official inquiry into the Profumo Affair, to call Michael Parker, Prince Philip's equerry, as a witness and question him about Ward's associations with Buckingham Palace.

Palace officials moved quickly to effect some damage control. Newspaper editors were asked not to draw attention to Profumo's associations with Princess Margaret and denied the rumors about Prince Philip. The editors were requested not even to print the denials. Only the *Sunday Mirror* failed to comply. Following a Fleet Street convention to skirt around libel laws, the *Mirror* reported that "the foulest rumor" in the whole affair was the involvement of Prince Philip. The newspaper self-righteously then claimed that was not the case, just as in a similar vein the press insisted years before that Princess Margaret was not involved with Group Captain Townsend.

In July 1963, Ward stood trial on trumped-up charges that he had lived off the earnings of prostitution, a ludicrous allegation that stood up only on perjured testimony obtained from a number of witnesses under duress. When it appeared that he was about to be found guilty, Ward, out on bail, committed suicide with an overdose of barbiturates and took many of the unanswered questions concerning the Profumo Affair to his grave—at least so far as the public was concerned. There is evidence that Ward, before committing suicide, wrote an extensive account of the affair to Henry Brooke, the home secretary. That letter has never surfaced. Whether Ivanov had consciously "turned" Ward so that the osteopath was prepared to set up Profumo for Ivanov or Ward merely bungled his MI5 assignment may never be known.

While the trial was in progress, a showing of Stephen Ward's portraits of various celebrities was taking place in a private London gallery, partly to raise money for his defense. It was a popular exhibition, and a number of portraits were sold at high prices. One evening, a tall, distinguished, silver-haired man came into the gallery and bought all the portraits of members of the Royal Family, Prince Philip, Princess Margaret, and the Duke of Kent among them. The tall figure, it was later revealed, was Sir Anthony Blunt, surveyor of the Queen's pictures.

For several more weeks the nation waited breathlessly for the publication of the Denning Report, the official judicial inquiry into the Profumo Affair. Prince Philip and Princess Margaret were relieved to find that their association with the central figures in the scandal was not mentioned.

The prime minister, Harold Macmillan, lasted only a few more weeks. His government narrowly survived the Profumo scandal, but it was clear he was politically doomed. He resigned in October 1963, citing ill health. He was, in fact, suffering acutely from a disease of the prostate. Macmillan was determined that his successor would not be the most likely candidate, R. A. "Rab" Butler, who had been an appeaser before the war and a defeatist during it. The Conservative party did not elect leaders, and there was a tortuous process by which the Queen would be "advised" whom to call upon to form a government.

Macmillan knew that the majority of the cabinet favored Butler and that, indeed, the Queen herself preferred him. He persuaded the lord chancellor, Lord Dilhorne, to fabricate the results of a private ballot to show support for Lord Home, the foreign secretary. The Queen called on Lord Home, later Sir Alec Douglas-Home, to form a government on the basis of a lie. Even though Home's political opponents in the Conservative party quickly discovered the deception, they all knew that revealing the scandal would be the final nail in the coffin of the government and the party. In the best—or the worst—traditions of party loyalty, they kept silent.

Almost immediately there was another spy scandal—again with the Royal Family involved—but it was to be covered up for almost fifteen more years.

Just weeks after Profumo resigned, Michael Straight, a onetime Soviet intelligence contact in the United States, confessed to the FBI that he had been recruited to work for the Soviet Union while at Cambridge. He identified the recruiting agent as Sir Anthony Blunt. Blunt, who had had a successful MI5 career and who had been a Soviet double agent all along, had become, in 1945, surveyor of the Queen's pictures. MI5 officers subsequently interrogated Straight, and he agreed to become a witness against Blunt if he were brought to trial in Britain.

But the last thing the British government of the day, the intelligence services, or indeed the Royal Family needed was a scandal of this proportion coming on the heels of the Profumo Affair. It was agreed that Blunt should be offered immunity and allowed to keep his post at Buckingham Palace and his knighthood in return for complete disclosure of his history as a Soviet agent.

Blunt grabbed at the offer of immunity but successfully evaded giving complete disclosure. In monthly interview sessions over several years he dodged, weaved, and danced around the questions posed by his MI5 interrogators. He never named colleagues who had also been agents except for those who had already been exposed or who were dead. He never divulged the reasons for his secret mission to Germany on behalf of the Royal Family after the war. He never revealed if he had continued to act as an agent after he left MI5 for Buckingham Palace or if he had played a role with Ivanov in the Profumo Affair.

It was only when Michael Straight's original confession leaked in 1979 that the prime minister, Margaret Thatcher, acknowledged that Blunt had been unmasked years before and allowed to remain free. The precise nature of his hold over the Royal Family remains obscure, but there can be no doubt that it existed. Even when Blunt developed cancer of the colon in 1971 and the opportunity arose for him to retire with grace, he insisted on retaining his post, as did Buckingham Palace.

The secrecy surrounding Blunt after he agreed to the immunity arrangement in April 1964 enabled the Conservative government to retain power for a few more months. In October 1964, they were defeated in a general election, and Harold Wilson formed the first Labour government in thirteen years.

The Profumo Affair had lasting implications beyond the whispers about Prince Philip and Stephen Ward's stable of available women. The scandal was a turning point for British society. The Establishment was never quite regarded in the same way again. The personal lives of politicians, peers, and indeed, Royals, would no longer be seen as sacrosanct by Fleet Street. Henceforth, reporters would pry with increasing fervor into areas hitherto considered off limits. There was a new appetite for the more salacious details of the private affairs of public people. This change of mores would have particular impact on the Royal Family in years to come.

Other postscripts to the Profumo scandal deserve noting. Profumo was fortunate enough to have a wife who stood by him after his name became synonymous with scandal and sexual impropriety. Ivanov was less successful. He received the Order of Lenin on his return to Moscow, but his wife left him. Profumo was also decorated. He spent the rest of his career doing charitable work and in 1975 was created commander of the British Empire. Thirty years after the Profumo Affair, after the collapse of the Soviet Union, Christine Keeler and

Yevgeny Ivanov met once again. They were brought together in Moscow by a British newspaper as a stunt and recalled the few minutes of sex that destroyed a government, a life, and a career.

Twenty-four

The Mountbatten Coup

There are few episodes in British politics since the end of World War II so staggering in their implications as the 1968 plot to overthrow the legitimate, democratically elected government of Harold Wilson and replace it with a "government of national unity" led by Lord Mountbatten, the self-appointed patriarch of the Royal Family. That year stood out as the most volatile in a decade of violence. Student unrest and industrial turmoil produced chaos in France and ultimately brought down the government of Charles de Gaulle. The United States was torn by antiwar demonstrations, civil rights protests, and widespread urban rioting. It was the year Dr. Martin Luther King, Jr., and Robert F. Kennedy were assassinated. And it was the year Lyndon Johnson refused to seek reelection as president.

In Britain, the political and economic fabric seemed to come apart. In Northern Ireland, Catholics demanded civil rights as vocally as did blacks in the United States. They were met with hostility and violence by the security forces and Protestants of Northern Ireland. Strikes and industrial strife exploded throughout the nation while British universities became the centers of antiwar protest and pro-disarmament demonstrations. In addition, racial violence threatened to erupt as belligerent right-wing politicians whipped up opposition to a wave of Commonwealth immigrants. Street fighting between police and protesters was common. Several potentially violent ultraleft fringe groups, who took their inspiration from Che Guevara, Fidel Castro, and Ho Chi Minh, emerged, alarming the Special Branch of the police.

Amid all these catastrophic events, Britain's economy was in free fall, and unemployment soared. The Labour prime minister, Harold Wilson, closed the London gold market and devalued sterling. The government's budget was one of the most punishing in history—stringent defense cuts, with large additional taxes on investments, income, corporations, cigarettes, alcohol, and gambling. The middle classes never seemed so cornered. The working classes never seemed so volatile. The military believed they had been let down by their political masters in colonial struggles in Aden, Cyprus, Kenya, and elsewhere. They had never felt so disaffected.

Behind the scenes, the British intelligence community—already racked by the search for traitors in its own ranks—assembled allegations that, incredibly, the prime minister himself had become a Soviet agent. Wilson had taken the party leadership after Hugh Gaitskell's death early in 1963 from a wasting disease, lupus, more commonly found in tropical climates. With CIA assistance, MI5 investigators discovered that the Russians had, some years before, worked on fabricating a chemical weapon that would induce the disease. Gaitskell had visited the Soviet Union some weeks before his death. But the investigators were unable to take the investigation any further.

Soon after Wilson had become Prime Minister, James Jesus Angleton, the CIA chief of counterintelligence, offered his MI5 opposite number, Martin Furnival-Jones, secret information on Wilson from an even more reliable source but only on condition that MI5 keep the information inside the intelligence community. Ultimately, MI5 refused to accept the condition, and Angleton refused to give further details. But MI5's own sources indicated a Soviet penetration of the Labour party, and a number of individual members of Parliament were unmasked. As a result, MI5 generally remained deeply suspicious of Wilson and his associates, who included several Britons with Eastern European backgrounds and business connections.

Some individual agents became convinced of the allegations and wanted to leak the information to Conservative newspapers and bring down the government. Furnival-Jones refused to do so, but inevitably word began to filter through the Whitehall corridors.

Wilson had barely scraped into power in 1964 but increased his parliamentary position in 1967. When the economic and social structures seemed about to collapse the following year, several extreme right-wing businessmen began to organize and fund private armies of mercenaries and "security experts," some of whom were retired officers of the armed forces and special forces. At least two loosely allied groupings became obsessed with the idea that a breakdown of law and order was imminent—not so farfetched in the tense atmosphere of 1968—and began to form a secret line of defense. Most of this activity was based in London, but a network of like-minded ultraconservatives emerged in other parts of the country.

The plans included lists of journalists and broadcasters who would take over newspapers and radio and television stations; military and police officers who would ensure that key installations were occupied; and local and regional bureaucrats who would form emergency administrations. The organizers used secret doomsday plans for governing a Britain ravaged by nuclear war. That those secret plans had become available suggests that these organizations were directed from a high level in the military or civil service. The organizers apparently lacked only one element; a high-profile figure who would arouse public support and confidence in a time of crisis.

At first, the armchair colonels preparing for the coup formed what was more a movement than a conspiracy—more like survivalists than revolutionaries. But it was a short leap from preparing for Armageddon to wishing for it. Before long, the focus of these right-wing groups switched to acting in order to prevent a breakdown in law and order, which was altogether different from acting to restore it.

The coup d'état in Greece served as an inspiration. There a junta of military officers had first taken power and purged left-wing and liberal elements, then in 1967 ousted the Greek Royal Family when it was believed they were planning a moderate countercoup. Ironically, the British royals had secretly aided the escape of Prince Philip's relatives from Greece, including King Constantine, his mother, the ardent former Nazi Queen Friederike, and Prince Philip's mother, Princess Alice. Princess Alice was secretly housed in Buckingham Palace, where she wandered the corridors in her gray nun's habit.

The CIA had actively encouraged the Greek coup, and the fingerprints of the CIA and MI5 can be seen on what became known as "the Mountbatten coup." Of two key figures known to be involved, one was a propaganda agent of MI5; another published a magazine heavily funded by the CIA. The first was Cecil King, chairman of the International Publishing Corporation (IPC) and publisher of the *Daily Mirror* and other newspapers and magazines. The other was Hugh Cudlipp, one of the IPC's chief executives and publisher of *Encounter*, funded by the CIA. King had been begging MI5 to let him publish exclusive scandalous information on Wilson to bring him down.

In May 1968, King and Cudlipp searched for a leader. The men who would be supported by the armed forces were too obscure to command the allegiance of the public. The men who might command the public's loyalty either were too closely associated with a party or were men the military believed to be suspect. According to King, only one man could win both widespread public confidence and the support of the security forces: Mountbatten.

Cudlipp arranged at least two meetings with Mountbatten. One took place at his estate, Broadlands. King was not present. Cudlipp appears to have drawn Mountbatten into a discussion of the disturbing state of the nation and the need for a strong leader, a peacetime Winston Churchill, to guide Britain through the rapids to calmer waters. Mountbatten agreed with Cudlipp, up to a point, but his suggestion for a strong leader is reported to have been Barbara Castle, a member of Wilson's cabinet. Still, Cudlipp must have been somewhat encouraged by these first soundings because within a few days he had arranged a second meeting, this time at Mountbatten's London home, with King and Cudlipp present.

In the meantime, Mountbatten reported something of his conversation with Cudlipp to his son-in-law, Lord Brabourne. Lord Brabourne told Mountbatten he was on dangerous ground and should cancel the meeting. Although very little is known about what was said between Cudlipp and Mountbatten at Broadlands, clearly there was enough talk of a disturbing nature to alarm Brabourne. Mountbatten declined to cancel the next meeting.

More is known about what happened at the second meeting because each of the participants left an account. The accounts conflict, however, with Mountbatten, his friend, Lord Solly Zuckerman, and Cudlipp agreeing on the broad issues and King disagreeing on almost every point. Mountbatten had called on his old wartime ally Lord Zuckerman, then the chief scientific adviser to the Ministry of Defense, to attend, but King, Cudlipp, and Mountbatten were alone together for some time before Zuckerman arrived. Cudlipp and Mountbatten say King outlined the difficulties that faced the nation, the economic hardships ahead, and the revolutionary forces at work in the universities and the trade unions. No doubt, as he was aware of the unsubstantiated and incredible allegations against Wilson, he vented his feelings about the prime minister.

King then painted a scenario in which the ordinary business of government broke down. It might be triggered by a final collapse of the pound, leading to runaway inflation; a strike of workers in a strategic industry, such as longshoremen, power workers, or miners; or a student revolt—or a combination of all three. It is important to remember that these scenarios appeared only too real in 1968. These were precisely the events unfolding in France. King suggested that once the crisis came, it would be necessary to proclaim an emergency government of national unity.

King wanted to know if, given such a crisis, Mountbatten was prepared to step forward as the savior of Britain and head a government of national unity. King had already crossed the line between preparing for a national crisis and attempting to direct it. Mountbatten's clear duty at that point was to end the discussion immediately and report it to the civil authorities. Instead, he betrayed an interest. He turned to Solly Zuckerman and asked for his opinion. Zuckerman did denounce the scheme, calling it "rank treachery," and left. Cudlipp followed him, leaving King and Mountbatten alone. William Evans, Mountbatten's aide, who was at the house but not at the meeting, says Mountbatten left the room and told Evans to interrupt him after a few more minutes and get King out of the house.

King's own account is remarkably different. He claimed that Mountbatten made the running, called the second meeting himself, and invited Zuckerman not as a referee or witness but as a defense expert and "one of the greatest brains in the world." Mountbatten is alleged to have described the appalling state of the nation rather than King, although there can be no doubt King agreed with him. And King claims Mountbatten introduced the Queen into the discussion, claiming that she was horrified by the state of the nation. King says that only then did he suggest that the Queen call for Wilson's resignation and appoint Mountbatten. King also claims he was the only one present taking notes and therefore insists his version is the more accurate.

Mountbatten's diary, quoted by his official biographer, Philip Ziegler, shows that he described the meeting as "dangerous nonsense." But there is evidence that he took the whole matter a good deal more seriously than that. Zuckerman's diary, also quoted by Ziegler, says that Mountbatten "was really intrigued by King's suggestion." Zuckerman was also very concerned about what Mountbatten had said to King when he, Zuckerman, was not there.

Mountbatten did refuse to have another meeting with King, writing to him that there was nothing he could do to help. But that was not the end of the matter. Although Mountbatten had a humanitarian, even radical, approach on many issues, he was almost obsessed with the idea that Communists would gain control of the trade unions. Marcia Williams, later Lady Falkender, served then as Harold Wilson's powerful political secretary. She claimed that both Wilson and herself were aware of the "coup" and believed Mountbatten was a prime mover. The plans, she suggested, went a good deal further than just idle talk, with detailed maps showing locations for military installations in the heart of London in Mountbatten's possession.

Ironically, the closest Britain came to a real breakdown occurred under the Conservative government. Wilson was defeated in the general election in 1970. He had timed the election campaign to coincide with the World Cup soccer tournament in Mexico, believing that the nation's men would be distracted by the event. England held the world soccer crown at the time. Victory in the tournament, which seemed likely, would produce a feeling of national euphoria and produce a vote for the status quo. England was defeated at an unexpectedly early stage, and Wilson was ousted on a wave of national despondency.

The Queen had genuinely liked Wilson and had established a close rapport with him. He was unusually direct and informative, filled their meetings with interesting gossip, and seemed interested in her contributions. She did not look forward to establishing a relationship with the new prime minister, Edward Heath, who seemed remote, unemotional, and too businesslike. The new administration soon experienced deep trouble. The Queen became deeply disturbed by the further divisions in the country caused by Heath's policies. He established industrial-relations courts to punish striking unions, sent union leaders to prison, and followed hyperinflationary policies.

In 1973, he found himself in a bitter confrontation with the National Union of Mineworkers over pay demands. The union of electrical engineers and other unions supported the miners, and Britons faced weeks of power blackouts for hours at a time. Virtually every factory was shut down four days out of seven. Millions of homes were lit by candles. Picketing became violent. Cornered, and faced with the frightening option of employing troops to man power stations, Heath's nerve failed. He called an election for February 1974.

The prospect of Wilson's return to power sent his enemies in MI5 into paroxysms once again. The network of right wingers with plans for the seizure of vital installations was revived. A clique of MI5 officers, close to open revolt, tried to obtain the details of the Angleton allegations against Wilson to leak them to the Conservative press. The mutiny in the making was put down, and subsequently there was a secret inquiry into the actions of several officers.

The Queen was acutely aware of the seriousness of the crisis. But while other heads of state might be worried by such matters, the Queen enjoys those instances which make her antiquated constitutional authority the focus of great events. If Heath won, he would face the same quandary as before: the possible use of troops against miners and power workers. If Wilson won, it would be a victory of organized workers over democratically elected government. She found both distasteful, and she guessed correctly what the results would be: a hung Parliament, with the Conservatives clearly defeated but with no overall majority for any party. Labour had 301 seats; the Conservatives, 296; and the Liberals, 14.

In normal circumstances, the Queen should have called on the leader of the party commanding the largest number of seats—Harold Wilson—and asked him to try to form a government. She was persuaded by Heath to allow him to continue in office until Parliament reconvened and try to remain in power through a coalition. The prospect of Mountbatten's being called on to form an emergency government was raised again. This possibility was not so outlandish as it may now seem. Mountbatten was entitled to a seat in the House of Lords and might have been able to win some support for an interim, emergency, but still parliamentary government until a new election could be called. But the Queen was worried that if Mountbatten's administration got into difficulties, it would embroil the Queen in party politics.

The crisis continued until Heath reluctantly accepted that he was unable to persuade the Liberals to help keep him in power. Wilson formed a shaky minority government and began at once to dismantle the Heath administration's antiunion legislation. There was no more talk of a coup. The following year, 1975, word of the "dangerous nonsense" that had been spoken at Mountbatten's home in 1968 began to leak out.

It was then that Mountbatten, Zuckerman, and Cudlipp, in an exchange of letters, agreed on their version of what had happened. Clearly, it was in their interests to portray the incident in the most anodyne and casual way. Wilson, now in power again, supported their version. It was King and Lady Falkender, though on opposing sides, who insisted Mountbatten had been the instigator of the coup that never was.

Twenty-five

The Queen Triumphant

T he year 1969 marked a turning point for the Royal Family. It was the year they changed from being the relatives of the monarch, deputized to perform public duties and constitutional functions within the British political system, to becoming the regular cast members of an ongoing Royal soap opera. The change literally happened overnight, in full view of a gaping public.

The tensions in the Queen and Prince Philip's marriage still appeared to remain a part of the past when, in 1964, their fourth child, Prince Edward, was born. But according to palace insiders, the marriage, filled with turmoil, had lost its emotional meaning for both. They still felt mutual respect, but undeniable differences existed. Had they been an ordinary married couple, they might have separated, perhaps even divorced. But the Queen believed that a breakdown of her marriage would have disastrous consequences for the monarchy.

They disagreed on Prince Philip's attitude toward his children. He was strict, critical, overbearing, and would humiliate Prince Charles, then in his teens, to the point of tears. The Queen made it clear that Prince Philip would only have a ceremonial role and deliberately kept him in the dark on political issues. They continued to disagree on his public persona. Philip enjoyed playing the irascible Prince and made public remarks that seemed at best thoughtless, at worst designed to provoke controversy. Sometimes, when Prince Philip expressed his opposition to majority rule in Rhodesia or his support for the reunification of Germany, he stepped clearly over the mark into the political arena.

Long separations between Queen Elizabeth and Prince Philip, purportedly due to their demanding schedules, nevertheless aroused speculation. Only a handful of people realized that the Queen, needing emotional fulfillment as much as any woman, had turned to another man for companionship. He was Patrick, Lord Plunkett, a former equerry of her father's, George VI.

The opposite of Prince Philip, Plunkett was handsome, sophisticated, and urbane, a seventh-generation aristocrat and a man of considerable artistic sensibilities and taste. Seven years older than the Queen, he had been deputy master of the Queen's household from 1954 and had the responsibility of designing the pageantry of Royal events and the elegance of state banquets.

The Queen found that he was someone she could confide in, turn to for emotional support and reassurance, and that he could be counted on to render an honest, apolitical, and compassionate opinion. She did with Plunkett something she was rarely able to do with Prince Philip—enjoy a discreet public outing. These "dates" were regular events, sometimes occurring as often as once or twice a week, over twenty-five years. Disguised as an ordinary, smartly dressed housewife accompanied by a man who looked for all the world like her husband, they would see a movie, often at the Odeon Cinema in Leicester Square, or dine at a quiet, favored restaurant where they would take a secluded corner table. The only other people in the know would be the Queen's detective-bodyguard, who would bring along a female member of the Buckingham Palace household or a woman police officer. Together they, too, would pose as a couple.

Even those who believed they recognized her must have decided they were wrong, that the woman in the head scarf and tinted spectacles in the back row of a cinema or orchestra of a theater or at the far table at a restaurant with an unknown man could not possibly be the Queen of England. The improbable—even the ridiculous—made such outings possible.

The two were never lovers. Like a number of men in senior positions in the Queen's household over the years, Lord Plunkett was a homosexual. But they did have a very deep affection for each other. When Lord Plunkett died in 1971, the Queen was heartbroken, the more so because his death came at the end of a long battle with cancer, during which she continued to see, support and cheer him. She created an ornate temple as a monument to him in Valley Gardens at Windsor and still visits it often in memory of her former companion and lifelong friend.

Both Prince Philip and Queen Elizabeth did agree that the British press had grown less deferential in its dealings with the Royal Family, reflecting and encouraging a negative attitude among ordinary Britons toward the Royals. The press had not only become more critical of Prince Philip's public posturing and the expense to the taxpayer of supporting the Royal Family. Reporters also appeared to be more intrusive. No longer satisfied by the official portraits and the strictly controlled photo opportunities at Royal events, photographers vied with each other for "candid" shots of the Royals in more natural surroundings. They would snap pictures of the Queen changing in a beach hut and of Prince Philip struggling into his riding gear in the front seat of a car. *Paris Match* published a bootleg photograph of the Queen, in bed, cradling Prince Edward in her arms. When the *Daily Express* published the same picture, the Queen demanded an apology. It was a sign of the times that she did not get it.

The sixties had changed the public perception of the Royal Family. In a decade filled with political and social conflict, old taboos were lifted from various aspects of public behavior and popular belief. To outsiders, the Royal Family seemed staid, distant, and behind the times. The reverence with which they had been held for generations had begun to decay. For the first time, individual members of the Royal Family came in for public mockery. The Queen's unusually precise accent and carefully rehearsed enunciation at public ceremonies was widely mimicked by television satirists on shows like *That Was the Week That Was* with David Frost as well as by stand-up comedians everywhere. Prince Charles's Dumbo-like ears were caricatured. Prince Philip's well-known bad temper and habit of crossing his hands behind his back were similarly parodied. The irreverent lampooning was symptomatic of a more serious problem. Britons were asking themselves about the relevance of the Royal Family.

There had been an early warning of the changes to come in the late fifties when Lord Altrincham, a young peer, criticized the monarchy as "second-rate" and claimed that the image created by the Queen in public appearances was one of "a priggish schoolgirl and captain of the school hockey team." It was true that the Queen's speeches were excessively formal, but that was largely because they could never be controversial and so were usually confined to colorless observations and superficially sincere expressions of goodwill. But the speeches made the still-youthful Queen appear vapid. Altrincham's criticism brought him public vilification, and he was slapped in the street by a loyal monarchist.

John Osborne, the playwright, joined the controversy, calling the entire monarchy "the gold filling in a mouth full of decay" and "a fatuous industry." The eminent British journalist and broadcaster Malcolm Muggeridge told Jack Parr's *Tonight Show* audience that the British were bored with the monarchy. For young intellectuals, on the eve of an era of protest, upheaval, and social and sexual revolution, it was becoming fashionable to believe that the Royal Family had become a moribund institution. It was not a development that went unnoticed in Buckingham Palace, where even the dullest courtier realized it was worse to be ignored than opposed.

This is not to say the Queen herself was no longer popular. A Royal visit to a town or borough still brought out the bunting and the cheering crowds. The Queen herself was still recognized, occasionally, as an accomplished diplomat on her overseas tours. Her personal charm on a visit to Ghana won over a hostile President Nkrumah and kept that country in the Commonwealth fold at a time when the Soviets were wooing them. Those who met the Queen were surprised at how natural, unassuming, and accommodating she could be with people from all walks of life. But the vast majority of the general public never got to see her that way. Television and newsreels had made it possible to view the Royal Family at close quarters more often, but instead of enhancing their image, the new media had merely made them more two-dimensional.

By the mid-sixties the dull, all too easily caricatured image of the monarchy was causing deep concern to the Royal Family, not so much in relation to the Queen's personal image but in terms of the future monarch, Prince Charles. In 1969, at twenty-one, Prince Charles was scheduled to be formally invested as Prince of Wales, the first such ceremony since the Duke of Windsor's investiture as Prince of Wales more than fifty years before and only the second such ceremony in three hundred years. The Queen, Prince Philip, and Lord Mountbatten believed it could be an opportunity to regenerate the kind of Royalist feeling that had surfaced at the Coronation, largely because millions had witnessed the ceremony on television for the first time.

Nigel Neilson, a public relations expert, specialized in discreet, subtle manipulation of the public image of superwealthy tycoons like

Aristotle Onassis and his daughter, Christina. Neilson had long believed that Prince Charles was a significant and underused Royal asset. Most people were aware of him only as a straitlaced youth with large ears whose dress, hair, and general demeanor were utterly conventional and, in the sixties, completely uninteresting. Neilson believed he could transform him into an intelligent, compassionate, immensely popular future King.

The Royal Family, however, does not hire public relations consultants. Instead, Neilson's company, Neilson McCarthy, hired Prince Charles's equerry, David Checketts, as a nonexecutive director. It was a means of training Checketts in public relations and channeling public relations advice to the palace almost unnoticed.

The impact on the image of Prince Charles was immediate and positive. Suddenly, he was seen as much more hip. He took up noncontroversial conservationist causes that portrayed him as compassionate. He lampooned himself in a Cambridge University revue, showing he did not take himself too seriously. Several reporters were invited to the palace to meet Prince Charles in person and were charmed by him. He was given training in how to handle interviews, something the Queen and her predecessors never had to do because they never gave them. His answers to difficult or impertinent questions in mock practice sessions were taped and endlessly analyzed by Checketts and Neilson.

In February 1968, William Heseltine replaced Comdr. Richard Colville as Buckingham Palace press secretary. One of his first decisions triggered a radical reevaluation of the Royal Family's relationship with the Queen's subjects. He told the Queen he wanted to accept a proposal by the BBC to make a full-length documentary on Prince Charles to be broadcast prior to the investiture as Prince of Wales the following year.

It was Prince Philip, encouraged by Neilson and Checketts, who suggested that the documentary be expanded so that the subject became the entire Royal Family. The documentary would not describe their formal life of Royal tours, official visits, and other public engagements. Instead it would portray them as no one outside the royal circle had ever seen them: as a family. Not an ordinary family, by any means, but recognizably human. It now seems an extraordinary volte-face for an institution so naturally conservative as the Royal Family to suddenly expose their inner selves to a medium as intrusive as television. The Royal Family's recognition that they were regarded by the rest of Britain as out of step with the pace of modern times is not the only factor that led them to make such an extraordinary decision.

Despite the many other less mundane diversions to occupy their time, the Royals are all television addicts. They avidly watch sitcoms, television dramas, and particularly soap operas that portray the daily lives of ordinary people. The reason is not hard to understand. It is virtually their only access to the real world outside the high walls of formality that surround them. It is their only way of seeing that world beyond palace life without themselves being seen. So understandably they eagerly accepted the opportunity to use television to show themselves to the public without actually having to perform their Royal roles.

Furthermore, as the constitutional purpose of the monarchy had declined, the Royal Family had taken on the role of representing both the state and its microcosm, the family. The documentary seemed a useful way to demonstrate that they were an ideal British family at precisely the time when the investiture of Prince Charles would underscore their constitutional position in the great panoply of state.

Richard Cawston, a BBC producer who specialized in a cinema verité documentary technique, was assigned the project. Up to then, no one outside their small circle of relatives, friends, and advisers had ever seen a member of the Royal Family except on the most formal occasions. Few members of the public had even heard their voices other than in public speeches. For the Royals, there are few unguarded moments.

But Cawston's camera crews were given unprecedented access to the Royal Family's private moments. The cameras became so ever present at Buckingham Palace and at Sandringham and Balmoral over the next several months that the Royals learned to ignore them. Soon they were behaving as if they really were speaking in private. To add the element of surprise, the whole project was carried out under conditions of complete secrecy.

The result was *Royal Family*, a film shown in Britain twice a few days before Prince Charles's investiture and later in 140 countries. While the degree of access became apparent with every sequence, the film contained nothing that proved controversial. But that was the whole idea. The documentary had been designed to portray the very ordinariness of the Royal Family within an extraordinary environment. Viewers saw games of charades, informal interaction between Queen Elizabeth and her husband and children, as well as meetings with ministers in which she became a model of efficiency. There were light moments, too, when, for example, Prince Charles, practicing his cello, snapped a string which struck Prince Edward in the face, causing him to run off in tears, and warm moments as when the family gathered to decorate the Christmas tree or when the Queen mixed a salad while her husband cooked steak on the barbecue. Both the Royal Family and the British public were delighted with the documentary. And for a while the film did enhance the Royal Family's popularity.

But the documentary also turned into a Pandora's box. Once admitted, the ravenous eyes of the television cameras never really left. *Royal Family* portrayed the Queen and her immediate family as warm, ordinary, essentially upper middle-class people. But the film also re-created them as characters in a television drama, not unlike two popular series of the day, *Coronation Street* and *Crossroads*, which portrayed the daily lives of ordinary people, with their familiar crises and resolutions and strong matriarchal characters. Instead of helping to reposition the Royal Family in the public view and confirm their relevance to British life, the documentary merely stimulated an insatiable appetite for information on their private foibles. It began the process by which the Royal Family reached the same level of celebrity as television stars. People felt they knew them. From being people who demanded awe and respect because of their social status and constitutional right, they began—very slowly at first—to be characters who might be liked or disliked. The media monarchy—the Royal soap opera—had been inadvertently launched. And as with all television soap operas, in the coming years, the plot lines and cliff hangers would become increasingly bizarre.

No one realized this at the time. And there is no reason why anyone should have. *Royal Family* seemed to be an unqualified success, bringing the Queen and her subjects closer together. The investiture ceremony of Charles as Prince of Wales at Caernarvon Castle in North Wales, on July 1, 1969, was also a success, though marred by terrorism. Welsh nationalists set off bombs immediately before and on the day of the ceremony. Two people were killed. The attacks did not affect the medieval pageantry of the investiture itself or threaten the safety of the Royal Family. The closest the Welsh nationalist extremists came to disturbing the stolid equanimity of the Queen, Prince Philip, and the youthful Prince of Wales occurred when an egg landed on the hood of the Royal Rolls-Royce.

It could not be claimed that the investiture had been a "second

Coronation," as had originally been planned. However, a much simpler innovation, introduced by the Queen a few months later, had a startling effect on her popularity. These were "walkabouts"—a conscious decision to shorten the distance between the monarchy and the people. Rather than simply ride in an open car or carriage so that her subjects, who had often waited hours, could see her, the Queen would leave her car to shake hands, chat, and sometimes receive bouquets and gifts. It was a nightmare for her bodyguards but a delight for ordinary Britons. Their pleasure at the Queen's informality was boundless. Some people would be reduced to tears at having had the opportunity to shake her hand and exchange a few words.

More than any public relations spin, television appearance, or Royal spectacular, this change in the Queen's behavior provided the needed boost to her personal popularity in the early seventies. At a time of considerable turmoil in Britain—industrial strife, shifts in government, nationwide power outages, product shortages, and economic malaise— the Queen, for a time, did live up to the old cliché which is so often used to justify the Crown's continued existence: that she is a symbol of stability in a changing world. Wearing bright solid colors so that she could be seen by all; carrying the omnipresent but surely empty handbag; assuming the graceful, regal, but not in the least proud or arrogant posture; and always ready with a consoling word, an engaging smile, or an unaffected, sincere interest in what someone had to say, the Queen, it seemed, was always the Queen.

But the upswing in the monarch's personal popularity had its downside. The public appetite for information, no matter how spurious, had become insatiable. Newspapers discovered that Royal stories sold newspapers and magazines. The best Royal stories involved either romance— forthcoming marriages, affairs, or pregnancies—or conflict—divorces, family arguments, or feuds. On no less than eighty separate occasions prior to the Queen's Silver Jubilee, stories were published in British and European newspapers that she was about to abdicate for one reason or another. She was preparing to divorce Prince Philip on at least seventy occasions and had become pregnant close to one hundred times. But much more anodyne material on the Royals also sold. There developed an apparently bottomless market for Royal hagiography of one kind or another.

At the moment of Britain's most serious crisis, in 1974, the Queen had a brush with death. She had broken off a visit to Indonesia shortly after the February election to deal with the constitutional crisis at home. As soon as Harold Wilson became prime minister, she was required to return to Bali. As the Queen's V-C 10 crossed over West Germany, it wandered into a zone used by NATO fighter aircraft for dogfight practice against unmanned drones. Mistaking the plane's radar blip for a radio-controlled target, a group of fighter planes closed in. Moments from being destroyed by missiles, the Queen's plane was identified, and the fighters broke off.

In 1977, the Queen celebrated the twenty-fifth anniversary of her reign, the Silver Jubilee. It was to be the high watermark of the Royal Family's popularity, a vast outpouring of affection for a monarch who, it seemed, had been perhaps Britain's only stable institution in a quarter century that had begun with optimism but had brought disappointment, gloom, pessimism, and then apathy. The ennui with which the Crown had been viewed just a few years before was forgotten. The Silver Jubilee echoed Queen Victoria's Golden and Diamond jubilees, which laid to rest the criticism following her long absence from the national scene.

For months before the climax of the Jubilee celebrations, the Queen, Prince Philip, Prince Charles, and to a lesser extent Princess Anne and Prince Andrew participated in a grueling series of public engagements in every region of the kingdom. On June 6, the Queen lit a thirty-foot-tall bonfire as a brass band of the Household Cavalry played the moving, patriotic strains of Elgar's martial "Pomp & Circumstance March No. 2." Across the entire nation, from hill to hill, from horizon to horizon, more bonfires were set alight until thousands burned, each within sight of one other.

The next day a Royal procession rode from the palace down the Mall to Trafalgar Square and up Fleet Street and Ludgate Hill to St. Paul's Cathedral. Over a million people, many more than had gathered for the Coronation in 1953, crowded the streets along the route. The Queen and Prince Philip sat in the golden state coach, Prince Charles alone on a black stallion. The Queen Mother, Princess Margaret, Princess Anne, and Princes Andrew and Edward shared three coaches. A poignant service of thanksgiving took place at St. Paul's, for it recalled an eventful and sometimes tempestuous period, and the Queen was clearly seen to have tears in her eyes.

After the hour-long service, the Queen strolled from St. Paul's to Guildhall, stopping to shake hands and exchange a few words with as many people as she could. Later, in a triumphant voyage, she sailed on the River Thames amid ship's sirens, whistles, colorful water fountains, and firework displays. Her reception seemed so warm, her personal contact with her subjects so successful, that she stepped up her schedule of tours and visits over the next several weeks. To those close to her and to the mass of people, it seemed she had never enjoyed herself so much as during the Silver Jubilee.

In those heady summer days of 1977, it appeared that the popularity of the Royal Family would now stay on this exalted plateau. Prince Charles's personal popularity, under the tutelage of Checketts and Neilson, had reached an all-time high. Even the testy Prince Philip seemed to have mellowed in middle age. The family that stood on the balcony of Buckingham Palace, from the oldest—the seventy-seven-year-old Queen Mother and Lord Mountbatten—to the Queen's youngest son—four-year-old Prince Edward—gave every indication of being united, happy, and stable. But the seeds of destruction had already been sown. A steep downward slope lay ahead. The next several years were to bring a slowly building crescendo of catastrophe.

Twenty-six

The Princess
and the Pauper

E ven as she celebrated her Silver Jubilee, the Queen knew that within weeks she would be forced to make an unprecedented announcement. Princess Margaret's marriage had been in difficulties for years. At its worst the marriage was a nightmare. Princess Margaret had twice been hospitalized in what appeared to be suicide attempts. One of her former lovers had committed suicide, and another had a breakdown.

By the mid-seventies, both the Princess and her husband were involved in relationships with other people. The first Royal divorce could not be long delayed, and despite her position as temporal head of the Church of England, which does not recognize divorce, she would have to sanction the dissolution of her sister's marriage. Princess Margaret had produced two children in quick succession—David, Lord Linley, and Lady Sarah. Armstrong-Jones had been created Lord Snowdon before the birth of his son, and for a short period of time, the two were happy. But Snowdon quickly tired of the tedious aspects of life among the Royals. He was an exceptionally talented photographer and continued to pursue his career. He became bored as he accompanied his wife on her round of royal duties, although no one would describe Princess Margaret's program of engagements as grueling.

Friends began to notice the friction that erupted between them. One friend of Snowdon's who had had reservations about the marriage from the beginning described them as two machine guns firing at each other with short breaks to reload. At one dinner party they were heard to fight over a painting that had been recently bought by the host. Princess Margaret did not like it. Snowdon did. The fight, perhaps typical of a married couple who no longer love each other, descended into insults about each other's taste. At another social event, Snowdon seemed to ignore his wife while chatting amiably with others. When Princess Margaret sought to get his attention, he was heard to shout, "Go away! You're boring me!" At another row at their home in Kensington Palace, a large and valuable Florentine mirror was smashed when Princess Margaret slammed a door too hard in violent frustration. One hostess even heard Snowdon boast that he could "get rid of her" anytime he wished.

A more serious argument grew out of their mutual infidelity. Both Princess Margaret and Lord Snowdon had sturdy sexual appetites, and both were capable of casting their eyes elsewhere. It was a period of unprecedented promiscuity, and among a wealthy London set, the Snowdons were very hip. Princess Margaret is reported to have had a short but destructive relationship with Anthony Barton, a member of a prominent vineyard-owning family and a friend of both. He had even stood as godfather to Princess Margaret and Snowdon's daughter. Princess Margaret, either racked by guilt or jealousy, reportedly told Barton's wife, Eva. Some of Snowdon's friends believed that he took the affair with equanimity because he was not himself guiltless.

There was a reconciliation, but Lord Snowdon was determined to establish his independence from the Royal Family. Unfortunately for Princess Margaret, she was often the butt of criticism of the increasing cost of maintaining the Royal Family during times of economic hardship. She became the target because politicians were reluctant to criticize the Queen, since doing so made them appear to be disloyal. As a result, they felt themselves free to attack her sister, whose constitutional functions were more vague. Moreover, Snowdon was determined not to be tarred with the same brush. He resented being forced to live in his wife's home, Kensington Palace, and established his own country estate in Sussex.

Snowdon bought Old House, a dilapidated mansion on thirty acres, and spent his own money, from a coffee-table book of photographs, on restoring it. He rarely consulted Princess Margaret, and when she saw the house after it had been restored, she hated it. Cynics have suggested that Snowdon intended that she hate it so that he could be alone there. When Princess Margaret realized her husband had established his own retreat, she decided to establish hers. An old friend, Colin Tennant, owned the tiny Caribbean island of Mustique, where he had established an exclusive tourist colony. He had offered Princess Margaret a large piece of property as a wedding gift.

It was a gift that had gone unclaimed, because Snowdon did not enjoy beaches and the sun. After Old House was complete, she claimed her gift and began building a home on the holiday island that she knew Snowdon would never want to visit.

In 1967, when Snowdon went on an extended assignment to Japan for the *Sunday Times*, Princess Margaret renewed an intimate friendship with Robin Douglas-Home, the nephew of the former prime minister, Sir Alec Douglas-Home. Robin Douglas-Home was an accomplished musician and sometime gossip journalist as well as heir to the Earldom of Home, his uncle's Scottish estate. Douglas-Home was in love with Princess Margaret and would not accept her decision to break off the relationship. Princess Margaret found herself in the middle of another intense and potentially scandalous romance. Douglas-Home was divorced, and a divorce between her and Snowdon seemed out of the question. When the Princess was admitted to the King Edward VII Hospital for undisclosed reasons, it was widely rumored in Fleet Street that there was a rift between her and Snowdon and that she had taken an overdose of barbiturates.

Margaret and Snowdon again reconciled while Douglas-Home's life and career went downhill. Notoriously unstable, he often talked of committing suicide. In 1968, he tried to sell his letters from Princess Margaret in New York, and when his friends ostracized him for this act of betrayal, he buried himself in loneliness and depression. He was found dead from an overdose the same year.

Princess Margaret and Snowdon's love was revived for only a short time. In 1969, they accepted the fact that their marriage no longer worked and that they could not obtain a divorce. They would allow each other the freedom to live separate lives for most of the year while maintaining the pretense of harmony on public occasions. The arrangement gave Snowdon the freedom to embark on an intense relationship with a woman young enough to be his daughter. Snowdon's friends at Old House were the Marquess of Reading and his family, who had an adjoining estate. The Readings had an attractive daughter, Lady Jacqueline, aged twenty-one. At Christmas, 1969, Snowdon, a charismatic thirty-nine, began a secret affair with her. Even given the diminishing standards of the day, it was at the very least a breach of hospitality.

The extent of Snowdon's feelings for her are unknown, but Lady Jacqueline told friends she was in love with him and wanted to marry him. Not for the last time in the matter of Royal love affairs, the British security services stepped in to break up the relationship by making the affair public.

The affair, which became increasingly serious, had remained secret for almost a year. The Royal Protection Squad and the Metropolitan Police Special Branch knew about it, since they were responsible for the Royal Family's safety and therefore had good reason to monitor Snowdon's movements and the people with whom he came in contact. Once the relationship threatened to involve the Queen in a scandal, a story was leaked to the New York *Daily News.* New York was chosen because reporters there were less likely to be aware of the original source of the leak. It was also hoped that a story emanating from New York would cause Snowdon to break off the relationship, while providing him with a measure of deniability.

As expected, the British press took up the story, and Lady Jacqueline, who had been vacationing in Gstaad, Switzerland, was besieged by reporters. Returning home, she confessed to her mother and father that the story was true, and Snowdon was banned from their home. Once more, Princess Margaret and Snowdon, partly for the sake of their children and partly because they were instructed to do so by the Queen, appeared in public together, posing as a happily married couple who had been the focus of sensational and baseless newspaper reports. But their appearance only served as a pretense. It took another seven years before they could extricate themselves from a now loveless marriage. Meanwhile, the difficulty of finding a fulfilling relationship outside her marriage began to take its toll on the Princess. Friends remarked that she had put on weight and drank and smoked more than usual.

In 1972, Princess Margaret spent several weeks apart from her husband at her home on the island of Mustique. Almost everyone else on the island had a companion. Although the Princess enjoyed the freewheeling lifestyle of Mustique's colony of less than a hundred wealthy Europeans and partied often, it was clear that she needed a man in her life. Colin Tennant, her old friend, resolved to find her one. He came in the unlikely form of an aimless young man named Roddy Llewellyn.

Tennant spent only a few weeks a year in Britain. In September 1973 he was staying on his impressive Scottish estate, known as Glen, and had invited Princess Margaret and others as houseguests for a week. Finding himself short of a single man to balance the numbers—Princess Margaret was the odd one—he called a London hostess he knew for advice. She mentioned the twenty-five-year-old Roddy Llewellyn as an agreeable young man, and Tennant invited him up from London. Llewellyn was the younger son of Harry Llewellyn, a wealthy Welsh landowner, equestrian, and horse breeder.

Harry, Roddy's father, knew several members of the Royal Family through the equestrian circuit. Roddy himself had breeding and good manners. He was handsome, with sharp, chiseled features, a fine jaw line and strong chin, and shoulder-length hair. He could be amusing and entertaining in a vapid way. But he had a mediocre education, no career, and worked reluctantly as a clerk researching genealogies in the offices of the College of Heralds in London for a subsistence wage. Despite his father's wealth, he was close to penury.

Roddy Llewellyn was introduced to Princess Margaret and placed next to her at lunch and dinner on the first day. They became lovers almost immediately. When the week passed, they agreed to see each other as often as they could, and several of Princess Margaret's circle of friends offered to invite them, separately, to weekends and dinners so they could be together. The basis of the relationship is easier to understand than it first appears. For Princess Margaret, Llewellyn was a stimulating and youthful lover who was completely captivated by her. In turn, Llewellyn seemed only too happy to be the illicit plaything of a Princess who had been one of the beauties of her day and who, at forty-three, was still very attractive.

They understood each other and had more in common than might at first glance be supposed. Both were second children living in the shadow of older siblings. Both lived comparatively pointless existences. Both were bored with life and were in desperate need of constant amusement.

At first, the relationship did them both good. Princess Margaret lost weight and regained her sense of enjoyment. She helped find Roddy a better job—although it only lasted two months—and she took him secretly to Mustique for a romantic holiday. But their relationship demanded too much secrecy. They obviously could not go out together on regular dates to the movies, the theater, or a public restaurant or simply see each other whenever they wanted. Llewellyn was aware that he was an unlikely match for Princess Margaret and uncertain where the relationship, heady at first, would lead. It has been suggested elsewhere that Princess Margaret's physical demands were overwhelming.

After more than a year of secret rendezvous and romantic escapes, Roddy Llewellyn had what amounted to an emotional breakdown. He took off unexpectedly for India for several weeks. India was at that time a magnet for wandering European hippies, many of whom were drug addicts who had to sell their blood to survive. When he eventually returned to Britain after a short sojourn in Barbados, he was admitted to Charing Cross Hospital for a complete rest. Princess Margaret had also been ill. The palace announced that she had a severe cold and canceled a series of engagements. In reality, she had again overdosed on sedatives, this time not seriously enough to be hospitalized.

Llewellyn recuperated at his family's home in Wales for several weeks. But they were reunited when Llewellyn, after joining a commune of well-heeled hippies on a fifty-acre farm known as Surrendell, near the town of Malmesbury in Wiltshire, appeared recovered. He visited Princess Margaret several times in London, then invited her to the commune for a weekend. On her first visit she brought the singer John Phillips, of the Mama and the Papas, and his wife, Genevieve. She came several more times, and her relationship with Llewellyn resumed its frenetic pace. They even returned to Mustique for another romantic vacation.

But there was no way to keep the relationship secret forever. There had been stories in several newspapers about their "friendship" and, in the scurrilous satirical magazine *Private Eye*, about lovemaking *sur l'herbe* at Surrendell. Ross Waby, an Australian journalist working for the *News of the World* in New York, managed to rent a house in Mustique while Llewellyn and Princess Margaret were there. He took the only photograph of them together. It was an innocent enough pose—sitting next to each other at a beachside table. To make it more interesting, the other couple at the table, Lord and Lady Coke, were cropped in the published picture.

Everyone now realized that Princess Margaret and Lord Snowdon's marriage had become a sham. Although the breakup of her marriage could not be entirely laid to Margaret, she bore the brunt of the criticism. She was portrayed as the spoiled and willful Princess, living off taxpayers' money, and as a wayward wife. Snowdon, whose work was widely admired, escaped much of the blame. It was now clear that the agreement the couple had made in private in 1969 would have to be made legal.

Divorce had played a role in two major Royal scandals, depriving one, King Edward VIII of his throne and a Princess of a husband. Now, at last, the unthinkable could no longer be avoided. In this instance, a man over whom the Palace had no real control simply demanded to be legally released from his marriage to a woman he no longer loved.

The matter was made more urgent by the fact that, unknown to anyone, Snowdon had a relationship of his own. He had spent six weeks in Australia shooting a documentary and had fallen in love with a member of the production team, Lucy Lindsay-Hogg, the ex-wife of television director Michael Lindsay-Hogg. He wished to marry her. If the Queen did not agree to allow her sister to divorce, Snowdon could have forced the issue in court. Like any other citizen, he had a right to a civil divorce, which the Queen could not deny him. Faced with the prospect of a court action against a member of her family, the Queen agreed to an amicable settlement.

The divorce became final in the spring of 1978. For all the great efforts of the Royals to avoid the stigma of divorce in the past, for all the past predictions of disaster, the heavens did not fall when the first Royal divorce was announced. By then Roddy Llewellyn had become almost a comic figure. Pursued relentlessly by the press, he swung erratically between cashing in and fleeing. He accepted $10,000 from a newspaper for a photograph of himself and fellow communards from Serrendell and pursued a recording career which was clearly based on his notoriety as Princess Margaret's "toy boy." He was charged with drunk driving after an accident in Central London when he apparently attempted to reach the safe refuge of Kensington Palace. He appeared on a television show and sang and was eviscerated by the critics.

The rest of the year was also a difficult one for Princess Margaret. She was again admitted to King Edward VII Hospital. This time doctors diagnosed hepatitis and ordered her to stop her heavy drinking for at least a year.

She was a physical and emotional wreck for several months—due not only to hepatitis and gastroenteritis but to the emotional strain of her divorce, the public humiliation of her relationship with Llewellyn and the physical and emotional changes brought on by giving up alcohol. In the years since, her health has given rise to some concern. A heavy smoker, she eventually had to have part of her lung removed.

The Queen adamantly refused to meet Roddy Llewellyn and made no secret of her distaste for his relationship with her sister. Prince Philip and Prince Charles regarded him as a good-for-nothing and wanted to horsewhip him. The Queen did recognize, however, that Princess Margaret was old enough to live her own life and, given the undeserved unhappiness that had come her way, had the right to whatever pleasure she could create for herself. The Queen Mother agreed to meet him informally. She liked him and enjoyed seeing her younger daughter radiant in his company. But she, too, was disturbed by the indiscreet antics of Princess Margaret and her young lover and the level of disrepute to which the affair had brought the Royal Family.

The relationship dragged on for almost two more years. The publicity surrounding the pair died as the press became bored with Llewellyn and the public no longer seemed to care about Princess Margaret's love life. There were more long sojourns in Mustique and many weekends with well-disposed friends. Princess Margaret even visited Llewellyn's parents with him, although they had made it clear they did not approve of the relationship. But by 1980 the bloom had gone from this particular rose. Llewellyn met Tania Soskin, a woman closer to his own age, and on their last visit to Mustique that winter, he confessed to Princess Margaret that he was in love with someone else and wanted to marry her.

Princess Margaret, then fifty years old, accepted the end of the relationship with grace, perhaps even relief. Knowing that Llewellyn was not the most emotionally stable of people, she may have been unwilling to risk breaking off the relationship herself. She was certainly not inconsolable, agreeing at first to attend Llewellyn's wedding, until she realized she was scheduled to be out of the country.

The nation and the Royal Family had found the entire spectacle at first amusing, then unedifying, and at the end somewhat pathetic. But the scandals surrounding Princess Margaret's personal life formed only a prologue to the disasters that were to come for the other members of the family, scandals that went further than simply causing embarrassment to the Queen. These new catastrophes rocked the House of Windsor to its foundations and brought not just the family but the institution of monarchy itself into disrepute. They were to leave the Windsor family shattered beyond repair and the prospect of the succession of Prince Charles and his descendants in serious doubt.

For the sake of clarity, it is necessary to deal with each branch of the family individually, but the full impact of the events covered in the following chapters can only be understood if it is recalled that the sagas involving Prince and Princess Michael of Kent, of Princess Anne and Mark Phillips, Prince Andrew and the Duchess of York, and Prince Charles and Princess Diana intertwine. The disasters that befell them and the scandals applied to their names occurred more or less simultaneously, compounding the blow to the family and the monarchy.

Twenty-seven

Princess Michael:
Crowned in a Far Country

I n the same year that Princess Margaret divorced, a new and spark-ling Royal came on the scene, bringing an unwelcome marital scan-dal with her and reviving debate on Britain's archaic anti-Catholic laws at a time when violence in sectarian Northern Ireland had increased.

She was the Royal who carries the burden of being Britain's least popular Princess, the former Marie-Christine von Reibnitz, Princess Michael of Kent. Her difficulties are partly due to the fact that she is married to one of the least well known and most determinedly private of all the Royal Princes, partly the result of her own poor judgment and provocative behavior. But it is largely the consequence of a concerted and mean-spirited effort on behalf of Buckingham Palace officials—and some individual members of the Royal Family—to ensure that the beau-tiful, willowy Princess be given a bad press.

Prince Michael is the son of Princess Marina of Greece and Prince George, Duke of Kent, George VI's and the Duke of Windsor's wayward brother. Prince Michael's brother, Edward, succeeded as Duke of Kent at age seven, when their father was killed in a plane crash in 1942. Prince Michael, born weeks before his father's death, grew up a hand-some, intelligent, and accomplished man, with a stable, if not especially glorious, military career in the Royal Hussars. He bore a striking resemblance to his grandfather, George V, and the last Czar, Nicholas Romanov, which he cultivated by sporting a beard exactly like his grandfather's.

The Kent branch of the Royal Family had fallen on hard times following the death of Prince Michael's father. There was no provision in the Civil List, from which Royal family members draw their income, for the widows of Royal Princes. So when the Duke was killed, his taxpayer-supported income ceased. The King and Queen could have adequately supported the widowed Duchess, Princess Marina, and her three children—the seven-year-old Duke, Princess Alexandra, and Prince Michael. They did help. But, humiliatingly, shortly after the war and again in 1960, the Kents were forced to publicly auction family art treasures, raising what now seem to be pathetically small sums of money and a fraction of what the items would be worth today.

Prince Michael lived in an elegantly furnished apartment in Kensington Palace, and his neighbors were the Queen Mother and Princess Margaret. But Prince Michael undertook few public duties and had no income from the Civil List. He was therefore able to maintain greater privacy than any of his Royal relatives. He was a prominent winter sportsman and liked fast cars and, discreetly, faster women. He had been close to Lord Mountbatten, who was something of a father figure. He got on remarkably well with Prince Philip, acted as an older brother to Prince Charles, and became one of the Queen's favorites. In 1977, he was thirty-five and had never married. He was the last Royal expected to be involved in a scandal of any kind.

One of Prince Michael's closest friends was his cousin, Prince William of Gloucester. In turn, Prince William's closest friend was a prominent British banker with whom he had been at Eton, Tom Troubridge. Troubridge was married to a remarkably beautiful Austrian aristocrat, Baroness Marie-Christine von Reibnitz, but the marriage does not appear to have worked for very long.

Prince William purportedly fell in love with his friend's wife, but how far that relationship went is unclear. In 1972, Prince William was killed instantly when the plane he was racing at a holiday air show crashed. It was a bizarre twist of fate for Prince Michael as well as for the Gloucester branch of the Royal Family. The father he never knew had been killed in a plane crash; now his cousin and friend. This second tragedy would bring him his wife.

Baroness von Reibnitz was deeply affected by the death of Prince William, as was Prince Michael. They were drawn together by the loss of their mutual friend. When her husband, Tom Troubridge, went first to New York and subsequently to Bahrain for lengthy stays on business, his wife did not accompany him. Before long, Prince Michael and the beautiful Baroness were in love. It seemed at first to be a hopeless match, similar to other Royal love affairs with divorced or married partners, the more so because the Baroness was Catholic and the Prince in direct line to the throne. Archaic British laws of succession forbade Royals marrying Catholics.

But Prince Michael and the Baroness were more aware than most of the state of Princess Margaret's marriage and the likelihood that Lord Snowdon would probably demand a divorce one day, there being nothing the Queen could do to stop him. Michael confided to Lord Mountbatten, who was something of a surrogate father, that he wanted to marry the Baroness but wanted above all to avoid a scandal. Mountbatten agreed to help pave the way. He used friends in the Vatican diplomatic corps to help the Baroness secure an annulment of her marriage—on the grounds he allegedly refused to give her children—and interceded on Prince Michael's behalf with the Queen.

Queen Elizabeth knew of the relationship, and while she had no particular regard for her cousin's taste in women, she was not prepared to stand in his way. She realized that once she had agreed to her sister's divorce, it would be unfair to obstruct Prince Michael's marriage. She agreed to ask the then prime minister, James Callaghan, for government approval of the marriage. But there were conditions. The first was easy. Prince Michael could keep his hereditary title and honors but had to stand aside in the line of succession to the throne, from which he was, in any case, distant. The second proved more difficult.

The Baroness would have to convert and join the Church of England and agree to bring up their children in the Anglican faith, which she adamantly refused to do. Dr. Donald Coggan, the archbishop of Canterbury, had imposed this latter condition, and without it, he refused to sanction a church wedding in England. Members of the Royal Family are forbidden to contract civil marriages.

A compromise was reached in which the Baroness agreed to bring up her children in the Anglican faith, but she could still not marry in England. The Baroness arranged a wedding in the ancient Roman Catholic church in Vienna. But just forty-eight hours before she was to walk down the aisle, the Vatican refused its permission for the marriage to take place. They objected to the arrangement on the religious education of any offspring born to the couple and stipulated that while they did not insist that Prince Michael convert to Catholicism, their children's upbringing must be in the Catholic faith. The Vatican's insistence on this arrangement was a bitter, humiliating blow. In England it revived memories of a sectarian prejudice that had been only shallowly buried.

The prohibition against members of the Royal Family marrying Catholics had its roots in the seventeenth-century struggles between the Protestant Establishment and the Catholic Stuart dynasty. But the belief that Catholics had an overriding loyalty to the Vatican continued well into the twentieth century and persisted in numerous anti-Catholic laws. Nowhere was this sectarian prejudice more institutionalized than in Northern Ireland, where, until the late sixties, more than half a million British citizens were disenfranchised and legally discriminated against in housing and employment because they were Catholics. The bitter conflict in Northern Ireland, where the Irish Republican Army (IRA) fought an increasingly bloody guerrilla war against the British army, had its roots in this sectarian prejudice. Ironically, the papal injunction against the marriage, sanctioned in part by the Royal Family, and the demand for Royal offspring to be brought up as Catholics resurrected the old saw that the Vatican demanded loyalty to the faith above loyalty to the Crown.

Prince Michael married the Baroness in a civil ceremony in Vienna that was much more subdued than had been planned. Much was made of which Royals came and which failed to appear. The Queen, Prince Philip, the Queen Mother, and Prince Charles stayed away. Princess Margaret was ill but would not have come if she had been well. Lord Mountbatten and Princess Anne attended, as did Prince Michael's brother, the Duke of Kent, and sister, Princess Alexandra. The battle lines were drawn on the wedding day.

The new Princess had been affronted by the public debate over her religion and, by implication, her fitness as a member of the Royal Family, as well as by the plotting, scheming, and negotiating that had been necessary for her to marry the man she loved. Much of her relationship with the Royals in the years to come would be based on that embittering experience. The Royal Family's failure to support the marriage only partially excuses the deliberate slap in the face she delivered to her new in-laws a few weeks later.

Returning from her honeymoon in the Far East, Princess Michael found herself in Paris. Long fascinated with the saga of the Duchess of Windsor and the Royal Family's long-standing feud with her and now believing there was an analogy between her own life and that of the Duchess, the Princess visited the Duchess's Paris home.

The Duke and Duchess of Windsor had been subjected to a long and often tedious exile following their marriage. The Duke's period as governor of the Bahamas had not brought him any kudos from the Royal Family. He had been allowed to attend the funeral of his brother, King George VI, in 1952 and to visit his mother, Queen Mary, on her deathbed the following year. But even those visits had deteriorated into acrimonious disputes over money. The new Queen's advisers had told her that a financial settlement between the Duke of Windsor and his brother the King was valid for the King's lifetime only and should not be continued after his death, which enraged the Duke. The exile and ice-cold distance from the Royal Family continued with occasional thaws. In 1965, the Duke visited London for an eye operation, and the Duchess was allowed to accompany him.

The Queen even visited the Duke of Windsor and exchanged a few words with his wife. A short time later, both were back in Britain for a memorial service for Princess Mary, the Princess Royal, the Duke's sister. Lord Mountbatten, the Duke's oldest friend, remained in contact with the Duke and sometimes acted as negotiator between the Duke and Duchess and the rest of the family. In 1969, Prince Charles made a private visit to the Duke, followed by several lesser family members, and three years later, the Queen herself visited the dying former King. She spent nearly ninety minutes alone with him, and while no one knows what was said, she emerged pale and upset. It is widely supposed that he made a deathbed plea for his wife to be acknowledged with the title "Her Royal Highness," which had always been denied her, and the Queen refused him. Two weeks later, he was dead. Keeping a secret bargain made in 1960, the former King of England was interred in the Royal Mausoleum at Frogmore, although he had once expressed a personal preference to be buried in the United States.

There was more than just sentiment involved in the attempt by the Royal Family to find a way to thaw relations. The Duke and Duchess still had a large collection of documents, letters, jewelry, ceremonial uniforms, and other possessions that the Royal Family sought. They wished to avoid the spectacle of an auction of the former King's personal property and possessions, but they were also worried that embarrassing letters between the Duke and his family, showing how petty the feud

had become, would be published. Most of all, they feared that the Duke
and Duchess had left either a manuscript to be published posthumously
or enough papers for an official biography which might also prove
embarrassing. Mountbatten constantly badgered the Duke about his
will. Having lived a full life and planning meticulously for his own
death, Mountbatten could not understand the reluctance with which
the Duke and Duchess considered their own mortality. Mountbatten
had to repeatedly urge him to leave various items to members of the
Royal Family.

After the Duke's death, Mountbatten tried unsuccessfully to have
himself appointed executor and Prince Charles chairman of a Duke of
Windsor trust. The Duchess and Maître Suzanne Blum, her attorney,
would not hear of it. Some items and documents were returned to the
possession of the Royal Family. It has been reported that Mountbatten
actually stole them. He continued to badger the Duchess for years about
her plans for disposing of the remainder of the estate, which would
upset and depress her.

The Queen Mother had been largely responsible for the continuation
of the feud after the war. She blamed her husband's death and the
change in the lives of her entire family on the Duke and Duchess. In
1976, she made a sudden gesture of friendship, offering to visit the
Duchess in Paris. The Duchess of Windsor believed the offer was
either hypocritical, it now being too late to have any point, or self-
interested, leading to another demand that her jewels be left to the
family, and refused to see her. The Queen Mother then sent her dozens
of roses.

The thaw over the years might have convinced the new British
Princess that it would be acceptable for her to visit the Duchess. The
old Duchess, now eighty-two, very sick and only intermittently lucid,
received the beautiful Princess Michael and her dashing husband with
evident pleasure, no doubt enhanced by the fact that Princess Michael
had addressed the Duchess by the title Royal Highness, long denied her
by the Royal Family.

The Duchess told the Prince some stories about his father, the Duke
of Kent, who had been the Duke of Windsor's favorite brother and the
only member of the Royal Family who enjoyed a good relationship with
the Duchess. She told the Princess it was a pleasure to have a beautiful
woman in the house again and thanked her for bringing a breath of
gaiety and fresh air into a home that had become a mausoleum. They

even talked of their respective difficulties in marrying the men they loved and how times had changed—Princess Margaret having just divorced that year.

The Duchess then gave Princess Michael a wedding gift of some jewelry—no doubt realizing the resentment the present would arouse in the rest of the family. To make matters worse, Princess Michael was quoted later as saying that the Duchess was a wronged woman and that historians would agree she had been unfairly treated.

The cordial visit with the Duchess turned the Queen, Prince Philip, and the Queen Mother against her. The feud never went as far as actually ostracizing the Princess—everyone liked Prince Michael too much for that—but there were some humiliating confrontations. The Queen recognized some jewelry Princess Michael had been given by the Duchess and told her never to wear it in her presence again. Unkind gossip items about the Princess and her relationship with the Queen began to appear—judicious leaks by palace officials.

The more Princess Michael demanded respect, the more the other Royals lampooned her. The palace let Fleet Street know that it was open season on Princess Michael. She was dubbed "Princess Pushy," "Our Val" for Valkyrie, and "Billiard Table Legs." Lord Linley, Princess Margaret's son, was quoted as saying he rated dinner with Princess Michael as a suitable Christmas gift for his worst enemy. Sometimes Princess Michael would retaliate with thinly veiled barbs against the Royal Family. She once pointed out in an interview that while most people referred to her as German, she had less German blood than her Royal in-laws. She could also go straight for the jugular. When she felt she had been betrayed by a friend, she sent her thirty silver coins— thirty pieces of silver—as a gift.

Throughout all this unpleasantness, Prince Michael remained devoted to his wife and she to him. The campaign of vilification became so heated that reporters were encouraged to check into the Nazi background of Princess Michael's father, Baron Gunther von Reibnitz, who had died in Mozambique in 1984 at the age of eighty-nine. It has been speculated that the encouragement came from officials at Buckingham Palace; others say that it came from a younger member of the Royal Family who particularly despised Princess Michael and who underestimated the hornet's nest that would be stirred up by the revelations.

Princess Michael's background had always been something of a mystery to the public, but it was no mystery to the Royal Family. Lord

Mountbatten, an acknowledged expert on the whole network of British and German aristocracy, probably learned a good deal of the story. He had met Princess Michael's father, and it would have been like him to try to find out why an Austrian aristocrat old enough to have held a World War II command had chosen to spend most of the postwar years in a German expatriate colony in Mozambique, remaining there, even during a civil war, until he died.

It is also routine for the British intelligence services to compile a detailed background check on people with close associations to the Royal Family. Investigators would not have had to look very far. There were files on Baron von Reibnitz at the Imperial War Museum in London, the United Nations, and the World War II document centers in Bonn and West Berlin. It is inconceivable that the Queen and other members of the Royal Family were unaware of Baron von Reibnitz's shocking past before it was revealed in the London Daily Mirror in 1985.

He had been born in Austria late in 1894 and fought in the German Army with distinction in World War I. He was twice decorated for valor, once with the Iron Cross, second-class. His Nazi party membership number was a low one, revealing that he joined the party as early as the late twenties. Those Germans who joined the Nazi party after 1933, when Hitler came to power, may be able to claim that there were political or social pressures to do so, but anyone joining the party as early as von Reibnitz had to have had a strong ideological commitment to its policies. A letter to Hitler in Nazi archives refers to von Reibnitz as a speaker at party election rallies.

In the years immediately after Hitler became chancellor of Germany, a power struggle took place between the Nazi's party's paramilitary wing, the Sturmabteilung, or Brownshirts, and the party hierarchy. Hitler launched a blood purge against the Brownshirts in June and July 1934, using his fanatical S.S. battalions, which became notorious during World War II. Von Reibnitz acted as a spy in the Brownshirts for Hitler's henchmen, Hermann Goering and Heinrich Himmler. He joined the S.S. shortly after the purge and was almost immediately promoted.

Von Reibnitz's career in the S.S. was undistinguished. He rose from the rank of S.S. *Untersturmführer*, equivalent to a second lieutenant in the U.S. Army, to S.S. *Sturmbannführer*, equivalent to a U.S. Army major. He took part in the invasion of Poland in 1939 but spent much of the rest of the war behind the lines in an annexed region of what is now

Czechoslovakia. There is no evidence he took part in any atrocities or worked at any concentration camps. In 1941 he sought the personal permission of Hitler to marry his second wife, Princess Michael's mother, a German Countess twenty years his junior. At one time she was suspected by the Gestapo of illegal contact with British agents. Her marriage to an S.S. officer was supposed to prove her innocence; in any case, the evidence against her was somewhat flimsy.

In 1944, when the Germans were purging many aristocrats suspected of disloyalty, von Reibnitz was ordered to retire from the S.S. on the grounds that he was still a practicing Catholic. His daughter, Marie-Christine, was born in January 1945. With Germany on the verge of collapse, von Reibnitz and his family found themselves in the path of Russian soldiers. They fled to American-occupied territory with few possessions. When the war ended and the S.S. was declared a criminal organization, von Reibnitz emigrated to the Portuguese colony of Mozambique, where he owned some property. His wife refused to join him there and took her daughter to Australia.

Her mother concealed her father's S.S. membership from her, but she grew up aware that her father had been a Nazi party member and had been a German officer. She visited her father in Mozambique as a teenager. Perhaps it should have struck her as suspicious that there were a number of Germans in their sixties residing in a colony there who appeared to have good reasons not to live in their native land. She says it did not. In 1966, when Marie-Christine turned twenty-one, she emigrated to England, using her old European title as an entrée to London society.

When the story broke in the *Daily Mirror* in 1985, Princess Michael claimed that the news that her father had been an officer in the S.S. came as a complete shock. Her mother, still in Australia, confirmed the report. Under pressure from Buckingham Palace to say little or nothing in response to the scandalous disclosures, Princess Michael issued a terse statement acknowledging the broad truth of the *Daily Mirror* report but pointing out she had known nothing of her father's war record.

It was obvious, considering the stringent background checks made by the security services, that Buckingham Palace must have known something about the late Baron's past. In order to keep the story alive, newspapers began to speculate about a palace cover-up. There had been no cover-up. But given the connections of Prince Philip to the S.S. by his sisters' marriages, the palace could have hardly objected to Princess

Michael's family background. People cannot choose their parents as they choose their spouses.

What had started as a spiteful piece of propaganda against Princess Michael now threatened to embroil the Royal Family itself and revive stories of their German and Nazi connections. Ordered to say nothing by the Queen, the Princess gave a television interview to try to win some sympathy. Princess Michael dissolved into tears during the broadcast, which, given the emotional strain she was under, seemed understandable. But public displays of emotion are despised among the Royal Family. The Queen, Prince Philip, and Prince Charles found the performance disgusting.

As soon as the story of her father's Nazi past no longer provoked interest, Princess Michael found herself involved in fresh scandal. Prince Michael had always lived in a comparatively frugal fashion, since he received no Civil List income. In order to support his new family and lifestyle, he had taken a number of business directorships—British corporations are always thrilled to have Royal Family representation on the board. Princess Michael, however, seemed always on the lookout for supplementary income and was alleged to have charged fees of up to $6,000 for public appearances. She became known as the "Royal for Rent" and "Rent a Kent." The Queen, outraged, ordered her to stop.

Princess Michael then turned to writing and produced two books: *Crowned in a Far Country*, about the misadventures of a Princess uprooted by arranged marriages, and *Kings and Courtesans*, about Royal mistresses. Both brought complaints that Princess Michael's work was at best highly derivative and at worst that parts had been plagiarized. One complaint from an author was settled out of court for about $30,000.

But the scandal that broke Princess Michael's heart came when newspapers intimated there was something more than friendship in her relationship with Ward Hunt, heir to a Texas oil fortune. Princess Michael was alleged to have known Hunt for nearly two years and to have visited him at his home in Dallas without her Royal husband. Hunt had visited her in London, and the two had also spent some time at the California home of a friend of Princess Michael's, Princess Ezra of Hyderabad.

Agents of MI5, acting after consultations with Buckingham Palace, leaked information that the forty-three-year-old Hunt planned another visit to London to see the Princess when Princess Michael was still recovering from the revelations about her father's Nazi background.

Hunt planned to stay at the home of Princess Ezra in fashionable Eaton Square. Reporters and photographers, tipped off by the palace, staked out the house and saw Princess Michael arrive in an apparent disguise. She stayed at the apartment until loyal members of the Royal Protection Squad, staking out the house, spotted the photographers and warned Her Royal Highness. Hunt returned to Texas the same day. The success of this operation led to another similar one against Fergie some years later.

The Queen did not enjoy her discomfiture—she understood that such scandals reflect on the entire family—but her avowed enemies among the Royals took the news with ill-concealed glee. It was a shot across Princess Michael's bows—a warning intended to bring her to heel—and it worked. But Princess Michael was to have the last laugh. In time, she and her husband patched up whatever damage had been done to their marriage, and while the other Windsor marriages were imploding, hers remained intact.

Twenty-eight

Princess Anne: The Princess in the Tower

T he losers in the genetic lottery are endowed with the worst traits of both sides of their family; such is the case with Queen Elizabeth II's only daughter, Anne, the Princess Royal. From her mother's side of the family she inherited the heavy Hanoverian jaw which makes her appear angry, sulky, or bored even in repose. From her father she got her quick temper, acid tongue, violent impatience, and hearty anti-intellectualism.

It was Prince Philip's contempt for the Windsor men—the Duke of Windsor, George VI, the Duke of Kent, and the Duke of Gloucester, whom he saw as a pathetic lot of weaklings—that made him determined that his own children would be made of sterner stuff. While he failed with Prince Charles, he succeeded with Princess Anne. Throughout her childhood, she fought like a young tigress with her brother, her mother, and her grandmother, becoming closest to her athletic, acerbic, stubborn, and demanding father. He only wished his eldest son could have been more like his only daughter.

A less than indifferent scholar, Princess Anne emerged from the chrysalis of a twelfth-grade education at the fashionable Benenden private school, looking, in the words of a newspaper columnist, "frumpy, grumpy and dumpy." She was neither sexy, pretty, or even graceful. The antithesis of sixties glamour, she was slightly overweight by the lean and hungry standards of the day. While she sported miniskirts and showed a generous, and in those days fashionable, breadth of thigh, the best that can be said of her is that she photographed well only on a

horse. Indeed, the cloistered world of amateur and professional equestrianism was where she found her happiness, her privacy, her mercurial
popularity, and her husband.

From the outset of her Royal career that began at the age of eighteen,
she has longed for, even sought, the ordinariness of private life. At the
same time, she was prepared, even enthusiastic, about Royal duties:
launching ships with aplomb, visiting regiments with muscular interest,
touring car plants, factories, and mines. But she refused to accept press
attention to, particularly press speculation about, her private life. And
from her teenaged years on, her relationship with the British press, and
therefore to a great extent the British public, has always been at best
tense, at worst open warfare.

She saw herself as the Princess in the Tower, a Rapunzel who longed
to let down her hair and escape to the arms of not a handsome prince but
an ordinary man.

Within a year of Anne's leaving school, her eldest brother, Prince
Charles, was invested as Prince of Wales. It was a reminder to her that
she would always be in the shadow first of one brother, then another.
Royal succession always leapfrogs women when men are in line. She
determined to find at least one endeavor in which she could shine
brighter than her brothers and preferably succeed despite of, or at least
regardless of, her Royal status. Inevitably, she focused on riding.

Like all the Royals, she had learned to ride as a child and was
thoroughly proficient. But in the year of the investiture, she bought
three first-class horses, hired world-class trainers, and for three years
rode three hours almost every day before breakfast, pushing herself at a
grueling pace. By 1970, she was a highly competitive Olympic standard
rider in the equestrian sport known as Eventing.

Few equestrians come to national prominence in Britain, although
horse trials and show-jumping events are often broadcast on television.
Princess Anne's obsession with the sport helped boost interest in the
1971 Badminton Horse Trials. She performed well among a field of
forty-eight outstanding riders from Britain and Europe and finished
fifth. The winner was a young British army officer named Mark Phillips.

Mark Phillips had first met Princess Anne in 1968, when he was a
member of the British Olympic Equestrian team in Mexico. Princess
Anne and her father had met him, along with other British athletes, on
their return to London. They met again on the equestrian circuit, often

rode together, and became friends. He was more accomplished, more experienced, and physically stronger, and she often sought his guidance and advice.

The same year, she showed astonishing courage by winning the Raleigh Trophy in the Individual European three-day event at Burghley, just weeks before she had had surgery for the removal of an ovarian cyst. Her victory brought her a range of honors, including Sports Personality of the Year and Sports Woman of the Year. But she missed being selected for the 1972 Munich Olympics.

By then, however, she was deeply involved with Mark Phillips, then a lieutenant in the Queen's Dragoon Guards. The Phillips family came from what in Britain is known as the county set—untitled, complacently comfortable, and following traditional pastoral pursuits, such as fox hunting and show jumping. Mark Phillips had performed unremarkably at the expensive and fashionable Marlborough private school and left with poor grades. His academic performance proved insufficient for admission to the British army's officer training college at Sandhurst, whose demands in that area can hardly be said to be stringent. He eventually was admitted after joining the army as a private soldier and as part of a quota of other-rank entries. He showed outstanding skill in only one area: riding.

By the time he became friends with Princess Anne, riding in equestrian events was his life; his career in the army was without glory. She had already had a number of boyfriends. One, Sandy Harpur, a rising young stockbroker, was Princess Anne's first great love and a man her family believed she would one day marry. Harpur had been given an insight into life behind the palace walls during his courtship and decided it wasn't for him. He unceremoniously dumped his Princess and married a fashion model.

Throughout months of speculation on a possible husband for Princess Anne, constitutionally at least, it did not matter whom she married, for her distance from the throne only increased the older she got. But life can be more complex than that. Another boyfriend she might have married, and with whom she has remained on intimate terms throughout her life, turns out to be an army officer who has had a fateful impact on the whole Royal Family, perhaps the future of the monarchy itself. He is Andrew Parker-Bowles, who later married Camilla Shand, a woman who was to feature prominently in the breakup of the marriage of Prince Charles and Princess Diana.

Parker-Bowles's father, Derek Parker-Bowles, became a close friend of the Queen Mother. His son met Princess Anne at her grandmother's home at Royal Lodge, Windsor. He pursued the Princess, ousting her then regular escort, Brian Alexander, son of World War II military leader Earl Alexander of Tunis. But the Queen intervened to break up the relationship. Parker-Bowles was a Catholic, and she feared the marriage of her daughter to a Catholic would cause another scandalous crisis. Parker-Bowles, a rising young officer in the Royal Horse Guards, was conveniently posted to West Germany, leaving the field open. Ironically, had Parker-Bowles been allowed to woo Princess Anne to the altar, the Crown might sit a little easier today.

Equestrian Richard Meade, one of Mark Phillips's closest rivals and challengers in the sport, also became a challenger for Princess Anne's hand. She enjoyed a romantic but superficial relationship with Meade. Her affair with Phillips developed slowly, as they became close friends, then, finally, and at first hesitantly, lovers.

Princess Anne's futile quest for privacy during her engagement to Phillips caused the relationship between the British press and Buckingham Palace to deteriorate. It seemed obvious that this man, with whom she was seen constantly at equestrian events, training, and at Royal Family gatherings, was a lover and therefore a marriage prospect. The palace denied a romance until the very moment the engagement was announced on May 29, 1973, leading the press to conclude they had been lied to and that all palace denials on every subject were worthless. Princess Anne and Mark Phillips claim that the realization that they were headed for love and marriage from companionship and platonic intimacy came to others before it happened to them. It is also true that the palace did lie to protect their privacy. But there was another reason why the palace tried to fend off speculation. Prince Philip and the Queen both hoped their daughter would change her mind.

Prince Philip did not like Mark Phillips, and such is the bond with his daughter, he would probably have distrusted any suitor. He particularly disliked Mark Phillips's equine sensibilities, the fact that he had a one-track mind—horses—and was unable to have a conversation that did not involve equestrian pursuits or the army. Prince Philip, as a career naval officer, looked down on the least fashionable arm of the military. He considered riding, in polo or in equestrian events, as a pastime. Phillips had made it a career. He may also have resented his expertise. It has been claimed that it was his future father-in-law who

coined the nickname "Fog" for Phillips. In fact, it had been his
nickname in his Sandhurst days. In English colloquial usage it means he
is thick, that is, stupid, and wet, a wimp, at least out of the saddle.

The Queen had also hoped for a more accomplished son-in-law with a
brighter future, but she at last realized that nothing would be gained by
trying to dissuade her stubborn daughter. It was Mark Phillips's ordinariness that enhanced his attractiveness to Princess Anne. Always
uncomfortable with the public aspects of Royal life, she saw in Mark
Phillips a means of escape into a more normal existence. It was a naive
hope, like a drowning man who drags his rescuer under. Rather than
find an ordinary life with Mark Phillips, she merely dragged him into
her extraordinary existence.

The wedding took place on a freezing morning, November 14, 1973,
in Westminster Abbey. Princess Anne refused to wait until the following spring and good weather, and her parents could not dissuade her
because they had also been married in November. Nine Royal coaches
and platoons of red-clad guards and cavalry—among them her former
boyfriend Andrew Parker-Bowles—rode to the nine-hundred-year-old
Abbey. In the words of one columnist, Princess Anne looked "as beautiful as ice" as she walked down the aisle to the sound of herald trumpets.
The public knew little of Mark Phillips except through the often acid
comments of press columnists. But in a joint television interview with
his bride prior to the wedding, and for which he had received weeks of
coaching from media experts, he appeared so dull, uninteresting, and
pompous that much of the press criticism appeared justified.

It was the worst possible time for an expensive Royal pageant. A
harsh economic winter was approaching, and everyone had become
aware of its icy clutch. Inflation, now rampant, was recalculated weekly. The Conservative government of Edward Heath began to prepare for
its confrontation with the underpaid coal miners, a class conflict that
would undermine, for several months, the stability of the state, the
economy, even the political system. Conservatives called for the welfare
state system to be cut back. One Conservative newspaper even claimed
it was possible to "get rich quick" on unemployment benefits. In the
past, Royal pageants have been distractions from hard times, but
Princess Anne's wedding, though not unusually lavish in itself, sparked
resentment among many who would soon be lining up for essential goods
in short supply. The honeymoon on the Royal yacht *Britannia*, which
cost $40,000 a day to keep afloat, also caused controversy.

But the Royal fans still came in the hundreds of thousands and braved the foot-stamping cold. And the press reported the ceremony breathlessly and the related minutiae in intimate detail, sometimes too intimate. A shop assistant who had been sworn to secrecy revealed the design of the lingerie that had been bought for Princess Anne's honeymoon.

In 1973, the conflict in Northern Ireland was escalating by the month. In normal circumstances, Capt. Mark Phillips would join his regiment there for at least one three-month tour of duty. This assignment had been judged too dangerous for the husband of a Royal Princess. Instead, he was posted to the Royal Military College at Sandhurst as an instructor, the same institution for which he had been judged academically ill equipped a few years before. With the posting came a subsidized home, not one normally provided a captain, but given to a colonel. And at fifteen dollars a week rent, they paid less than an average family for public housing.

The economic and constitutional crisis that erupted just a few months after the wedding helped to make the criticism of such favoritism more shrill. Then, just five months after their wedding, came an unprecedented assault. A man tried to kidnap Princess Anne from her official car as gunfire echoed down the Mall to Buckingham Palace.

Just days before, the Queen had had a narrow escape when her plane strayed into a NATO air training zone, was mistaken for a robot target drone, and came within seconds of being shot out of the sky by a wing of fighter planes. The Royal Protection Squad, Special Branch, and MI5, aware of the possibility of an assassination attempt on a member of the Royal Family by the Provisional IRA, had ordered a review of all security.

Princess Anne and Captain Phillips had gone to a charity movie screening in Newgate Street earlier in the evening. An Austin Princess limo, carrying the Princess, Phillips, a lady-in-waiting, Rowena Brassey, one bodyguard, James Beaton, and the chauffeur, Alexander Callendar, drove up Fleet Street and across Trafalgar Square to the Mall for a ride of what would have been just a few minutes. Following them, unnoticed, was a white Ford Escort driven by a man named Ian Ball.

Halfway up the Mall, Ball swerved in front of the limo, forcing it to stop. He leaped from the car, rushed at the limo pointing a .22 handgun, opened the door, and pointed it at Princess Anne. Beaton, the bodyguard, was already out of the front door of the limo and in firing position. Ball shot him twice. Beaton fired back but, badly wounded, missed. When he tried to fire again, his pistol jammed, and he took cover to try to free the mechanism.

"Come with me! I want you for two days!" Ball screamed at Princess Anne. Callendar, the chauffeur, grabbed Ball and was shot in the chest. There was a tug-of-war between Ball and Phillips, each holding one of Princess Anne's arms. Beaton could not free the firing mechanism on his Walther automatic, but he pointed it at Ball again. Ball countered by pointing his at the Princess. "Drop it or I'll shoot her!" he said. Beaton, who was in any case holding a useless weapon, did so.

Beaton was still on his feet despite his wounds. He pushed himself into the limo and tried to shield Princess Anne. He swung the door at the attacker to try to knock him off his feet. Ball shot him twice more. Princess Anne tried to calm Ball when a passerby, ironically, a journalist, Brian McConnell, intervened and was also shot. A police constable, Michael Hills, on guard duty at nearby St. James Palace, joined the melée and he, too, was brought down by gunfire. Only when a passing car blocked Ball's escape vehicle and police reinforcements, summoned by the wounded Constable Hills, began to arrive did Ball give up and run. He was brought down from behind by a detective, Peter Edmonds. The incident had lasted ten minutes.

For a time at least, the Royal Protection Squad and Special Branch believed that the attack was part of a wider plan and that Ball had not operated alone. Other members of the Royal Family were in various parts of the world: the Queen and Prince Philip in Djakarta, Indonesia; Prince Charles in Los Angeles; and Princess Margaret, with her boyfriend, Roddy Llewellyn, in Mustique. All were placed under maximum security protection, which was particularly embarrassing for Princess Margaret.

It was even feared that the kidnap attempt was a signal for a coup. The crack Special Forces regiments, the paratroopers, SAS, and some units of the Royal Marines were placed on alert, and other units of the army were confined to barracks.

Ball was quickly judged to be a lunatic and sent to a maximum security institution for the criminally insane from which he has not since emerged. However, for an apparent madman, he had planned his kidnap attempt meticulously, arranging false identities and documents and leaving behind kidnap demands with precise instructions. He had been following the Princess and Captain Phillips for weeks and had prepared one kidnap attempt in Spain a short time earlier. There was no public inquiry into the incident. The flow of information from both the palace and Scotland Yard was carefully controlled, and the insanity decision avoided a full trial. It is virtually a tradition that those who attack British Royalty are ipso facto insane.

What was most frightening to the Royal Family was that—insane or not—had Ball been an assassin bent only on killing the Princess, he would certainly have succeeded and stood a good chance of escaping. Though Beaton had been brave—he had willingly put his life at risk to save the Princess—a single bodyguard with an unreliable weapon could not protect two lives. Royal protection obviously had to be stepped up. In fact, it remained lax because the Queen insisted that the Royals could not exist behind the kind of blanket protection that governs the movements of other heads of state, such as American presidents.

The marital relationship of Princess Anne and Capt. Mark Phillips was always tempestuous. He found life under the microscope too pressured. His army career was ruined because he could not pursue the normal avenues of promotion and had to avoid conflict, which is, of course, the whole point of being an army officer. No one believed he was suited to the post of instructor at Sandhurst. His military experience did not support it. He seemed ill at ease at public Royal events and diffident in private gatherings.

After two years, the Queen bought him a 730-acre farm, Gatcombe Park, for nearly $10 million, while he went to agricultural college to learn the ways of a gentleman farmer.

Meanwhile, Princess Anne found it as difficult to adjust to the role of army wife as her spouse did to the role of Royal husband. Horses became their only binding interest, and in 1976 Princess Anne was selected for the British Olympic team in Montreal. It was the peak of her career in the sport. Her performance was mediocre by world standards, although getting there was an enormous achievement, one forged by her own iron will. It had nothing to do with her Royal status.

She turned her attention to having a family and became pregnant the following year, giving birth to a son, Peter Mark Andrew Phillips, in November 1977. She insisted that the child have no title, the first step in a campaign to extricate her family from the Royal burden. But soon after the birth of her son, weaknesses in their marriage began to surface. Even relatively trivial arguments became explosive.

One reason had to do with Princess Anne's own innate stubbornness. According to friends she was never wrong. In turn, her husband tended to see each disagreement as questioning his manhood, which was already severely challenged by the circumstances of his marriage to a Princess. Worse, both had a bizarre view of intrapersonal relationships. It is a fundamental rule of riding that the rider must master the horse at all times and never allow the mount to rule the rider. Neither had a sophisticated education in human relations, and both saw each other as a horse that needed to be mastered. But relationships need give-and-take. Purportedly, Princess Anne was so incensed at her husband's behavior on a Royal tour that she locked him out of her bedroom. He kicked the door in. Buckingham Palace denies the story.

Determined to make a career independent of his wife, Phillips devoted arduous days to his farm and months of the year to professional equestrian pursuits, such as specialized schools, sponsored events, and the like. These pursuits meant that he and Princess Anne were often apart while he was in the company of women who were still committed to riding careers and who admired Phillips for what he was—one of a handful of world-class horsemen.

In 1979 a new detective was appointed to the rota of Princess Anne's bodyguards. Peter Cross was a thirty-one-year-old ladies' man. The turmoil in her marriage to Mark Phillips, the realization of her sliding popularity, and the fact that Princess Margaret performed fewer and fewer Royal duties impelled Princess Anne to take on a greater burden of Royal obligations. Her industry and stamina, particularly on behalf of the charity Save the Children, earned her the title Princess Royal, bestowed by the Queen in 1987. In 1979 and 1980, she visited Portugal, West Germany, Thailand, the Gilbert and Ellice islands, New Zealand, Australia, the Bahamas, Canada, Cyprus, France, Belgium, and Fiji, as well as participating in a full calendar of duties in Britain. Although Phillips went with her on a number of these tours, she became close to Cross. After only ten months on the Royal Protection Squad, following an investigation by other members of the squad and MI5, triggered by a complaint by Captain Phillips about his familiarity with Princess Anne, Cross was fired.

Cross almost immediately offered a story of his "special relationship" with Princess Anne to British newspapers. There were at first no takers, but in 1985 one Sunday newspaper did publish the sensational allegations, leaving readers the impression that Princess Anne was in love with her bodyguard. It was even claimed that after he had been dismissed from royal protection Princess Anne continued to stay in contact with him.

In May 1981, Princess Anne gave birth to her daughter, Zara. Cross claimed that Princess Anne called him at home the same night to tell him of the successful delivery and that she was well. It is not unusual for bodyguards to become father confessors, even surrogate brothers, to their charges. There have even been cases in which the protected and the protector fall in love. There was never any public confirmation of the bodyguard's allegations. Cross himself was subject to a campaign of vilification by the palace and Scotland Yard, and Fleet Street's rival newspapers were led to stories which portrayed him, with some justification, as a compulsive womanizer.

By the time the allegations against the Princess were published, the eight-year-old Royal marriage was effectively over. They agreed to lead separate lives, to stay together for the children's sake, but to give each other the freedom to live their own lives with discretion. Phillips took every advantage of the situation but was incapable of restraining his jealousy when his wife used the same freedom. Mark Phillips's name had already been linked with a prominent BBC news reporter, Angela Rippon, although she has always denied there was a relationship between them. A Canadian public relations consultant, Kathy Birks, was also pursued by reporters after they were discovered having breakfast together at a hotel. Several prominent horsewomen, including the American rider Karen Lende, have also been linked with Phillips.

And according to allegations made in court papers several years later, Phillips had had a child out of wedlock the same year the Peter Cross allegations appeared in the British press. Schoolteacher Heather Tonkin claimed that Phillips had a one-night affair with her in a hotel in Auckland in 1984, just days before his eleventh wedding anniversary. The child, named "Bunny," was born the following August.

Although Phillips was alleged to have filtered money to her under the guise of consultancy fees, she eventually sued for paternity. There was an out-of-court settlement. Princess Anne was aware of Heather Tonkin's telephone calls to Gatcombe Park, as was MI5, which taped them.

Anne, too, was reported to have male companions, including the actor Anthony Andrews, who became famous in the United States as one of the stars of *Brideshead Revisited* on the high-quality Public Broadcasting

System (PBS). At the time of one meeting in Paris, Andrews was shooting a television drama series in which he portrayed, ironically, the Duke of Windsor. Andrews has always countered that he and his wife, Georgina, were friends of both Princess Anne and Mark Phillips and that the relationship never went beyond that. Another man said to have been an intimate friend of the Princess's was Maj. Hugh Lindsay. He died in a skiing accident in 1988 while on vacation with Prince Charles.

In August 1989 the couple legally separated, for by then Princess Anne was in love with another, younger man and was determined to divorce Captain Phillips and marry him. It was an affair remarkably similar to Princess Margaret's with Peter Townsend nearly forty years before and, even in changed times, as potentially explosive. Worse, it occurred when other family scandals and disasters had begun to shake the foundations of the House of Windsor.

Comdr. Timothy Laurence first met Princess Anne in 1981, when he was a young naval officer in the crew of the Royal yacht *Britannia*. He left the *Britannia* to command a naval patrol boat, *Cygnet*, on secret counterterrorist duties off the coasts of the Republic of Ireland and Northern Ireland, intercepting arms supplies to the Provisional IRA. In 1988 he became an equerry to the Queen. Princess Anne and Laurence worked on a number of projects together, and behind the protective walls of Buckingham Palace, they became lovers.

But in April 1989, love letters from him to Princess Anne were stolen and sent to the *Sun* newspaper. The public revelation that the still-married Princess was in love with another man breached the agreement she and Phillips had made to keep their separate private lives discreet. The legal separation, which came a few weeks after the theft of the letters, was inevitable.

Laurence's involvement with Princess Anne came as a surprise to a number of Buckingham Palace officials, although it was not news to the Queen. Senior courtiers were furious and wanted Laurence to resign. He offered to do so, but the Queen refused to allow it. It was her personal support for him that permitted the relationship to continue when her advisers tried to undermine it. And it was not just her courtiers who were against the relationship. The Queen Mother objected to the affair and never changed her view. Prince Andrew and Prince Charles also expressed reservations. In their view, the fact that Laurence held posts working for the Royal family may have disqualified him from becoming one of them.

But there may also have been an additional reason. Laurence is of Jewish descent. His family had changed their name from Levy. There has always been a despicable undercurrent of anti-Semitism in the British aristocracy and Royalty, and that may have played a role in their opposition.

Under British law it takes two years of legal separation to set the groundwork for an uncontested, no-fault divorce. Princess Anne and Mark Phillips were prepared to settle amicably, but for Princess Anne and Laurence there remained a lengthy, tedious wait to get married. They also faced more opposition from the establishment, the circle of palace officials and from the family. The Queen had determined that she would not allow her daughter's potential happiness to be ruined as Princess Margaret's had been. She insisted that all obstacles be set aside so that her daughter could marry the man she loved. When Laurence completed his three-year term as equerry, the Queen awarded him the Royal Victorian Order, a personal decoration from the monarch rather than the state. In the arcane haiku of British honors, it was confirmation that he had her personal support against all comers. Laurence took up a post at Dartmouth Naval College to sit it out.

Princess Anne would be free to divorce in the summer of 1991, although she would not actually do so until March 1992. But no one could have known in 1989, when the legal separation was negotiated, that 1992 would be the Queen's *annus horribilis* (Year of Horror). That would be a year when the intricately constructed façade of the House of Windsor would come tumbling down, perhaps severely damaging the edifice itself. For while Princess Anne's marriage had been slowly deflating, the marriages of Prince Charles and Princess Diana and the Duke and Duchess of York were about to implode.

Twenty-nine

Fergie: Games Without Frontiers

T here have been few more unseemly Royal spectacles than the one
broadcast to Britons on a summer's night in 1987. For many years,
one of the BBC television shows least likely to make it to PBS in the
United States has been a slapstick game show called *It's a Knock-out.*
Opposing teams, usually representing small British towns or villages,
compete in contests that involve duels with inflatable weapons, races
over surreal assault courses, games with giant balls, and inevitably,
dunks in large vats of water. It is what the British think of as "good
clean fun," and it so appealed to the European sense of humor that it
was expanded into a pan-European version, *Jeux Sans Frontieres* or
Games Without Frontiers.

That night, the British television audience was confronted by members of the British Royal Family—Prince Edward, the Queen's youngest
son, and the Duchess of York, known as "Fergie"—cavorting on opposing teams in a special edition of the show, *It's a Royal Knock-out.* The
Duchess, dressed in medieval-style costume, took part in the undignified antics associated with the games with lusty bravado, intervening
on occasion to spray camera crew, spectators, and teammates with
champagne. Prince Edward, similarly enthusiastic, set about his role in
the games with gusto. Other team players included Christopher Reeve,
Jane Seymour, Sheena Easton, and Meatloaf.

The British had never seen members of the Royal Family behave in
such a blatantly unself-conscious and undignified way. The participa-

tion of the Royals was emphasized not only by the insertion of the word "Royal" into the title but by the set, modeled on a fourteenth-century Royal tournament, and the location, the grounds of a castle which, for economic reasons, had long before been turned into a theme park. It was as if the younger generation of Royals decided to lampoon the whole fabric of Royal pageantry and dignity. For many Britons it was compulsory but painful viewing.

At a press conference after the event, Prince Edward was asked if he felt the spectacle helped to trivialize the Royal Family. He became upset and flounced away, sulking.

It's a Royal Knock-out had been Prince Edward's idea. But the star of the show had been Fergie, the Duchess of York. Appropriately, for the entire six years that the Duchess would be a member of the House of Windsor, life was to be one long *Jeux Sans Frontieres*—with slapstick battles, belly laughs, guffaws, and the occasional unexpected dunk in the water. Over the years she has been called by many names—Duchess of Pork, Freebie Fergie, Freeloader Fergie, the Redheaded Rover—even sometimes by her given name, Sarah Ferguson. But it was as Fergie that her friends knew her and the public got to know her. It was to be her misfortune, among many misfortunes, that the word Fergie fitted nicely across a deep five-column tabloid headline.

Sarah Ferguson grew up in a ten-bedroom Edwardian country house set on fourteen acres, near Sunninghill, Berkshire, about fifty fast minutes by road from London and a canter from the Queen's estate at Windsor. Her father, Maj. Ronald Ferguson, was untitled but came from a family related to a posse of dukes. It was a predominantly military family, traditionally providing officers who rode escort to the Royal Family, the kind who like to keep their military titles long after their retirement from the service, in lieu of a more aristocratic handle. This is precisely what Major Ferguson did.

Major Ferguson and his wife, Susie, had two daughters: Jane, in 1957, and Sarah, in 1959. Apart from the army, the major's primary interest lay in the patrician pursuit polo. He became one of Britain's best polo players, and since polo matches are social events as well as sporting encounters, he became friendly with other leading players, among them Lord Mountbatten and his nephew, Prince Philip. The contact led to invitations for shooting weekends to Sandringham and other Royal gatherings. Sometimes the children went along and met the

Royal offspring. At one polo match in 1967, a photographer took a picture of seven-year-old Prince Andrew chatting to a nearly eight-year-old Sarah Ferguson. At the time it hardly seemed significant.

The Ferguson marriage had settled into a complacent groove when it suddenly derailed. In 1972 the couple were vacationing on the Greek island of Corfu. Among various guests at the holiday home was Hector Barrantes, a wealthy, world-class polo player from Argentina. Barrantes had lost his wife and unborn child in a traffic accident and was recuperating. Susie Ferguson fell head over heels in love. Two years later, in 1974, the Fergusons divorced, and the following year Susie Ferguson became Susie Barrantes and moved to Argentina.

Sarah Ferguson was by then sixteen, with freckles, a voluptuous figure, and a great shock of bright Titian-red hair, her outstanding feature. She was not pretty. She had inherited the round, masculine face with high cheekbones that made her mother and father pass almost for brother and sister. But she had plenty of personality, energy, and enthusiasm, and that covered a multitude of blemishes. An academic failure, she tried secretarial school without enthusiasm, then landed a job in public relations.

But she was not from the kind of family in which women work. Women married. After a visit to her mother and stepfather in Argentina—a four-thousand-acre ranch with its own polo field and a stable of some of the world's finest polo ponies—she realized that she would either have to marry well or turn out a lot of press releases to live comfortably.

Her first taste of love occurred when she met Kim Smith-Bingham, scion of a wealthy horse-breeding family, who worked as a stockbroker. Improbably, they had first encountered each other when he was working on a ranch in Argentina and she was staying with her mother. They resumed their acquaintance in London and became lovers. By the 1980s, Sarah had emerged as a leading member of a large pack of young women from wealthy backgrounds, most of whom were on the husband hunt. Fashionably dressed in something akin to the preppie look and comfortably housed and entertained in a golden ghetto centered in Sloane Square, they became known as Sloane Rangers.

Smith-Bingham lived for much of the time in Verbier, Switzerland, a fashionable resort where he had a business selling and renting ski equipment. It was during a lengthy stay there with him that Sarah met a former racing-car driver, Paddy McNally. He was twenty-two years older than her and something of a rascally middle-aged playboy. Grand Prix racing had made him rich, and he lived in a large Verbier house known as "the Castle," a magnet for visiting ski bunnies and McNally's well-heeled friends. Soon Smith-Bingham was out of the picture, and Sarah became part of McNally's court.

The relationship was to last four fun-filled years. Life at the Castle was by no means formal. The only rules were never to bore or be bored and no drugs. Every visitor had a schoolboy nickname. McNally was Toad, Sarah was inevitably Fergie. McNally's friends—British businessmen, politicians, and the occasional Lord—would drop their names at the door and become Beano, Ratty, Bentles, Ollie, and Wiggy. Large quantities of alcohol were consumed at the local disco, the Farm, beneath the local hotel, the Rhodania, which stayed open until daylight. Hangovers were left behind on the ski slopes the same morning. Fergie and Paddy McNally were a perfect match for a while. She was little more than a child wishing to appear adult, and he was feeling his age, wishing he were young.

Sarah—Fergie—stayed at the Castle for long periods but never fully moved in. She remained in London for much of the year between stretches with McNally. While in London she would often see a young woman who was the envied heroine of the Sloane Rangers for having brought down the big game in the Great Husband Hunt. She was Princess Diana, wife of the Prince of Wales. They knew each other because Sarah's father, Ronald Ferguson, had capped his career in polo by becoming polo manager to the heir to the throne. When Sarah hobnobbed at the polo fields, she would meet the Princess. Occasionally there were lunches in smart restaurants in Belgravia and South Kensington. In Ascot Week, 1985, Princess Diana swung an invitation to Windsor Castle for her friend. At dinner the first night, Fergie found herself seated next to Prince Andrew, Princess Diana's brother-in-law. It was not an accident.

At the time Prince Andrew was the World's Most Eligible Bachelor. Whereas Princess Anne had inherited all the worst aspects of the Windsor countenance, Prince Andrew had inherited the best. In 1985, at twenty-five, he was at the peak of his popularity. He was handsome and photographed even better than he looked. He was athletic and was enthusiastic on public occasions. He had returned from the Falklands War with Argentina a hero. He had a reputation as a stud. In headlines and general conversations he was just "Andy."

In temperament he was the opposite of his brother, Prince Charles. It is doubtful that he has read a book since he was at Gordonstoun, the hearty, physically tough private school that has become the alma mater of Windsor males, and his tutors may question whether he read many even then. As a child he was boisterous, arrogant, and incorrigibly *méchant*. A palace footman who became so enraged at his teasing and practical jokes struck him a heavy blow in a Buckingham Palace corridor. He immediately offered his resignation to the Queen, but she forgave him. "Let's hope it does him some good," she responded.

At Gordonstoun he was known as "the Great I Am" for his arrogance, unnecessarily loud voice, boastfulness, and overpowering personality. That at least was one nickname. Another referred to his oversized buttocks. He made it clear he felt he need do little work. "I already have a job to go to, ha-ha," he would tell pupils and masters alike. He was the only one of the three Windsor children the school decided not to appoint head boy in his senior year. The irony of all his boorishness is that Prince Andrew desperately wanted to be liked for himself and not because he was the Queen's son. As a result, almost everyone despised him.

After Gordonstoun—he scraped through final examinations—Prince Philip pushed him into the navy. It was just as well, since his grades did not qualify him for a leading university. Both senior officers and lower ranks had the same reaction to him as his schoolfellows. He is once said to have told a senior officer he could call him Andy. "You, Sublieutenant, may call me sir!" the officer snapped back. Lower ranks who disliked Prince Andrew arranged for biological material of various kinds to find their way into his food.

Prince Andrew became a helicopter pilot and was posted to the Royal Navy's 19,500-ton aircraft carrier *Invincible*. In 1982, Argentina invaded the half-forgotten British possession of the Falkland Islands in the South Atlantic, asserting a long-disputed claim. The Argentine junta had carried out the invasion in a desperate bid to boost its popularity among a severely repressed populace and unite the nation. They did not allow for the possibility that the policy cut both ways. Prime Minister Margaret Thatcher, an election looming, used the opportunity to boost her own popularity and unite Britain behind her in a war.

A task force led by the *Invincible* sailed to the Falklands to win the windswept islands back. Prince Andrew, to his credit, insisted he be allowed to take part in the campaign, and his mother, the Queen, to her credit, supported him. She told the prime minister she would not be able to stomach other British mothers sending their sons to be killed if she declined to send her own to submit to equal risk. But few believed there would be a battle. The United States, the United Nations, and the Organization of American States (OAS) were trying hard to find a diplomatic solution.

Prime Minister Thatcher declared a two-hundred-mile exclusion zone around the islands and warned Argentina that any ships entering the zone to supply the army of occupation would be sunk. But when a British submarine spotted the *General Belgrano*, an antiquated former U.S. Navy destroyer that had survived Pearl Harbor, she was sunk without warning. As it turned out, the Argentine destroyer was outside the exclusion zone and heading away from the islands. The Queen expressed grave reservations about the sinking, which cost hundreds of lives, but Mrs. Thatcher, who had given the explicit order, defended the action. War was now inevitable.

Prince Andrew flew Sea King helicopters during the six-week conflict, and there is no question that his life was in danger. His missions included acting as a decoy against deadly Exocet low-level missiles and antisubmarine patrols. He also dropped Special Forces units on the Falkland Islands, but the British military never reveals details of such missions. His most dramatic mission came at the height of the conflict when the Argentine air force bombed a British supply ship, *Atlantic Conveyor*. As the ship burned and with the attack still under way, Prince Andrew rescued several crew members from the air. In June, Argentina surrendered, the junta collapsed, and Mrs. Thatcher celebrated. The Falklands had cost 255 lives and 778 wounded on the British side and an undetermined number—in the thousands—on the Argentine side.

It was after the Falklands War that Prince Andrew earned his nickname Randy Andy. He had been something of a womanizer early on, inevitably, perhaps, because he was not only handsome but his status made him a magnet for young women looking for a husband or just a night to remember. At sixteen he had fallen in love with Canadian Sandi Jones and after a romantic night asked her to marry him. She realized they were both too young and told him so.

Kirstie Richmond had been another girlfriend whom he knew from schooldays and who spent many weekends at Windsor and Sandringham. But once he joined the navy he opted for a series of high-profile

young women, dating Carolyn Seaward, who was a Miss United Kingdom, fashion models Gemma Curry and Vicki Hodge, Nikki Caine,
daughter of the actor Michael Caine, and many others. Prince Andrew's
reputation as a lover was, however, not quite deserved. Some former
girlfriends have said he was overenthusiastic, and the fun ended soon
after it began.

Shortly before the Falklands War, he had begun seeing a controversial young American woman, Koo Stark. A beautiful, languid aspiring
actress, she had taken roles in what has been called soft pornography,
which were really simply very racy Grade B movies with little merit.
After the war, Prince Andrew took her and two other friends to Mustique to recuperate amid the sun and surf. Newspapers that discovered
the affair made much of Miss Stark's career. After the BBC had carried
a clip from one of her movies on its evening news broadcast, the media
began to speculate on her suitability to marry into the Royal Family.

The Queen liked Koo Stark, and everyone accepts that she was a
calming and maturing influence on Prince Andrew. It was Prince Philip
who convinced his son that the affair could go nowhere and both would
be hurt if they persisted. Koo Stark behaved admirably throughout the
period she was linked with Prince Andrew and since. She spurned all
offers to tell her story to newspapers and maintained his confidences.
Not all his girlfriends were so discreet.

The Koo Stark affair, and the constant use of the sobriquet Randy
Andy in relation to Prince Andrew, forced the Queen and Prince Philip
to find their son a suitable wife with whom he could settle down. They
did not want a playboy Prince in the family. It was natural to turn to
Princess Diana for help. She had been a childhood friend of Prince
Andrew's and a confidante after her marriage to his brother. When her
friend Sarah Ferguson complained over lunch that after four years
Paddy McNally showed no signs of marrying her, Princess Diana
thought of her brother-in-law.

After Ascot Week, Prince Andrew began to date Sarah Ferguson. She
saw him at his Buckingham Palace apartment, went to the ballet with
him, and visited friends' palatial homes on weekends. But she also spent
time with McNally in Ibiza, an island off the coast of Spain, where he
was staying with friends. Under Princess Diana's guidance, she began
reeling in the big fish. By the end of the year, she was invited to
Sandringham for the family New Year celebrations, a sure sign of
acceptance into the Royal circle. She also had a BMW and a preengage-

ment ring to show for the six-month-old relationship. By then, on Princess Diana's advice, she had removed all her belongings from the Castle at Verbier.

In February 1986, Prince Andrew invited Fergie to Floors Castle in Scotland—one of his regular getaways—for the weekend. Late the first night, in one of two adjoining bedrooms, Prince Andrew went down on one knee and asked her to marry him. She accepted, but told him if he wanted to tell her the next morning it was a joke, she would understand. The next morning, he said he still wanted to marry her.

Sarah Ferguson was not the kind of woman the public had expected Prince Andrew to marry. Somehow they believed he would find a more traditionally beautiful wife, the demure daughter of an Earl or a Duke, perhaps, a popular fashion model, even an actress if she kept her clothes on. But Fergie was boisterous, toothy, loud, and not particularly pretty, the sort of young woman who had been captain of her school hockey team or who might have lost her virginity in the tack room.

The usual security checks were carried out on Fergie, starting in September 1985. The intelligence officers who conducted it made discreet inquiries in Geneva and Verbier, where McNally had homes, and were disturbed by the relationship. A story that appeared in a British newspaper the weekend Prince Andrew proposed under the headline "Andy Girl in Cocaine Castle" and claiming that cocaine had been part of the Castle lifestyle had been purportedly engineered by MI5 to break up the relationship. Drugs were available at Verbier, but McNally had banned them from the Castle set. He sued the newspaper and won an out-of-court settlement.

The Queen was disturbed by Fergie's past relationships and worried that she would prove unsuitable for Royal life. It was only after a prolonged interview with the Queen Mother and the intervention of Princess Diana that the Queen relented and gave her consent in March to a July wedding. Fergie became an immediate media star, joining Princess Diana as the woman of the moment. Columnists agreed her party personality and jolly hockey-sticks enthusiasm would breathe fresh air into the cobwebbed corridors of Balmoral and Buckingham Palace. Another Sloane Ranger had bagged the Big One, and now she was having a honeymoon with both the public and the press. It would not last long.

A week before the wedding, Princess Diana and Fergie were involved in a reckless escapade. It was Prince Andrew's stag night, and Princess

Diana, Fergie, and several other friends gathered for their own party at a Belgravia apartment of the Duchess of Roxburghe. By prior arrangement, three women's police uniforms were brought along, and late in the evening, Princess Diana, Fergie, and a third woman, Pamela Stephenson, went out to a fashionable nightclub, Annabel's, on Berkeley Square, dressed as police officers.

The original plan had been to crash Prince Andrew's stag night, but the location was too secure. So they went to Buckingham Palace, took charge of the front gate, and when Prince Andrew arrived, closed it in the path of his car. Realizing something was amiss, he threw the gears into reverse, executed a high-speed two-point turn, and headed off as his detective, in the front passenger seat, called a red alert. The incident was over a few moments later, but when it was reported in several newspapers, it appeared more irresponsible than just a harmless prank. It seemed that the future Duchess of York was leading the future Queen of England astray.

The wedding at Westminster Abbey on July 23 showed Fergie at her most boisterous. That morning, Prince Andrew had been officially given his grandfather's old title, Duke of York, which meant that Fergie would become Duchess of York. Her pearl-studded, puff-shouldered gown, with its seventeen-foot train beaded with her coat of arms, was voluminous, ostentatious, and tasteless. It seemed the more so because Fergie is not a woman whose figure lends itself to wearing fashionable clothes with elegance. After the wedding, the Duke and Duchess embraced and dived into a passionate and lingering kiss on the balcony of Buckingham Palace.

The Duchess made goggle-eyed faces at the crowd. It was fun, the thousands in the Mall enjoyed it, but captured by still cameras and on television, her appearance lacked dignity, a failing that permeated everything Fergie did over the next several years. There was a waddling, goggle-eyed, guffawing quality in many of her public appearances, whether it was an off-the-cuff remark or a public pratfall. She ran across a London street to retrieve a bouquet from an admirer, only to go into a slapstick slipslide, desperately waving her arms to keep balanced. When someone yelled, "I love you," during a speech, she remarked, "See you outside."

This kind of behavior, refreshing at first, quickly paled. Fun-loving Fergie became Freeloading Fergie and Freebie Fergie when it was learned that she parlayed her Royal status into free airline tickets, hotels, gifts, clothes, and other perks in return for promised publicity. Bills that did arrive were often unpaid. She never realized that despite their enormous personal wealth, the Windsors can be frugal with their own money.

The public's love affair with Fergie was already waning when she gave birth to her first child, a daughter, Beatrice, in 1988. While her unrestrained sense of fun and high-spiritedness had endeared her to the public, the Queen and Prince Philip had begun to find her grating. Even her friend Princess Diana decided to distance herself. There were reports of raucous food fights down the corridors of Buckingham Palace and childish practical jokes. They conjured up images of the teenaged heroine of a schoolgirl comic crying, "Yikes, for the high jump again!" when caught eating after lights out by the head girl.

The slide began when Fergie took off for Australia for several weeks—her third long trip in eighteen months—leaving Princess Beatrice behind with a nanny. She was criticized by the press for being a neglectful mother, although she was merely following the established Windsor way. Almost overnight, Fergiemania melted away, and Fergie bashing became the new sport.

The Yorks decided to build their own home, ignoring the availability of more traditional styles—Georgian, Edwardian, and Victorian country houses—that abound within an hour or two's drive of London. It was modeled on a split-level ranch-style house the Duchess had seen for only a few minutes on a visit to the United States. It cost $12 million to build and was an assault on the senses not only because it was tasteless in itself but because the house appeared totally out of place in its English country setting. It was no place to raise a branch of the Royal Family.

By no means the worst example of the Yorks' poor taste involved one of the bathrooms. At Fergie's behest she had a lavatory seat installed which played "The Star-Spangled Banner" when an occupant sat down. She was unable to find one that played "God Save the Queen." The press immediately dubbed the house Southyork, after the fictional Texas ranch of the Ewings in the drama series *Dallas*.

Money had been a recurrent problem in the York household. Prince Andrew earned regular naval pay plus a generous Civil List allowance, but Fergie complained she had little access to ready cash. A photo spread of the Yorks with Princess Beatrice appeared in the tabloid *Hello!* magazine, for which $250,000 allegedly changed hands. Another $120,000 was paid for an interview in a British newspaper. Her desperate need for financial independence was also behind her creation of Budgie the Helicopter, a character for children's books along the lines of Thomas the Tank Engine. She announced that the royalties would go to charity, but it was discovered that only 12 percent had been earmarked for charitable uses. Budgie made Fergie an estimated $150,000 in book sales in two years. However, Budgie led to further controversy when it was discovered Fergie's work bore a marked similarity to a book published in the early sixties, *Hector the Helicopter*.

Fergie became pregnant with her second child in 1989. By then the rot had set in. Prince Andrew's Royal duties had caused many separations; his naval career, many more. But he had begun to spend part of his shore leave away from Southyork, and some of Fergie's high spirits had begun to bore him. Theirs had been an essentially physical relationship seasoned by a boisterous back-slapping friendship that Prince Andrew had found refreshing at first. As emotionally immature as the rest of his family, he mistook comfortable familiarity and sexual compatibility for love. He became impatient with her wildly fluctuating weight and self-indulgent overeating. And he became embarrassed by her public behavior—her screaming across the street at people she knew, running with an undignified, waddling gait in public, making childish faces at the cameras, and her inane running commentary on everything around her. On several occasions Prince Andrew would intervene as Fergie was about to say something potentially embarrassing, telling her: "Shut up! Just shut up!"

Increasingly isolated from her husband, finding palace officials overbearing and judgmental, her calendar of public appearances oppressive and dull, and the atmosphere among her in-laws tense, she began to look elsewhere for companionship. One of the men she turned to was Steve Wyatt, a charismatic Texan. She met him on an official visit to Houston in November 1989, when she was nearly five months pregnant. Fergie knew his mother, socialite Lynn Wyatt, from the Palm Beach polo playing set. Fergie was staying at the Wyatt mansion in Houston when she was introduced to a tall, rugged, tousle-haired man who looked as if he had stepped off the cover of a "bodice ripper" romance novel.

For the next four days, Steve Wyatt was constantly at her side. He showed her the Wyatts' sixteen-thousand-acre ranch in south Texas, accompanied her to the theater and opera, and kept her amused. It was the beginning of a friendship that would help shatter the Yorks' already unstable marriage. Wyatt kept up the friendship with long phone calls to Southyork after Fergie had returned home, and a few weeks after he met her, he flew to Britain on business and joined her at a weekend shooting party. She introduced him to Prince Andrew, who also befriended him, and Wyatt introduced Fergie to a friend of his, Johnny Bryan.

In March 1990, Fergie gave birth to a second daughter, Princess Eugenie. Six weeks later she left for a vacation in Morocco without her husband or youngest child. The party included Princess Beatrice, a nanny, a pair of Royal Protection Squad bodyguards, and Steve Wyatt. They spent five days at an exclusive resort hotel at Agadir, paid for by Wyatt. They continued to see each other in London on their return.

The trip with Wyatt had already caused a furor at Buckingham Palace before Steve Wyatt's private jet had touched down at Agadir on the outward journey. It was almost certainly then that a concerted campaign was begun to expel Fergie from the Royal Family. Because virtually nothing the Royals do can remain secret from their protectors, by the time Fergie and the party returned to London, every detail of the vacation was known. Just a few weeks later, another trip with Wyatt took place, this time to Cap Ferrat on the French Riviera. And Wyatt was with her again when she flew to New York the same summer to visit her dying stepfather, Hector Barrantes, in a hospital in New York.

Britain's intelligence agencies now kept a close eye on Wyatt, and not only because they were suspicious of his blossoming friendship with the Duchess of York. Robert Lipman, Wyatt's natural father, had been jailed in London in 1968 for killing a teenaged girl during a drug and alcohol binge. Oscar Wyatt, his adoptive father, did millions of dollars' worth of business with Iraq, and his brother, Doug, was connected with a bizarre New Age cult into which intelligence agents feared Fergie might also be recruited. She had already expressed interest in some aspects of unconventional medicine and received treatment for muscle pains by sitting under a pyramid in the consulting rooms of a Greek mystic.

Freddie von Mierers, the founder of the Eternal Values cult, was a bisexual conman and fantasist who claimed to come from the "Planet Arcturus" with a mystic message from aliens. Beautiful women who had been recruited into the cult claimed that they had been subjected to humiliating sexual practices and cheated out of large amounts of money.

Doug Wyatt was not alleged to have been involved in any wrongdoing, but his involvement in the cult had led to a bitter legal battle between him and Robert Sakowitz, his uncle, over the family fortune.

Surveillance by British intelligence also revealed that Wyatt had had a sexual liaison with Lesley Player, a woman with whom Fergie's father, Maj. Ronald Ferguson, had also become infatuated. The Queen, wary of another scandal, told her daughter-in-law to stop seeing her new lover. She did not. Palace officials, consulting with the Special Branch and MI5, wanted more. They wanted Fergie out of the picture, too. But they understood that a Fergie unhitched from the Royal Family might be more dangerous than a Fergie under their control.

Another Royal marriage breakup posed serious problems over and above the public scandal. The collapse of previous marriages involved Royal women, Princess Margaret and Princess Anne. That custody of the children should go to their mothers was never in question. But Fergie, it was supposed, would demand custody of Princess Beatrice and Princess Eugenie, and she would win unless it could be demonstrated that she was somehow unfit. Theoretically, she might take them away from Britain and outside the control of the Royal Family.

So a plot was hatched to discredit the errant Duchess. Mysterious men with military bearing had already begun laying the groundwork, holding clandestine meetings with newspaper reporters and offering information on the Duchess that only insiders would know. Scores of photographs that had been taken of Fergie on her vacation with Steve Wyatt in Morocco had been copied and were in the hands of intelligence officers. In the last weeks of 1991, a set was brought to Steve Wyatt's vacated apartment at Cadogan Square and left on top of an armoir in a spare bedroom, positioned so that anyone cleaning the tall windows from the inside would see a mysterious package. What was inside was not to come to light until early the following year, the *annus horribilis* of 1992. And by then, the greatest scandal of all was also about to overwhelm the Windsors: the bitter, public breakup of the marriage of the heir to the throne.

Thirty

Charlie's Angels

A lmost from the first stirring of puberty, a harem of available but not always suitable women were only too eager to fling themselves at Prince Charles. But this tidal wave of sexual availability washing at the feet of the heir to the throne contains one of the many contradictions of his life. For while he has always possessed the potent aphrodisiac of wealth and rank, he has also been acutely aware of the need to be as discreet as a bishop.

Over the years he became adept at keeping the public gaze away from many of his partners, using love nests obediently provided by his close male friends or by employing smokescreen of platonic companions to put the press off the scent of his real girlfriends. One of the reasons given for his exile to the Spartan pleasures of Australia's remote Geelong Grammar School for his final year of school concerns his abiding love for an unsuitable young woman. In truth, Prince Charles was a virgin until he attended Cambridge University.

For his first passionate affair, at the age of nineteen, he chose—or was chosen by—Lucia Santa Cruz, a tantalizingly beautiful postgraduate student four years his senior and the daughter of a Chilean diplomat. She had been working closely with R. A. "Rab" Butler, the master of Trinity College and Prince Charles's mentor. He was only too happy to play matchmaker for the heir to the throne and gave the Prince the key to the master's lodge for clandestine meetings with the delightful Lucia.

But there was never any chance that she might one day marry Prince Charles. She was a Roman Catholic, a foreigner, and an assertive intellectual who would never have adapted herself to the Royal role. She became the first of "Charlie's Angels," as the press dubbed his coterie of girlfriends, to marry far less eligible but far more suitable men.

Butler found himself called upon to vacate the master's lodge a little too often. The Queen eventually gave Prince Charles a ten-room cottage at Sandringham to entertain, which he used often. One of the women suitable enough to be introduced to the family circle was another Cambridge student, Bettina Lindsay, daughter of Lord Balniel and a descendant of King Charles II. She spent many weekends at Balmoral and Windsor in 1968, but the relationship cooled as Prince Charles added to an impressive scoresheet of daughters of the titled, rich, and landed.

When Anthony Holden published an official biography of Prince Charles, he was unable to squeeze the phrase "Prince Charles enjoys a normal healthy sex life" past censorious Buckingham Palace officials. According to Holden, Prince Charles's girlfriends, not all of them serious, included Lady Leonora Grosvenor, daughter of one of the then wealthiest landowners in the world, the Duke of Westminster; her sister, Lady Jane Grosvenor; Lady Victoria Percy and her sister Lady Caroline, Lady Henrietta Fitzroy; Lady Charlotte Manners; her cousin, Elizabeth Manners; Lady Cecil Kerr; Lady Camilla Fane, daughter of the Earl of Westmoreland; Angela Nevill, daughter of Prince Philip's then private secretary; Caroline Longman, daughter of a prominent British publisher; Louise Astor; Georgiana Russell, daughter of diplomat John Russell; Laura Jo Watkins, daughter of Adm. James Watkins of the U.S. Navy; Rosie Clifton, who later married a friend of Prince Charles, Mark Vestey; Sabrina Guinness, of the brewing family; and Fiona Watson, whose ample enticements were subsequently displayed across eleven pages of *Penthouse* magazine.

Another love, Davina Sheffield, seemed at one stage to be ranked high among the marriage prospects. However, she was abruptly dumped when a former boyfriend revealed details of a long and intimate relationship. And Prince Charles went so far as to propose to two women: Lady Jane Wellesley, descendant of Napoleon's nemesis, the Duke of Wellington, and Anna Wallace, known as "Whiplash" for her acid tongue and quick temper. Both women passed stringent approval tests of the Queen, Prince Philip, and the Queen Mother. Both women turned down Prince Charles flat. Lady Jane simply had no wish to live the kind of life intended for a future Princess of Wales and Queen of England. On the other hand, Anna Wallace became infuriated with some of Prince Charles's idiosyncrasies and said she did not love him.

Some women went to extraordinary lengths to awaken some passion in the Prince of Wales. On a trip to Fiji, Princes Charles was alone in the swimming pool of his host, the then Fijian minister of finance. His stunning daughter, Jeanette Stitson, stripped naked and joined him, to the astonishment and delight of the future King.

But the love of his life was Camilla Shand. They had moved in the same circles for years, she as a social butterfly in the dying world of British debutantes who dated a succession of wealthy members of the military caste, he as the polo-playing Prince of Wales and nominal leader of youthful society. They met in 1972 when he was twenty-three years old; she was a year younger. As is often the case with enduring romances, they became good friends first, drawn together by her vivacity, and relative to the Prince, informality and easy grace.

She came from the immensely wealthy Shand and Cubitt families, who had built the prestigious London districts Belgravia and Mayfair on land owned by the Duke of Westminster. Her father was Maj. Bruce Middleton Shand, her uncles Lord Ashcombe and Sir Geoffrey Howe, a leading figure in a succession of Conservative governments. As Camilla pointed out at their first meeting, her great-grandmother was Mrs. George Keppel, the longtime lover of Edward VII. Her grandmother, Sonia Cubitt, Keppel's daughter, used to call his great-great grandfather "Kingy."

Camilla had had numerous boyfriends, but there was one with whom, friends say, she was "obsessed." He was Andrew Parker-Bowles, the same young Guards officer who had dated Princess Anne, to the Royal family's dismay, and had been conveniently posted to Germany. Parker-Bowles had the reputation of being something of a swordsman in romantic matters. He had openly dated other women during his relationship with Camilla and seemed to care little when Camilla dated Prince Charles. To complicate matters further, Parker-Bowles and Prince Charles were friends.

Prince Charles was not ready for marriage when he fell in love with Camilla, in part because he was still required to serve a period in the Royal Navy, which would involve long periods at sea. Moreover, he was emotionally very immature. He knew how to behave with women socially, but he had little knowledge of relationships. He had learned not to show his emotions, and as a result, he had taught himself to repress them. Some of Charles's restraint is due to his distant relationship with his father, some from his spartan education, some from being "a Royal" and therefore tied to a predetermined set of duties, and some simply from being British. The British are not a breed that communicates feelings easily or well.

In 1973, Prince Charles missed an opportunity to express the depth of his feelings for Camilla. Andrew Parker-Bowles was back on the scene, Prince Charles was scheduled to spend several months at sea, and Camilla Shand expected some indication that the relationship had a future. She got none. A few weeks after Prince Charles sailed, Parker-Bowles asked her to marry him, and she accepted.

Desperately unhappy, Prince Charles turned to the one adult male with whom he had a deep, trusting, loving relationship. His philosophical, introspective, sober bent and interest in art, architecture, and history helped alienate him from his father, who had no time for intellectualism and had hoped Gordonstoun would turn his son into a tough, down-to-earth, hard-playing, hard-working hearty like himself. The Prince turned instead to Lord Mountbatten. Mountbatten developed such a close relationship with his great-nephew that Prince Charles referred to him as his "honorary grandfather" and made it obvious he was closer to him than his own father.

Mountbatten had encouraged Prince Charles to play the field as much as possible and not to marry too soon. It was good advice, but it contained a very strong element of self-interest. Mountbatten wanted to strengthen his blood ties to the Windsors with another Mountbatten marriage. From the time his granddaughter, Amanda Knatchbull, was a child, Mountbatten had hoped that he would be able to convince Prince Charles, nine years her senior, to marry her. He hoped to keep Prince Charles occupied until his granddaughter was old enough to marry. He allowed Prince Charles to bring various girlfriends to Broadlands, the Mountbatten estate, where they could spend time together in privacy but also where Mountbatten himself could keep abreast of developments.

Prince Charles tried to forget Camilla, but social life in London would bring them together on innumerable occasions. They continued their friendship, and after the birth of the Parker-Bowleses' first child, Thomas, in 1975, Prince Charles stood godfather. By then the Prince had realized that he had made a tragic error in not pursuing Camilla with greater ardor. It was now too late. No matter how much they loved each other, no matter how desperately they wanted to be with each other, they could never marry. Over a period of years, it was to make Prince Charles even more introspective and morose than ever.

In 1977, Prince Charles was snapped out of his morbid state of mind for a period when he began to date Lady Sarah Spencer, daughter of the Earl Spencer. Beautiful, fun loving, and irrepressible, she brought a light into the darker corners of his life. They saw each other regularly and in 1978 went on a skiing holiday together to Klosters, the fashionable Swiss resort Prince Charles favors. Amid speculation that the Prince had found a future Queen, Lady Sarah brought the relationship crashing to a halt, telling reporters that she did not love the Prince and would never marry a man she was not in love with.

As damaging as the words themselves was that she had talked of her relationship to the press at all. Lady Sarah was through.

By then Mountbatten was ready to arrange the marriage of Prince Charles to his granddaughter. The Prince was thirty and Amanda Katchbull was twenty-one and, so far as Mountbatten was concerned, perfect Royal material. Mountbatten had advised Prince Charles to marry someone very much younger than himself, a woman who would grow to love him rather than marry him out of love. She should be young so that she would be less likely to have had prior relationships that might cause a scandal. Youth would more likely make her "trainable" in Royal routine, duties, and traditions and, of course, make her more likely to do as she was told. He could personally vouch for Amanda on all three counts. The Queen Mother was aware of the plan, and she waged a concerted campaign against it. The Queen remonstrated with Mountbatten over his matchmaking efforts, trying to fend off Mountbatten's ambition. Prince Charles, though not in love with Amanda Knatchbull, was prepared to go through with it. It was she who refused.

Mountbatten's ambitions were abruptly cut short in August 1979. He had been spending part of his summers at his family's Classiebawn Castle estate near Mullaghmore, County Sligo, in the Republic of Ireland for years. The Provisional IRA had scored numerous successes against the British that year, one of particular violence that marked the tenth anniversary of the current conflict in Northern Ireland. Aware that he might be at risk, Mountbatten checked every year with the intelligence services, Special Branch, and the local police in County Sligo before staying at Classiebawn.

With remarkable ease a team of IRA assassins gained access to Lord Mountbatten's fishing boat to plant a fifty-pound bomb the night before the assassination. Mountbatten's party headed out to sea to harvest lobster pots and were observed from the shore by at least two assassins, who probably had backup from several more. While Mountbatten was at sea but visible from the shore, the bomb was detonated by a high-frequency radio signal. Mountbatten was killed instantly. One intelligence estimate was that twelve men and women took part in the assassination. No one was successfully prosecuted.

The murder of Lord Mountbatten had a profound effect on Prince Charles. It was the second great tragedy of his life—the first was the loss of Camilla—and it left him rudderless. That Lord Mountbatten, a man of action, adventure, and bravery, full of life and ideas, who had always feared growing old, sick, and useless, had died as he might have wished provided little comfort to those who loved him. At his state funeral at Westminster Abbey, broadcast live on British television, millions saw the heir to the throne fighting to control his tears. That a man might cry at the funeral of someone he loved and confided in seems natural enough, but in the Royal Family, to whom emotion is something that needs to be hidden, it proved an embarrassment. Prince Philip was contemptuous.

Just weeks after the assassination, Andrew Parker-Bowles was posted to Rhodesia among the staff of Lord Soames, who had begun to bring about an orderly transition from white rebel rule to democratic majority rule and legal independence. One can only speculate whether the posting came just as Prince Charles needed the emotional support of Camilla Parker-Bowles or whether it was arranged for that purpose. But during the period Andrew Parker-Bowles was away, Camilla and Prince Charles became closer than ever and he even more dependent on her.

In 1980, when Prince Charles was in an emotionally vulnerable state, the pressure on him to find a wife continued. He was thirty-two years old. The difficulties of finding a suitable bride would only increase as he got older. He was already faced with a situation in which he might be middle-aged, or even an old man, before he succeeded to the throne. In the meantime, it was his duty to beget another heir. No other heir to the throne had found himself with the same problems in finding a wife, given the lack of suitable foreign princesses, the unprecedented press attention that would be given to a courtship, and the need to find someone inexperienced so that former boyfriends would not sell their stories to the newspapers, let alone the fact that the Prince himself was in love with another woman.

It was the Queen Mother who had the solution. One of her closest friends, Lady Fermoy, had a granddaughter, Lady Diana Spencer, the sister of Lady Sarah, whom Prince Charles had already dated. Another sister, Lady Jane, was married to a rising Buckingham Palace official, Sir Robert Fellowes. Through them, Charles already knew Diana.

Lady Diana Spencer was the youngest of the daughters of the Earl Spencer and easily the most physically attractive. In 1980, at the age of nineteen, she had a round, open, childlike face, almost a Lolita look, with a clear, honeyed complexion, large, expressive blue eyes, her features framed by a thick blond pageboy cut. About fifteen pounds overweight, she had a voluptuous figure. Later, her features would become finer and more chiseled, the weight would drop away, and she would change from being merely attractive to being a genuine beauty of her generation. Prince Charles was nearly thirteen years older than her. While he attended Cambridge and enjoyed the first years of adulthood, she was a mere seven years old. They had little in common other than a few friends and acquaintances. Her sister Sarah and Neil McCorquodale, her new husband, were still friendly with Prince Charles. Tragically, perhaps the one thing they truly had in common was that they both came from severely dysfunctional families.

Lady Diana's maternal family had a bizarre history. They were descended from Frank Work, who had been raised in Chillicothe, Ohio, in conditions of extreme poverty. Work had become a "robber baron" millionaire in New York through a chance association with "Commodore" Vanderbilt, who had encouraged Work to become a stockbroker. Work had two socialite daughters, Frances and Ruth. Frances married a penniless Irish aristocrat, James Boothby Burke Roche, and left to live in England at a time when it was fashionable for American heiresses to marry into titled European families. But Frank had strenuously opposed the match and disowned his oldest daughter.

Frances had three children—two twin sons and a daughter—by Burke Roche, second son of the First Baron Fermoy. She left her drunken and often violent husband after ten years of marriage, and Frank Work took her back, raising the children as Americans. Frances's scandalous promiscuity led to repeated clashes with her father, and in 1905, when she married her Hungarian stable manager, she was again disowned. Frances's sister also had a scandalous life. Her marriage to Peter Cooper Hewitt ended when she discovered that her husband had been keeping a secret wife and daughter.

Frank Work had a deep-rooted contempt for the British and for aristocracy of any kind and sought to tie up his heirs with a complex, impenetrable will. When he died in 1911, he left instructions that his grandchildren had to change their names to Work, never leave the United States, marry only American citizens, and that Maurice Burke Roche, the elder of the twins by only a few minutes, must renounce his claim to the Barony of Fermoy.

Frances and her children voluntarily disinherited themselves, leaving some $15 million to Ruth, who promptly redistributed the inheritance among them. Maurice, after the deaths of his grandfather, uncle, and father in rapid succession, became the Fourth Baron Fermoy in 1920. He married Ruth Sylvia Gill, Lady Fermoy, in 1931. The Fermoys and King George VI and Queen Elizabeth had been friends before the accession, and after the deaths of their husbands, Lady Fermoy and the Queen Mother continued their friendship.

Lord and Lady Fermoy had three children, Mary, Frances Ruth, named for Frank Work's daughters, and Edmund. Frances Ruth married Edward "Johnnie" Spencer, Viscount Althorp, who inherited the family's Earldom and became the eighth Earl Spencer in 1975. In 1969, after four children, she abandoned her husband for millionaire businessman Peter Shand-Kydd. The children became the center of a bitter custody battle, which the Earl Spencer won. Frances's own mother, Lady Fermoy, had supported the Earl Spencer during the legal wrangling. The dispute badly scarred all four children, most severely their youngest daughter, eight-year-old Lady Diana.

Prince Charles and Lady Diana Spencer had met on several occasions, but the Prince did not take notice of her until early 1979, five months before Mountbatten's assassination. The Queen Mother had promoted Diana as a possible bride because she still feared Mountbatten's maneuverings to install Amanda Knatchbull as his wife. She arranged for Diana and her sister Sarah to be invited to Sandringham for the weekend. Prince Charles took her out on a number of dates after that, but it was not until the following year that he began to look upon Diana as a possible wife. She visited Highgrove, Prince Charles's estate in Gloucestershire he bought for $1.5 million early in 1980; he had her invited into the Royal Family circle at Sandringham, Windsor, and Balmoral.

One of the people to whom he introduced Diana in the spring of 1980 was Camilla Parker-Bowles. She approved of Diana, but like others in Prince Charles's circle, the approval was based on a misconception.

Diana seemed young—almost too young—for Prince Charles, but this was all to the good, for she was clearly inexperienced. Her view of the world was shaped by pop-song lyrics and romantic novels. She was so poorly educated that she had left school without the equivalent of a high school diploma. She could barely hold a conversation without blushing. Those who knew her only slightly concluded she would be malleable.

The Queen Mother approved of Diana because she, too, believed that she would give the family no problems, that she came from the right social background, and because she could be trained in the ways of the Royal Family. The Queen and Princess Anne found her shallow. Prince Philip agreed, but he could see why his son found her physically attractive and was only too happy that he had not chosen someone with Prince Charles's own morose, introspective, overly intellectual temperament.

For her part, Lady Diana was infatuated with Prince Charles. And little wonder. He was her first serious boyfriend, had enormous wealth, great rank, and during their days of courtship, appeared to be sensitive and attentive. His staff, family, and friends went out of their way to ensure them some privacy, giving her a false impression of the kind of life they were likely to lead after they were married. Her own friends were envious, her family encouraging. There seemed no better match. She had the chance to become the Queen of England.

The public took immediately to Lady Diana. In the autumn of 1980, when speculation that the relationship was serious began to mount, she was working as a kindergarten teacher's aide and sharing a West London apartment with two girlfriends. She seemed so ordinary and unassuming despite her title, her family's vast wealth, and her privileged background. She became "Shy Di," a Cinderella who had tried on the Prince's glass slipper and found it fit.

In the third week of January 1981, thirty-three-year-old Prince Charles proposed to twenty-year-old Lady Diana during a weekend at Highgrove. He asked her to think about the answer, but she was almost immediately insistent that the answer was yes. The official announcement was made a month later, and the wedding was set for July.

No wedding of a Prince of Wales had taken place for nearly a hundred years, and this one, with the added spice of a beautiful and very ordinary and appealing young woman as the bride, seemed irresistibly romantic. Interest in the Prince and his shy, blushing bride-to-be exploded throughout the world. Newspaper and magazine editors found a new icon in Diana, a woman whose expressive eyes and slightly embarrassed smile could make covers fly off the newsstands.

But it was not a fairy tale. Behind the scenes, both Prince Charles and his future bride were racked with doubts almost immediately after the wedding was announced. Both began to realize how different were their separate worlds—their tastes, their education, their interests. Prince Charles desperately sought reassurance from members of his family that he was doing the right thing in marrying a woman barely out of her teens. Prince Philip told him it was crucial that he marry and produce an heir. He also advised his son that if the marriage did not work, while there could be no divorce, an arrangement could be made whereby the couple could live separate lives in private so long as they maintained a façade of happiness in public, an indication, perhaps, of the true state of the Queen's own marriage.

Lady Diana had her own second thoughts, and they went deeper than Prince Charles's doubts. Just a few days before the scheduled nuptials, with millions waiting for the wedding of the century, she tried to call it off.

The incident has been put down to prewedding nerves by Prince Charles's supporters, who leaked selected details of the incident years later. But the cause was actually a furious fight the couple had had over Camilla Parker-Bowles. Six months before the official engagement was announced, Buckingham Palace had been outraged by a story that had appeared in a British Sunday newspaper. The story suggested that Lady Di had been smuggled on board the Royal train to spend the night with Prince Charles. The smuggling incident had been vehemently denied by the palace, and it seemed at the time that the vehemence stemmed from the suggestion of impropriety on the part of Lady Diana, whose unsullied reputation had been part of her intrinsic appeal.

The *Sunday Mirror* refused to retract the story. But it now seems that it did get some of its facts wrong. According to British journalist James Whittaker, the woman smuggled aboard the train was Camilla Parker-Bowles.

Lady Diana may or may not have been aware of the identity of the woman, but she knew that it had not been herself. She was certainly aware of the special friendship Camilla Parker-Bowles enjoyed with Prince Charles. So when, a few days before the wedding, she opened what she believed was a wedding gift, she was outraged to find it was a gift Prince Charles had bought for Camilla—an expensive bracelet inscribed "Fred to Gladys," Charles and Camilla's pet names for each other. She held her anger for several hours, but at a palace cocktail party that night, to the astonishment of the guests, she exploded in tears and fled from the room.

Lady Jane Fellowes, her sister, who had a divided loyalty as the wife of a senior Buckingham Palace official, spent almost twenty-four hours with Lady Diana. For most of that time, Lady Diana insisted she would not go through with the wedding, that Prince Charles did not love her, and worse, loved someone else. The Queen, told that the wedding might have to be canceled, ordered Prince Charles, wisely, not to intervene.

A plan was drawn up to have the wedding postponed, and palace officials tried to come up with some story that would stand up to scrutiny. The Queen decided that if Lady Diana still did not want to go ahead with the marriage after twenty-four hours, the wedding would be called off, and the family would weather the storm. Gradually, brought around by Lady Jane, Lady Diana was persuaded to proceed with the marriage. The tense day passed. The wedding of the century was on.

Thirty-one

Fractured Fairy Tale

P rince Charles and Lady Diana were married on July 29, 1981. It
was unquestionably the most watched Royal event in history. A
combined worldwide audience of some 700 million people saw it live on
television. Millions more watched its highlights on extended television
news broadcasts in every corner of the globe. Hardly a magazine or a
newspaper failed to place photographs of the wedding of the century on
covers and front pages. The defining image was of the Prince, in full
naval uniform, giving his bride a chaste, yet tender, romantic, and
loving kiss and of the bride melting as she received it.

It had been a ceremony of grandeur and poignancy. In a break with
tradition, the wedding was held at St. Paul's Cathedral rather than in
Westminster Abbey, making the processional route longer. Of the
hundreds of thousands who lined that route, down the Mall, across
Trafalgar Square, up to Fleet Street and Ludgate Hill, some had camped
out for three days. Prince Charles himself had narrated a documentary
on the intricate wedding arrangements for the wedding to be shown on
British television the night before.

If there were any flaws in the relationship between the Prince and his
bride, they were invisible. The romantic story became so popular that
no one had an inkling that they were not deeply in love. But in a
prewedding interview staged for television, the couple were asked if
they were in love. "Yes, of course." Diana giggled and blushed. "Whatever that means," said Prince Charles.

Lady Diana had played almost no part in the planning; it was almost
all done by Prince Charles himself and Lord MacLean, the Lord Chamberlain. The night before the wedding a fireworks display lit up Hyde
Park, packed with fifteen thousand people, and massed bands of the

342

Brigade of Guards and the Choir of the Welsh Guards performed. The evening ended with the likenesses of the bride and groom etched out in sparking fireworks.

The wedding day itself was one of pageantry on a scale not witnessed since the Coronation nearly three decades earlier. The bells of St. Paul's rang for thirty full minutes while a dozen magnificent horse-drawn Royal coaches, escorted by platoons of mounted guards in their eighteenth-century uniforms, carried the members of the Royal Family from the palace. The guests who filled the great cathedral reflected the changes in British politics and society since earlier royal events of similar grandeur. In place of the bevy of European monarchs were African and Middle Eastern ruler and heads of state.

The Earl Spencer had been recovering from a stroke but insisted on his right to walk his daughter up the aisle on her wedding day. He did so, painfully, slowly, but courageously. The archbishop of Canterbury, in performing the marriage ceremony, pointed out the many thousands of references in newspapers, magazines, and on television to what seemed a fairy-tale romance.

"Fairy tales usually end with the simple phrase 'They lived happily ever after,' " the archbishop said. "Our faith sees the wedding day not as a place of arrival but as the place where adventure really begins. Those who are married live happily ever after only if they persevere."

In light of what was to happen, it was a poignant sermon.

Prince Charles and Princess Diana spent their honeymoon at Broad-lands, the Mountbatten estate where his father and mother had gone for their wedding night, and on the Royal yacht *Britannia*, whose sailing destination over the next fourteen days was kept a closely guarded secret. Estimates vary as to how long the couple were truly happy. The longest is six months. From there it was all downhill.

Princess Diana and Prince Charles thoroughly enjoyed their honey-moon, but there were two blazing rows that were omens for the future. Several days into their honeymoon, photographs of Camilla fell out of Prince Charles's diary. Princess Diana was furious that he should have keepsakes of his supposedly former girlfriends where he would see them every day. She eventually calmed down, but Prince Charles foolishly compounded the problem. One evening he wore a pair of cufflinks inscribed with two intertwined C's, which Princess Diana took to stand for Camilla and Charles.

On their return to England, Princess Diana found herself thrown into the everyday tedium of Royal routine. She found herself cut off from her friends and with little in common with her new in-laws. Only after living together for a few weeks did the newlyweds realize how far apart their real interests were. Princess Diana expected, with some justification, to have unlimited and uninterrupted access to her husband, but his position involved a heavy calendar of public duties as well as a heavy commitment to his personal interests, which excluded his wife. As a result, she became lonely, bored, and, she felt, excluded. The Prince, who had seemed so attentive and sensitive, now appeared distant, undemonstrative, and uncommunicative.

There were bitter disputes with Prince Charles's staff over his calendar; with Prince Charles himself over the amount of time he spent playing polo; and over the Royal Family's obsession with blood sports—fox hunting, grouse and pheasant shooting, and other country pursuits that the Royal Family have traditionally taken part in but which Princess Diana, like many Britons, finds cruel and revolting. She came to despise the way in which Prince Charles allowed himself to be swayed by his mother and bullied by his father. She resented the gilded cage she found herself in, unable, most of the time, to go anywhere without a Royal Protection Squad bodyguard. Some forty members of the staff left Prince Charles and Princess Diana in five years, many of them after clashes with Princess Diana.

Just about everyone had underestimated Princess Diana and the effect she would have on Prince Charles. Instead of being the compliant, obedient bride and bearer of Royal heirs, she proved herself assertive and demanding, even willful. Prince Charles had been used to assertive, domineering women. His mother ruled her household; his grandmother had ruled hers. His sister, Princess Anne, had bullied him unmercifully, and his aunt, Princess Margaret, was also assertive and demanding. He had no idea how to handle Princess Diana and had only two reactions to conflict: to collapse or run away.

Princess Diana became pregnant in the fall following her marriage and produced a son, Prince William, heir to the throne, in 1982. Despite the generations of tradition which demanded that she give birth at one of the Royal residences, Princess Diana insisted on a hospital birth and got her way. It was a long and arduous labor, but motherhood had a momentous effect on Princess Diana. As mother of a future King, she quickly realized that she had assumed a position of power in the Royal Family that nothing could take away from her. She held the future of the monarchy in her arms. And as a mother raising her child, she had a tangible role. Prince Charles still waited in the wings for his life's purpose to begin.

Pregnancy and the first months of motherhood also brought an emotional strain that further damaged her relationship with her husband. Prince Charles, neither demonstrative himself nor understanding of expressed emotion in others, saw his wife's emotional outbursts as merely undisciplined. Princess Diana began to do almost anything to get attention, including what have been since called "suicide" attempts. When she was three months pregnant with Prince William, she tumbled down a flight of stairs. She was not seriously hurt, but Prince Charles's reaction was callous and unfeeling. On another occasion she is reported to have slashed her wrist with a lemon slicer, at best an unusual instrument with which to attempt suicide. On yet another occasion she is said to have thrown herself at a glass cabinet in despair and on another to have taken a slight overdose of sleeping pills.

Later, when Princess Diana was being treated for depression and for the emotional root causes of her eating disorders, she would review these incidents and call them suicide attempts. Psychologists usually refer to such events as "suicidal behavior" rather than suicide attempts, an important distinction. Suicidal behavior means self-destructive acts which could ultimately lead to a suicide attempt, successful or otherwise. The distinction would be lost when these incidents were later revealed to an astonished public.

After the birth of Prince William violent arguments ensued between Prince Charles and his popular young wife. She overheard a telephone conversation between her husband and someone she assumed was Camilla. As she listened, her husband said, "No matter what happens, I'll always love you."

The tensions between Prince Charles and Princess Diana threatened to become public some weeks later, on the morning of a major annual event in the British calendar, Remembrance Day, similar to Memorial Day but without the holiday atmosphere. Prince Charles and other members of the Royal Family were scheduled to attend the annual ceremonies, but on the morning of the event Princess Diana wanted to stay home. Prince Charles would no more have considered not attending a scheduled Royal event than a president would consider not giving a State of the Union address. Such duties are part of his raison d'être, indeed his only raison d'être. To Princess Diana they are merely boring.

Prince Charles arrived without her, explaining that his wife was sick, and her seat on the rostrum was taken away. Minutes later, Princess Diana appeared, having changed her mind. Prince Charles was embarrassed and humiliated and visibly angry.

The most serious arguments centered on his continuing relationship with Camilla Parker-Bowles, which Princess Diana believed was improper. She suspected that their friends and his staff helped keep secret clandestine meetings with her when he was away from home. She began investigating the contacts between Prince Charles and his former girlfriend. Whenever she arrived at Highgrove or Kensington Palace after Prince Charles had been there alone, she would press the redial button on his private phone. On many occasions, she found herself connected to Camilla's country home.

The fairy-tale sheen on the romance began to show signs of tarnish in the public eye in the year after Prince William was born. Stephen Barry, a former valet, had left the Prince's employ following numerous clashes with Princess Diana. He had written a book which portrayed their domestic life as less than perfect—she was immature and petulant; he was sulky, undemonstrative, and weak. Partly in order to quell speculation that all was not well, Prince Charles and Princess Diana arranged for a documentary to be made portraying their home life. It was not nearly as successful as previous attempts to portray the homelife of the Queen. Prince Charles admitted that he talked to the plants in the garden at his home at Highgrove to encourage them to grow.

Despite the strains in their relationship, in 1984, Princess Diana became pregnant for the second time and in the same year gave birth to another son, Prince Henry. But after his birth, their four-year-old marriage to all intents and purposes ceased to be a real union. They had separate bedrooms, arranged deliberately conflicting schedules, and spent only weeks of every year together. Prince Charles spent his private time at Highgrove, where he would be visited by Camilla Parker-Bowles. Princess Diana lived Monday to Friday at Kensington Palace and visited Highgrove with the children on weekends, which often turned unpleasant. The staff would overhear Princess Diana call her husband "a shit" and "a fucking bastard." After such scenes, Prince Charles would retreat to work on his garden and talk to his plants.

That the marriage had failed was known to their friends and families. On occasion, their children witnessed arguments and were visibly distressed. After one fight, Princess Diana locked herself in the bathroom, audibly weeping. Prince William shoved tissues under the door for his mother, which upset Diana further, for it brought back memories of her own unhappy childhood, when she had witnessed numerous violent arguments between her mother and father. Princess Diana confided the truth to Lord Althorp, her younger brother, with whom she was extremely close. Prince Charles did not need to confide the truth to his mother. She had witnessed and overheard fights between her son and daughter-in-law in which Princess Diana screamed a string of obscenities. And she knew in detail from the Royal Protection Squad and from MI5 that all was not well with the marriage.

That the British intelligence services should judge that they had a legitimate interest in the personal life of a future head of state should be no surprise. But it is shocking that beginning in 1984 the intelligence services stepped up their surveillance of the Royal Family. It included not only telephone monitoring, which has been routine for many years, but listening to private conversations inside Highgrove and Prince Charles's home at Kensington Palace.

Princess Diana's public image improved year by year, while her marriage deteriorated and Prince Charles's public popularity declined. The press began to portray Prince Charles as something of an eccentric. In his continuing search for a paternal soulmate, he became a close friend of the philosopher Sir Laurens van de Post, one of a breed of intellectuals whom his father despised. He became obsessed with what he believed was a decline in architectural standards and publicly railed against the changing skyline of eighties London. In a documentary on his views on architecture, he took the controls of a wrecker's ball and tried to knock down a building he hated. He became interested in Buddhism and organic farming and sponsored an isolated community of Scottish crofters where he spent weeks working in the fields. Newspapers began to describe him as the "Loony Prince."

Princess Diana, on the other hand, appeared to be the perfect loving mother, vastly different from Royal mothers who left their children to be cared for by nannies. She seemed to revel in the kind of Royal visits that showed kindness and concern, as opposed to those that involved pageantry and tradition. She visited hospitals, drug rehabilitation centers, and senior citizens' homes and sponsored charities and charity concerts, particularly for children and AIDS research. The other Royals

did so, too, but there was something about Princess Diana's youthful
joie de vivre, her careful balance of aristocratic bearing and open accessibility, that endeared her to the public.

Year by year, she appeared to have grown more beautiful, more
photogenic. Scores of magazines fought for an excuse to carry her
photograph on their covers. She simply outshone the other Royals. On
the rare occasions when they appeared together, the waves and cheers
seemed to be for Princess Diana rather than for the heir to the throne.
It made Prince Charles at first amused, then jealous, then depressed.

But Princess Diana was in pain. She had deep emotional problems
caused by the tensions in her marriage and the strain of living a public
lie, of being an icon and living in the public gaze. She had had recurring
weight problems from the period before her marriage when she struggled to lose sixteen pounds before her wedding. After the birth of her
first child she had starved herself to lose weight and went on a series of
eating and vomiting binges. The cycle of bulimia and anorexia dogged
her health for several years. Prince Charles had little patience for his
wife's health problems. When she fainted during a public appearance
because she had had too little to eat, Prince Charles scolded her for
embarrassing him. She was unable to carry the burden of living a public
lie without stress and sought first psychiatric and ultimately astrological
and occult help. Ultimately she realized that her unhappy marriage had
become the root of her eating disorders.

By 1987, when they had been married six years, Prince Charles and
Princess Diana were spending little time together. Prince Charles went
to the Kalahari Desert with Sir Laurens van de Post to commune with
nature and discuss philosophy, then to Italy to study Renaissance
architecture and to paint. He returned to Britain, but it was another
two days before he saw Princess Diana. A few weeks later, Prince
Charles attended the wedding of Amanda Knatchbull, whom Lord
Mountbatten had once hoped Prince Charles would marry. Princess
Diana boycotted the event. Later that year, the Prince and Princess
visited victims of severe flooding in Wales, but they arrived and left
separately. Comparing the pattern of their schedules, newspapers noted
that they were apart for up to six weeks at a time and seemed to relish
the separation.

The intelligence services meanwhile kept Princess Diana under close
surveillance for any signs that her relationships with other men were in
any way improper. She had had a number of friendships with men with

whom she was seen publicly. One was with Maj. David Waterhouse, a Household Cavalry officer who escorted her to a rock concert featuring David Bowie and watched by eighty thousand people at London's Wembley Stadium.

There was safety in those numbers, and it was an event at which Prince Charles would have been unspeakably bored and out of place. But when she was photographed leaving a late-night party at a friend's West London home with the major, she became distraught and, weeping, begged the photographer for the film. Her pleas—and some bullying from a bodyguard—won her the roll of film.

The intelligence agencies became interested in another male friend, Capt. James Hewitt. Princess Diana had been traumatized by a fall from a horse as a child and had been encouraged to take riding lessons to overcome her fear of riding. Hewitt, a cavalry officer, was chosen to teach her to ride. The friendship persisted after the lessons ended, and Princess Diana is reported to have written letters to Hewitt during the Gulf War in 1991. Intelligence sources say those letters were intercepted and read by MI5 agents.

A third man who came to the attention of the intelligence services was James Gilbey, a former Saab dealer and marketing manager of Team Lotus, the Grand Prix racing team. He is also a member of the Gilbey's gin distilling family. Princess Diana had known Gilbey for two years before she married Prince Charles, and he had continued to be a confidant. An intelligence report says that on at least one occasion in 1989, Princess Diana visited Gilbey at his home in Lennox Gardens, Knightsbridge, at eight-thirty in the evening with one of her Royal Protection Squad bodyguards, David Sharp. She entered alone and did not reemerge until 1:00 A.M., when she pulled a hat down over the upper part of her face and ran to a car in which Sharp waited for her.

Telephone conversations between Princess Diana and James Gilbey were frequent and routinely taped by the intelligence services. Two of those taped conversations, in phone calls in late 1989 and early 1990, were later to be published as the so-called Squidgy Tapes. As we shall see, sections of those tapes contained remarks which could be interpreted as indicating an improper relationship developing between Gilbey and the Princess.

In 1991, Princess Diana finally decided that she could stay in the marriage no longer and desperately sought a formal separation. But she knew that the Royal Family would move heaven and earth to keep the marriage from dissolving. No marriage of an heir to the throne had ever ended in divorce. It seemed unthinkable that a divorced or even separated Prince of Wales could ever be King. Innumerable discussions, magazine features, and newspaper articles prior to their marriage made mention of the fact that no matter how unhappy they were, Prince Charles and his wife could never go their separate ways.

At some point in 1991, Princess Diana took stock of her marriage and her future in the Royal Family. She believed she had two choices: She could go on living an unhappy lie, never have a public relationship with a man she loved and who loved her, and risk raising her children with the same warped emotional values as her husband and his family. Or she could escape.

She decided to escape. But in order to bring about a separation which left her public stature untarnished and the custody of her children unchallenged, she would have to fight a brilliant campaign.

Together with her brother, Lord Althorp, Carolyn Bartholomew, who had been for years her closest girlfriend and confidant, James Gilbey, and a number of other friends, Princess Diana agreed to a plan to allow details of the true state of her marriage to become public. Princess Diana knew Andrew Morton, who was a Royal correspondent and author of a number of books on the Royal Family. Through a mutual friend, Morton had advised Princess Diana on a number of occasions about her relationship with the press in general. And it was Morton's name that came up when Diana plotted her escape from the Royal Family. Diana agreed to allow her friends to reveal the secrets of her marriage to Morton. Once the details were in the open, she believed, there would be no alternative but divorce.

The result of a series of interviews given to Andrew Morton appeared in the book *Diana: Her True Story*. It was a historic journalistic coup. It detailed the struggle with bulimia and anorexia, the alleged suicide attempts, Princess Diana's growing contempt for Prince Charles and his callous indifference to and emotional distance from her. It was, for the British public, a shattering insight into their marriage. The book would be published in the *annus horribilis* of 1992.

Thirty-two

The Year of Horrors

T he Queen herself would call the year 1992 *annus horribilis*, or "year of horrors." It was a year filled with catastrophe, humiliation, and scandal, the year when the Royal Family's most closely guarded secrets came bursting forth like seeds from a ripe pod. Each month brought a fresh revelation, a new twist to what had seemed an exhausted plot, even before the British public had come to terms with the last. It was a painful, agonizing process analogous to the steady stream of revelations during the Watergate period. And just as Watergate damaged not only the president but the presidency, so the *annus horribilis* damaged not only the individuals at the center of the scandals but the entire institution of monarchy. The Royal Family was falling apart, and as it did so, inevitably, the purpose of the monarchy would itself be questioned.

The Royal Family celebrated the New Year at Sandringham, but few members of the family could have entertained high hopes for 1992. Open warfare had exploded among the Royals. Princess Diana tried to distance herself from Fergie as her sister-in-law's public image segued from boisterous and fun-loving to greedy and selfish. Princess Diana and Prince Charles were both aware of the impending publication of Morton's book. Another book, *Diana: A Princess and Her Troubled Marriage*, by Nicholas Davies, was also being prepared. Its sources included Prince Charles's friends. Yet a third book that the Queen was not looking forward to reading was *Royal Fortune*, which detailed the private wealth of the family.

Princess Anne, who had an ill-disguised contempt for both her sisters-in-law, knew that she would suffer the trauma of announcing her final divorce from Mark Phillips in the coming year. Members of her family continued to reject her lover, Tim Laurence. Capt. Mark

Phillips, meanwhile, celebrated New Year at Val d'Isere with his girlfriend, travel executive Jane Thornton. Fergie, constantly fighting with Prince Andrew, planned her own skiing vacation and counted the hours until January 3, when she could leave. There was an inauspicious start to the New Year for Princess Michael of Kent, too. She broke her nose while riding and was not well enough to fly to Switzerland to her daughter, Gabriella, who had broken her leg skiing. Prince Michael went instead.

Prince Charles fell into a tense mood during the first week of the year. Out fox hunting with the Meynell Hunt in rural Derbyshire in the English Midlands, Prince Charles was besieged by antihunt campaigners. He lost his temper and shouted abuse at them as the crowd heckled their future King. The following day, Prince Charles had another outburst when he took his sons to Sunday church services at Sandringham without their mother. A number of people, disappointed not to see the Princess of Wales, shouted, "Where's Di?" Always sensitive about his popularity in relation to his wife's, he shouted back: "She's not here today—so you can go and get your money back!"

On January 14, 120 photographs of the Duchess of York—Fergie—on vacation in Morocco with Texas millionaire Steve Wyatt were brought to Scotland Yard by attorneys for a British newspaper. The newspaper had been given the photographs after they were found in Wyatt's apartment—left there deliberately by British intelligence agents so they might find their way to the newspapers.

The newspapers could not publish the photographs for copyright reasons. A legal question was also raised about the right of possession of the prints. But the *Daily Mail* published an account of what the photographs showed, among them a shot of Wyatt with his arms around Princess Beatrice; Wyatt and Fergie together and obviously on friendly, if not intimate, terms. The photographs in themselves proved nothing, but they were enough to deeply humiliate Fergie and infuriate Prince Andrew.

Fergie had just returned from her skiing trip to Klosters in Switzerland when the storm broke over the photographs. Hoping to escape some of the press battering, she went with her father, Maj. Ronald Ferguson, to a charity polo tournament in Palm Beach. Once in Florida, she caused another controversy by attending a dinner at an exclusive country club that was alleged to be a little too exclusive—it discriminated against Jews and blacks. On the return flight, Fergie behaved badly, disturbing passengers, throwing packets of sugar around the cabin, pulling a bag over her head, and arguing with cabin staff.

Other passengers in the First Class cabin were appalled, and accounts quickly made the newspapers. By the end of the month, a poll published in a daily newspaper said that Britons believed that Fergie was the person who had done the most harm to the Royal Family. Prince Charles, the poll said, remained popular, but Princess Diana was rated twice as popular as the Queen herself.

On her return, the Queen and Prince Philip summoned Fergie to a painful interview. Prince Andrew had been angered and humiliated over the accounts of the Morocco vacation that had been published in the newspapers. From that point, the marriage was as good as over, and over the next several weeks lawyers began secretly negotiating a separation. As her relationship with Wyatt cooled, another male friend appeared on the scene—a tall, balding Delaware businessman, John Bryan. Bryan, a friend of Wyatt's, had had a mercurial business career in the United States. Fergie claimed he was her business adviser, negotiating various deals on her Budgie the Helicopter character and investing the proceeds from Budgie and other coffee table books she had edited or contributed to, about the Royal family.

Less than a week after the newspaper poll lionized Princess Diana and excoriated Fergie, Princess Diana was in trouble for one of the few times in her public career. She took delivery of a $110,000 German-built Mercedes. The depressed British car industry believed it was wrong for the Princess to buy a foreign car when Jaguar made luxury cars at least as prestigious. A public outcry ensued, and she found herself forced, reluctantly, to send the car back.

Later that month, Prince Charles and Princess Diana visited India, arriving separately. Twelve years before, Prince Charles had visited the Taj Mahal, a temple and monument to love. He vowed then that he would return one day with the woman he loved. But when Princess Diana visited the temple on February 12, she was alone. The Prince was two hundred miles away at a British business forum. The Princess allowed herself to be photographed at the Taj Mahal in a series of wistful wide shots, with the great temple towering in the background. They emphasized her loneliness and isolation.

The following day, the Prince and Princess were together at a polo match in Jaipur. In an attempt to show some unity and affection, Prince Charles bent to kiss his wife. She turned her head at the last moment, and Prince Charles was left delivering an inexpert peck on her ear. Prince Charles was visibly embarrassed and annoyed. It was clear to everyone—at last—that this was a marriage with severe problems.

Back in London, a storm gathered over the Royal Family's finances. The precise nature of the personal wealth of the Queen had been a subject of speculation for many years. It is a complex subject because some of the Queen's wealth is personal, some of it is held by the state, and it is not always clear which is which. Sandringham and Balmoral, for example, are owned by the Queen personally, while Windsor and Buckingham Palace are owned by the state. Very little of the Queen's personal fortune is disposable. She has a vast philatelic collection, founded by her father, containing some of the world's most valuable stamps, but it is unlikely that she would ever be able to sell significant parts of it. She has a huge collection of art, but a public outcry would occur if she decided to auction valuable paintings.

An assessment becomes even more complicated, since the Royal Family's right to a subsidy from the government—known as the Civil List—stems from a pact in which income from some of the Royal Family's estates was handed over to the government. (The value of those estates far exceeds the $15 million in Civil List payments.)

Investigations into the Queen's wealth in 1992 suggested that she was worth up to $8.5 billion and had significant holdings in a wide range of British and foreign companies, including North Sea oil corporations, RTZ, the mining conglomerate, General Electric, and other multinationals. Prince Charles's personal fortune has been put as high as $200 million. The Royal Family is exempt from laws that demand disclosure of holdings in public companies. All of their holdings are placed in a corporation known as Bank of England Nominees. The transactions of Bank of England Nominees are secret. The Queen at that time paid no income or inheritance taxes.

Speculation about the Royal Family's finances always raises hackles in Britain and was particularly divisive in 1992, when the country once more fell into a recession, when the Conservative government's economic policies failed and the prosperity of the eighties rested on a collapsing foundation.

At the end of February the Queen visited Australia, only to be affronted by the upsurge in republican feeling there. John Keating, the prime minister, made it clear that he favored abolishing the rank of the monarchy in Australia, where a governor permanently represents the Queen as head of state, and establishing a republic.

In early March there were further indications of a split in both Prince Andrew's and Prince Charles's marriages. Princess Diana had become a patron of the marriage-guidance organization Relate, and in a speech at the organization's Family of the Year Award, she remarked: "I have seen the tears, the anguish, the raw emotions, the hurt and the pain caused by the split between couples."

Palace officials tried to suggest that she was talking about the many visits she had made to Relate's gatherings and to the conflict in her parents' marriage and those of her friends. But her comments seemed to be an unmistakable reference to her own marriage and that of her brother-in-law. The same week, stories that lawyers for both Fergie and Prince Andrew were negotiating a separation surfaced for the first time.

Those negotiations were not going well. According to palace sources, Fergie was demanding a multi-million-dollar settlement, and officials were concerned she might take her two daughters to live abroad. There was also deep concern that having written a history of Queen Victoria and Prince Albert and a series of children's books, she might be tempted to secure her future with a book about her life inside the Royal Family. On March 18, the Queen had a last meeting with Fergie and Prince Andrew over their marriage and asked them to reconsider. Palace officials were convinced that Fergie had been leaking details of the breakup to newspapers to force a quick settlement. In fact, it now seems more likely that Princess Diana had more to gain by a rapid breakup of the marriage, for it would pave the way for her own departure.

On March 19 the Palace officially announced Andrew and Fergie's separation. Fergie was removed from the Royal schedule and would be asked to perform no more public duties. In a private off-the-record briefing, Charles Anson, the Queen's press secretary, admitted that "the knives were out for Fergie at the Palace" over her behavior. He said she was "unsuitable for Royal and public life." Some of his remarks were reported, and Anson was forced to apologize. But the Queen refused to accept his resignation, a sure indication that, although indiscreet, his remarks mirrored the Queen's own view of her daughter-in-law.

A week later, Princess Diana took her children skiing at Lech in Austria. They were joined there by Prince Charles. While they were away, Princess Diana's father, the eighth Earl Spencer, died in a hospital of a heart attack. He left an estate worth $89 million. Princess Diana flew home to prepare for the funeral, and photographs showed Prince Charles giving her little comfort during her time of grief. At the funeral on April 1, Prince Charles and Princess Diana arrived separately, Prince Charles just minutes before the service.

Princess Diana left a wreath on her father's coffin with a card that read: "I miss you dreadfully, darling Daddy, but I will love you always." Prince Charles did not stay for the cremation and returned to London for another Royal engagement. The public could witness in sharp relief the contrast between the weeping Princess Diana, with her poignant message for her late father, and her somber but distant husband. It was yet another indicator that there was no longer any affection in their marriage.

While newspapers still speculated over Prince Charles's behavior, Princess Anne announced that she planned to divorce Mark Phillips. Days later, the divorce case was heard at Marylebone Court, with only two attorneys representing the couple. The divorce was not entirely unexpected. They had been separated for longer than the legally required two years. But it raised speculation over the much more controversial issue: her likely remarriage to Capt. Tim Laurence. Just a few days before the announcement, she had returned from a vacation with Laurence aboard her new thirty-five-foot, $125,000 yacht. Unknown to the public, there were deep divisions inside the Royal Family over Laurence, with Princess Anne insisting she would marry him by the end of the year—and in a church wedding. The Queen Mother led the opposition to her wedding plans, and several palace officials were disdainful of the relationship with Laurence.

The news of the divorce proceedings was soon eclipsed by Fergie's sudden disappearance from Southyork. As part of the separation deal, she would quit the $7.5 million house, which had been paid for by the Queen. On March 23, Fergie was discovered in Phuket, Thailand, where she was vacationing with her children and several members of her staff at the $1,500-a-night Amanpuri Hotel. With her was John Bryan, her financial adviser.

After several days with Fergie, Bryan returned to Britain and met with Prince Andrew to brief him on further details of the separation. He denied he had anything other than a business relationship with the Duchess of York and said he had gone on vacation with her to help her wind down. Fergie did not return to Britain until May 8. Her exotic vacation had lasted thirty days and had ended in ugly scenes at Djakarta airport when Fergie demanded that British embassy officials protect her from a group of photographers following her. On her return, she held lengthy discussions with Prince Andrew over their marriage breakup. To the consternation of palace officials, it seemed that the couple still left open the possibility of a reconciliation. The palace was determined to discredit Fergie once and for all.

The following day, May 10, Prince Charles made a fool of himself on national television. He had agreed to a documentary on his fascination with crofting on the remote Hebridean island of Berneray, off the coast of northern Scotland and one of the most remote corners of the British Isles. He was shown digging potatoes, lobster potting, and waxing lyrical about the joys of organic farming and the idyllic, primitive lifestyle on the islands. Given that crofters live at subsistence level and are among Britain's poorest citizens, it was a foolish enterprise at best. But what made British viewers cringe was the sight of Prince Charles singing "Auntie Mary Had a Canary" off key at a musical evening known as a ceilidh. It portrayed the Prince as unceasingly remote, temperamentally morose, and out of touch.

Princess Diana did not watch the documentary. She left that day for a tour of Egypt, where, as on her tour of India, photographs emphasized her loneliness. Prince Charles was disappointed by the reception given the documentary and left the next day for Turkey on a painting vacation.

In Britain, other members of the Royal Family had gathered for the Windsor Horse Show. They were still reeling from yet another survey of attitudes about the Royals that showed their popularity at an all-time low. A majority believed they lived too luxuriously, were out of touch with the rest of the nation, and set a bad example of family life. The same day, the Queen tried to discover from Fergie if there was still a chance for a reconciliation with Prince Andrew. She invited her errant daughter-in-law into the backseat of her car and spoke to her for over thirty minutes.

When Prince Charles and Princess Diana returned from their separate vacations, they were scheduled to go together to the World's Fair in Seville, Spain. Again, neither made any attempt to show any affection for each other, and news footage and photographs showed that they appeared somber and pensive and tried to avoid making eye contact in public.

Andrew Morton's book *Diana: Her True Story* appeared in the last week of May and proved a bombshell. It detailed for the first time the true state of the Royal marriage: Princess Diana's eating disorders, her depression, her suspicions of her husband's relationship with Camilla Parker-Bowles, and her alleged suicide attempts. It portrayed Charles as an emotionally distant, uncaring husband, obsessed with his own interests and his Royal duties to the exclusion of his wife and family. Almost simultaneously, another book, *Diana: A Princess and Her Troubled Marriage*, was published. In part, the latter portrayed Princess Diana as a petulant, self-centered, emotionally unstable, and immature woman incapable of understanding her husband's problems and the demands on his time. Prince Charles was also shown to be cold, his behavior at times bizarre and his love for Camilla unending.

What stunned Britons most was not the revelation that the marriage was in trouble—that already appeared obvious—but the depth of the problems, the couple's obvious distaste for each other, and the extent of the sham that had been publicly perpetrated during the years of their union. Some Britons naturally supported Prince Charles and refused to believe the allegations in Morton's book. Many—possibly a majority—supported Princess Diana. But it was clear to all that the marriage had collapsed and a constitutional crisis lay just ahead.

The British government had considered trying to suppress Andrew Morton's book, which was far the more sensational of the two. Books upsetting to the Royal Family had been suppressed before, notably *Living With the Queen* by a former palace official, Malcolm Barker. Barker's allegations included the claim that a number of palace staff had been involved in a homosexual gang rape on board the Royal yacht *Britannia* and that the incident had been covered up.

But there were legal grounds to suppress Barker's book. Palace officials are contracted not to write memoirs. Although some booksellers refused to stock Morton's book under palace pressure, there was little that could be done to suppress it. Palace officials and journalists friendly with the palace disputed Morton's allegations. He was pointedly criticized in television interviews and talk shows over the enormous amount of money he stood to make from his sensational revelations. But there was, for once, no escaping the truth. Princess Diana and Prince Charles were obviously locked in a loveless marriage.

As the *London Sunday Times* began serializing the book in June, members of the Royal Family and their circle of friends took sides in the now-open warfare in the family. The Queen chose to invite Camilla Parker-Bowles into the Royal box at a polo game at Windsor. Princess Diana visited her friend Carolyn Bartholomew, a known source for the book. It was an eloquent confirmation that the contents were true and that Princess Diana had approved her friend's interviews with Morton.

That year's Ascot races on June 16 provided a bizarre spectacle. Fergie and her two children, Princess Beatrice and Princess Eugenie, seeming outcasts from the Royal Family, watched the Royal procession from a public area, waving and cheering boisterously as ever. Princess Diana and Prince Charles were together at Ascot. After appearing to leave together, they separated after only half a mile. On the second day of the race meeting, Fergie was once again in the public enclosure with her children, but this time they were joined by Prince Andrew, who appeared to be enjoying himself. Princess Diana sat in the Royal box, but Prince Philip pointedly ignored her.

On June 23 the Queen, Prince Charles, and Princess Diana held a crisis conference on the state of her marriage. The Queen won an agreement that Princess Diana would maintain a dignified silence as the debate about the Royal marriages intensified. Princess Diana promised she would make no public statements and keep all her public engagements, including those with Prince Charles. She was also told that the most she could gain was an informal separation, which in effect already existed.

The crisis among the Windsors was now so deep that two events that should have emphasized family unity only emphasized the rifts in the Royal Family. On July 18, Lady Helen Windsor, daughter of the Duke and Duchess of Kent, married a long time boyfriend—art dealer, Tim Taylor at St. George's Chapel, Windsor. It was a subdued event in comparison to other Royal marriages. The Royal Family attended the ceremony, but the divisions seemed obvious. Prince Charles would not have come but for the fact that his polo team had been eliminated from a tournament and he was unexpectedly free. Princess Diana kept her distance from her husband and at one time turned her back weeping. Fergie had not been invited, and Princess Anne also came alone. In the evening, all the key members of the Royal Family left for other engagements.

Just over a week later, the Queen celebrated forty years on the throne. In other circumstances there would have been a series of public events, but the Queen staged only one state banquet to mark the anniversary. The Royal Family had hoped to avoid the fortieth anniversary's fueling the debate over the future of the monarchy, but on August 2, a former defense minister, Alan Clark, launched an unprecedented attack on the Royal Family, calling them, with the exception of the Queen herself and Princess Diana, "vulgar and brutish," and urged the abolition of the monarchy.

It had been a painful year so far, but it would get worse. For weeks there had been speculation about a possible reconciliation between Fergie and Prince Andrew. They had been seen together several times and appeared to be enjoying themselves. They had even celebrated their sixth wedding anniversary together. Prince Andrew began to talk in private about eventually saving his marriage. He secured an invitation for Fergie to Balmoral in mid-August for two weeks and hoped that they would begin to settle their differences. But Fergie had also been seen on several occasions with Bryan, at Brighton's Sea Life Center in New York City and at a friend's wedding. The prospect of a reconciliation disturbed members of the intelligence services who had both Fergie and Bryan under close surveillance.

On August 9, Bryan, Fergie, and her two children arrived for a week's stay at the $1 million Le Mas de Pignorol villa in the South of France near St. Tropez for a one-week stay. Within twenty-four hours of their return to Britain, Bryan discovered that intimate photographs were being syndicated across Europe. He tried desperately to win injunctions against *Paris Match* and the *London Daily Mirror* to prevent publication of the photographs, but he failed. On August 19, the *Daily Mirror* published a series of pictures showing Bryan sucking Fergie's toe, kissing and hugging her, and the Duchess of York sunbathing topless. Worse, the entire scene appeared to have taken place in front of the children.

Fergie appeared at the breakfast table at Balmoral that morning to find her in-laws buried in several copies of the *Mirror*. One was tossed across the table at her. Princess Anne was openly contemptuous; Prince Philip, stonily silent. Prince Andrew, his hopes for a reconciliation shattered, asked detectives if it was possible his wife had somehow been drugged. After toughing it out at Balmoral for a few more days, Fergie left the palace and the Royal Family, it seems for good.

There were immediate demands for an inquiry into how the photographs could have been taken. While Fergie no longer had a security staff, the little Princesses still merited bodyguards. The villa where they stayed was isolated and surrounded by vegetation, and local police had added additional security on the orders of the French government. One Italian photographer, Daniel Angelli, was credited with having taken the photographs, but he denied being at the villa. According to intelligence sources, the photographs were actually taken by two photographers with the aid of MI5 agents. The purpose was to discredit Fergie, destroy any hope of a reconciliation, and eliminate any negotiating power she had with the Royal Family. After publication of the photographs she would count herself lucky to keep custody of the children. Inspection of some of the photographs confirms that they were taken from at least three different angles almost simultaneously and over a period of some twenty minutes.

Almost immediately thereafter MI5 was suspected of being involved in the release of audiotapes of conversations between a woman believed to be the Princess of Wales and a male admirer, believed to be James Gilbey, her longtime friend and a key source for Andrew Morton's damaging book. A British newspaper, the *Sun*, had been sitting on the tape for months, uncertain of the legal implications of publishing its contents. Scooped by its rival the *Daily Mirror* on the Fergie photographs, it published details of the conversation for the first time.

The conversations had taken place at the end of 1989 and in the first days of 1990. Most of the talk back and forth appeared to be innocuous chat, but individual comments were shattering. Throughout their conversation, Gilbey calls Princess Diana "darling" and whispers, "I love you, I love you, I love you." At another he says, "Kiss me, darling," and there is the sound of the two blowing kisses at each other. On a number of occasions he calls Princess Diana by the pet names "Squidgy" and "Squidge." "That's all I want to do, darling," he tells her. "I just want to see you and be with you."

Princess Diana returns his affection and makes pointed references to their marriage: "After all I've done for this fucking family!" she says, and refers to her life inside the Royal fold as "torture."

But as important as the tape itself was its provenance. Ostensibly it had been taped by a seventy-year-old retired bank manager, Cyril Reenan, using a scanner which can pick up car phone signals. But examination of the tape shows that it had been recorded at Princess Diana's end of the line—which was a land line—and not at Gilbey's end, which was the car phone. Furthermore, it had been taped, then rebroadcast so that it would be picked up by amateur eavesdroppers and passed on to the press. Reenan himself believed he was used by "some behind-the-scenes sinister element."

The release of the "Squidgy" tapes caused a new furor inside the

Royal family over intelligence-service monitoring of their telephone conversations. Ironically, it did little to damage Princess Diana's reputation among the British public despite the implication that she had had an intimate relationship with Gilbey. According to intelligence sources, the monitoring of the telephone conversations, the private conversations, the mail, and other private activities inside the Royal Family is regular, if not routine, and is stepped up at times of crisis. During the breakup of each of the Royal marriages, monitoring by MI5 became intense.

Why and at whose order the "Squidgy" tapes were rebroadcast so that they might eventually be made public remains a mystery. But it seems an obvious effort to discredit Princess Diana at a time when it was believed that she and her friends were winning the war inside the palace. In fact, publication came at the wrong time. It had been expected that the tapes would surface long before Morton's book and counter many of the allegations contained in it. By surfacing when they did, the tapes merely did further damage to the chances of keeping the marriage intact.

By mid-September the Queen began consultations with selected historians, theologians, and constitutional experts on whether her son could still ascend the throne one day if his marriage failed. A "brain trust" was asked to draw up a secret report on how Princess Diana and Prince Charles could part leaving Prince Charles still free to become King.

In November, Prince Charles and Princess Diana visited South Korea on an official visit together, amid unfounded rumors—fueled by the palace—that there had been a sudden reconciliation. That the rumors were baseless seemed evident. Princess Diana looked miserable; Prince Charles, bored. Only when her husband was elsewhere did she appear relaxed and happy. They returned to a fresh controversy: a newspaper's account of a conversation between Prince Charles and Camilla Parker-Bowles that took place in 1989 and appeared to confirm all of Princess Diana's suspicions of the nature of the relationship.

British publications held off publishing the entire transcript until the Australian magazine *New Idea* did so.

Prince Charles was mortified to read intimate details of his conversation with Camilla. It was far more explicit than Princess Diana's with James Gilbey. He told Camilla: "Your great achievement is to love me." Together the couple plotted a secret meeting at the home of a friend, and both expressed disappointment that their time together would be cut short by one of Prince Charles's engagements. No one could doubt the nature of the relationship of an otherwise mature man and woman having the following exchange:

CHARLES: The trouble is, I need you several times a week.
CAMILLA: Mmmm. So do I. I need you all week. All the time.
CHARLES: Oh, God, I'll just live inside your trousers or something. It would be much easier.
CAMILLA: What are you going to turn into? A pair of knickers? (*laughter*) Oh, you're going to come back as a pair of knickers!
CHARLES: Or, God forbid, a Tampax. Just my luck! (*laughter*)
CAMILLA: You are a complete idiot! Oh, what a wonderful idea!
CHARLES: My luck to be chucked down a lavatory and go on and on forever swirling round on the top, never going down . . .
CAMILLA: (*laughter*) Oh, darling!
CHARLES: Until the next one comes through.
CAMILLA: Perhaps you'll come back as a box.
CHARLES: What sort of box?
CAMILLA: A box of Tampax so you could just keep going.
CHARLES: That's true!
CAMILLA: Oh, darling! Oh, I just want you now.
CHARLES: Do you?
CAMILLA: Mmmm.
CHARLES: So do I.
CAMILLA: Desperately, desperately, desperately . . .

There is a tendency to equate the intervention of the security and intelligence services with the clandestine battles of the Cold War and to assume that the ornate corridors of Buckingham Palace are as far removed from the interest of the British intelligence agencies as the hearth of the average citizen. In fact, monitoring the activities of the Royal Family and their friends and acquaintances has been high on the priorities of British intelligence since before World War I. The reason is simple. The monarchy embodies the state and the security of the monarchy—from infiltration, subversion and from its own foolhardiness—is the security of the state.

The modern British intelligence community is composed of MI5, which is responsible for counterintelligence, counterterrorism, and national security, and MI6, responsible for intelligence gathering outside of the United Kingdom. MI stands for military intelligence, but the agencies are no longer directly connected to the armed services. They share the data gathered by GCHQ, which is a computer and communications locus based in the English market town of Cheltenham and which monitors telephone calls and collects and analyzes satellite intelligence. The Special Branch of the Metropolitan Police and other regional police departments also perform counterterrorism and state security functions similar to those of MI5. Each branch of the armed services also has an intelligence department with specific intelligence gathering and counterintelligence functions.

Both MI6 and MI5 have been in existence in one form or another for over eighty years but their work has been so shrouded in secrecy that for most of that time their very existence has been denied. That there is an organization called MI5 was only officially confirmed in 1989 and the existence of MI6 was formally acknowledged in 1992. MI5—motto: "Defende Regnum" or "Defend the Kingdom"—has about two thousand full-time agents, more than half of them women. There are, however, many more agents in place in British institutions, including major newspapers, the British Broadcasting Corporation, the British parliament, all major and several minor political parties, leading corporations, and the upper reaches of the Civil Service. Since the collapse of Communism and the end of the Cold War, most of its work deals with counterterrorism, primarily in Northern Ireland, and MI5 spends about $500 million a year. Stella Rimington, director general of MI5—the first woman to head the agency—has denied that MI5 is responsible for spying on the Royal Family. But in fact, a proportion of MI5's work has always been directed at protecting the monarchy and that protection has always involved some degree of covert surveillance.

During the reign of Queen Victoria, before the existence of professional intelligence agencies, the then Prince of Wales, later Edward VII, was under almost constant surveillance and detailed reports of his gambling and womanizing were filtered to the Queen and her prime ministers. Edward VII remarked several times in personal correspondence that his mother seemed to know everything and he could not imagine where she got her information. Surveillance has continued down four generations of Royals.

The intelligence services' intrusion into the lives of the Windsors intensified during the 1936 Abdication Crisis. The private life of Wallis

Simpson, later Duchess of Windsor, was thoroughly investigated at the specific instructions of George V. The technology available for electronic surveillance in 1936 was primitive by modern standards but it has been confirmed by Sir Percy Sillitoe, who headed the agency after World War II, that both Wallis Simpson's and Edward VIII's telephone conversations were bugged, that their mail was intercepted and read, that agents were planted in their household, and that even after the abdication the Duke and Duchess of Windsor were the subject of unremitting scrutiny.

Surveillance of the modern Royals by the intelligence services takes several forms. Every telephone conversation is recorded and processed by GCHQ on behalf of MI5. In the past this would have been a laborious process but computer technology has enabled the British security services to monitor the telephone conversations of thousands of British citizens. According to a confidential source who was at one time a highly-placed intelligence officer, monitoring devices automatically trace calls and listen for key words, each of which is given a number. When journalists, politicians, and suspected terrorists in Northern Ireland are being monitored, for example, the key words are usually those that apply to terrorism or extremist politics.

When the Royals are under scrutiny, the key words apply to sex, love, marriage, and marital disputes, because sex scandals and marriage break-ups are matters considered most likely to undermine the monarchy. Terms of intimacy or endearment, abusive words and vulgar expressions and expletives, are given very high numeric values. The computer adds up the number of key words and their numeric value and gives each conversation a number, so that an intelligence agent can see at a glance if any particular transcript is worth reading in full.

So flexible is this system that slang, jargon, and an individual's idiosyncratic expressions can be factored in. The transcripts of conversations between Prince Charles and Camilla Parker-Bowles and the "Squidgy" tapes of conversations between Princess Diana and James Gilbey contain large numbers of words and expressions which might be expected to be given high numeric values by a computer monitoring program.

The conversations are monitored at GCHQ by special units of seven people known as "gatherers." One group of gatherers is charged solely with monitoring the Royals. Circulation of the sensitive material is limited to intelligence chiefs and a clique of top level civil servants.

Some, but not all, of the information and none of the raw data is made available to the Queen and the Prime Minister. It was information compiled by gatherers that led the Royal Protection Squad to transfer bodyguards who had become too close to their Royal charges, as in the case of Peter Cross and Princess Anne. In a similar case, another member of the Royal Protection Squad was transferred because information from the gatherers revealed he had become obsessed with Princess Diana.

In addition to their telephone conversations, private conversations are sometimes recorded, either by bugs placed in royal residences or by agents using high tech laser devices first developed for surveillance of civilians in Northern Ireland. These project a laser beam on to a windowpane and detect the vibrations made on the glass by a human voice on the other side of the window. The vibrations are translated into digital information and reproduced by computer as script. Such high intensity surveillance is carried out only when more routine surveillance has detected a situation that needs to be followed up. At the height of the crisis over Prince Charles and Princess Diana's marriage, even her most mundane conversations were monitored with these devices.

Another form of surveillance involves electronic homing devices fitted into the private vehicles of all the Royals. Both the Duke of York and Princess Diana have for various reasons in the past eluded their personal bodyguards. At those times homing devices have been used to track their whereabouts.

Personal friends and acquaintances of Princess Diana, Princess Anne, Princess Margaret, and the Duchess of York have also from time to time become the subject of similar MI5 surveillance. According to a confidential source, a British army officer who had developed a platonic friendship with Princess Diana was given an overseas posting when it was revealed by the gatherers that he wanted to try to take the relationship somewhat further. Journalists covering the Royals have had their telephones bugged and, in some instances, their homes burglarized—all in the name of state security.

Such a profound intrusion into private life seems shocking and unnecessary, but the Royal Family accepts the fact that some surveillance is inevitable, if only to support the continuing operation by the Royal Protection Squad, which protects the Royals at close quarters, and the British Army's special forces regiment, the SAS., which provides additional protection during public appearances and when the Royals travel. Since the attempted kidnapping of Princess Anne, for example, all members of the Royal Family have undergone special training at the SAS headquarters in the southern English town of Hereford, in using firearms, escaping from bonds, and practicing unarmed combat.

What the Royal Family finds objectionable is not the fact that surveillance takes place—although both Princess Diana and Prince Charles had private security agencies sweep and debug their homes in a bid to limit surveillance during the height of the marriage crisis—but the use to which the information has sometimes been put. In the case of Fergie, the Duchess of York, it seems clear that information on her relationship with Steve Wyatt and John Bryan, gathered by electronic surveillance, was used to discredit her, first by planting photographs of her vacation with Wyatt in Wyatt's vacated apartment where they were bound to be discovered, then by arranging for her to be photographed with Bryan in the South of France.

The motivation for the dirty tricks campaign is not hard to understand. The Duke of York appeared incapable of controlling his wife and unwilling to accept that his marriage was breaking up. It was considered possible that the Duchess of York would take her children outside of British control and it became crucial to organize her ouster from the Royal circle rather than allow her to leave it on her terms.

The leaking of the "Camillagate" and "Squidgy" tapes is more difficult to fathom. The "Squidgy" tapes of an intimate conversation between Princess Diana and James Gilbey were recorded and rebroadcast over a number of nights in a deliberate bid to ensure that they were picked up by someone with a scanning device. That suggests an official leak—an attempt to publicly discredit her at a time when she had widespread support. The "Camillagate" taping—an incriminating conversation between Prince Charles and Camilla Parker-Bowles—appears to have been an unofficial leak, possibly by an employee of GCHQ, either for financial gain or simply out of support for Princess Diana. There has been speculation that Princess Diana herself or someone acting on her behalf recorded the Camillagate tapes and had them leaked.

The *London Daily Telegraph*, suggesting that Princess Diana was in fact behind the Camillagate leak, praised her ingenuity in an editorial: "A woman in her position, whose marriage has irretrievably broken down, who may at some future time have to enter divorce proceedings and face a crucial ruling on custody of the children, needs a card or two in her hand."

The conversation between Prince Charles and Camilla had taken place nearly three years earlier, but a police officer told reporters he had been on duty at Highgrove in the early spring of 1992 and seen Camilla and Prince Charles locked in a passionate kiss. On November 14, Prince Charles spent his forty-fourth birthday quietly at his home at Highgrove. It was the unhappiest of his life. He was the center of the most damaging public scandal in Royal history, his accession to the throne was being questioned, and his personal and deeply embarrassing conversation with Camilla was on everybody's lips and had become an international joke.

Just as it seemed nothing worse could happen, a fresh catastrophe struck. On November 20, fire erupted inside Windsor Castle and spread quickly through the 185-foot-long St. George's Hall, the State Dining Room, and the Crimson Drawing Room and Grand Reception, used for state occasions. Prince Andrew led rescue efforts, and millions of dollars' worth of antique furniture, paintings, sculptures, mirrors, and other works of art were dragged out of the path of the fire, filling the quadrangle of the castle. The Queen, visibly shaken, rushed to the scene as firemen battled to contain the damage to the nine-hundred-year-old structure.

No one was seriously hurt, but within twenty-four hours the extent of the damage was assessed at $150 million. An entire section of the castle had been destroyed, and many works of art had severe smoke and water damage. It seemed symbolic of the damage already done to the House of Windsor that year that Windsor Castle itself—the Royal Family's favorite home and the place from which the family takes its name—should be so severely scarred.

Peter Brooke, the government's heritage secretary, announced almost immediately that there would be a full restoration at taxpayers' expense. But even amid the sadness over the tragedy for the Royal Family, demands erupted that the Royal Family contribute to the cost of restoring Windsor Castle.

The fire and the controversy over who should bear the expense became the deciding factor in the Queen's decision to pay income taxes for the first time. The Queen's finances had been the subject of intermittent debate all year, and each fresh controversy seemed to fuel the debate. The Queen agreed to pay $2 million in taxes on a proportion of her fortune—actually only a token—but balked at the idea of full disclosure of her assets. Civil List payments were restricted to the Queen Mother, Prince Philip, and the Queen. The other members of the family would continue to live on their significant personal fortunes, assisted by the Queen and Prince Charles. But this was expected to save the taxpayer only $1.3 million.

At a speech in London four days after the fire, the Queen made her first reference to the traumatic year. "In the words of one of my more sympathetic correspondents," she said, "it has turned out to be an '*annus horribilis*'." She already knew—and the public didn't—that Prince Charles and Princess Diana had agreed to a formal separation.

The panel of constitutional advisers had told the Queen there was no specific bar to Prince Charles being crowned King if he were separated, or even divorced, but there could be a crisis if he wished to remarry. Princess Diana and Prince Charles agreed to separate. But Princess Diana had won key concessions. She would be allowed custody of the children, her own official royal household, and her share of Royal assignments—to be carried out her way. There was very little the Royal Family could do to stop a rival court, centered on Princess Diana, from emerging. Her enormous popularity with the British public had grown too strong.

On December 9, John Major, the prime minister, rose in the House of Commons and made the historic announcement that the heir to the throne and his wife were to part. Although it was widely accepted that the marriage had collapsed, the announcement was sudden and there were gasps from the packed House. Major declared that there were no plans for a divorce and that Prince Charles remained heir to the throne, with his eldest son, Prince William, next in line.

"And there is no reason," he said, "why the Princess of Wales should not be crowned Queen in due course." But there were those who could not agree that the succession was unaffected as Major claimed, and a number of legislators told reporters they believed that Prince Charles should step out of the line of succession and allow his son, Prince William, to become heir.

The process of setting up two separate courts—one around the Prince of Wales and one around the Princess—had already begun. In order to keep rivalry to a minimum, all engagements would be in the hands of a single secretariat with orders to ensure that important appearances do not clash. It was agreed that Princess Diana would continue to live in Kensington Palace despite the hostility of her neighbors, Prince and Princess Michael of Kent and Princess Margaret. Prince Charles was given an apartment at Clarence House, the palace where the ninety-three-year-old Queen Mother keeps her television continually tuned to closed-circuit racecourse commentaries designed for offtrack betting. Prince Charles would continue to live at Highgrove unless his engagements kept him in London, and Princess Diana would spend weekends at her family's country home, Althorp.

Three days after the announcement, what should have been a happy event inside the Windsors was also bathed in controversy. The announcement in September that Princess Anne was to marry Cmdr. Tim Laurence in December had been virtually swamped by the more salacious controversies of the summer. It was a small, private ceremony in Cathrie Church near the Queen's Scottish home at Balmoral. Any chance of a family reunion, or even a family rededication, was marred. Neither of her sisters-in-law, Princess Diana or the Duchess of York, were present. The Queen Mother, who neither approved of the divorce nor the remarriage, refused to attend, citing a previous engagement. At the very last moment she was persuaded by the Queen to go for the sake of family unity.

Royals are forbidden to contract civil marriages in Britain, and the Queen had no wish to insist that her daughter marry in a foreign country, as Prince Michael had been forced to do. The Church of England, however, does not recognize divorce. The conundrum was solved by arranging the marriage in the Church of Scotland. The Queen is head of the Church of England but not the Church of Scotland.

Only a few years ago, such a pragmatic solution would have been viewed as hypocritical, and the Queen Mother remained adamant that the decision to allow Princess Anne to become the first Royal to remarry in such a manner was morally indefensible. It certainly made a mockery of the sacrifices that had gone before. If the thought crossed Princess Margaret's mind as she watched the ceremony that the same solution could have been provided for her, then she confided it to no one.

The year ended on yet another note of controversy. The Queen's speech on Christmas Day is one of the holiday's traditions in Britain— begun by her grandfather, George V. Every Christmas Day millions of Britons gather around televisions and radios to hear the only direct address to the British people the monarch ever makes. The Christmas speech of 1992 was leaked to a daily newspaper, which printed the text in full on December 23. Although the transcript was in no way controversial, it did refer in a general way to the controversies surrounding the Royal marriages, and the Queen thanked the many thousands of citizens who had sent messages of sympathy and support to her.

> Like many families, we have lived through some difficult days, this year. The prayers, understanding and sympathy given to us by so many of you in good times and bad have lent us great support and encouragement. It has touched me deeply that much of this has come from those of you who have had troubles of your own. As some of you may have heard me observe, it has been a somber year. . . . There is no magic formula that will transform sorrow into happiness . . . but inspiration can change human behavior.

The Queen had worked for days on a speech that would strike precisely the right tone, neither ignoring what had happened during the year nor making too direct a reference. She was outraged by the leak, and the palace took the unprecedented step of suing for breach of copyright. The newspaper, the *Sun*, apologized, and there was an out-of-court settlement.

So ended the *annus horribilis*. The divided family gathered for Christmas and New Year, but there were two absentees, Fergie and Princess Diana. Fergie was simply not invited, emphasizing her estrangement from the family. Princess Diana made it clear she did not want to be invited and sent Prince William and Prince Harry to Sandringham with their father while she spent Christmas with her brother, the ninth Earl Spencer, and sister, Lady Sarah McCorquodale, at Althorp. In many ways the Royal Family Christmas and New Year were like the Christmases and New Years of the past. Most of the family traditions remained unbroken. But there was an air of tension, and for some, depression. For the first time in the family's history, the future seemed in doubt.

Epilogue

S ome five months after the disastrous fire that consumed St.
George's Hall and other areas of Windsor Castle, there was another
fire that symbolized tragedy and loss in the Windsor family. It was less
spectacular than the castle blaze and was watched by far fewer people.
There was no live television coverage, no dramatic interviews or hero-
ics. There was no attempt to intervene to save the treasures that went
up in smoke. But it was a no less significant blaze for all that.

On April 18, 1993, hundreds of personal effects of Prince Charles
and Princess Diana were taken out of storage at Windsor Castle in two
large trucks and driven the one hundred miles to the Prince's country
home at Highgrove. They were stacked in a bonfire and burned. They
included an ornate chess set, figurines, sets of china, Japanese minia-
tures with delicate mechanisms, and other artifacts. All had, over the
years, been gifts to Princess Diana and Prince Charles. In their new
separate lives, neither wanted them.

It was the final chapter of their marriage. A new chapter of division
and rivalry had begun. That same week, the *London Daily Mail* emphasized the fact that Britain now has, effectively, two Royal Houses—the
House of Charles and the House of Diana. In a study of the first five
months of separate engagements, the newspaper reported, Princess
Diana attracted five times as many spectators, twice as many reporters,
and more than twice as many photographers than her husband.

Fergie, meanwhile, attracted fewer spectators in the first months of
1993. Following her humiliating exit from the Royal Family, she wisely
opted for a low profile. But doing so failed to keep her out of the
headlines. Lesley Player, a beautiful polo-playing divorcée with whom
her father, Maj. Ronald Ferguson, was allegedly obsessed, revealed

details of a shocking double affair. She said she had had affairs both with Steve Wyatt and, with Fergie's connivance, Major Ferguson. There was more depressing news for Fergie when a woman from San Francisco, Peggy Caskie, claimed she had had unprotected sex with John Bryan some three months after she learned she was HIV positive. Prince Andrew, meanwhile, had returned to his Randy Andy bachelor days, but with greater discretion than in the past.

The first half of 1993 marked the final retreat from the Royal Family for Princess Anne. For a time Tim Laurence lived in Princess Anne's quarters at Buckingham Palace, and those Royal courtiers and palace officials he had known as equerry had to get used to calling him "Sir." Weekends were spent at Gatcombe Park, which was still farmed by Phillips and where he keeps an apartment. The first of the Queen's children to divorce, the first Royal to remarry, the first to deny her children titles, there was only one step left in her plan to escape the restriction of Royal birth. She announced that she would leave the palace to make her home in a spacious, seven-room apartment in a fashionable block in London's Pimlico district.

It was a symbol of the life she hopes to lead—private, ostensibly middle class, outside the center of Royal life and with children who will be known as plain Mr. and Miss rather than Prince Peter and Princess Zara. The escape had been plotted as if it were from a prison, but by the time it was accomplished, the House of Windsor had become more like a burning building. In its own way it was just as desperate, just as longed for, and just as successful as Princess Diana's flight.

In the summer of 1993, the British public was still trying to come to terms with the prospect of a future coronation ceremony, one with the same gleaming pageantry and splendor of so many coronations past but with a glaring and unique difference. At this future coronation, the King and Queen will ride in separate processions, take separate vows, and ride to separate homes. In some ways it is a logical climax to the story of a dysfunctional family: dysfunctional monarchy.

But this scenario, in which the King and Queen of England live separate lives with separate courts, is unlikely. According to insiders, Princess Diana intends to divorce Prince Charles when their two years of separation are over in early 1994. She may then take a title other than Princess of Wales, although she would be able to keep Princess of Wales until Prince Charles remarried. If there appeared any prospect that Princess Diana intended to remain legally married to the heir to the throne, Prince Charles would almost certainly divorce her rather than allow her to set up a rival monarchy.

In early 1993, the Queen commissioned a detailed report on the Royal Family's future role, part of a plan to keep the monarchy alive in Britain well into the twenty-first century. A committee of historians and constitutional experts were told to design a streamlined monarchy, reduce the number of members of the Royal Family engaged in Royal duties, and cut back on the number of Royal events. The experts were told to envisage a divorced Prince Charles assuming the throne. Significantly, however, a secondary plan, in which Prince Charles steps out of the line of succession in favor of his son Prince William, was also commissioned, along with an assessment of the effects of such a plan on the monarchy.

The committee is not expected to report to the Queen until 1994, and there is little chance that the results will ever be made public except insofar as its recommendations for a streamlined monarchy are put into effect. Palace insiders suggest that the future of the monarchy now rests squarely on the shoulders of the Queen and her longevity. She was sixty-seven years old in 1993 and can look forward to surviving into the second decade of the twenty-first century.

By then Prince Charles would be in his mid-sixties and his heir, Prince William, in his thirties. At that stage it might be possible for Prince Charles to step aside and allow his son to become King and rejuvenate the monarchy. But that plan depends on Prince William developing into a character that the British public wants badly to see on the throne. If in his mature years he possesses the same traits of some of his Windsor forebears—the weakness of character, the emotional dysfunction, and addictive personality—then the British monarchy may be doomed.

But the likelihood of the Royal children—Prince William, Prince Harry, Princess Beatrice, and Princess Eugenie—growing up better adjusted than their parents, grandparents, and great-grandparents seems, alas, remote. The whole history of the Windsors suggests that they are doomed to repeat the cycle. That is their tragedy.

Select Bibliography

QUEEN VICTORIA

Hibbert, Christopher. *Queen Victoria in Her Letters and Journals.* New York: Viking, 1981.

Longford, Elizabeth. *Victoria R.I.* New York: Harper & Row, 1968.

Wintraub, Stanley. *Victoria—an Intimate Biography*, New York: Dutton, 1988.

EDWARD VII

Aronson, Theo. *The King in Love.* New York: Harper & Row, 1986.

Battiscombe, Georgina. *Queen Alexandra.* London: Constable, 1962.

Hibbert, Christopher. *The Royal Victorians.* Philadelphia: Lippincott, 1982.

Martin, Ralph. *Jennie.* Englewood Cliffs, NJ: Prentice-Hall, 1990.

GEORGE V

Gore, John. *King George V.* London: Murray, 1981.

Lang, Theo. *The Darling Daisy Affair.* New York: Atheneum, 1966.

Nicolson, Harold. *King George V.* London: Constable, 1968.

Pope-Hennessey, James. *Queen Mary.* London: Allen & Unwin, 1959.

Rose, Kenneth. *King George V.* New York: Knopf, 1910.

EDWARD VIII

Bloch, Michael, ed. *The Secret File of the Duke of Windsor.* New York: Harper & Row, 1989.

———, ed. *Wallis & Edward: Letters 1931–1937.* New York: Summit, 1988.

Bocca, Geoffrey. *The Woman Who Would Be Queen.* New York: Rinehart, 1955.

De Launay, Jacques. *Secret Diplomacy of World War II.* Omaha, NE, 1960.

The Duke of Windsor. *A King's Story.* New York: Putnam's, 1951.

Higham, Charles. *The Secret Life of the Duchess of Windsor*. New York: Doubleday, 1986.

Marx, Samuel. *Queen of the Ritz*. Indianapolis, IN: Bobbs-Merrill, 1982.

Ziegler, Philip. *King Edward VIII*. New York: Ballantine, 1990.

GEORGE VI

Bradford, Sarah. *The Reluctant King*. New York: St. Martins' Press, 1990.

Hough, Richard. *Born Royal*. New York: Bantam, 1986.

LORD MOUNTBATTEN

Hatch, Alden. *The Mountbattens*. New York: Random House, 1965.

Ziegler, Philip. *Mountbatten*. New York, Knopf, 1985.

QUEEN ELIZABETH II

Higham, Charles, and Roy Mosely. *Elizabeth & Philip*. New York: Doubleday, 1991.

Pearson, John. *The Ultimate Family*. London: Michael Joseph, 1986.

PRINCESS MARGARET

Dempster, Nigel. *A Life Unfulfilled*. New York: Macmillan, 1984.

PRINCESS ANNE

Campbell, Judith. *Portrait of a Princess*. London: Casell, 1962.

Parker, John. *The Princess Royal*. London: Hamish Hamilton, 1988.

PRINCE CHARLES AND PRINCESS DIANA

Davies, Nicholas. *Diana: A Princess and Her Troubled Marriage*. New York: Birch Lane Press, 1992.

Holden, Anthony. *Charles Prince of Wales*. London: Weidenfel & Nicolson, 1992.

_____. *Their Royal Highnesses*. London: Weidenfeld & Nicolson, 1988.

DUKE AND DUCHESS OF YORK

Hutchins, Chris, and Peter Thompson. *Fergie Confidential*. New York: St. Martin's Press, 1992.

Seward, Ingrid. *Sarah, the Life of a Duchess*. New York, St. Martin's Press, 1991.

MISCELLANEOUS

Cannadine, David. *The Pleasures of the Past*. New York, Norton, 1989.

Costello, John. *Mask of Treachery*. New York: Morrow, 1988.

_____. *Ten Days to Destiny*. New York: Morrow, 1991.

Fox, James. *White Mischief.* New York: Random House, 1982.

Goldsmith, Barbara. *Little Gloria, Happy at Last.* New York: Random House, 1982.

Goralski, Robert. *World War II Almanac.* New York: Putnam's, 1981.

Martin, Kingsley. *The Magic of Monarchy.* Boston: Little, Brown, 1966.

Oxbury, Harold. *Great Britons.* London: Oxford University Press, 1985.